SUMMER'S
SNOW

Carly H. Mannon

Author's Note:

This book contains subject matter that might be difficult for some readers, including blood and gore depiction, child abuse recounted, death of a parent, emesis, grief depiction, murder, physical and emotional abuse, sexual content, references to sexual assault, trauma and nightmares, and violence.

SUMMER'S SNOW

Carly H. Mannon

The Continent

The Mountains of Rei

Ankaa

Crater Lake

Galorian Mountain

Swan Lake

Haldrin

Montevalle

The Death Tree

Sanserria

Bellport

Desdemon

Hahnaley

Valora

Daire Hills

Chiaran

Halcon Rainforest

Sossulla

Alara

Reyna

Thymis Islands

Padmar

Malvada

Oscuri Island

White Sands

Beryllia

PROLOGUE
Diana

T he stars knew how to send a message.

Trees beyond the open stained-glass windows stood lifeless, burned black by a fire started during a lightning storm. The following morning, we were hit by a blizzard, a late summer's snow.

Something was coming.

I sat perched in one of the window seats of the library and stared out at the palace gardens as I stitched rows of beading on my sister's gown. I'd hoped that the monotony of the task would soothe my nerves.

It didn't work.

The stars' warning had me fearing for our future, that the peace we'd had in the seventy-seven years since the Blood Treaty would not last. Such shifts in nature always meant great change was coming, whether it was for better or worse was yet to be determined.

Lost in my reverie, I lost focus on my embroidery, the needle piercing my finger. As I held it out from the window, the blood ran down my hand. Two red drops landed on the snow outside of my perch. As the red marred the white, images invaded my vision.

The walls of the room were black as night, the space empty except for seven mirrors of various types and sizes. In the center was the largest, the most intriguing—the most dreadful. The frame was made from obsidian, inlaid with moonstones and shimmering stardust, a large crystal at its peak. As I stood before my reflection, the glass shimmered. The surface of a still lake broken by a dropped pebble.

Broken castles covered in ash and thorns. A drop of poison muddied clear water as it unfurled. A dragon roared as thunder erupted. The earth cracked and broke apart as a piercing scream of agony rang. Then, out of that fractured snow-covered ground, what rose from it...

Gods save us all.

The images shifted.

Two children, little girls about 5 years old. They were familiar, I'd seen them so many times now. Turned away from me, they held hands. One with hair dark as night, the other golden like the sun. They felt like...hope. The flame of a candle in the darkness. In flashes, I watched them grow into adulthood, to their twenty-second birthday—their fates on that day.

I went to them and placed my hands on their shoulders. They began to turn to me, but before I could see their faces, before I could warn them, I was brought back to my present.

The two girls were my daughters, twins like myself and Alesia, whom I would bear within the next year. The girls already grew in my womb—tiny sparks of light—but I would never know them. I would not survive their birth. There was to be another war, one that would cause total destruction of our continent as it stood. Our way of life, their way of life, would be shattered.

My hands shook. I knew that Dominic's, my mate, and my union would be powerful. The stars had declared it so in the vision I had when I met him. I thought the five years of war for our liberation was the accumulation of that. How wrong I'd been if this was what the stars had intended all along.

But there was still hope.

Tears blurred my vision as I looked back to the snow. From my fallen blood, a sprout emerged through the ice and slowly unfurled. A blood red rose grew in its place.

My daughters would know great heartbreak and tragedy, but they would be as tenacious and strong as a rose sprouting from the frozen ground.

The tears streamed down my face as I mourned the fact that I would never get to see them grow, play, love—at least not closely, not as I should have as their mother. It was no wonder now that I had never held them in my visions. I would only ever observe from afar, separated by death's veil.

Though I would never know them, I knew that Dominic, my sister, and her mate would raise them to be strong, intelligent, and kind. My daughters would be fearless leaders that showed compassion, that protected our people and each other at any cost.

I gathered my now blood-spotted needlework and stepped down from the ledge.

As much as I wished I could stop time and fate from taking them from me, I wouldn't be idle. The stars' prophecy could not be changed, but I would protect my daughters in any way I was able. I needed to give them every chance to survive the darkness to come.

I knew exactly where to start.

CHAPTER 1
Nic

Only an hour after sunrise and the streets of Sanserria were already packed.

My skin prickled in the chill of the morning air, though the late June sun was warm upon my face. Nearly everyone in Sanserria was out in preparation for the ball tonight. The perfect day for a crown princess to sneak out of the palace unnoticed.

I reached for my scarf, ensuring it remained covering the bottom half of my face and braided black hair, as I made my way down to the open-air market in the city's southernmost square. I quickly wound between all the humans, High Fae, and vast multitude of faeries buzzing about on their own missions. If any of their glances turned my way, their gaze didn't linger for long. I'd gotten very good at hiding in plain sight, at moving in a way that didn't stand out.

Even if I had to be disguised to do it, being surrounded by the people of our country, Hahnaley, founded by my parents, gave me a sense of connection to them. A sense of belonging.

Today marked the first of a series of celebrations honoring the Blood Treaty of the Four Kingdoms, signed one hundred years ago on this day. Colorful paper lanterns and streamers were hung across the street from terracotta tiled roofs of white stucco buildings. The Treaty celebrations only occurred once every twenty years, so the entire city was buzzing with excitement. It was one of the few times the royalty from each kingdom came together in one place.

This year's revels would be even larger considering the Summer Solstice, falling on the last day, would also be my twin and my twenty-second birthday. The year in which all fae finished the ascent into the height of their magic.

Turning a corner, my gaze caught on a human woman. She looked to be in her early thirties, her shoulders hunched forward as she begged for money at the border of the square. I could see her much too prominent cheek and collarbones from where I stood, but what struck me were her eyes. They shone with a weariness that spoke of lost dreams and broken hearts.

As demi-fae, my mother and Aunt Alesia had grown up penniless in the slums with their human mother. Prior to the great war, humans were given the least of the resources by the much more powerful and long-lived fae, surviving on scraps and resilience. The demi-fae fared no better, often treated as outcasts, fitting in neither with the humans nor faeries. Because she knew all too well what it was to starve, after the defeat of the High King, Diana, my mother, vowed to make this new country better for the humans and other faeries. Before she died, she'd sought to eradicate the poverty she experienced growing up and had been successful. This woman shouldn't have been in this situation—it was unacceptable.

I could hear her over the noise of the streets and shoppers as I neared. "Please, anything you can spare. For my children." Some of those that passed by gave her coins, but most only gave her pitying glances. None seemed surprised.

The woman was looking away as I neared. In her profile, I could more clearly see her bones jutting sharply against her sallow skin. I kept my tone calm, my cadence slow, not wanting to startle her.

"Why are you here? What happened?"

The woman jumped anyway, her eyes going wide. "My—my husband passed away four months ago. He was ill. Now I have no way to earn money to support my children. They're ten and eight...I have tried to find work myself but there is nothing."

My chest tightened at her words, the wrongness of them. "The crown should provide you with any food and shelter you need, as well as resources to find fair work. Why haven't you gone to them?"

She glanced down, shaking her head. "I did. They said they could do nothing for me, that the funds were gone." Her shoulders rounded further, shielding her from the world that had already taken so much.

I went still, even as my blood heated. I took a breath to steady myself. "Do you have housing?" The woman nodded. "Can you give me your name?"

"Ruth—Ruth Maia," she whispered. I committed the name to memory.

"Ruth, someone from the crown will be in touch to help you. In the meantime, take this." I reached into my pocket and took out a large sum of coins—gold, silver, and copper. "It should be enough for you to pay for your housing and feed your family for a few months."

"Thank you, thank you so much." Tears of relief streamed down Ruth's face.

I touched my hand to her shoulder, my eyes softening. "You don't need to thank me. You should have never been in this situation, but I promise it will be rectified. You will be able to provide for your family."

The woman said her thanks again before turning away. I took a moment to process before I continued down the street, my gait now more focused as I processed what this meant. Sanserria hadn't been like this the last time I'd come nearly half a year ago. I vowed to find answers when I returned to the palace.

We'd had no restrictions in coming here until our father died nine years ago. My twin sister, Misha, and I were no longer allowed into the city without chaperones after that. Our stepmother, the interim queen until we became of age, didn't believe that royals were to *mix with the civilians* except in a regal capacity. Detached, only seen from afar, like good little princesses on an ivory pedestal. I burned at the thought—the asinine rule. My parents would have never enacted such a thing. They loved the people.

My hand compulsively reached for my necklace as I thought of them. Our mother had gifted my sister and me matching pendants before we were born, a tiny four-pointed knot with a circle threaded through the openings. Mine was silver, a ruby embedded in the center, while my sister's was gold with an emerald. They were small and plain, the chains delicate but magically strengthened to never break. We never took them off, her first and last gift to us, in remembrance.

By now I'd reached the market, winding through stall after stall among the busy shoppers. In my perusing, I found the sweets Misha liked best and was searching for jewelry to complement Eve, Alesia's mate and godmother to my sister and me. As I did so, I passed a traveling blacksmith selling different tools, baubles, and weapons. While I perused them, my eyes caught on a dagger.

At first glance, it was a plain weapon, only distinct by the hilt fashioned into swan's wings, but its glint hinted at a composition of Galorian silver. A metal found beneath one mountain in the north, only able to be worked by the skill of the goblins that inhabited the tunnels beneath, forged in the fire said to have been gifted by the gods themselves, and the only metal that could be bonded to rowan wood ash.

My finger pointed through the glass case. "Excuse me, can I see that dagger?"

"You sure, miss? I have some hair pins or combs that may suit you better. Handmade by the nereids with pearls and coral." He indicated the velvet-lined case next to it.

"No, thank you," I said, irritated at the insinuation that females should only be intrigued by decorative things. Not that I wasn't interested in those as well, they were indeed gorgeous, but the assumption was grating.

The tradesman shrugged and opened the case to hand me the dagger as well as its plain leather sheath. It had none of the usual precious stones or ornamentations the more affluent fae liked their weapons to have. It was, however, perfectly balanced, the swan's wings giving it a touch of elegance. The trader had definitely mistaken its composition, or he wouldn't have it displayed so openly.

"How much for this?" I asked.

"Ten gold pieces."

My eyes narrowed. The tradesman might have not understood how valuable a weapon he'd displayed, but regardless, he was trying to use my gender against me in bargaining.

"A high price for such a plain weapon. Price gouging is illegal, you know. Maybe you can give me a fair one, or I can flag down a guard to come have a look instead." Without breaking my gaze, I inclined my head to the royal guard standing just behind my right flank, thirty yards away, leaning against the wall of a fabric shop.

The blacksmith scowled. "I'll go down to eight." I continued to stare at him, unwavering. Silence always made the less practiced merchants jumpy.

"Fine. Five."

I smiled under my scarf as I handed him the coins. "Nice doing business with you."

The price was still much too high for a plain silver dagger, but a bargain for Galorian silver. It wasn't the fairest deal, but any blacksmith worth his salt would have been able to identify the rare metal—and besides, he'd offended me.

"Pretty faeries like yourself have no need for weapons like that." A male said as he came up behind me, then brushed his hand along my low back, drifting lower until it reached my ass. "You're gonna hurt that soft slender hand on such a sharp blade."

My muscles locked into preternatural stillness as I told myself not to make a scene. I really did—but I couldn't let him get away with touching me like that. With his unfoundedly high self-esteem, I knew it was unlikely the first time this male had groped a female without consent.

I would make it his last.

"Oh yeah, maybe you can show me how to wield it later?" I crooned with faux sweetness, tucking the sheathed blade into the back of my belt as I turned to face him. I met his gaze eye to eye.

The High Fae always thought themselves the most beautiful of the sapien races and the most powerful. With his beady eyes that were much too close together and a nose too small to fill the expanse of his face, he alone was proof this wasn't true.

He leered, taking his time as his gaze roamed up my body. "Maybe if you play your cards right, beautiful."

Bile rose in my throat. All I'd wanted this morning was to enjoy time in the city with the people, and this male had to ruin it.

I swallowed it down as I leaned in closer to him, whispering, "Maybe so. Although, I have been told I'm pretty good with my grip on a sword..." I slammed my knee into his groin, then took the hand he'd used to grope me and spun, successfully breaking the bones in much of his wrist and fingers with a satisfying crunch.

"You broke my hand you stupid bitch!" The male shrieked in pain.

"You will *never* lay your hands on a female again without her explicitly requesting it—though by the looks of you, that's unlikely to be the case." I snarled, pushing him away from me. He stumbled and crashed into another merchant's cart of fruit. Apples, pears, and oranges spilled into the street.

Shit.

"What's going on?" Another burly male said as a group of three of them came over to him, easing him back onto his feet. There were too many eyes on me, too many ears pricked in our direction. The royal guards pushed through the throngs of people, making their way to us. Not wanting my stepmother to know of my secret escapes into the city, I took off down a side street, then turned into an alley to escape them.

Unfortunately for me, the males had followed closely behind. And while I was faster, they knew this area better. The city's new buildings and redone streets confused me. I turned a few more corners and slammed into a dead end.

The stone walls were smooth, no ladders or low-hanging roofs I could pull myself onto for an escape. The males' footsteps neared, coming closer much too quickly. Cursing myself, I started trying doors and windows. The first three I attempted were locked.

"Hey, I think she came this way!" One of the males shouted just around the bend. I stilled, about to pull out the daggers tucked into the shafts of each boot to defend myself, but before I resorted to that, I tried the last and final door which, thank the Mother, opened.

I darted inside. My gaze remained toward the alley as I turned, closing the door behind me with a soft click. Then I stepped backward, directly into what felt like a broad chest. The stranger whose room I'd burst into wrapped his arms around me. He held me tightly as his hand came up to cover my mouth.

"*Shhh,*" the stranger whispered into my ear as he kept me pressed into him, his scent vaguely reminiscent of a rainstorm and crackling embers surrounding me. The male shifted and looked through a crack in the blinds near the door as the four males rushed into the dead end.

My heart thundered in my chest as the logical part of my brain told me I should be thankful for his help, that I'd gotten myself into this mess by bursting into what was clearly a complete stranger's bedroom. But the longer I stood there, the angrier I became that yet another male thought he could manhandle me and I would play along without a fight.

The voices outside slowly faded as the males took their search elsewhere.

"I think they're gone," the stranger said, his voice deep with an accent slightly different from ours, one I oddly couldn't place even in all my travels. He released my mouth and turned me toward him, his hands resting on my arms as he looked down at me. Somehow in all the running, my scarf hadn't slipped to reveal my face. My one stroke of luck.

My eyes came level to his chest. His hands, though gentle, held me tightly as they steadied me. I lifted my gaze to meet his. Short, wavy black hair, tan skin, and pointed ears denoted him as High Fae, but his eyes were what set him apart. A dark silver. Striking.

"Great, now you can get your hands off me." My hands pushed against his chest.

He resisted the move, his grip unfaltering, but not tight enough to hurt. "That's all you have to say...not even a thank you?" He broke into a feline smile as I tried to shrug him off again.

I snorted and wondered how much trouble that smile had gotten him out of before now.

"What were you doing running from them? Caught stealing?" He said as he cocked an eyebrow.

I remained silent, peering at him through narrowed eyes. I didn't owe him an explanation.

"The evidence suggests so. Running, hiding in alleyways, face covered—what did you take?" His eyes gleamed with intrigue.

"Enough, prick. Time to let me go before I make you." Ice flickered at my fingertips before I pulled the power back into myself. I would only use the magic as a last resort, it was too much of a tell to my identity.

"So ungrateful—"

Before he finished, I struck with the heel of my boot, coming down onto his instep and driving my other knee into his stomach, using my hands around his neck for leverage. The breath was knocked from him, his hands loosening as I rushed for the door. But before I could undo the latch, he grabbed my forearm, jerking me back.

I turned, slid, and twisted under his arm, coming up behind him and kicking the back of one knee so it crashed to the floor, forcing him into a kneel. The male grunted in pain as I ran for the backdoor.

The stranger snagged the back of my shirt before I could reach it and pulled me back. I hit the side wall with a loud thump. While I was off balance, he pinned my hands at my side in each of his, then used his much larger body to press against me, effectively blocking any more of my movements.

"Well, that wasn't very nice after I saved your life, little thief." Rather than angry, his tone held a hint of amusement. His silver eyes danced as if he'd enjoyed the challenge.

"I didn't steal *anything*. Some males just can't take no for an answer." I snarled. "And I would have killed them all before they touched me, so no, you didn't save my life. You just saved the alley from being painted red. I neither need nor want your help, and if you don't let me go in the next five seconds, what was nearly their fate will become yours." I said as I struggled against his unfaltering grip. The ease with which he kept me trapped only fueled the anger flooding my veins.

"Ah, that explains the one nursing his hand," he mused, seemingly unbothered, but his breaths came more quickly from our struggle. "And I'm sure you'd try your hardest, sweetheart, but you couldn't kill me. Besides, it looks like I have the advantage now." He smiled tauntingly.

I moved to bring my knee up to his groin again, but he blocked it with his thigh, which was then wedged between mine.

"Saw that one coming, fool me once and all, but I would rather you not try that again. I'm very fond of those parts."

I clicked my tongue. *Prick.*

"But I will make a deal with you. I will let you go if you give me your name. It's not often I'm given such a challenge. It's...exhilarating."

"Go to hell," I hissed as I twisted my arm, temporarily breaking his grip. Before my fist could connect with his jaw, his forearm blocked me, that hand once again pinning my arm now at my side.

"So aggressive." He chided, but humor flicked at the corners of his mouth. This male was insane. He must've had a death wish.

"Come on, sweetheart—" he crooned, still thinking he could wear me down into giving him my name. He had no idea what he was asking.

"Call me that one more time," I dared.

He smiled wickedly and leaned in closer to my face, "Sweet—"

Faster than lightning I took my opportunity, headbutting him. There was a sickening crunch, and his grip on me loosened for just long enough. I slid beneath one of his arms toward the door, my scarf catching on the buttons of his shirt. The fabric slid down, revealing my braided hair and face as I pushed away from him. I didn't pause to note if he'd seen me as I bolted for the door, yanking it open. As I ran into the alley, he thankfully did not follow.

Asshole.

My heart pounded as I made my way out of the winding streets and continued to the edge of town, where I could finally catch my breath.

I pulled out the small box of chocolates I'd tucked into the pouch at my belt, their soft fruit-filled insides splattered and staining the pink paper wrapped around them. Ruined. I couldn't even replace them as I'd gotten blood on my shirt from breaking the stranger's nose and a slowly forming knot on my forehead from the impact.

As I walked along the road, nothing more than the worn track of wagon wheels through the grass behind a set of townhomes, I tossed the box into a garbage bin. Reaching back to adjust my shirt tail that had been pulled loose in the fray, I also noted the loss of the Galorian dagger I'd tucked there.

I cursed under my breath. I'd only wanted to enjoy a morning in the city before being bound to a week's worth of royal events, only to find that my parents' social programs had been cut and becoming a beacon for every jerk in the city.

Pissed off and empty handed, I began the long walk back to the palace.

CHAPTER 2
Misha

I sat on the floor of my sister's closet, staring at her vast jewelry collection laid out before me in its glass case, set on the soft patterned rug. Our chambers were across the hall from one another in the western wing of the palace, the proximity a necessity. As twins, we'd never been separated for more than a day.

Nic's room was all deep blue walls, white crown molding, and a canopy bed with a plethora of pillows all in white or cream. Huge paned glass windows filled all of one wall with double doors that opened onto a small balcony overlooking the lake on the palace grounds. The opposite was full of bookcases overflowing with her eclectic collection of novels, tomes on battle strategy, and histories of all the sapien races and magical beings. Besides two large chairs for reading, a fireplace, desk, and some end tables with stained-glass lamps, not much else filled the space.

My twin's room would have been hugely boring if she hadn't let me cast tiny red and yellow roses, my favorite, and white calla lilies, hers, winding up the walls from the earthen floors, covered in various patterned rugs. The blooms gave the room much needed color and life, thanks to my earth magic.

Nic's closet was much like her bedroom, hyper-organized with everything separated by type and color. It made it so much easier to borrow from her, which I did often. Nic had excellent taste and an obsession with fine clothing and jewelry. Her collection of sparkly things could rival a dragon's hoard.

As I sat, my fingers slowly twirling the golden blonde hair I'd inherited from my father, I thought of tonight and the four kingdoms finally coming together. I thought of seeing *him* again.

Julian and I first met at my father and stepmother, Adrienne's, wedding ten years ago. We'd been children, each barely into adolescence. In that short time, we'd forged a friendship, sustained by letters delivered via ravens.

My parents and his father, Josiah Warin, had been reluctant allies in the Great War, but never friendly. He was allegedly horrible and morally corrupt, but a necessary ally. He and his eldest son, August's, stormcasting abilities were the reason the rebels stood any chance against the former king's now extinct dragons.

The only reason Julian had attended my father's wedding was that Josiah had died several years before from a blood disease, similar to the one that had taken our own father. His mother, Sena, then became the ambassador to Montevalle, the northernmost kingdom, and brought him along in an effort to improve relations between the North and the other countries. My sister and I have never met his older brother August, the now king. He didn't attend the wedding, and no one outside his own country has seen him since the Blood Treaty's inception one hundred years ago. According to Julian, his brother prefers his privacy.

Julian and I have since bonded in the mutual loss of a parent. He attended our father's funeral with his mother to pay their respects, the last time we'd been together, but he'd always been there for me in our letters, helping me through my grief. He let me express my heartache and vent in anger at my father's loss, receiving more tear-stained pages than I cared to admit. Julian allowed me to express myself in a way I couldn't to my family, even my sister. An outlet that helped me to heal, drawing me from my depression and back into the light.

Only Nic knew of our correspondence, nothing could ever be hidden from her. I worried that if my aunts found out I was writing with Josiah's son, the man they so vehemently disdained, they would forbid us from speaking.

Even now the thought terrified me because I was desperately in love with him.

I refocused, again debating which earrings would fit my gown best, as Rasalas snoozed by my side, his tail intermittently flicking back and forth across the floor. The massive jaguar had only been a cub when my sister and I found him abandoned during a tour of the jungle in the southern part of our kingdom, near my mother's home, thirteen years ago. The little cub came to me, bloodied from some attack, and began purring in my arms immediately. I knew I had to take care of him, had to help him heal and grow strong enough to return to the wild. No force in this world could have caused me to abandon him. Though how the little beast knew I would be such a pushover, I'll never understand.

I gave Ras a scratch on the chin, and he purred contentedly in response. I planted a quick kiss on his nose before returning to pick through the silver and gold scattered before me, adorned with sapphires, diamonds, rubies, and more, each piece expertly and beautifully crafted. *And Nic says I'm the flashy one.*

"What are you doing here?"

I jumped and shrieked, my heart pounding as I turned to see my sister leaning against the doorframe. Ras continued flicking his tail, utterly unbothered. I glared at him. The overgrown fur ball could have warned me.

"Shit Nicky, you scared me. My life just flashed before my eyes." I said as my heart rate slowed. I swore instead of part human, Nic was part wraith with the silent way she was able to slink around.

"Don't you have enough jewelry from Mother in your own room?" She lifted one eyebrow, arms crossed.

"I do, but nothing seems to fit just right with my gown and it looks like your gold threader earrings will be perfect." I plucked them up and held them to my ears to demonstrate, the emeralds glinting in the light. "You have to let me borrow them." I gave her my most dazzling smile.

Nic's head tilted, her dark brown eyes narrowing as she saw straight through my charms, but I was sure she would let me borrow them, anyway. Perks of the bond we had as twins.

"Come on Nicky, gold doesn't flatter your complexion like it does mine." It was a truth that would benefit me. Her pale, almost moonlit skin was much better suited for silver tones.

"Ouch, Meesh...but fine, they're yours." She pushed her black hair over her shoulder before crossing her arms.

"How was the city?" I asked, noting her stiff posture. Her secret trips usually eased such tension, but that clearly wasn't the case today.

It was funny, Rasalas was the wild animal, but every time we tried to release him back into the rainforest outside Alara, sobbing uncontrollably as I did so, the jaguar always ended up scaling the walls of our manor there and climbing back into my room. Eventually, Father had given up and let me keep him, my overgrown feline shadow. Nic, however, could get too restless when confined to the palace walls. Not that she resented being a princess or the duties that came with it, only the arbitrary rules that kept her confined.

"No, it's Asshole Day in the city evidently." Nic's brown eyes darkened. Normally the trips into the city eased her irritability, but her posture was tense as ever as she stood in the doorway.

My eyebrows shot up. "Ohh, what happened?" I leaned back onto my hands, eager to hear more. That's when I noticed the shadow of a bruise forming on her brow, the blood on her shirt that clearly hadn't come from her.

"Males," Nic sighed, before moving to sit next to me on the floor as she launched into her story of handsy males and rooms in hidden alleyways.

"How did you get away?" I chuckled, amused at how much of a challenge the last male was for her and how clearly irritated she still was.

She shrugged. "I headbutted him."

I fell to my side, laughing as I laid on the ground. Nic's irritation finally cracked as she smiled down at me. That male was sure to be nursing some horrible black eye, much worse than hers. The poor guy had no idea what had come crashing into that room with him.

I wiped the dampness from my eyes as I sat up again. "Well, make sure you get any cuts or bruises healed away by Eve before we get dressed later. I'm sure she'll get a kick out of your story, but Adrienne will be upset if we aren't the perfect picture of a sweet, demure princess for the ball." I pantomimed my hands under my chin, the picture of innocence.

Nic's nose wrinkled in annoyance. "Speaking of our stepmother, have you heard anything about the social programs' funding being reduced?"

"No, I thought the council was in charge of that?" I told her, confused. Between tutoring and training, Nic and I hadn't attended many of Hahnaley's royal council meetings, Adrienne ensuring us that it wasn't necessary until we turned twenty-two and began preparation for our own coronations the following year. "Where is this coming from?"

"There was a mortal woman in town. She was in a bad situation and had come to the crown for help, but they told her there was no funding. I gave her what I could and promised that we would be in touch." Nic's eyes flared with heat.

"What the hell—" I scoffed. "Mother created those programs. They're endowed—the highest priority. The funding can't just be cut."

Nic stroked a hand down Rasalas's back. "We can ask Adrienne later. I would suggest we go to her chambers now, but I'm sure she's locked in there primping or whatever she spends so much time doing."

I shook my head. "We can't go now, anyway. Alesia said she wants to train. She couldn't find you this morning so she told me to tell you."

My sister's hand stilled on Ras, her brow furrowing. "She wants to train eight hours before the ball is supposed to start?"

Our aunt had significantly upped our training in the past months, not only readying us to be at the center of so many powerful fae this week but also because of our nearing birthday. In our twenty-second year, we would reach our full capacity for magic, and she wanted us to be fully prepared to handle such power.

"You know her, she doesn't believe in days off." I stood, reaching for her hand. "Come on Nicky, that's plenty of time for me to kick your ass, have Eve heal your bruises, and then I can help you with your makeup and hair. All before the first guests arrive."

She laughed as she took my hand, standing with my assistance. "In your dreams, sister," she said before turning to change out of her bloodied shirt.

I waited in her room until she was done, admiring the tiny flowers along her dark blue walls, sprucing them up where they needed it. They climbed up her many bookshelves as well. I was flipping through one of her many novels when she emerged a few minutes later. Then we made our way down the wide halls of the palace.

My sister and I crossed into a gallery that would lead us into the gardens, the walls lined with art—canvases and sculptures from local artists in Hahnaley as well as gifts from the other kingdoms. As we walked, we passed one portrait of our deceased mother and father, the size of which spanned greater than my height.

Beneath Diana's bronze face, framed with nearly black hair identical to Nic's, which even painted portrayed the joy everyone said she radiated, hung the Galorian silver sword she used in battle. Sapphires decorated the hilt, the blade emblazoned with an old, forgotten language. The Mercedelmar, loosely translated to the *Mercy of the Sea* in her first language, one of many spoken by humans. Alesia still carried its twin, the Iradelmar. *Wrath of the Sea.*

My father's own massive battle sword, Luxien, hung beneath my father's likeness, the blonde hair and blue eyes he and I shared. The hilt and top portion of the blade a gleaming gold etched with roses and thorns. Nic and I paused in front of this tribute to our parents, remembering.

Sometimes I still went into their empty chambers to touch my father's shirts, the soft fabric that would caress my cheek every time I laid my head on his shoulder as a child, to smell his scent of cedar and sandalwood that somehow lingered after all this time. Sometimes I needed it, needed to feel close to him again, the father who'd loved us so unconditionally—who'd promised to always be there to protect us, yet still gave us the power to protect ourselves. Father had always seemed so strong, so invincible—the most powerful High Fae male on the continent, torn from us by a common blood disease.

When he died, I thought I'd never get over it—never survive it. The High Fae were supposed to be near immortal, yet here Nic and I were, so young, with both parents gone. Even the best of healers couldn't save them—no amount of magic could have stopped it. And while the pain of their loss had receded over the years, the jagged scar remained. Thank the gods for my sister and aunts. All of which would undoubtedly comfort me now, lost in melancholy as I thought of our parents. Never invalidating my feelings, but still pushing me to more positive thoughts. Father would've wanted that, would've wanted my sister and I to not think of him with sadness, but joy at the memories we'd made. Joy for the future, of what today would bring.

But days like today, ones where we would experience something he should have been present for, always sat heavily on my heart.

Before the grief could crest in my chest, Nic took my hand, her eyes conveying the same sadness but also comfort in our mutual loss. We turned away from the image of the mother we'd never met and the father that loved us for only thirteen short years. Then we continued down the steps and into the rose garden, heading for the woods to the north of the palace.

"Are you anxious about tonight?" Nic broke our silence.

"Yes and no...I don't know. It's been nine years since I've seen Julian." I sighed.

"But you write to each other almost weekly."

"I know but what if it's not the same in person? You can be whoever you want in letters." I pictured Julian the last time we'd met. Tall, with a lanky build with tightly-curled black hair. The dark skin he inherited from his mother, and gray eyes from his father. He'd been beautiful even then, when we were all in that awkward stage of adolescence. In building our friendship, I found him to be kind and funny in a way that catches you off guard. I felt like we could spend our entire existence laughing together if given the chance.

"Come on Misha, that isn't true." Nic nudged me with an elbow. "You have only gotten to know each other better in all that time. I'm sure it will feel more natural than anything."

I supposed she was right, but a heaviness still dwelled in my chest from the fear that tonight would be a letdown, that he didn't care for me as I did for him.

"Don't overthink it, sister. You are ridiculously gorgeous, smart, funny—you light up every room you walk into. Even if you hadn't been making him fall in love with you the past ten years, I'm sure he and every other male tonight will be falling at your feet." Nic said as she squeezed my hand tighter.

My twin, my biggest supporter. I smiled back at her.

We arrived at the clearing and passed through Alesia's wards for silencing and detection. As we stepped out of the trees, we saw our aunt leaning against one of the far trunks, waiting for us. She looked so much like our mother, like seeing her portrait come to life.

Alesia was one of the lead generals in the war against the High King, fighting alongside Mother and Father. She was the best remaining warrior in our kingdom, and stories were still told of her ferocity in battle. So while she could be an absolute tyrant during these training sessions, my sister and I both knew that her instruction was invaluable. It also stirred a quite bit of pride in us that such a celebrated warrior was our aunt.

"It's about time, you two." Alesia tucked a piece of her dark hair behind one ear, more rounded than other High Fae, similar to ours thanks to the human heritage we all possessed from her mother, Marisela. She'd never met her fae father, and her mother had never spoken of the male that had abandoned her and her daughters after their birth.

Our aunt made her way toward us. "I spelled the area with wards, so anyone passing by won't be able to see or hear us and will find themselves on an urgent mission elsewhere," she said with her slight accent. Alesia was always secretive in our fighting lessons, but to go through this much trouble only meant one thing.

"We're training with rowan ash?" Nic's eyebrows rose. "Today?"

Rowan trees nulled the fae's magic, healing, senses, and strength, rendering them essentially human—therefore vulnerable. But because children between the faeries and humans were so rare, so difficult to conceive, and the ash illegal except for use by the royal guards, it was not common knowledge that the rowan tree's wood, berries, and ash affected us only partially. No one knew the reason for this, for why we were less susceptible. I was sure an alchemist somewhere would one day determine the cause. Until then, I was thankful for the advantage.

"Yes, and don't worry, Nic. It's a very low dose and will be worn off by the time we return to the palace. It will only last a couple of hours," Alesia assured us as she took out the small black pouch.

I wrinkled my nose, just because I understood the advantage of training with it, didn't mean I enjoyed it.

"Wipe that sour look off your face Misha." Alesia barked. "If you think this is bad, we could go visit the Tribe of Khutulun again."

I paled as I thought of our time in the Halcon Rainforest training with the tribe of warrior fae. While all the members of the matriarchal society were lovely and the training impeccable, the humidity and mosquitoes were monstrous. I didn't think I could ever see another bug net again without wanting to light it on fire.

"Alé, that's not funny. I'm going to be sick just thinking about the size of those roaches." I grimaced as if I could feel their pokey, little legs. It had been two years and I still couldn't stop myself from skewering the little bastards on thorns whenever I spotted them.

Alesia chuckled as I shuddered at the memory. "Then stop wrinkling your nose and get over here," she said, then began with what she always reiterated in these lessons. "You want what others perceive as a potential weakness, to be your strength. If you are struck with a weapon of rowan wood, Galorian silver, or are exposed to the ash, your enemy will expect you to fall easily after. This training proves them wrong. It gives you the element of surprise and the upper hand. Magic is your gift, not your crutch. With or without it you, my nieces, are still a force to be reckoned with."

Once we reached her, Alesia blew a pinch of ash into our faces. It felt like coming out of a deep sleep when I hadn't fully awakened. Groggy and sluggish, my sight and hearing somewhat dulled, and my magic at half its usual capacity. The woods around us lost their brightness and the ever-present background noise of the forest was quieted.

To warm up, Alesia had us run around the clearing several times, then put us through different drills for strength and balance. Following this we took up bows to practice our archery, hitting different water targets Alesia cast for us as she flung them into the air at random. Nic's and my birch arrows pierced every one, all while we dodged the ice arrows Alé cast back at us with her magic, the water element she and Nic shared.

Afterward, we took a break, catching our breath and drinking deeply from the cool water Alé cast into carafes for us.

"How are your shields, girls?" Our aunt stood above me as I sat on the ground, my elbows resting on my knees.

She hadn't meant physical. I ran a mental hand over them, the shields that protected my thoughts. I looked up at her. "Solid as ever."

Alesia turned to Nic, who only nodded from where she stood. "Good. Your shields should never come down, even with the ash and exhaustion."

I knew why my aunt was worried and wondered if this was the real reason she'd wanted to train. With the gathering of the royals, there would be many powerful fae in one place. Though we were allies, bound by the Blood Treaty, some were less friendly than others.

Alexander Deimos was the brother of our stepmother, Adrienne. They were High Fae arising from the southernmost peninsula and had been a part of the High King's court prior to the rebellion. In those times, Alexander was Governor of the southern portion of the continent, which after the war became

Reyna, the country he now ruled as King. Adrienne had been their ambassador in the capitol and one of the High King's top spies. The flipping of the Deimos to the rebels aided the cause greatly as the information they fed to the others saved them on countless occasions.

The Deimos' power was the reason they were able to glean such information, why Adrienne had been so valuable to the king as a spy. Unlike the elementals, as my family and I were, their magic was that of coercion and manipulation of the mind. While powerful, their gifts could be resisted with strong mental shields, which our father and aunts trained my sister and me to build as soon as we were old enough to understand. Our aunts had gone so far as to bring in other mindcasters to train us in it. Because for those with less than impenetrable defenses, the Deimos' attacks could be lethal. There were stories told from the war in which the siblings destroyed other faeries' minds, killing them instantly, and made soldiers take their lives upon their own swords, all without lifting a finger.

I shuddered, remembering the last time we'd seen Alexander. Nic and I'd been sixteen, visiting Reyna. I'd felt his power edge toward mine, testing the boundaries, the walls. To no avail but still—he'd tried. One look at Nic told me he'd done the same to her.

We trusted Adrienne, she'd never attempted to push our mental shields like her brother had, but we would always be wary of Alexander after that.

After what Alé deemed was enough rest, Nic and I prepared to spar. We used no magic, only our hands and practice weapons. The short swords, arrows, and daggers were spelled for training so that if one of us landed a hit on the other, we would feel the pain of being struck but without the bodily damage. Alesia determined it was important to feel the force of the blow, training us to never drop our own weapons or lose focus. Doing so, even for a moment, left you vulnerable.

"Remember that your skill only matters as much as the opponent you are up against. Determine their weaknesses and tells, everyone has them. Once you do so, even the most skilled opponent can be beaten," Alesia instructed us. Her reliance on pickpocketing to obtain money for food as an adolescent had caused her to develop eagle eyes. She spotted our tells instantly and trained them out of us.

My twin and I lined up, facing each other. "Come on Nic, I know you're slow, but don't make me wait all day. You need all the time you can get to make yourself presentable for the ball later." I baited her.

Nic was susceptible to anger. This made her a fierce opponent, but could also leave her vulnerable if the emotion controlled her.

My sister smirked as she circled me, short sword clutched in her left hand, not falling for my attempt to annoy her. "You should be the one more worried about that, Meesh. It takes you half an hour just to get your eyeliner right."

"Excuse *me* for wanting to look my best at all times." I scoffed. "Some of us care what other people think, Nic."

She only shrugged at my retort. Nic acted like she didn't care one bit about how anyone else saw her, but I knew better.

"Girls, get on with it. You're wasting time." Alesia barked from the edge of the ring.

"Fine," I twirled my sword as I took up a defensive stance. Feet staggered, weight even. "I guess Nic can take getting her ass kicked for the second time today."

"Excuse you," Nic spat. "I kicked *his* ass." Then she lunged.

I had a feeling that would do it. Having anticipated the move, I blocked her sword easily. My sister's pride was always an easy target, and now we were getting somewhere.

"Sure Nicky, whatever you have to tell yourself next time you get pinned."

With this she truly attacked. I blocked her sword with my own, then counter-struck. We sparred with the blades for a minute when she became a bit too bold and lunged for me, leaving her weight uneven. I dodged the attack but used her position against her. With my foot hooked under her leg, I knocked her off balance. Nic dropped to the ground, and I trapped her sword under my boot, blocking her from striking back up at me.

I smirked but didn't have much time to celebrate as she quickly let go of her now useless sword, spun, and knocked my own feet out from under me. I landed hard on my back and swiftly one of Nic's knees was on my chest, dagger already at my throat.

"Yield," I sighed as my sister pinned me.

"Nice use of your sister's temper, Misha, but remember to be looking for the counter strike before you gloat. And nice escape maneuver, Nic. That hidden dagger pull has gotten faster. Go again." Alesia twirled her hand. "Only hand to hand this time. No weapons."

Nic smirked as she stood and held out a hand to pull me to my feet. We dropped our weapons to the side.

"I'll get you this time, Nicky."

"Sure, sure," she smiled, and we repositioned.

We went through several more practice matches, Nic and I each winning equally. Then we each took turns with Alesia, who we rarely ever beat, but training against her was better than anything else. No one was faster, more cunning, or dirtier in her tricks. Once in a different ash training session when I'd thought her down, she'd thrown actual dirt in my face. I'd reflexively blocked it, but in that quick loss of concentration, she'd had me beaten. It was a dishonorable tactic, but a good lesson—in matters of life and death, you couldn't trust your enemy to fight fair. Never trust them to follow the rules.

If you want to survive, find a way to cheat before they do.

When the ash wore off we ceased with the training, Alesia deeming it enough, and the three of us made our way back to the palace together. My heart felt lighter afterward, the exertion a balm to my nerves.

Only a few more hours separated me now from everything tonight would bring.

CHAPTER 3
Nic

After showering away the grime from training, Misha and I stood together at the marble vanity in her bathing room, it and the gilded mirror taking up all of one wall. An orange tree in full bloom grew in the corner, its branches arching along the ceiling painted to mimic the sky at dawn.

Misha helped me put a few drops of oil on the ends of my hair as it fell in loose waves down my back. Hers was already done with one side of it braided and pulled half up, the rest falling in a cascade of golden curls.

As I looked in the mirror, our shared features became clear. The same round eyes, slightly upturned noses, and full lips of our mother—the features that marked us as twins.

"Okay now get your dress on, then you can help me into mine." Misha backed away, admiring her work.

I stood and threaded dangling crystal and silver earrings through my earlobes that matched the rings and diamond studs in my upper cartilage. "Will do, sister," I finished and turned from the mirror, then slid my gown from its hanger on a hook at the closet door.

The style was simple to don and once dressed, I helped my sister step into her voluminous skirts. I used the corset strings to tighten the bodice slightly, enhancing her shape without pulling so tight that she would be uncomfortable.

Misha then stepped into her heels and stood to face the tall full-length mirror on the opposite wall. As I watched, she cast her earth magic, the gift she shared with our father. Roses appeared all along her skirt, bodice, and sleeves, the petals varying from the palest peach to a vibrant magenta.

"You make that look so effortless Misha." I touched my fingers to one of the silk-soft petals, admiring the beauty of her magic.

She smiled and gave a quick spin, skirts fluttering around her like a sunlit flower. "Now let's see yours, Nicky. I know you can't be going in just that."

My jaw dropped in mock outrage as she laughed.

I looked down at my sleek silver gown. She was right, I was planning to add some embellishments. I brought my right leg just out of the slit in my skirt. Ice crystals formed on my skin in a lattice pattern, just far apart enough that you could still see my skin underneath. The crystals began at my toes and continued up my leg to the top of the slit, then to the right side of my waist and chest, finally they reached the top and weaved in with the delicate strap. Little crystals of frost also shone in my hair like dispersed stars catching in the light.

"Gorgeous, sister. I see you're taking the Ice Queen nickname seriously tonight—try not to blind anyone too severely with your sparkles," Misha gestured to the glittering crystals, waving her fingers.

I shot her my middle one in response.

Misha burst into laughter. "Okay, *moody.*"

My sister was now practically bouncing with excitement. She walked to the end of the vanity where two boxes were waiting. The ball was to be a masquerade and inside were the masks made for tonight.

Opening the nearest one, Misha pulled out a mask wrought into vines and intricate flowers. It perfectly fit her floral beauty, her blue eyes accentuated by the rose gold.

The other held mine, plain silver silk to match the fabric of my dress with no other adornments as I'd already added plenty to my dress. I placed it on my face carefully, locking it in place with simple sticking magic.

"Let's go find Alesia and see where Adrienne wants us." I turned from the mirror, and we walked out of her bathing room together.

Misha's bedroom walls were sage green, with nearly every flower you could think of winding up the walls—a visual encyclopedia of Hahnaley's flora. Her bed had an ornate, hand-carved wooden frame depicting roses, with pillows and a duvet in various shades of pink.

I plucked one of the blooms winding up a bookcase, a deep red rose. Breathing in its rich scent, I twirled the stem between my fingers, careful to avoid the thorns.

Alesia waited for us at the end of the hall, leaning on the stone rail of the stairs that would take us down to the main level of the northern wing. She looked annoyed, but radiant, in a black sparkling gown with a plunging neckline. A mask of intricate black lace hung from her fingers.

"There you are, girls. Adrienne is going to lose her mind if you two are late."

"I'm surprised she notices anything not concerning herself as much as she stares into those mirrors of hers," Misha quipped and I snorted. Alesia gave us a reprimanding look, but the corners of her mouth lifted, in on the joke. She never quite got along with our stepmother and while cordial, Alé didn't pretend to care for her.

Misha and I liked Adrienne well enough. She was never overly kind, but just kind of *there*. Though she could come off as rather pretentious and obsessed with appearances. Alesia, however, could not stand to be around our stepmother. When our father decided to remarry years after the loss of our mother, my aunt was understandably upset. Afterward, they didn't speak for weeks. Though my father made sure we knew it was a pact between countries, not love.

Political allies rather than true husband and wife. He could never replace what our mother was to him, the other half of his soul.

It was unheard of that our father decided to marry after finding and losing his mate. But Father took the welfare of our country very seriously, so he underwent a marriage of mutual political benefit to Adrienne which served to perpetuate a greater alliance with the Reyna and strengthen the peace our countries share. I would have thought that the Blood Treaty was enough to do so, but I supposed he'd wanted something stronger.

Alesia, Misha, and I continued down the corridor, turned the corner, and saw Adrienne standing with her brother. Alexander was over 500 years old—Adrienne over 750. All High Fae lived such long lives they were essentially ageless, retaining youthful appearances for millennia. They could have each stood next to a human in their late twenties and appeared the same age.

"Hello, girls." Adrienne greeted us as she turned and pushed her long, glossy hair over one shoulder, just a shade darker than her white silk gown. Half of her tanned face was concealed in a white, feathered mask that accentuated her pale blue eyes. "We were hoping you would arrive before our other guests."

Misha's hand tightened on mine at our stepmother's slight.

On Adrienne's right stood her brother, the pair nearly identical in appearance. Alexander wore a white dress jacket and pants, accented with the deep purple of Reyna, and a matching mask to his sister. The king looked at us and said nothing.

He gives me the creeps, Misha said to me with her eyes. I returned the feeling.

"But you both look beautiful, as always," Adrienne gave us each an appraising look. "Come, it's time." She turned to head down the grand hallway as we followed.

Closer to the ballroom, the halls were affixed with the fern green banners of our kingdom. The Hahnaleyan crest of a golden tree with its roots flowing into a river encircling its branches. The green represented my father's earth element, the gold my mother—the color of the setting sun hitting the ocean waves.

The entire palace was strewn from the earth, rock, and water by our parents' magic. White stone comprised the walls and ceilings, frequently covered with various plants, moss, and flowering vines. Crystal chandeliers of glimmering pale gold hung from the domed ceiling, lit with faerie lights sitting in blooms casting everything in an ethereal glow. Intermittently waterfalls streamed from splits in the rock walls, the water flickering softly in the light.

Eve stood waiting at the carved wooden doors that would take us to the ballroom, her ombré gown glowing peach and orange, radiating the warmth of sunset. Her hair was left loose, the black, tightly-wound voluminous curls accentuating her high cheekbones.

Our godmother's dark brown eyes lit up as she saw us. "Ah, my little nieces. You two are stunning tonight," Eve gushed as she gave Misha and me tight hugs. She released us and faced Alesia, her warm brown skin turning rosy as she blushed and greeted her mate with a kiss. "And gorgeous as always, my love."

Alesia and Eve had met and been mated during the Great War. A brief, informal ceremony amidst the chaos and death surrounding them. They'd wanted to celebrate life, Eve said—wanted to know that even if the next day was their last, they would spend it together.

"Adrienne. Alexander. Nice to see you two as well." Eve smiled and bowed slightly to them both. Adrienne politely returned her smile. Alexander showed no reaction outside of a quick nod. Even if she felt the same, Eve tolerated them much better than Alesia, always projecting kindness and warmth. A different kind of strength.

After the greetings, my aunts donned their masks like the rest of us. Eve's an orange silk, decorated with peach blossoms cast by Misha.

Because we were the hosting kingdom, we would be the last to arrive, making a grand entrance just as Adrienne liked. Guards slowly opened the heavy wooden doors, carved to depict a woodland scene with all manner of fae, human, and creature. The sounds of music and revelry from the ballroom serenaded us from where we stood before quieting to a soft melody.

Alesia and Eve joined hands and entered first. They were announced as they made their way down the steps to join the party.

"Ready?" I turned to Misha and took her hand. She matched my smile but the emotion didn't reach her eyes. I gave her hand a reassuring squeeze as we entered.

"Misha Camila Sancrista Briar and Nicole Maria Sancrista Briar. Crown Princesses of Hahnaley." The royal guard announced as we made our way down the steps.

I took in the ballroom before us, spinning that red rose between my fingers. Towering trees sat in each corner, their branches coming up to trail along the ceiling covered in dark mother-of-pearl, a gift to our mother from the nereids. Faerie lights scattered across it, shimmering like stars in the night sky as they depicted the many constellations.

We descended the earth-strewn stairs, the railings covered in winding roses of every color at our sides. As we reached the bottom, the attendees, mostly Hahnaleyan citizens, parted for us. They were dressed in various finery, billowing ball gowns and embroidered suits worn by the fae, humans, nymphs, sprites, and goblins, all differing in style but all nonetheless beautiful. We made our way through them toward the moss and stone dais, where the thrones resided.

Misha's and mine were created to mimic our mother's—silver, tall backed, and embedded with the emeralds, sapphires, and rubies native to our region. The tops crested like waves in the sea. We split and moved to stand in front of them. I rested the rose I'd been carrying on the throne's wide arm.

The soft music went quiet before the next announcement, building the feeling of anticipation, as everyone watched the top of the stairs.

"Alexander Emile Deimos, King of Reyna, and Adrienne Tarra Deimos Briar, Queen of Hahnaley."

Adrienne glided down, taking her time before she sat between us on our father's grand throne in the center of the dais. The chair was gilded in gold, formed from twisting vines speckled with lilies and roses throughout, cast by his magic. Adrienne sat at last, all eyes on her, as she waved to the conductor for the music to renew.

Our stepmother lavished in the attention she received as the guests lined up to greet us and pay their respects. It was something my sister and I would have rather skipped, preferring to mingle in a less formal fashion, but what Adrienne wanted, she got.

As we sat awkwardly upon the dais, Misha's posture was taut, scanning the room as everyone returned to their mingling. The royal family from Desdemon, the famed air elementals, interrupted her search. They greeted Adrienne first, then we stood as they turned to us.

"You two have grown so much." Orelia Shaw, our mother's best friend, said as she looked up at us with dark green eyes. The petite fae hugged Misha, then me. My arms wrapped around her full figure, comforted by her motherly presence. After a moment, the Eastern Queen stepped back, tucking her long blonde hair behind a pointed ear, to allow her husband, Cedric, to greet us.

"Hello, girls," he said softly. Because the King of Desdemon wasn't nearly as exuberant as his wife, his tall stature could have been construed as intimidating, except for the warmth that cascaded from his soft hazel eyes. I smiled as Cedric tucked us into his broad chest, his wavy brown hair and full beard grazing the top of my head.

Orelia then stood by her husband, reclaiming our attention. Each wore matching masks depicting different forest scenes. "You both look so much like your parents. It's almost as if I'm looking at my old friends again." Her eyes welled up with tears as she touched a hand to each of our faces.

As Orelia fawned over us, we heard a high-pitched squeal. We turned to see Gemma, the burgundy skirts of her gown twirling around her as she rushed around her parents to grab us into hugs. As we embraced, I rested my cheek on her auburn hair.

"Oh, I've missed you," the youngest Shaw exclaimed, hazel eyes like her father's beaming with excitement. Her parents smiled at their youngest daughter's exuberance, the ever-indulgent parents.

Lorraine, their older daughter, stood just behind, greeting us with a tight smile and slight bow. Her rigid posture was accentuated by the long-sleeved emerald gown, equally green eyes bright beneath her peacock-feathered mask. The neatly braided coronet atop her head had not a single brown hair out of place. In the odd way magic sometimes worked, she hadn't been gifted with air as the rest of her family but was rather a mindcaster like he Deimos, fond of illusions.

Gemma broke apart from us to stand near her mother again, and as she did so, Evander approached us. The eldest. He wore the colors of the East, a pale blue jacket and pants accentuated with gold detailing that matched the blonde hair that fell to his shoulders.

"Princess Misha," Evander greeted my twin with a bow, then took her hand, kissing her knuckles in a chivalrous gesture. He turned to me with the same greeting, but as he straightened his hazel eyes locked with mine beneath his mask that resembled an eagle's wings. "Nic, would you do me the honor of being my partner in the opening dance?" he asked softly.

"I will." My cheeks warmed as I felt Misha's gaze on me, trying and failing to hide her smile as she looked between us.

"Excellent, I am very much looking forward to it." Evander broke into a smile of his own, and my breath caught. The royals from Desdemon stepped aside as more of the Hahnaleyan courtiers and civilians came to the dais to pay their respects.

After a while, Misha moved to stand beside me again. "Dancing with Evander, huh?" she whispered and gave me a quick jab to the ribs with her elbow.

"Yes," I responded coolly, keeping my gaze on the room and smiling at all those still approaching us in greeting.

"Come on, Nicky, I know you're freaking out inside. He's so tall and that *face*...oh my gods." She feigned a swoon. As she continued to tease me, I scanned the room, and my gaze caught on the male now walking up to the dais. Now it was my turn to mess with her. Misha was so caught up in her teasing that she hadn't yet noticed him.

The male was much taller than I remembered, which made sense considering Misha and I were only thirteen at our father's funeral, nearly nine years ago. He'd been fifteen then, but had clearly grown up since, losing the awkwardness we'd all possessed at that age. I recognized the dark brown skin he'd inherited from his mother, black hair cut close to his head, and the fluid grace he'd always possessed. Though the scruff along his jaw was new. As he approached, his gaze was only for Misha. A male caught in the siren's snare.

"You're not even listening to me." Misha frowned, then turned to see what I'd been staring at. "What could possibly—"

When she saw him, she stopped breathing altogether. "...Julian."

My sister, who'd just been mercilessly teasing me, now stood utterly speechless.

"Misha." He said her name like she was the only being in existence, the source of all the light in his world. He took her hand and kissed it with a bow. "Nicole," Julian greeted me with a similar motion, then quickly addressed Adrienne with her title and a respectful incline of the head.

Julian then made his way back to my sister. "Misha, may I have the first dance?" he asked, taking her hand again.

"Of course," she said shyly, but her face glowed like the sunrise.

Julian guided her down the steps with their still connected hands and led her, side by side, out onto the floor. They walked in silence, Misha too nervous to begin their conversation. She looked back at me, and I gave her a reassuring grin.

The music was starting, and in the next moment, Evander returned for my hand as well, leading me onto the floor with the other royals, the only ones that would participate in this opening song. Only one seemed to be missing. Julian's brother, the King of Montevalle.

As we reached the floor, Evander took my right hand in his, the other hand coming to my waist. As the violins and woodwinds played we began dancing together, spinning as the waltz called for it. Evander's hand tightened on my waist as he brought me back into him, making my stomach flutter.

"I am thankful you agreed to be my partner. It appears I have the best in the room," he told me, an appreciative smile on his lips.

"The same could be said of you." I gazed up at him, quite a few inches taller than me, as I peered at his face through my lashes.

"My dancing prowess is exaggerated by the skill of my partner," he replied humbly. A blush heated my cheeks at his compliment.

Breaking our eye contact, I spied Julian and Misha across the floor and could see they were talking now. He leaned into her ear and said something that made her throw her head back in laughter, clinging to him as she did so. My sister was absolutely stunning as she beamed back at him. Joy thrummed in my chest to see her initial shyness had worn off as they danced. I hoped for nothing but her absolute happiness. My sister had been through so much already. If anything or anyone ruined this night for her, I would turn them to nothing but frost upon the ground.

Evander guided me through the last verse of the song. As the music came to a close, we gave the other the customary bow. Before he led me back toward the dais, he paused. "I promised the next dance to Gemma, but I hope we will dance again tonight?" He asked, hazel eyes brimming with anticipation.

"I suppose I can save one more for you," I teased. He smiled again, his hand lingering in mine before he left me to find his youngest sister.

As Evander walked away, I turned and headed toward the edge of the room, searching for a glass of champagne now that all the required royal formalities had been completed. I found a server with a tray and took a glass with a note of thanks.

Scanning the room, I searched for my aunts, hoping to join them when I felt a presence behind me. A tingling awareness played at the base of my neck—the charge in the air before a storm. As I turned to investigate the feeling, it spoke.

"There you are, sweetheart."

CHAPTER 4
Nic

My stomach dropped.

"Or should I call you, *princess*?" The voice continued in its deep cadence, accentuating my title. I faced him fully then. Even in plain, though finely made, black clothing and a simple black mask covering half his face, I would have recognized those silver eyes anywhere.

"I believe you have mistaken me for another," I feigned ignorance, my face cool and aloof, even as my heart panicked in my chest. I stepped around the stranger from the alleyway to head back toward the dance floor, hoping to lose him in the crowd.

Of course, he followed me. After this morning, I should have known better than to think he would just let me walk away.

"Oh, I don't think I have, *Nicole Maria Sancrista Briar.*"

Shit, shit, shit. He must have recognized me the moment my scarf fell.

"I helped you this morning and you still can't give me a moment of your time." His voice sang with amusement. "Or maybe it isn't you..." the male continued, talking to himself as he walked just behind me, his long strides easily keeping up with mine. "Although I found something in my room after you ran off that was rather interesting, a deceivingly plain dagger...but I guess if you aren't her, I will have to keep looking for its owner. I would hate to return it to the wrong person."

I stopped walking. In my panic over being recognized, I'd forgotten about the weapon.

"Ah, now I've gotten your attention." His lips were pulled upward in a feline smile as I whirled on him. I wanted nothing more than to knock that insufferable grin right off his face. Again.

"You attempt to hold women captive and now you're a thief? After you so wrongly accused *me* of being the same?" I hissed, lowering my voice.

"I will admit that was uncharacteristic of me," the male said. His tone seemed genuine, but it wasn't an apology. Of course, this prick wouldn't have the capacity to admit that he was wrong.

"Fine, you found me...now are you going to give it back?"

"I will, but I would like to dance with you first," he countered.

I glared at him. "Absolutely not."

"I saw the gleam in your eyes this morning, sweetheart. You certainly enjoyed fighting with me—scared you'll enjoy dancing too?"

"You're right, I certainly enjoyed smashing your nose in."

"Such sweet words you whisper," he said, his hand going to his heart as if he were moved by them. "I offer a compromise. We dance and as penance, I will let you step on my feet as much as you wish. Then I will give you the dagger back."

"You do realize this is extortion," I snapped.

"Maybe." He shrugged. Prick.

I considered his offer. One dance and then I would have the Galorian dagger back, or I could tell him to forget it and lose it forever. My pride told me to refuse him, dagger be damned. But then I considered how quickly he'd recognized me, that my scarf falling was all it took. If I danced with him, I could glean who else he'd shared the events of the morning with. Possibly keep him from telling anyone else.

"Fine." I conceded. The male broke into a triumphant smile as he offered his arm. Gods, it made him more handsome.

I hated him even more for it.

Begrudgingly, I took his arm as I let the male lead me onto the dance floor as the next song began, another waltz. A flutter of anxiety settled into my gut, I was going to hate myself later for agreeing to this.

He took my hand in his as I placed my other on his shoulder. Then his arm snaked around my waist, drawing me into him, closer than the respectable distance Evander had put between us. I scowled at him, which only made his unabashed grin rise. The male was playing with fire, but it was like he knew it—liked the thrill of it. He must have been absolutely out of his mind.

We began to dance, moving in union with the other dancers. He was surprisingly graceful, meeting each step perfectly. His spins were practiced, fluid.

"Why are you so good at this?"

"Practice."

My eyes rolled at his non-answer. I timed my steps so my next one landed on his foot. The sharp point of my heel successfully hit a tender spot. He exhaled in pain as I internally gloated.

"There she is," he hissed, gripping my waist tighter. I ignored how it made my stomach drop. He kept dancing without missing a step. "I've unfortunately been to quite a lot of balls," he offered after a moment.

It couldn't have been many in our country, I was sure I would have recognized him. If his face didn't cause him to stand out, his stature certainly did.

"What reason does a back-alley creep like you have to attend balls?"

The male laughed in response. "I will tell you *if* you tell me why you were out in the city, disguised and causing so much trouble this morning."

"No—how did you recognize me?"

"Your hood slipped and your face is...distinct." He replied evasively, leaving something out—something critical.

In the silence that fell between us, I pressed my body into his as we turned, feigning that I needed to lean into him for balance—a distraction, attempting to draw his attention from my other hand.

"I don't have the dagger on me, sweetheart. I wouldn't be so foolish to bring Galorian silver here where anyone could snatch it off me."

Gods damn him, I leaned back, putting distance between us again. "I don't know what you're talking about."

"Oh, you don't? Then I must assume you weren't searching for it and instead just can't keep your hands off me—you are more than welcome to continue." He smirked. "You know for someone who denied being a thief this morning, your hands are rather deft."

"Are you ever in your incessant prattling going to tell me something useful? Like your name? You know mine. It's only fair."

"I didn't expect you to be so curious. Warming up to me, sweetheart?" His silver eyes gleamed as they met mine.

"No," I bit back, responding too quickly as I looked away. His gaze remained on my face, searching it, and we fell back into silence.

Maybe I was more curious than I wanted to admit, but if I knew his name, I could have the guards bar him from attending any of the other Blood Treaty events. That's the reason I gave myself.

After a moment he broke the silence. "I guess I should tell you. You are going to find out, eventually."

My eyes met his again, confused, as the song finished and we came to a stop. He was still holding me, his silver gaze locked into mine. "My na—"

"There you are," Julian interrupted as he and Misha walked toward us. The male and I both dropped our arms and turned to them. But Julian was speaking to him, not me.

"Brother, I wanted to introduce you to Misha and her sister, Nic, but I see you've already met," Julian said with a nod toward me.

Brother.

My heart seized. It couldn't have been—it wasn't possible.

"Misha, this is my brother, August." Julian continued with the informal introduction.

The stranger greeted my sister with a bow. "It's a pleasure, I've heard wonderful things from Julian." He said and she smiled, blushing slightly as she appraised him. She'd noticed how handsome he was as well, a trait he and Julian shared.

They didn't favor each other much in appearance, but now that I looked at them side by side, I could see the resemblance. Julian was nearly as tall, though his build was more long and lean. His skin tone was darker, his hair a similar black but a different texture—tightly wound curls instead of the loose waves of the male at my side, but Julian had the same silver eyes.

Funny how I hadn't noticed, they didn't burn the way his brother's did.

Julian's brother. The stormcaster. The reason all the High King's dragons were dead...and the stranger from this morning.

August Warin, King of Montevalle.

The stars had a cruel sense of humor.

There was no crown, no hint of his identity. He hadn't danced in that first round with the other royals. Though I noted Julian wasn't wearing a crown either. I kept my expression as blank as possible, but I was sure my sister could sense the tension radiating off me.

Misha looked between us, "How did you two—"

"Would you mind if I stole my sister away for a moment?" I interrupted, turning to Julian and praying he wouldn't think me rude.

"Not at all," he said as he let go of my sister's hand, gently squeezing it before he did so.

I nodded to him with a polite smile of thanks before grasping Misha's arm and walking toward the edge of the room, both males watching us go.

My sister began talking a mile a minute as soon as we were out of earshot. "Nicky, when did you meet August? Julian says he hates balls and never dances at them. Then we saw you two together and were both a bit stunned. How did you get him to dance?" Misha spewed her questions all at once as we walked arm in arm toward the far end of the room.

"I didn't. He asked me." Though asked was much too kind a word for it. I searched the ballroom for a server with more wine.

"*Really.*" Her eyebrows shot up. "Who knew you'd be so popular with the royal males, sister? Do you think he and Evander will fight over you for the next dance?" Her face lit up as if the idea excited her.

"What?" I shook my head. How had her thoughts even taken her there? I stopped walking and turned to her. "No. Where did you get that idea from?"

"The way he was looking at you," Misha smirked. "The way you were looking at each other, really. I could cut the tension with a knife," her hands mimicked cutting the air.

"You are delusional." I pointed at her as I finally saw a server with champagne. I grabbed a glass and immediately took a drink. Then two more.

"I am not, I could see it. We all could." Misha shrugged as she grabbed a strand of my hair, playing with the end. "And you two looked like you had *quite* a bit to say to each other."

"That's because I met him this morning," I whispered to her, switching to the language spoken by our Mother and Alesia growing up. Faeries rarely deigned to learn human languages, giving us some semblance of privacy.

"What? When? Why didn't you tell me?" She accused, converting into the language as well.

Knocking back my glass of champagne, I finished it and was already on the hunt for another. "I did tell you—I didn't know it was him." I wished she would keep her voice down.

"This morning, but..." my sister paused, then erupted into laughter as the realization dawned on her. "*No*," She drew out the word with wide eyes. "That was him? But how—why? What was he doing in the city?"

"I don't know," I said, my tone curt as I set the empty glass down on another's server's tray and briefly thanked him as I took another.

Misha continued laughing, hysterically now. "Oh my gods, this is too good," she said as she wiped a tear from her eye. "And now you two will have to spend the week together. Gods bless us all, this is going to be fantastic."

"It will absolutely *not* be fantastic." I hissed as Alesia and Eve joined us.

"Nic, were you dancing with August Warin?" Alesia asked me. Her brows furrowed at our use of her native language. Good gods, had everyone really seen? Did everyone know who he was except for me?

"Yes," Misha beamed as I glared.

"It's been a century. I forgot how handsome he is," Eve joined, to which Alesia's eyes narrowed. "Though of course I only have eyes for you, my heart," she added, her hand coming to her mate's cheek. Alesia's gaze softened as she leaned into the gesture.

"Isn't he though?" Misha said, responding to Eve's initial statement as she leaned toward our godmother. "And did you two see how he was looking at Nic?"

"We did," Alesia answered instead, the sharpness back in her eyes. She wasn't nearly as happy about this as Misha seemed to be. "You two looked...intense. We also saw *you* dancing with his brother." My aunt crooked a brow at my sister.

"We met Julian at Father's wedding, Alé. You know this. I had to dance with someone." Misha evaded, feigning indifference with a dismissive wave of her hand. "But just wait until I tell you how Nic and August met. You are going to die." Misha successfully directed the attention off her, taking Eve's hands in her own. The two gossip-mongers smiled at each other.

"I'm not doing this right now," I said as I walked off, done with the conversation. Misha stayed with our aunts, relaying my adventure in the city this morning. At least she had the forethought to cast a silencing ward around them before spilling. It was no secret to our aunts that I occasionally snuck into the city, but I had hoped to keep this one escapade to myself.

Luckily, one of the councilor's sons approached at that moment, asking me for the next dance—a welcome distraction. Once the song was over, I made my way back to the edge of the room, now wanting to take a break outside on the terrace.

As I walked I removed my mask. Most of the other guests had done so as well, over the allure of hidden identities and wanting to be seen. I tucked the mask into a bit of magenta bougainvillea climbing the high walls of the ballroom, concealing it for retrieval later.

When I turned around, I was unfortunate enough to again run into the last male on earth I wanted to see.

"Nicole."

"*August.*" My lip curled at the name he'd conveniently kept from me.

"You're angry." He too was now maskless, nothing impeding what I might have thought was concern in his eyes.

"Wow. Royal and observant. I could swoon." I stepped around him.

His mouth pressed into a tight line. "To be fair, I was in the process of telling you who I was before our siblings interrupted us."

"No," I growled. "Fair would have been telling me when you first approached me tonight. Or better yet, this morning when you recognized me. What were you even doing in the city, anyway?"

"The Crown Prince of the North, August Warin." Adrienne strode up to us with the smile she reserved for those she hoped to charm. "Though it is King now isn't it? My apologies." My stepmother purred.

I prayed to all the gods she hadn't overheard us as I shot him a look that said the same. His eyes flared with intrigue, but through them, he conveyed he would keep our meeting this morning to himself.

"Adrienne," August responded coolly. He turned his head to her, keeping his body angled toward me.

My stepmother didn't seem to notice. "We were greeted by your brother earlier, such a charming young male, but no sign of you. It made me think that you'd decided to skip another of these Blood Treaty celebrations. I am thrilled that is not the case, but I was disappointed we didn't have a formal greeting from you earlier."

Adrienne did so love to be bowed to upon her throne, I thought as ice filled my veins.

"I was otherwise engaged," August said, his tone cold.

Adrienne's eyes hardened, unaccustomed to being so disregarded before she looked between the two of us. "Such a long time it's been. Pity none of us were invited to your coronation. Fae royalty so rarely changes."

"Indeed," he said.

"Well then, I do hope you enjoy your evening. I'd hate for this to be the last time you grace us with your presence." Adrienne smiled but appeared to bristle at his curtness. She finally turned her attention to me. "Nic."

I repeated the gesture but remained silent, intrigued by the coldness that seemed to radiate off August in her presence. He set his silver eyes back on me as my stepmother walked off, back to the party and sauntering among the many guests.

When she was out of hearing range, he turned back to me. "How could I have told you who I was this morning? You ran off before I had the chance. Also, it's...complicated."

"Fine—let's uncomplicate it. We'll pretend it never happened." I began to walk away again.

"Nic, I brought drinks." It was my sister that interrupted this time, walking over to us with Julian, two shots of elderberry liquor in her hands. I wondered where in the world she had gotten them.

"Misha, you don't drink alcohol," I said, my eyebrows pinching together.

"Of course not. They're for you. Looks like you could use them." She smiled mischievously as I gave her my coldest glare. Her eyes lifted to say, *am I wrong?*

"Fine, give them to me." I took the shots one by one and threw them back as my sister smirked, she too removed her mask and began twirling it around her fingers.

Julian arrived next to her with two glasses of wine, giving me one and holding onto the other. "Thank you," I smiled at him.

August cocked an eyebrow. "None for me, brother?"

"You are more than capable of getting your own glass, brother," Julian responded, a playfulness in his voice.

August's lips twitched up as he walked toward one of the servers. He gave me a glance before he left, his gaze lingering.

Julian was grinning at me now, his dimples on full display. "I heard you're the one that broke my brother's nose this morning. He didn't tell me what happened, but I am quite impressed. It is rare that anyone gets one on him like that. The healer was forced to rebreak it in order to reset it." He had the same mischievous gleam in his eyes that I so often saw on Misha.

Misha grinned up at him as he spoke. She sure had told a lot of people what happened between me and the King in the North, and quickly.

"How many people do you intend to tell Misha?" I hissed.

"Relax, Nicky. I just told our aunts and Julian. I won't tell anyone else, promise." She held her pinky finger up. I wasn't sure I believed her, but locked mine with hers, anyway.

Thankfully, Gemma and Evander chose that moment to walk up. As they approached, I gave my sister a look that meant this conversation was over. She sighed but nodded in acquiescence.

"There you are, my favorite twins," Gemma exclaimed. Evander smiled at her exuberance in the way older brothers do.

Misha nudged her. "Gemma, you remember Julian, from Father and Adrienne's wedding?" She gestured to him on her other side.

"Of course," Gemma said, nodding.

"Lovely to see you again," Julian responded, with a dip of his head. He addressed her brother similarly. "Evander."

"Julian," he returned. Both smiled politely, though each stood rigidly, the air between them thickening. I wondered what Evander knew of the Warins from his travels, if he had ever been allowed into Montevalle in his role as ambassador.

"Are you excited about the Hunt tomorrow?" Misha patted Evander on the arm, her words bringing the males' attention away from each other, easing the tension.

"Yes, very much so. Gemma has grown into quite the equestrian." Evander inclined his head toward his youngest sister, hugging her into his side. "She may even win it all."

Gemma's cheeks warmed. "I am not so sure about that. Misha has an unnatural affinity for riding. She always beat us in races growing up."

"Not to mention impeccable aim with a bow," I said. "Considering we won't be able to use our magic to catch the beast, that puts my sister at an advantage." Misha excelled in archery, and I in swordsmanship. She would have the definite edge between us tomorrow.

"Though Evander is also well practiced in archery. You nearly won the last one didn't you brother?" Gemma peered up at him.

Evander nodded. "I came in second, just behind the impressive Alesia Sancrista."

"Is there anything you aren't good at Evander?" Misha gave me a sly wink, too quick for the others to catch.

"Julian, it will be your first Hunt as well. Are you looking forward to it?" I turned toward him, not wanting him to be left out of the conversation, though he didn't appear to mind.

"Yes, of course." His words were stiffer, more formal than they'd been when it was just my sister and me.

"Come on, Julian." Gemma teased, dropping her arm from around her brother as she shifted to face him. "What talents are you hiding from us? You have just heard about ours."

"I guess you will just have to wait and see." Julian evaded, a soft smile playing on his lips that gave nothing away.

"So the Warins will be participating?" Evander asked, his eyes probing.

Julian nodded in the affirmative. He shifted, somehow taller now, as if he towered over Evander, though they were of the same height.

"Ah, I just...wasn't expecting that." Evander shrugged, clasping his hands behind him. "I know that Josiah always sat them out because—what were his words—'our little competitions are silly, meaningless trifles.'"

Discomfort settled in my gut. A quick glance told me that Misha felt the same, her arms crossed in front of her. Gemma's eyes widened slightly.

"Yes, well," Julian began, chuckling. "My father had his beliefs, but my brother and I do not share in them. We very much look forward to participating in all that the Blood Treaty celebrations have to offer." He surveyed the room behind me. "Speaking of, my brother looks like he may be in need of my company. But before I go," Julian turned toward my twin, his face softening as their eyes met. "Misha, may I have your next dance?"

"You may." The two shared a look of promise, their fingers grazing, as Julian walked off toward the opposite end of the ballroom.

"So tell us about your travels, Evander. You must have seen much of the continent in your work as ambassador for the East," I said, facing him more fully. The male still seemed off after making that comment about Josiah.

Luckily, the change in topic seemed to brighten his demeanor. "Yes, I am lucky to have seen much of what our beautiful countries have to offer." His eyes were bright and clear as he spoke. "I will always be partial to the East of course, but the white sands of the south are mesmerizing. As well as the southern part of your own kingdom. The cliffs, lush jungle, and sapphire waters of Alara may be my favorite place outside of home."

"Oh, that is where our mother and Alesia are from." Misha clapped her hands together. "It is beautiful, isn't it? We haven't traveled often in the past years, but it is mine and Nic's favorite place."

My heart warmed as Evander spoke in admiration of my mother's home. "Yes, there is no other like it," I agreed. Alara would always be special to my sister and me.

At that moment, my eyes caught on Adrienne as she finished dancing with one of the Hahnaleyan lords, heading back toward the dais.

"Excuse us," I nodded to Gemma and Evander as I gave Misha a look. My twin understood what I was trying to convey—now was the time to talk to our stepmother about the funds.

"You haven't seen the last of us," Misha promised them both, as she hooked her arm through mine.

We walked across the floor toward our stepmother, now talking with another High Fae, a member of the royal council.

"Hello Zaran," I nodded to him in greeting, then turned to our stepmother as I let my arm drop from Misha's. "Adrienne, we need to speak to you for a moment...privately."

"Oh, girls. Why so serious? It's a celebration." She smiled radiantly as she gestured toward the gathered guests before taking a drink of her pale honeyed wine. "We can speak later."

Misha's eyes grew hard. "I think this would be better addressed now."

Adrienne stilled, assessing each of us. "Of course. Excuse us, Zaran." She inclined her head to the male. He bowed to each of us before rejoining the party. "What is it?"

I stepped closer, my voice low. "I saw a woman begging on the streets in town this morning. She said that she had gone to the crown for assistance and was told there was no funding for her."

"You know you cannot be in town without a guard, Nic. It is much too dangerous, you never know who is lurking in some of those neighborhoods." She chided. "If you can so easily leave, I'll need to speak to the guards personally about enhancing the border wards."

I caught the threat in her words. The perimeter of the royal grounds was securely warded to keep anyone from passing through them without a proper escort, all except for the guards and royal family. This was why I'd always strived to avoid being caught. If she knew how often I left, breaking her rules, she'd find a way to ward me in.

"Is it really so dangerous?" I inclined my head. "Or is it to keep us from the people, to see what has become of them and the programs we've promised?"

"Nic," Adrienne tsked. "I would never intentionally keep this from you. If you and your sister ever took the time to attend the council meetings, you would know this."

Dread settled in my gut. My stepmother had been the one who'd assured us it made no difference if we attended, not until the year before our coronation. I bit my tongue before it could lash out at her. *Liar.*

"You never answered our question." Misha cut in, her voice steady even if her face conveyed that same unease. "Why was the funding for the social programs cut?"

Adrienne waved her hand at the opulence surrounding us. "We had to host the celebration of the Blood Treaty. Those resources don't come from nowhere." She stated easily as if this is a perfectly satisfactory response before taking another drink of her wine.

"And the council agreed to this?" I sneered.

"I don't answer to the council, Nic. The council answers to their queen." She rebuffed as she straightened. We were eye to eye now.

My own spine steeled in response. "Those programs could have been funded for a year with half the cost of the extravagance here tonight."

Adrienne met my glare. "These celebrations are only hosted once every twenty years, it has been sixty since the West hosted last. We needed to show strength to the other countries. They need to see that we are strong and flourishing."

"The other countries we have been at peace with for a hundred years?" Misha angled her head. "How could you possibly fathom that letting our own people starve and beg on the streets could be construed as strength?" Distaste shone in my sister's eyes.

"Come on, girls, don't be so dramatic." Adrienne shook her head and laughed. "Let's discuss this at the end of the week when the celebrations are over. There is a council meeting scheduled for then. I will let you look over the ledgers yourself to make sure everything is funded to your liking."

"Fine, but that discussion will happen." I turned to walk away with Misha.

We'd been too lax in the last several years, more focused on our studies and training than on the politics of our own court. And in that time, Adrienne had used our kingdom's riches for what she valued most, displays of extravagance and wealth—what she considered to be power. But Misha and I were no longer going to allow her to do so at the expense of the people.

There were much more effective ways to show our allies and enemies how powerful we were, ones that didn't cost a drop of gold or silver.

I was still bristling at the conversation with Adrienne when I walked outside minutes later, the stuffiness and confinement of the ballroom suddenly too much for me. I needed fresh air to cool off.

I slipped out a side door to avoid the patrons on the main terrace and stepped into the grass. Slowly I reached down, unbuckling my heels and sliding them off my feet so they wouldn't sink into the earth. I sighed at the feeling of the soft grass beneath my feet, letting the tension leave my body as I walked, hugging the palace wall as I approached the rose garden.

As I came around a corner, I heard voices and paused. They clearly hadn't heard me approaching, my barefoot steps on the grass too soft for even their fae ears to detect. They were alone on a side balcony, also escaping the crowd. I couldn't see them from where I stood pressed against the wall, but I tilted my head to listen.

"So the Briar princess, are you still serious about her?" *August.*

"Since the moment I laid eyes on her ten years ago, brother. She is the most divine creature I have ever seen." Julian's tone had a reverence when talking about Misha, a devotion. She was going to be over the moon when he told her how he felt.

"Beauty tends to blind, brother. The princesses are young, untried, and have been surrounded by influential fae. It would be wise to discern which of those has impacted them. Which carved them most in their image."

My blood thrummed in my veins. August was a fool. He didn't know my parents or aunts at all if he thought they had attempted to make my sister and I into anything but what we were. Though being molded to my mother's selflessness, my father's patience, Alesia's bravery, and Eve's kindness could have only been a good thing.

"As you did for me?" I heard Julian chuckle in response. "I've already seen all of Misha's darkest parts. Nothing you or I discover about her could make me shy away. And something tells me she would refuse to be anyone's whetting stone. Nor would her sister—those eyes are much too cunning. Though I think you know that as well as I do, brother, with the way you watch her. Tonight has been quite an unexpected turn of events. I didn't think anyone would ever catch your eye."

August let out a refuting snort. "I wouldn't say that, though she is indeed...intriguing. She has more spark than one would think with her reputation for coldness. It is surprising, really—like no one that spoke of her really knew her at all."

"You have a lot to say about a female you claim hasn't caught your attention."

"What I have to say does not mean that my interest is lasting. She is still proud and unreasonably arrogant for her youth and inexperience. Any interest I find in her will pass by the time we return home."

A pang went through my chest.

"There is nothing more I would love than to see than you proven wrong, brother." Julian chuckled.

"You should return to your princess. You could be collecting more of her smiles instead of wasting time out here with me," August told Julian, who wordlessly gave his brother a clap on the shoulder and took his advice.

I left then as well, having heard enough.

As much as I hated to admit it, August's words struck a familiar chord, a familiar hurt I had worked to bury deep. Overhearing him, reliving that moment in my head, only succeeded in making it return. Not only that, but August had insulted my family's influence, said I was proud and naïve as well as hardly interesting enough to be only passing entertainment for him.

Because my sister's happiness meant more to me than my own, I'd considered letting go of the anger I held toward August after this morning for Misha's sake. The last thing I wanted was for anything with us to come between her and Julian. After what I'd overheard, I knew I wouldn't be able to.

I made my way back inside, still holding my shoes in my hand. As I re-entered the ballroom, I grabbed another glass of wine. To hell with tonight, my stepmother, and August Warin.

CHAPTER 5
Misha

T hey are madly in love."

"No way," Gemma scoffed. "They hate each other—they're practically at one another's throat."

Catching our breath after a particularly lively dance, Gemma and I perched ourselves on the sill of one of the many ceiling-high, arched windows. She used her air magic to call a breeze through the opening, cooling the grand ballroom.

Gemma was a year younger than Nic and me, yet already held significant skill over the element. Nearly as powerful as her brother already, who was over sixty years her senior. In Fae families where the heir was the most powerful, not the eldest, she seemed most likely to one day take her parents' throne.

As we sat we made a game of guessing the other guests' conversations, laughing to ourselves the more ridiculous our theories became.

The lemon-scented breeze fluttered through my hair. "Hate is not the opposite of love, Gem. They're two sides of the same coin."

Gemma rolled her eyes. "There she goes, storming off. See?" She lifted her chin as the female faerie, flipping her lavender hair over one shoulder, walked away from the male she'd been fighting with. "She can't even stand to be near him."

"But his *eyes*, Gemma. Look at them. They hold such longing for her." I clasped a hand to my chest. "Watch. I give it less than a minute before she's looking back to see if he followed her." Which the male indeed had, his long brown hair flowing out behind him as he weaved through the other revelers.

"Impossible. Do you want to make a bet on it?" She held her hand out to mine.

"Winner gets a piece of jewelry from the other?" I proposed. Gemma nodded, and we shook on it. "Time starts now. One minute." Leaning back against the window's edge, I watched the seconds flip by on the clock sitting high on the far wall, the face glowing pale like the moon at its fullest.

Not twenty seconds later, the lavender-haired female neared one of the exiting doors, looking back behind her as she did so. The male was no more than ten meters behind. As their eyes locked, I swore I saw something give in the female's hard gaze.

"Hah!" I pointed. "She just looked over her shoulder! I bet they're off to find an alcove where he can grovel and beg her forgiveness, then *make up* in." I grinned triumphantly, holding out my hand.

"Fine. You won." Gemma sighed, slipping off a bejeweled ring shaped like a branch of cherry blossoms, the golden stem and pink sapphire blooms wrapping around the band.

I slid my winnings onto my right index finger. As I held my hand up to admire it, I saw Nic returning from wherever she'd snuck off to. Her shoes hung at her side in one hand, a glass of red wine in the other. At first look my sister's face was calm, perhaps a touch distant—but her eyes were murderous.

"Nic!" Gemma beamed as she waved her over.

My sister stopped short, as if Gemma had broken her out some deep thought, then made her way over to us.

"We were just playing the most wonderful game." Gemma leaned forward onto her hands from where she sat, all thoughts of losing our wager forgotten. "Care to join?"

"No, but I can listen." Nic leaned against the wall next to us, looking out at the crowd. She was clearly still fuming over our conversation with Adrienne.

Gemma shrugged before glancing about the room again. She knew us too well to take it personally.

I leaned around the window edge to face Nic better. "Sister, has Evander returned to take you up on that second dance yet?"

She took another sip of dark wine. "Not yet."

"But you would like him to." I smiled coyly.

Gemma gasped, her head spinning back toward us. "You two would make such a great pair! Imagine you and my brother—we could all spend so much more time together."

As if summoned by the mention of his name, Evander appeared, walking toward us after finishing a dance with Adrienne. "Sorry to interrupt you, ladies." He gave Gemma and me a quick nod, then a curious glance once he realized where we sat. "Nic, may I have this dance?"

"You may." She set down her now empty glass, her eyes finally thawing as Evander took her hand and led her to the center of the floor.

We watched them go, but Gemma and I weren't left alone for long as a courtier from Hahnaley came to ask her hand for this dance as well. She hesitated as she glanced at me, not wanting to leave me there alone.

"Go ahead, Gem, I was just planning to hunt down a server with a dessert tray," I reassured her before standing, my hands smoothing my skirts.

Gemma gave me a small smile of thanks before taking the man's hand and letting him guide to the floor. As they walked away, I turned to make my way toward the top of the room.

In my search, I felt a warmth climb up my spine toward my neck. Turning to investigate, I saw Julian making his way toward me. I didn't know if it was good or pathetic how attuned my body already was to his presence.

"Misha," he said, and I couldn't help the smile forming on my lips. That warmth I'd felt grew to expand in my chest, right where my heart resided.

"There you are, you disappeared for a bit," I said then immediately regretted it. I should have been playing it cool, and now I'd admitted that I'd been looking for him.

"Yes, I apologize for that. I accompanied my brother outside for a moment. He usually avoids balls and parties of this size. They tend to drain him."

"Ah, I know what you mean. Nic can be the same way." I spun Gemma's ring around my finger, unsure of how to stand or what to do with my hands in his presence.

"I was actually hoping that you and I..." A nervousness crept into his gray eyes. "That we could get a breath of fresh air ourselves in the gardens. You've always described them so beautifully, and I would love to see what you've done with them in person."

"Of course." I nodded my head in agreement though my heart thundered in my chest, unsure if I was ready to be alone with him—truly alone for the first time tonight. This male might very well be the ruin of me.

Julian gave me a breathtaking smile before taking my hand, the simple action soothing me and making my breath catch all at once. We exited the ballroom, walking out onto the terrace where several guests were enjoying the clear summer night. With his hand in mine, I led him down the steps toward what I most wanted to show him.

Sneaking a glance up at him, I wondered what my parents would have thought of Julian. In my heart, I hoped they would have loved him as I did, even if they abhorred his father. My father and aunts had always taught my sister and me to never judge someone by their history, so I hoped my parents would've given Julian that same courtesy, and my aunts as well once I divulged our story to them.

No matter which partner I chose, I always knew it would have to be someone that could see me, all of me, and love me fully—unconditionally as my father loved my mother. Looking into Julian's eyes, at the light that shone there, I felt in my heart that he would. He already had in a way, helping me through the darkest parts of my grief—never wavering in his friendship with me in those cherished letters.

"You created all of this?" Julian looked around in awe as we entered the rose garden, a maze of winding pathways that led to different alcoves, all of it covered in lush summer blooms in every color. Deepest red to white as snow. He touched his fingers to the petals of a soft pink rose, his other hand never leaving mine. My heart left my chest and started beating there where we were joined. I nodded, unable to form the words.

"Breathtaking." He said of the roses, but his eyes were locked on mine. I wondered what the stars were thinking when they'd made him so perfectly.

Before I melted entirely under the intensity of his gaze, I tugged on his hand to bring him into the center of the garden where a small stone temple sat. Large limestone columns surrounded its circular base, vines of pink tea roses climbing each one. We ascended the steps to the center, now able to see the labyrinth of the gardens from all sides. Once at the top, I cast out floating faerie lights, the entire place igniting in an incandescent glow.

"This place is extraordinary." Julian turned, finally letting go of my hand to walk around the edges and take in the view.

"It is, isn't it? I was told by my father that it was a favorite of my mother's. He is the one that initially grew the roses for her since they were her favorite. I've just expanded them."

Julian turned away from the edge, facing me again from across the space. "It is truly one of the most beautiful things I have ever laid my eyes on."

My cheeks heated at his compliment. "Just one of them? What could possibly outshine it?" I teased, leaning against one of the pillars. I banished the thorns so only soft rose petals grazed my back.

"I can think of several things."

My heart sank as my eyes drifted down, the petals along my skirt beginning to wilt under my gaze.

"Like your face, radiant as the sun from the moment I first saw you."

My eyes snapped up as Julian began to walk toward me.

"And your eyes when they're filled with laughter or lost in thought. The way you move as you dance, so graceful, so effortlessly mesmerizing—or even the rare moments where you stand completely still, the ideal grace that no artist could ever fully capture."

I stood motionless, unable to think—to breathe—as he made his way to me.

"The way you curve your letters in your writing, even the small smudges where your tears fell, letting me see your pain. All are so breathtakingly beautiful, but compare nothing to your soul, Misha—to your kind and fearless heart." He came to stand in front of me, just inches between us, as I pressed myself harder into the pillar. My gaze drifted down to his collar, the embroidery there I hadn't noticed. Tiny silver roses and thorns shimmered along his lapel.

Julian's fingertips went to my chin, lifting to bring my eyes back to his. The gray in them churned like storm clouds just before rain. "Though my favorite view might be right now, when you look at me with those deep blue eyes that breathe light into the darkest reaches of my soul."

"That's quite the list," I whispered, so entranced by his words, terrified of breaking the spell they'd cast over him and me.

Julian moved his hand to cup my face gently. "I mean every word. No thing or place or person could ever outshine *you* to me." He moved in to kiss me, and though I very much wanted him to, I placed my hands on his chest to halt him.

"Aren't you worried about what our families will think? What your brother might think?" His heart beat wildly against my palm, its rhythm in tune with my own. My concerns of over my aunts still plagued me, but I also didn't think I could ever let him go. Not after his admission.

His hand lifted to brush back a strand of hair from my face. In his touch, I felt a spark, a hint of the lightning that flowed through his veins. "My brother has only ever wanted my happiness. You give me that. Your letters were the air

I breathed for so long. He will accept whatever makes me most happy. That's you, Misha."

I ran my finger over those embroidered roses as I smiled, finally letting myself bask in his words as I pulled him nearer, closing that final space between us.

Julian's hand shifted to cup the back of my head as he leaned into me, then pressed his lips to mine. The tenderness of it rattled me, down to the very core of my soul.

He moved his hand to the nape of my neck, and slowly the kiss changed as we became more passionate, unable to get enough of one another. His fingers entangled in my hair, holding me captive as my mouth opened for him, and his tongue slipped in to caress my own. With his other arm, he clutched my waist, pulling me even closer to him.

The hunger I had for him should have scared me, it couldn't have been sane to have wanted someone this much.

"You have no idea how long I've waited to do that," Julian whispered as he pulled back, his lips pressing soft kisses down my neck.

"Eleven years?" I shivered under his touch.

His lips curved up against the bare skin of my shoulder. "Yes, love. Since I first laid eyes on you."

I ran my fingernails over the back of his head. "It was the same for me. Even when we were so young, I think I knew what you would come to mean to me. My friend through every laugh and heartbreak."

Julian lifted his head, chuckling as he kissed my nose. "I don't know if that's better or worse, knowing you felt the same and having to wait all this time."

"Regardless, I wouldn't change anything about this moment, about tonight. It's better than I could have ever dreamed." I confessed and pulled his lips down to mine again.

As our lips met for the second time, we became lost in our own world—in each other. Surrounded by roses and the shimmer of faerie lights.

CHAPTER 6
Nic

S ister!"

Misha burst into my room, abruptly pulling me from my alcohol-induced deep sleep. My head pounded from last night's wine and the late hour in which I finally made it to bed. She went to the far wall, full of floor to ceiling windows and doors that led onto a balcony, before throwing open the curtains. The soft light of early morning poured in.

I wondered if I laid still enough she would think I was asleep and leave.

"Nicky, wake up. I have to tell you about last night—" my twin said as she jumped onto the bed and landed painfully on my calves.

Who was I kidding?

"Meesh, what the hell," I grumbled into my pillow, still face down. "What time is it?"

"Time to get your ass up and listen to me." She bounced herself on the mattress, shaking me. I rolled over reluctantly, keeping my forearm over my eyes to block the sunlight. *Gods curse me*, it couldn't have been more than thirty minutes past sunrise.

"Fine, what is it?" I groaned.

Misha grabbed my arm and threw it off my face. "Julian kissed me last night."

I squinted open my eyes to glance up at my sister. She was radiating pure bliss, her wide grin so bright it made even my headache dim a bit.

"Oh, that's great, Meesh. See, I knew he would feel the same. You had nothing to worry about." Definitely not after witnessing the way Julian was looking at her all last night. The poor male was so far wrapped around her finger it wasn't even funny. Adorable though.

"I know, I feel silly thinking about it now. He told me how he feels, and it was the absolutely most romantic thing I've ever heard, even better than all those novels you read—*don't* play coy Nicky," she accused, pointing a finger at me. "I know you sneak them in late at night like we don't know you love them." My sister winked then grabbed one of several on my nightstand, flicking through the pages for good measure as my face burned. I quickly snatched it from her, stuffing it under my pillow as she laughed. Gods, if she didn't keep that to herself I may have to strangle her.

Misha continued, still riding her high from last night, "I feel like my heart soared into the clouds and is never coming down. And his lips, the way he—"

"Misha—enough." My face pinched and my sister laughed again.

"But now I have to tell our aunts about him, right?" Misha's amusement dimmed as worry seeped into her eyes. "What if it doesn't go well? You know how Alesia feels about the Warins."

"Eve will be happy if you're happy. You could fall in love with a dryad that spends half their time as a willow tree and she would be thrilled for you. But Alesia—yeah, she'll be the tough one."

My sister sighed. "Okay...will you go with me?"

"No."

"Ugh—" my sister groaned dramatically as she threw herself into the pillows next to me. "But she is going to be angry that I hid this from her. What if she doesn't understand?"

"She will support you no matter what, just be honest with her. But don't get it wrong, Alé will absolutely make you squirm first."

Misha pondered this for a moment, looking out my floor to ceiling windows as the early morning light flooded in, and wrinkled her nose at the thought. Alesia and Eve were designated as our godparents after our birth, a title neither took lightly. As our maternal figures, they were going to be hurt that Misha had hidden this from them, especially considering how important Julian had become to her over the years. Though Eve would take the hurt in stride, Alé was going to give her at least some hell.

"Consider this Nicky." My sister turned onto her side to face me, ready to change the subject. "What if Julian and I end up together, and you and Evander do as well—" my sister saw the look on my face and cut me off before I could interrupt her. "Don't give me that look, you can't run from love forever. Just think of how fun it would be to both be in love at the same time."

I smiled at her enthusiasm but shook my head. "You are counting your flowers before they bloom, sister. We talked and danced last night—that's it."

Misha rolled her eyes. "Fine Nic, be a pessimist. You can't forever think everyone will be like—"

"Nuh uh. No." I cut her off. "We are not bringing that up—and I am not a pessimist, I'm realistic. I am not going to start romanticizing a life with Evander just because we danced a few times." Evander might have a beautiful face and jawline and a scent reminiscent of summer wind through a meadow, with a voice that could charm just about anyone...but I'd been there, done that. The hurt wasn't worth it. It never would be.

"But I know you, sister—too well. If Evander starts showing you *too much* interest, it will scare you off. If you think he isn't showing *enough*, you will think he isn't serious. There is no winning with you. Promise me you will take in his advances with an open mind?" Misha pressed.

"Fine, but I am not rushing into anything. Besides, who is to say that he will be the one for me, my mate? Orelia was over three hundred years old when she married Cedric, and Mother was nearly one hundred and fifty when she mated with Father. Who's to say that my match won't come along then? We are turning twenty-two in a couple of days, I can surely spare a few decades or centuries looking for my *one true match deemed by the stars*," I waved my hands up toward the molded ceiling. "Males do it all the time and no one gives them any trouble."

It was true. There had always been a double standard when it came to being married or mated among the fae. The males would be seen as noble and romantic if they waited centuries for the right partner; females that did the same were seen as undesirable. *Fuck that.*

"Besides," I continued. "A mate could very well be your worst enemy instead of your one true love. A perfect adversary."

Misha scoffed. "Bless the Mother, Nic, that is an old fae tale. You are going to be alone forever with that attitude."

"Better alone and happy than bound to someone who turns out to be a complete prick when their mask comes off." I leaned back into my pillows, satisfied I'd won.

"Ugh, forget it! You are insufferable." Misha shook my bed as she jumped off, then pulled my white, embroidered duvet with her. "Now get up, lazy bones. You're going to make us late for breakfast."

I scrambled to grab the blankets before they too hit the floor. "It's always *you* that is late to breakfast, Misha, not me. You must really have it bad if the thought of seeing Julian again has made you this eager to be on time for once." I called after her.

"Yes, that and the promise of pancakes." Misha walked backward toward my door. "But seriously, get up. I'm not walking down there by myself." The blonde tornado made her way back out of my room as quickly as she'd run in a few minutes ago, leaving the door wide open.

I groaned as I stood then fixed my bedding. Walking sluggishly, I closed the door before making my way into my attached bathroom. The floors, walls, and ceiling were all covered in similar tiles of dark turquoise, their mottled appearance making the colors vary uniquely on each square. The whole effect made you feel as if you were walking under the sea.

After washing my face and braiding back my hair, I dressed in my black leathers with dark burgundy accents and pulled on riding boots that nearly reached my knees. The top of this set came up high on the neck, with small cap sleeves covering my shoulders that would allow for greater freedom of movement for archery, not to mention keep me from sweating too much with skillfully placed venting if the hunt ran into the late morning.

Then I grabbed my weapons from my closet. Daggers in each boot, a yew bow, and a quiver of birch arrows across my back. I thought of the Galorian dagger I'd lost, that August *still* had, and felt a resurgence of my anger from last night. There was no way in hell I was talking to him again unless it was under duress, even to get the dagger back. I would rather stab myself in the thigh with it first.

I made my way across the hall and into Misha's room. My sister was already fully dressed in matching leathers, but in a warm caramel with cream accents, and lounging on her pink velvet sofa with Rasalas purring contentedly on the ground beneath her.

"Ugh, finally."

"Misha, it has been at most fifteen minutes since you left my room."

"It felt like an eternity." My sister drawled then jumped up, her dexterity keeping her from catching one of Ras's paws or tail underfoot. The great cat only continued to purr, completely unbothered by my sister's sudden movement, used to the chaos that was her.

We walked down to breakfast in silence. Misha because she was quietly buzzing with excitement at seeing Julian again, and me because my head still ached.

Surprisingly, we were not the first to arrive in the dining hall at this early hour. Alesia, Eve, and the Warins were all already at the table. I was instantly jealous of the Shaws for getting the luxury of sleeping in with no Misha Briars to wake them. Adrienne would inevitably arrive last, making her entrance a spectacle. I also noted the lack of tension in the room. I would have thought there would be more awkwardness between the Warins and our aunts based on the history with their father.

My sister gave me a subtle nod as we entered, wanting me to sit by Alesia so she didn't have to be grilled just yet. I rolled my eyes in response but did so anyway. Eve sat on Alé's other side, across the table from August and Julian. Misha went down to sit by her.

"Good morning, mija. How are you feeling?" Alesia asked as I sat and reached for the kettle, then methodically prepared tea just how I liked it.

"Fine," I grumbled as she chuckled, knowing all too well how I was actually feeling.

After filling my plate for breakfast, I reached back for my tea, now cooled enough to drink, and I looked up to see August watching me. I glared back as I took a sip, refusing to yield by being the first to look away.

In response the corners of his mouth flickered upward just slightly, suppressing a smile as he held my gaze. After a few moments he slowly returned his gaze back to Eve, whom he had been in conversation with before my sister and I'd arrived.

Prick.

Thankfully, in the next moment the Shaws joined us. Orelia and Cedric entered first followed by their children. The first two patted my shoulder as they passed, then Misha's, before finally sitting on the other side of August.

After greeting everyone warmly, Orelia launched into asking my sister how she enjoyed her first Treaty Ball, then lamented that she didn't get to see us more often, and finally admired how much she and I had grown up since last year. I also overheard her guilt tripping my sister that we would all visit them more often in Desdemon. Misha, being unable to disappoint anyone, readily agreed.

Lorraine sat across from me next to Julian, Gemma at her other side. Finally, Evander took the seat next to mine, my breath going shallow at his proximity and remembering how we danced last night.

"How are you this morning, Nic?" he asked me as he reached for the kettle.

"Good," I lied with a small smile. "And yourself?"

"Amazing. We went for a run this morning. We wanted to get the day started and ready ourselves for the Hunt to come later. Such beautiful walkways and trails you have through the gardens and the nearby woods. It was all so stunning in the early morning light."

I had to stop myself from wrinkling my nose. "Yes, the trails are beautiful. We run them often. I am glad you all got the chance to enjoy them." Just the thought of running right now made my stomach turn.

"Well, those two did. I hate rising before the sun." Gemma grumbled as she filled her own plate. "It should be illegal to be up before the birds," she yawned.

Julian chuckled in agreement, still looking a bit sleepy from his late night with my sister. Thank the gods I wasn't the only one worse for the wear this morning. Though he did appear more lively since Misha arrived. They were sneaking glances at each other adorably from across the table. My sister had a slight pink blush across her cheeks and was obviously holding back a smile as she intermittently pretended to be intrigued by Eve and August's conversation and made more promises to Orelia that we may or may not be able to keep.

"Good morning everyone." Adrienne held out her arms as she and Alexander entered the room, he in black riding leathers and she in a gauzy white gown, train billowing behind her, and a golden crown she'd commissioned for herself atop her intricately braided hair. She would not be participating in the Hunt then.

They walked to the opposite end of the table, Adrienne sitting at the head and Alexander to her right next to Misha. My sister subtly scooted a bit closer to Eve.

"Nervous for the Hunt?" Evander asked, pulling my gaze from my sister and back to him.

"Nervousness would indicate a lack of preparation," I said as Alesia gave me a nudge. *You better be able to back up that arrogance.* "And I do have the best trainer on the continent," I added to appease my aunt, nudging her right back.

"Of course, the legendary Alesia Sancrista is renowned for her skill with a bow," Evander said as he nodded to her in appreciation.

"Good thing I'm overseeing this year to give you all a chance then." Alesia had won two of the last four Treaty Hunts, my mother won another. Sancrista's were the ones to beat, apparently.

"Maybe I will actually stand a chance against your proteges," Evander said.

"Maybe." Eve piped up from Alesia's other side. "Or you could end up on the same team and benefit from the lineage."

"Teams?" Misha gaped. The Hunt had always been an individual event. The first to slay the symbolic stag won. My sister, nor any of us really, wanted to share in the glory.

"We decided this year to make it a team event. To further demonstrate our camaraderie and mutual alliance." Adrienne said from the head of the table, having overheard us.

Julian leaned forward to whisper to me conspiratorially, "And likely to prevent the brawls."

I smiled knowingly at him. Fae blood ran hotter than humans', and not just in temperature. We were territorial and aggressive beings by nature. Put a bunch of fae in competition with one another and likely someone would be snarling by the end.

"Ah yes, like at the last one," Evander whispered to us as well.

"Who fought last at the last one?" I tried to keep my voice low now that the other end of the table had fallen back into their own conversation. My eyes caught Misha's as she viciously glared at me. She hated feeling left out.

I gave her a nearly imperceptible nod, *I'll tell you later.*

Her eyes narrowed. *You better.*

Evander's voice lowered further. "Your aunt and Alexander."

I whipped my head back to Alesia, eyebrows raised.

"Don't look at me." She put her hands up innocently, then continued eating like it was nothing.

"Eve?" My eyebrows shot up my forehead.

My godmother turned to us and discreetly cast a silencing ward from her fingers encasing just she, Alesia, and me. "The bastard almost ran my horse and I off into a ravine. Freja stopped us from going over, but just barely." She said of her beloved paint mare. "We were centimeters from being splattered on the rocks. Then he tried gaslighting me into thinking I'd imagined it." Eve hissed. Her dark eyes heated at the memory.

"She broke his jaw and several ribs," Alesia added.

My mouth fell open. "Didn't you try to stop it?"

"You know you can't stop a duel between two fae once it's begun, Nic, even the informal ones. It's a good way to get yourself hurt. Besides, I was enjoying every second. I saw the whole thing. He was getting what he deserved." She said with a glimmer in her eye, an appreciation for the brutality that laid dormant in her mate.

Eve smirked and shrugged as she uncast the silencing ward.

I turned to face the others. Gemma was grinning at me. "I can read lips."

CHAPTER 7
Nic

I caught up to Eve as we left the dining room, heading to the stables. Misha and Julian walked ahead of us side by side. They were pointedly ignoring the other, trying to look like they weren't together, and failing spectacularly.

"Auntie—"

"You only bust out the *Auntie* when you want something, Nic." Eve cut me off.

I gasped, a hand to my chest. "And what if I was just coming up to say how much I admire you and your brawling skills?"

Eve arched an eyebrow, shooting me a wry look.

"Okay," I conceded. "My head is pounding—please help me." I gave her my best puppy dog eyes in the hopes she'd use her healing powers on my wine hangover.

"Oh fine, Nicky," Eve laughed. "You can relax with the theatrics. I swear, the drama of you and your sister." She brought her hand behind my head to my opposite temple as her healing energy pulsed into me with a warm golden light, and I immediately began to feel the ache dissolve. I wrapped my arm around her waist as we walked and took in her unique scent, reminiscent of sun-warmed freesia.

As her magic poured into me I whispered to her, "Since when are you so friendly with August Warin? You and Alé always made it seem as if you hardly knew him." They had been in conversation with each other, Alesia joining in occasionally, for most of the breakfast.

"Well we haven't seen him in a hundred years, and back then we didn't really have the chance to get to know him during the war from being stationed on different fronts, and then the war council meetings were always so heated. August rarely attended those—I suspect avoiding his awful father. Who can blame him for that? All of us only came together in the final push, but he tended to keep to his own regiments. Surprisingly, he really is quite charming." She laughed as I rolled my eyes at her response, the sound like bells on Winter Solstice.

Eve went on, "August was inquiring where exactly in the southeast of the continent I am from. He told me that one of his current council members in the North grew up in a nearby region."

I turned to look at my aunt, my headache finally disappearing as she healed me. "And are you from the same place?"

"We are," she said excitedly. "She is from Sossulla as well. Though I didn't recognize the surname. I asked if they had joined him on the journey, you know how lovely it is to reminisce with another about your homeland, but he said that they had not. He and his brother traveled here alone. So odd for a pair of royals don't you think? The Shaws brought at least fifteen of their own household staff." Eve dropped her hand from my temple, wrapping it instead around my shoulders as she'd finished healing me.

I couldn't help but snort at her words. The Shaws always arrived with an entourage. But her saying that the Warins came alone intrigued me. If he said none of their court came, then who fixed August's nose after I broke it? Surely someone had come with them...but if they weren't on the palace grounds, where were they?

"Oh hush, Nicky." Eve hugged me closer to her side as she chuckled. "Like you've ever been a light traveler."

"I like to look nice, Auntie, you know this. And you can never have too many options."

By this time we'd reached the stables. Eve gave me a wink as she went to stand near her mate. I went to the back to say hello to our stable staff, then leaned my shoulder into one of the wooden columns.

"We will begin by explaining the rules of the Hunt." Alesia began, drawing all of our attention.

Everyone turned to look at her as Julian came to stand just behind my sister at the back of the group. Misha kept her eyes forward but she was biting her lip to hold in a grin. Her fingers reached back to intertwine with Julian's behind her.

Very inconspicuous, sister.

The Hunt began several millennia ago as a symbolic tradition celebrating the gods and the story of the Mother, all of their true names long forgotten with the passage of time. It was written that tens of thousands of years ago, when only the humans and the naturistic faeries roamed the earth, like the pixies, gobins, and nymphs, the Father ruled in the heavens. One of several deities, but the most powerful—the King of the Gods. He watched the beings on earth and felt loneliness. He yearned for what they had: love, family, friendship. None of the other gods suited him for this and he remained alone through the passage of time.

One day the Father spotted a human woman, with long brown, braided hair riding on a horse with her bow strapped to her back. Entranced, he watched her day after day as she hunted and provided for her family. Eventually, he disguised himself as a human man, hiding his large feathered wings and ethereal beauty as he went to her.

The human woman was initially wary of him, but after they would meet in the forest day after day, talking and laughing, and she slowly began to trust him.

They fell in love, and when he was honest with her about who and what he was, she did not shy away, was not afraid. In their trysts, they conceived the Son. He was born as the first High Fae, and eventually became first High King of the continent, holding all of the elemental magic as well as that of healing and the connection to animals. Curiously none of the stories mentioned storms or mindcasting...legends say different gods bestowed those gifts to the fae.

Though the gods no longer walked upon the earth as they once had, the Hunt was upheld as a tradition in the days before the Summer Solstice to honor the Mother who upon her death ascended to goddess to join the Father in the heavens. It was held on horseback as she once rode, though the High Fae in general were very fast, faster than most common horses as we ran. But these stables held only Areion horses, a breed that was so swift and light of foot, that they flowed across the earth like mist.

"Each participant will draw one of three stones." Alesia held them up in her palms. Jade, lapis lazuli, and carnelian. "The team that finds and downs the stag first wins. You will also not be allowed to use your individual gifts." She set the rocks back in their bowl, then reached for iron bracelets. "These are spelled to restrain your magic, but not to impede your speed, healing, or other senses. They can be easily removed in the case of an emergency, but you will be disqualified once they are unbound. Besides this, there are no rules." Alé gestured toward two of the Royal Guard standing behind her. "Santiago and Fitz will help you with your horses."

Alesia held out the small bowl holding the stones, the top veiled so that no one could peek at them within. "Time to choose your teams."

Everyone except Adrienne, Orelia, and Cedric stepped up. The Shaws looked as if they'd decided to stay behind to keep Adrienne company, leaving the competition up to their three children.

I remained back, leaning against my post as everyone stepped forward to claim a team. Watching warily, I hoped to be paired with anyone but August.

Eve reached in first, pulling out a small jade stone. Next went Gemma with lapis lazuli, the gold flecks sparkling within the deep blue, then Misha drew jade. She and our godmother grinned at each other before linking arms and whispering conspiratorially.

Julian drew carnelian, pocketing the soft red stone. Evander took jade as he went to stand near my aunt and sister. Lorraine pulled carnelian, and finally, Alexander drew lapis. August and I were the only ones left, so he and I would draw different stones regardless, of which I was grateful for. He motioned for me to go first. I stepped forward, reaching in and pulling out a carnelian, meaning he was stuck with lapis.

Following this, we each donned the iron cuffs to block our magic. These weren't like the rowan ash. I felt the same with them on, all of my fae senses still heightened. But I tried to call ice to my fingertips, it wouldn't come—the power blocked off from me. I knew if I tried to winnow it would be the same.

"Nicky, trade with me," my sister whispered as we turned the corner to collect our tack before going to the horse stalls.

"No, Misha."

"But then you can be teamed with Evander and me with Julian." She said as she lifted her saddle from its stand.

"Everyone already saw what we drew," I said as I reached for my own. "We can't switch now or it will be obvious. Besides, it's not like anyone actually cares about the teams. You know everyone is still treating this like an individual competition."

"No, I suppose not." She huffed, shifting the saddle to rest on her leg. "Fine, but I'm going to smear the ground with you, Nicky," Misha said before leaving to enter the stall of her beloved palomino mare, Hyacinth.

I walked into the adjacent stall for Luthien, my blood bay mare, letting her nuzzle my hand before saddling her. After I finished, she dropped her head, hoping for ear scratches and I obliged, pressing my forehead to hers as I did so. Luthien began lipping my leathers and I gave her a playful pat on the neck. She knew better, but she was cheeky.

Just as I was leading her out, August came toward me. I attempted to veer away, but he blocked me with his much larger figure.

"I am not explaining the rules to you again, August. You should have pulled your head out of your ass and listened the first time."

"Cute." He deadpanned as I tried to walk around him. Unsurprisingly, he cut me off again. Luthien then became interested in the male and started sniffing his shoulder. August turned to her with a smile, scratching at her ears, which Luthien leaned into. *Traitor.*

"Stop that," I nudged my horse who would apparently do anything for attention. "Are you lost?" I faced him again.

"I am returning this. You left last night before I had the chance to." August said as he held out my Galorian dagger. "A deal's a deal."

"That easily? No more extortion you want to attempt?"

"Would it be successful?" His mouth curved up.

"No." I pulled back Luthien, who'd begun to nudge August's shoulder for more scratches.

"Is that so?" His eyes sang with amusement at both me and the horse.

"Brother," Julian interrupted, clapping August on the shoulder. "You have your own lovely teammate, do stop pestering mine. If you don't, I'm going to have to accuse you of subterfuge."

August held my gaze another moment, but then begrudgingly turned to his brother.

Julian lifted his chin toward a stall farther down the stables, "Misha picked out a horse for you, a buckskin stallion, eighteen hands tall. Should be large enough to hold even your ego."

I snorted a laugh, my hand coming to my mouth to smother the sound.

August left us with a shake of his head, walking over to the horse his brother indicated without acknowledging his joke—and without giving back the dagger.

Julian then turned to me with a wink before approaching the horse Misha picked out for him in the stall adjacent to Luthien's. A black mare, Celosia, my sister was fond of and one of our fastest.

"Okay everyone, let's get set," Alesia called.

I led Luthien out of the stables before stepping into the stirrup and swinging into the saddle. The sky was a cloudless blue, the sun just high and warm enough to clear the grass of any remaining dew. A perfect morning.

August rode up beside me. "Here." He held out my Galorian silver dagger.

Reaching my hand out, he placed the hilt in my palm, our fingertips brushing as I felt a jolt of electricity that shouldn't have been possible considering the iron bands he also wore. I leaned down to tuck the knife into a spare space in my boot as I rode, then sped up, wanting to put distance between us.

He easily kept up with me. "Now the silent treatment?"

I continued to ignore him, riding as if he wasn't next to me. Luthien continued her easy trot, acting as if she didn't feel the press of my heels urging her to go faster.

"Come on, sweetheart. Surely you can't hold a grudge forever."

"Stop calling me that." I snapped.

"And why would I ever do such a thing?"

"Because it's idiotic."

"What should I call you then? Princess?" As my eyes narrowed, his smile grew. August faced forward again to guide his horse through the trees.

"What about Ice Princess? Ice Queen? No, I've heard people already call you that one." He pulled his horse in front of mine, each nickname he tested growing stupider by the second.

I slid from Luthien's back and grabbed a palm-sized stone from the ground, all without the mare breaking her trot.

"Snowflake—" then hurled it at the back of his head, striking him with a hard thunk. August hissed in pain, his face whipping back to where I rode.

My hand was placed at my brow as I looked up into the forest canopy. "How odd. You must have riled a pixie."

"Sounds like we have a winner, *Snowflake*."

My smile turned into a sneer as I rode away, aiming around to the far side of the clearing. I had a feeling I'd only made things worse for myself when it came to him.

CHAPTER 8
Misha

G ods, they bicker like small children," I mumbled to Julian as we watched Nic ride away from August, the latter watching her go.

I ran my hand down Hyacinth's neck, and she whinnied happily in response. She'd been a gift from Father on our thirteenth birthday, just a foal at the time, given weeks before he died. If our Royal Steward had allowed it, I'd keep her in my room along with Ras. The horse pressed her head into my shoulder, and I gave her a kiss on her velvet-soft nose.

"Yes, but it's wonderful entertainment. I hope I get to see your sister kick his ass in person this time." He swung onto Celosia.

"They should hate fuck each other and get over it," I said dryly as I did the same.

Julian hesitated, processing my words, then roared with laughter. "I don't even know what to say to that. I'm speechless, love." He continued laughing.

I looked at him, still slightly taller as we were seated in our saddles, and a plan began to form in my head.

His eyes narrowed. "Oh no, what is that conniving head of yours scheming?"

"You'll just have to be patient and see." I nudged Hyacinth with my heels, riding after my sister.

Nic guarded herself more than anyone because of her past. The only male my sister had ever allowed to get close to her had deceived her, horribly. So much so that the betrayal had made her closed off to any future suitors. Nic did seem open to Evander though, but she still needed to loosen up a bit to fully return his interest or risk running the male off. Though my intuition told me that nothing could scare August away.

All of the participants were lined up in the clearing behind the water barrier Alesia cast to demarcate our starting point. She was on her own dapple gray mare, Antiope, facing us. She would be riding with us but only observing, making sure that everything went as it should.

"On my mark," Alesia said, everyone going fatally still. She then held up her hands, hesitating.

"Go!"

We took off from the start, heading for the main trail into the woods surrounding the palace to the North.

Gemma, Evander, and I broke through first to lead the pack. Nic, Eve, and August not far behind. Lorraine, Julian, and Alexander were edged out into the rear. We flew through the trees, the sounds of birds chirping and smaller animals running for cover all around us.

Not much later we came across the stag's trail. I was just behind Evander and Gemma now, the two of them neck and neck. The cuffs might have blocked their magic, but the Shaws still rode like the wind.

Suddenly the trail of the stag split into three, all of them appearing legitimate. Gemma didn't hesitate to follow the trail on the right, Evander broke left. I followed his tail.

I smiled to myself as more were caught by the false leads. The three were identical, but the left *felt* right. I looked over my shoulder to see my sister hesitate, then choose the middle trail, followed by Eve then Alexander. August went right behind Gemma. Lorraine and Julian then went left, just a few paces behind Evander and me.

Our trail took us to a small stream, shallow enough to easily wade across, but it slowed us down. It only took me a few moments to pick up the stag's trail once on the other side. I hurtled down its path, now in the lead, Evander close on my heels.

I finally caught a glimpse of the magically-crafted stag of light through a break in the trees and galloped after it, urging Hyacinth to take us faster. She obliged, loving the chase as much as I did. We were of one mind, one body, lighter than the wind and sunlight.

Evander and I raced after the stag, slowly catching up to it as we dashed through the forest. I was dead even with Evander weaving through the trees, Lorraine and Julian just behind. Any of us could have been the first to take down the stag at this point. Only a few more meters and I would be in range. I dropped my reins and drew my bow.

From the corner of my eye, I saw Lorraine shoot forward so she was even with us, sacrificing the accuracy of her shot for speed. Then suddenly, her horse rammed toward mine. Hyacinth whinnied as she veered to the left to avoid a crash, knocking me off balance and putting us headed directly for a muddy river bank.

The mud brought us to a hard stop, nearly launching me forward out of the saddle. Hyacinth sank almost immediately to her knees, and every struggle she made to break free caused her to sink even deeper. The horse let out a panicked screech, terror alighting in her eyes. If she didn't calm down, she would break her own legs in her struggle to escape.

"Hyacinth, shh." I rubbed her shoulders and neck while I tried to soothe her. "You're okay." She stopped struggling as I stroked her and spoke in that calming tone, even as my own hands were shaking.

"Misha, are you okay?" Julian abandoned the chase when he saw what happened, coming back around for us.

"Yes, but I need to get her out." I tore off the iron cuffs, the Hunt be damned, and used my magic to clear the mud from her legs. Once she was free, I hardened it so we could climb out of the pit. Back on solid ground, I dismounted. Hyacinth was calmer but still breathing heavily, her pulse racing. Eve and Alesia arrived then.

"Is everything okay?" Eve said as she swung off Freja.

"It will be." I handed off my reins to Julian now that Hyacinth was calm. "Check Hyacinth will you, Eve? See if she needs healing. I'll be right back."

I stalked toward the others, Julian stayed behind with my aunts and looked to be filling them in on how Lorraine sabotaged me.

As I walked, I saw Evander had been the one to successfully shoot the stag, and while normally I would be disappointed to lose, at this moment I didn't give a damn. I cared about my horse and how she was almost severely injured thanks to Lorraine's foul play.

She was about to be aware of just how much.

CHAPTER 9
Nic

We caught up to where the others ran down the stag, still fuming at myself for being led astray by that false trail. Eve figured it out first and bailed, tracking back. I realized half a second later. August, Alexander, and Gemma were just behind me in joining the others.

Evander won and was holding the symbolic light-filled antlers as he rode over with Lorraine, though I didn't see Misha, Julian, or my aunts with them. It was odd, I thought for sure Misha would be the one to win when I realized we'd taken the wrong path.

I was still about fifty meters away when I saw Misha stalking toward them from out of the dense woods near the river, clearly fuming. Julian wasn't far behind her, worry as well as anger was also etched on his face. Neither had their horses.

Just before she reached Lorraine, Misha jumped up and grabbed hold of a tree branch. She swung her legs and twisted, using her momentum to hit Lorraine square in the chest with her boots to knock her off her horse. Lorraine hit the ground hard on her back.

Oh hell.

I pushed Luthien into a gallop toward them.

Misha landed in a three-point stance. Lorraine quickly rolled and did the same, rather impressive for the force Misha put into that kick. I'd been the one she'd first practiced that particular move on, knocking the breath out of me for at least a minute.

Misha was roaring. "She could have broken her legs!"

"It was an accident!" Lorraine shouted back.

Misha snarled her reproof. But luckily for Lorraine, a moment later she stood and backed off before it could become an all-out duel, though her eyes still burned with her fury.

"You're not even worth the trouble of a fight." Misha spat as she stalked away, back to Eve and Alesia, who led both Hyacinth and Celosia next to their own horses.

By this time I'd reached Julian, who quickly filled me in on what sent my sister into her rage.

Misha took Hyacinth's reins from Alesia and leaned her head against the horse's, gently rubbing her neck and speaking to her in hushed tones. Julian left me to make his way over to her, taking Celosia's reins from Eve. My aunt was then free to check on Lorraine, to heal any possible damage that Misha had caused as Alesia began riding over to me.

"Come on, you beautiful, vicious thing. Let's get you both back to the stable before a war is started." I overheard Julian tell my sister. Misha still looked furious, her eyes blazing, but Julian was smiling at her like she was the most magnificent thing he'd ever seen. They walked back to the stables together, leaving the rest of us behind.

Alesia now rode next to me as we made our way to Evander. "Not the sister I thought would get into a brawl today."

I cocked my head. "I don't know what you mean. I'm the epitome of peace and serenity."

Alé snorted at my sarcasm.

"Evander, congratulations," I said as we reached him.

"Yes, it was quite the hard fought win. Your sister is an excellent rider. Though I'm sure the after events will be much more memorable this year." He chuckled.

Lorraine cast her eyes downward at his remark. She may have felt no shame for how Misha and Hyacinth were affected, but she did seem somewhat apologetic that her actions overshadowed her brother's win.

The others all offered their congratulations to him as well. Once done, everyone remounted to make our way back to the palace. I rode next to my aunts toward the back of the group where we were less likely to be overhead.

"And here I thought Misha got her humor and good-naturedness from you, Eve. But it turns out she has your brawling tendencies as well." I joked with her as we rode back side by side.

Eve grinned. "Who do you think taught her that move, Nicky?"

CHAPTER 10
Nic

Returning to the palace, I bathed off the sweat and grime from the morning. Afterward, I made a quick stop in the East Wing, then made my way to my aunts' chambers. They were just down from mine and Misha's rooms.

I knocked softly before opening their door. "Alesia?"

The mixed scent of my aunts, freesia and jasmine, and the soft glow of sun streaming through the windows onto their goldenrod walls welcomed me. Growing up, Misha and I would come here to sleep with Alesia and Eve when we wanted to be close to them, making little parties of it. When we were children, this included hot chocolate and faerie tales. Now it included playful palace gossip and copious amounts of wine.

"In here," Alesia called just before she exited their connected bathroom in a fresh shirt and pants.

"Can you help me with something?"

"Of course, mija. Anything." She walked toward me, finishing the tail of her braid as she went.

"I'm looking for Mother's dress, the one she wore to the initial Blood Treaty signing. I looked in her chambers and closet, but I wasn't able to find it."

Alesia's brows rose. "That's quite the dress for dinner, Nic. May I ask why you want to wear it?"

I explained to her about the day before, the mortal woman in town, and our confrontation with Adrienne at the ball. When I finished, Alesia was as angry as Misha and I had been.

"She had no right to do that, sitting queen or not. Your father and mother implemented those programs for the people. It is a dishonor to their name to take even a cent of the funding."

"I know, I'm still pissed. She said she needed to do it to 'demonstrate power' to the other kingdoms. She needs a reminder of who the real power in Hahnaley belongs to, and whose throne she's keeping warm." I didn't care how old and powerful Adrienne Deimos was. The West was ours.

Alesia chuckled darkly. "Say no more—it's down in the vaults." She nodded to the door as we turned to leave.

"You know your mother wore that dress for the same reason. A show of power." Alesia hooked my arm with hers. "Diana wanted the other rebel leaders to know that she may only be half fae, but she was one of the strongest in the room, if not *the* strongest based on battles won. She was a formidable sight." Alesia sighed wistfully. "Because of her and Dominic's strength, they were able to add much to the treaty to prevent another war. It was their idea to make the blood oath, so no one would dare betray the others."

"What was in the blood oath to make it so unbreakable?" I asked, curious.

"That I don't know, only the eight that were present for it do. Your parents, Orelia and Cedric Shaw, Adrienne and Alexander Deimos, and Josiah and August Warin—taking his mother's place after she died in battle. I know what was written after, we all do, but there are terms known to only those that were originally bound by it. Though you and your sister would have replaced your parents in the magic's eyes and would now be considered bound as well."

I nodded, pausing a moment before speaking again. "In your stories, Mother is always so courageous, so strong. I wish we could have known her, even for a little while." Even if we'd lost our father much too young, we'd never even gotten the chance to know her. To be held by her or hear her laugh.

"I do too, mi vida. But she lives within you and your sister, just like your father. I see so much of them in you both, not just in looks, but in the way you carry yourselves. And you know how much they loved you. Even before you were born, your mother and father did everything they could to ensure you lived a blessed life."

My heart swelled at the gesture. "I know...but we also had two amazing godmothers. Misha and I are grateful to have you and Eve."

Alesia reached her arm down, squeezing my hand. Unconditional devotion gleamed in her dark eyes. Misha and I might have grown up without our mother, but our aunts did all they could to make up for it. We had always been surrounded by so much love.

She and I then reached the stairs, taking the flights down to the lowest level of the palace. As we did so, we walked in silence, my mind circling. The training, the dress, what it represented—

"Alé, what was the war like?"

Her brow furrowed. "You and your sister have studied it, Nic. You know what happened."

"Yes, the semantics, the history. But the actual act of war—battle. You, Father, and Eve have been training us for so long, but...how was it to actually fight, to kill?"

Alesia took a deep breath. "War is always horrible, Nic. Even when fighting for the most valiant of causes, violence should always be a last resort. In the Great War we fought for liberation from the High King, who was a true monster, but his soldiers, those that fought for him...not all were so. Some were just people like us that ended up on the wrong side. And those deaths never leave you, Nic. Taking a life always leaves a mark."

I nodded my head solemnly.

"But know this, Nicole." Alesia paused, her hand stilling me as she turned to face me in the stairway one step above. "If anyone ever puts a blade to *your* throat, your family's, an innocent's—you do not hesitate. *They* made their choice of violence—you give it to them." Alesia's eyes burned with her words. "We trained you and your sister this way for a reason. If the time ever comes, and I pray to the gods every day that it does not, defend yourself and those you love. Defend those that cannot defend themselves. And do not for one moment feel guilty for it. They chose their fate when they came for you and yours."

Her words weighed heavily on me, but I could feel their truth. No, when it came to those I loved, I would not hesitate. Gods, help anyone that threatened them.

My aunt saw what she needed to in my eyes, the resolution, and nodded.

We finally reached the last few steps that would take us to the vaults. Near the catacombs and sealed by magic, only a Briar or Sancrista could open it. I placed my palm on the large iron door. The locking mechanism began unraveling with a series of melodic clicks and swung open.

Much of our parents' royal jewels, crowns, and other valuables were stored here, as well as relics, old scrolls, and books deemed too valuable and fragile to be displayed in the library. Alesia led me to the right, toward the far side of the cavernous space. There, encased in glass, hung my mother's dress.

"I've forgotten how beautiful it is," I whispered as I lifted my gaze to its dark form, a specter on the wall.

"Yes, handcrafted by goblins. They made it especially for her. They saw the way she fought on the battlefield, not just for High Fae and humans, but for the other faeries—for them. They gifted it to her just before the treaty was signed. Diana was the people's chosen, the champion of humans and beings so long deemed lesser by the High Fae. She had and would always fight for them.

Wearing this she became a symbol of that. And no one underestimated her when she wore this."

I stood there for a few moments picturing it—picturing her—gently touching my fingers to the glass before I broke the silence.

"If memory serves, Alé, didn't they make one for you as well?" I crooked an eyebrow at her.

Alesia let out a low laugh, her eyes sparkling. "That they did. Let's grab it for your sister, shall we?"

CHAPTER 11
Misha

L ounging on my aunts' large cream couch, I braided, unbraided, then rebraided bits of my hair, when Alesia returned to her chambers.

"Ah, I just came from helping your sister. It seems I am very popular today." She said as she strode into the room. "I left something for you in your room, cariña."

"Really?" My eyes beamed as I shook out the last little braid and sat up. "I can't wait to see what it is."

My excitement quickly faded as she neared, and I remembered what I'd come here for—what I needed to tell her. I took a deep breath to steady my courage before I spoke. "I have something to tell you, Alé."

"You do? And what's that?" Her smile remained as she sat down next to me.

I looked down at my hands, fiddling with the rings there. "Julian and I have been writing for years. Ever since we met at Father and Adrienne's wedding. And now...I...I think I'm in love with him."

"Is that so?" She said, and I ventured a peek up at her.

Her eyes were narrowed at me, but her lips looked like they were holding in amusement.

"I thought I would ask for forgiveness instead of permission, knowing how you felt about his father, though I guess really I am asking for both. I'm sorry I kept this from you."

"Misha, you humble me." My aunt laughed. "Did you really think I had been unaware of your correspondence with the young Warin Prince all these years?"

"You knew?" I gaped at her, "—this entire time?"

"Of course, Misha. Did you really think that I don't know everything that happens with you and your sister?"

"But you never said anything."

"I think you were enjoying your little secret, and I could see the positive effects his letters were having on you, especially after we lost your father. You needed a friend so badly, even more than we and your sister could provide. He was adding light to your life in your darkest moments. I wasn't going to take that from you. Though I am offended that you tried to hide it from me and Eve for so long." My aunt's eyes darkened, conveying her hurt.

"Hide what from us?" Eve walked in from the hall. After assessing our faces, her eyes shone with understanding. "Oh! This is about Misha and Julian. Finally coming clean are you?" my godmother grinned.

I threw my hands up. "You both let me believe you didn't know this whole time?"

"We weren't the ones keeping secrets, mi vida. You were," Alesia said. "We knew you would share with us when you were ready."

"I just didn't think it would take so many years," Eve added as she sat on my other side. The three of us now on the plush couch together.

"I'm sorry, I really am. I never meant to hurt you by keeping it from you—either of you. I misjudged how you would react. But you do approve, though? Of our relationship? I don't think I could stand it if you didn't." I said, looking between them both.

Alesia took a moment, her dark eyes wary. "I cannot say that I am completely without worry, given who his father was."

My gut clenched, even though her words were fair. It was why I'd been hesitant to tell them in the first place.

Eve sensed my distress and interjected. "But we did see how he stared at you last night, how he looked after you today during the hunt. There is no doubt of his devotion. And more importantly," My godmother touched my cheek gently. "We saw how you looked back at him."

Still, Alesia was hesitant. "We know little of him, Misha, nearly as little as the brother that raised him. It will take time to know if he can be trusted with your precious heart." Her hand gripped mine.

"I am sure he will, darling," Eve said, then whispered in my ear. "Don't fret too much over it, your aunt never likes nor trusts anyone upon meeting them. It's been her fatal flaw for over two centuries." Her voice teased.

Alesia's fae hearing of course missed nothing. "My trust must be *earned*. Not in pretty words, but by action. But *your aunt*," she pointed to her mate over my shoulder. "—believes everyone to have good intentions as soon as she meets them."

"That may be so," Eve scoffed. "But once my good favor is lost, it is gone forever, with no hope of recovering it."

"And that is how we fell in love," Alesia smirked. "Our mutual loathing of the same beings."

I laughed, leaning into Eve's embrace. "So you will have an open mind?" I looked back at Alesia, the fate of my heart hinging upon her next words.

Reading my expression, her face softened. "Of course, mija. If he proves himself to be worthy of you, nothing would make me happier."

I lunged forward, hugging her to me. "Thank you. You don't know how much this means to me."

"We do, darling." Eve said, then both of my aunts squeezed me in a hug between them.

"Nic is right, I'm a horrible secret keeper," I whispered, wiping my eyes. My aunts couldn't help but laugh, and I joined in with them.

"Now—" I sat up straight. "Tell me about what you've left in my room."

CHAPTER 12
Misha

I left my room and crossed the hall to my sister's chambers, Rasalas prowling silently at my side. As I was about to reach for the handle to her door, Nic opened it.

"Nicky..." My gaze roamed from her head to her feet. "I don't know whether to be terrified or in awe of you."

She had her black hair pulled back into a harsh braid, not a strand out of place. Her earrings were crafted like daggers, their little silver blades covered in tiny diamonds and teardrop rubies hanging from their tips. But the real sight was our mother's infamous gown of fine black chainmail.

The dress hung off her body like liquid, catching and shimmering in the light like the spilled ink. The neckline was a draping cowl that hung low with long sleeves that came to her hands in a point that encircled her middle finger. A thick belt of studded black metal encircled her waist along with rounded metal cusps that came over her shoulders like scaled armor—our mother's Blood Treaty dress.

Diana had been wise enough to know that the convening to create the pact was the true last battle of the Great War, so she wore a dress made for a warrior.

"I could say the same of you, sister."

My mouth turned up into a full grin as I gave her a twirl in Alesia's dress that was twin to her own.

While Diana's was dark as a moonless night, mine was the color of dawn, a chainmail of pale gold. But while her dress went low, mine came high on my neck into a collar, my arms bare except for the capped shoulder plates. On my head, I wore a crown made for me by our father, the golden spikes of which mimicked the sun's rays.

I grasped my sister's arm. "Adrienne is going to shit herself."

"Only if you don't blind her first." Nic poked my arm and I feigned offense. She smiled and said truthfully, "You are absolutely dazzling, sister."

We walked hand in hand down the hall then stairs to the terrace where dinner would be held beneath the stars, passing through the outward leading doors fifteen minutes later than Adrienne asked us to be there.

"You remember what we discussed?" Nic murmured to me.

"Of course," I answered, my stomach fluttering with excitement. My magic had grown impatient under my ribs, eager to play.

The other royals were milling about on the large terrace that faced the lake. We continued in locked hands as we passed through the open glass doors and down the steps. Then we released the damper on our power.

A crown of ice formed to rest on Nic's head, the crystals sparkling like diamonds. Tiny vines formed on my own crown, coiling around the golden spikes. Small roses bloomed at their tips and little thorns pushed out from the stems. Behind her on the earthen floor, Nic left a trail of jagged ice while behind me was a path of winding vines, thick with both thorns and roses. Rasalas entered on my other side, his large head coming under my hand as he stared the others down, assessing them.

"Girls," Orelia beamed. "We were wondering where you were. We didn't know you had such a grand entrance planned, but I'm glad we waited for it." She smiled as she embraced us.

The others looked to us like this was planned as well, like it was all part of the evening... everyone except Adrienne. Our stepmother had gone utterly still. Something dark flashed in her eyes before her lips curled up in a smile.

"Indeed. The elemental magic is always so—" Adrienne waved her hand as if looking for the right word, "—amusing."

"*Amusing*...indeed," Alesia said with a snake's smile back at Adrienne from where she casually leaned on the terrace railing in a gown of cobalt blue, the wind fluttering through her skirts and unbound hair as if she were a vengeful sea goddess.

Then the entire lake rumbled.

The waves of Alesia's power came up so high they would've soaked the terrace had they not hit her shield, the water crashing as if striking glass behind her, the sound like thunder. After a few moments it finally settled, and our aunt hadn't moved an inch, her eyes locked on Adrienne.

Everyone went silent at her power, the might of her magic displayed with half a thought. An example of the element she and Nic shared that had pushed the tide of so many battles in the rebels' favor. Though if Nic's power was already comparable to Alesia and Diana's, and mine close to surpassing my father's, the amount we would bear after we ascended to our full potential in our twenty-second year would be unfathomable.

Adrienne's smile tightened. "Well, now that we've all finally made it, we can be seated. I hope the first course hasn't gone cold."

The heads of the long table were typically furnished for the hosting king and queen. Because Adrienne was the interim Queen of Hahnaley until Nic and I could come of age next year, this was where she sat—in our Father's former place in a golden gilded chair, high backed and its seat tufted with fern green velvet, much more extravagant than the others. A throne for the reigning sovereign. The opposing head was left empty with no place setting.

Nic disregarded the seating placards, approaching the other end of the table, our mother's place, and without even a wave of her hand crafted a throne of ice. It was taller and grander than Adrienne's, sparkling like diamonds in the light. Nic sat without explanation.

Alesia sat to Nic's right, her eyes singing in approval of her niece. Evander sat between them, a warm smile coming to my sister's face as he took his seat next to her. Then August moved to sit in his place setting, the seat directly on her left.

I may have snuck down earlier in the evening to flip the name cards, ensuring he would be seated next to where my sister intended to be. Evander too.

Nic looked at me through narrowed eyes as she suspected what I had done. I shrugged my shoulders innocently.

"Nicole, you must have missed your place setting. You are sitting there, next to Eve." Adrienne said coolly as her eyes moved to a chair in the center of the table, then back to my sister.

"I thought I would give a taste of what it will look like this time next year when we are all again gathered for mine and Misha's coronation. Although for a proper picture, it is *you* that is in the wrong seat." Nic responded with an equally icy smile, then took a drink of the dark wine one of the servers poured for her.

Adrienne's pale blue eyes were piercing as she took in my sister, her ice. She seemed like a snake still before a strike. But after a few moments, she relaxed back into her chair. "Of course, *Princess*." She crooned, toasting Nic with her own glass. "We will all be excited to rejoin again to celebrate the ascension of you and your sister next year."

Julian was seated on his brother's other side, where my name placard now rested next to his. I briefly wondered if there were many left that I hadn't switched tonight. The staff did seem bewildered as to where everyone began to sit, quickly scrambling to adjust. I would have to apologize to them later for the trouble.

I reached for the chair, but before I sat, my magic covered it. Vines grew and ran up the side, coiling around the arms and seatback. From them sprouted full pink roses with yellow centers and more thorns, the length and width of two fingers. My own chair was now as tall and intricate as Nic's.

The magic drew Adrienne's eye from my sister. I couldn't help but wink back.

"You look enchanting tonight," Julian whispered, his eyes darkening as he took me in, and reached for my hand under the table.

"Oh thank the gods, I was worried I'd be stuck between my own siblings." Gemma sat on my other side. "I see them enough as it is." I couldn't stop my snort of laughter in response. That was indeed where she had originally been placed.

Ras moved to sit between Julian and me. He sniffed his arm curiously where his hand held mine.

"Misha, you described rescuing a *kitten*." Julian kept his hand frozen, not daring to move. "You made Rasalas sound like a lap cat...this is a beast." He looked mildly worried that Ras would take a chunk out of it. A valid concern.

"He *is* a lap cat," I scoffed. "And to me, he will always be the sweet little cub I found in the jungle." I cooed as I let go of Julian to scratch down Ras's spine. The jaguar leaned further into my touch. As I spoke, Rasalas finished his appraisal. Releasing a deep rumbling purr, he pushed his head to Julian's hand.

"He likes you." I beamed. Animals always were the greatest judge of character.

Julian gave him a scratch behind the ear. After which Ras relaxed and laid down between us. "I can't believe I just pet that thing." He said as he looked up from the great cat and back to me, amazement filling his face.

The first course was served and conversations began, mostly idle talk and catching up between the royals that had not seen each other in several years or decades. Gemma, Julian, and I discussed our own lives and travels. Julian enraptured Gemma with his tales from the north. I knew about them already from his letters, but watching him describe his home in person, the joy lighting his face as he did so, was breathtaking in itself.

During the third course, I snuck a glance at Nic. She and Evander were deep in conversation, smiling and laughing intermittently with one another. Occasionally, Alesia or Eve would jump in as well from where they were seated on his other side. Nic was pointedly ignoring August on her left, and at first glance, it would appear he was doing the same. Though the male sat just so Nic would happen to be in the corner of his gaze at all times.

"Misha," Gemma said, pulling me from my gaze at the other end of the table. "I heard there isn't anything planned for tomorrow to set up for the Summer Solstice celebration. Does this mean we will get to go down to the beach? The one here is the prettiest I've ever seen."

The coast was about a mile from our palace. It consisted mostly of high limestone cliffs, but there were a few places that could be climbed down to reach small stretches where gold sand met sapphire blue water. Nic often practiced her watercasting there with Alesia while I worked on my earth manipulation in the forest with Eve.

Julian leaned toward us, his brow furrowed. "I thought sirens dwelt in the waters off the western coast."

"Oh, they do." I gave him a playful nudge with my elbow. "But they don't come into the shallows. We've never seen them anywhere near the beaches. You have nothing to worry about."

"But do be careful you all." Orelia chimed in from where she sat on Gemma's other side. "Sirens are unpredictable and can be particularly vicious if they feel their territory is threatened."

Alexander looked toward us from where he sat across from Orelia, at Adrienne's left hand. "You wouldn't have to worry about the creatures at all if you exterminate them, as was done off the southern peninsula."

"What do you mean?" I sought clarification, hoping my ears had misled me.

"Just what I said. The sirens were a problem for the ships off our coasts. So, Reyna's guard dealt with them."

I gaped, horrified. "You killed them—all of them?"

"There were likely a few that escaped, but they were wise enough to not return. They must have found other tribes of their sisters to join—away from our waters."

Nic's head inclined toward us, having just caught the end of our exchange. "How could you do that? The fae and sirens can live peacefully, so long as proper precautions are kept and we avoid encroaching on their territory." My sister's eyes burned furiously.

Alexander looked down the long table at her and added matter of factly, "They attacked our people, causing numerous fatalities. It was affecting our trade. They are monsters and nothing more. They needed to be put down."

Nic leaned back into her throne, letting out a low, bitter laugh. "And what exactly constitutes a monster to you? Many things kill and aren't labeled as such. To be clear, the sirens do not attack all faeries or humans, they only harm *males*." Nic accentuated the word. Evander blanched as she went on. "The stories say it's not even all males, just the ones that have harmed a female. Any female, faerie or human. The sirens can smell the reek of the offense and seek vengeance for their sisters. Our father never worried about plugging his ears to deafen him to the sirens' song on his sea travels. It makes you wonder, if a male fears the sirens' voice, what is he hiding?"

Silence fell over the table as she and Alexander stared each other down.

Cedric coughed, breaking the tension. "That is what the stories say, but the sirens may eventually devolve into seeking out any being as a food source. Better to be safe than sorry these days."

"Perhaps." Alesia ran a finger around the rim of her wine glass. "Dominic could always be a bit too cavalier in some instances. Though we would never consider extermination of an entire species just because of interruptions in monetary gain." My aunt's tone was scathing.

The water elementals always felt a connection to the other water-blessed faeries—the naiads, nereids, sprites, and sirens. The sirens particularly, as they themselves had once been water elementals before going permanently into the sea several millennia ago—before evolving into what they were now.

Eve intervened with a smile, placing a steadying hand on Alé's. "As my family said, there are plenty of ways to avoid conflict with the sirens. I think we would all come to regret annihilating them like the Etherii did to the firecasters."

Gemma's brow furrowed. "The firecasters?"

August spoke for the first time since the dinner started, and Gemma jumped slightly at the sound. "Many forget, or feign ignorance, that at one time all four elemental High Fae were prevalent on the continent. That is until the firecasters were destroyed over 600 years ago by the Etherii." His storm gray eyes danced with violence at the mention of the High King's familial line.

He went on, "They were the rarest elemental, but the most powerful. It was thought that a firecaster's flame could burn through almost anything, even shields and wards. Some even say they were more directly descended from the Gods than the Etherii, making them the greatest threat to their rule. As they were impervious to dragon fire, the crown feared a coup with firecasters at the helm would stand a chance at overthrowing their rule, so they eradicated them."

Nic watched him carefully. "If the firecasters were so powerful, how were they so easily killed?"

August turned. The rest of us were silent, listening to his story, but he seemed to speak only to her. "The stories say it *wasn't* easy. Over a century the Etherii sought them out and placed spies in the villages where they lived, watching them for months, sometimes years. These spies befriended the fire-wielders, waited until their guards were down, and incapacitated them with the berries or ash of the rowan tree. Then they killed them."

Nic said too quietly, "Cowards."

"Indeed." August smiled at the violence in her tone. "The Etherii weren't known for their upstanding tactics, and since their prized dragons were ineffective against them, they were required to resort to such methods."

"But the firecasters were all volatile—dangerous." Adrienne interjected from the opposite head of the table, the only one of us old enough to have possibly met a fire elemental. "The magic could not be checked. Unlike the other elements, fire only brings destruction."

August reluctantly pulled his gaze from Nic to Adrienne, all the warmth vanishing from his gaze. "Do the farmers not burn their fields at the end of the season to clear the weeds and waste so new life might grow? Yes, fire can be destructive, but more often than not new life rises from the ashes, including the food many of us eat. One could also justify the extermination of *any* magical race with the right argument. After the firecasters and sirens, who will be deemed most dangerous next?"

His anger seemed to stem from more than his connection to the fire-blessed, the lightning he bore so similar, but from that the stormcasters like him and Julian were currently the High Fae with the rarest magic and among the most powerful. After all, August's lightning was no small part of how the war against the High King was won. It wasn't a stretch to assume that they, in the vast minority, could be painted as the next volatile group by another that sought to diminish their threat.

Alexander gave him a slowly unfurling smile. "Such an admonishment of the extinction of a species, coming from the male that killed nearly all the dragons himself."

"I did what had to be done to win the war. The cost is not lost to me." August's jaw clenched. "But you'll do well to remember, my actions handed you the throne upon which you now sit."

Alexander's pale blue gaze sharpened, and August gave him a cruel smile, further baiting him.

He opened his mouth to retort before Adrienne interjected. "This topic has turned bland. The fire beings have been gone for decades—centuries, and no fae has been born with the gift since. Surely there are more current events to discuss."

The Reynian King sat back in his chair, though he still seemed primed to lash out after August's insult, his tan skin flushed. Rigidity remained in August's posture as well, and I wondered just how binding the Blood Treaty actually was.

"Ah yes," my sister said, her fingers circling the rim of her glass. "Shall we discuss how the social programs in our country are thriving, stepmother? About all the good they've done for faerie and human alike?"

Adrienne inclined her head, then waved her hand dismissively. "No one cares to hear about such trivial things, Nic." She took another sip of her pale yellow wine.

"No matter." Nic's eyes sparkled with delight. "I suppose it can remain between me and Niall."

Niall, the Treasurer of Hahnaley's Royal Council.

Adrienne choked on her drink. Swallowing and composing herself, she said, "Oh?"

"I ran into him earlier in the East Wing. Such a kind man, isn't he? He told me all about our coffer's surpluses this year. How all that gold was just sitting around or going toward luxury items for the palace."

Cedric glanced at his wife, as if checking if she could also sense the animosity between Nic and Adrienne. Orelia gave his hand a quick squeeze.

"How curious," Alesia purred. "I haven't noticed any additions."

"Indeed," Nic smiled. "But not to worry. I made sure it was allocated to the social programs instead. Now they are more well funded than ever. Niall and I came up with such great ideas on how to expand the services the crown offers to humans and faeries alike. I can't wait to share it all with you at the next Council meeting, Stepmother." She leaned back into her throne of ice with ease.

Adrienne had gone still, the only motion was the firelight flickering off her white pleated gown. Finally, she broke into a smile that was hardly genuine. "I'm so glad you were able to oversee everything to your liking. Such a sympathetic queen you will make one day, Nicole." She raised her glass to my sister across the table.

Nic matched the gesture. "One day very soon."

CHAPTER 13
Nic

Standing alone at the terrace railing, my fingers brushed over the singular petals of the calla lilies growing on the other side.

As I took another sip of wine, I looked over at Misha and Julian sitting with Evander and Gemma, smiling and laughing while Ras lounged at their feet. They hadn't snuck off yet, but they couldn't stop giving each other heated looks. I smiled to myself. Misha deserved this.

"That was quite the entrance." August came to stand on my other side. I reluctantly turned to him, putting my back to the others. "For most elementals, the complexity of what you and your sister cast is all their magic will ever amount to. But for you two...those were party tricks."

"Maybe." I shrugged at his implication.

He turned, facing me as he leaned on the stone railing. "Humility doesn't suit you, Snowflake."

My eyes narrowed, remembering how he'd called me proud and unreasonably arrogant last night, but I held my tongue. I wasn't going to give him the reaction he was hoping for, even if he insisted on using that ridiculous name.

"You and Adrienne seemed...at odds," August said, plucking one of the calla lilies and bringing it to his nose.

"I could say the same of you." I thought of the night before when he'd been so cold to her at the ball.

"Fair enough. Though I am curious as to what's happened between you."

"And why would I share that with you?"

"You don't have to. I'm just intrigued as to the cause. Though you should know that seeking power for selfish ambition is never satisfied. You'll only ever want more until you'll do anything to get it. It corrupts completely."

I snorted. "Says a king. Why are you so sure that my challenging Adrienne is selfish?"

"I am actually guessing it is the opposite, based on your defense of the sirens. They are beings that could do nothing to benefit you in turn for their protection. Seeking power to defend those who cannot defend themselves, those that cannot benefit you in turn is...admirable." August's eyes gleamed as they met mine. Then they flitted to the others as he changed the subject. "How did your sister come to tame such a creature?"

I glanced over my shoulder. Julian had just leaned down to pet Ras again. The great cat didn't stir except for a contented flick of his tail. "Misha has the kind of heart that could entrance the most ferocious of beasts. It's effortless."

"Maybe so," he said, still gazing at the jaguar over my head. "All monsters do seem to have their...obsessions." He said as he brought his gaze back down to mine. August's silver eyes were darker now.

"Nic," Evander approached on my other side.

I turned to him, grateful for the interruption. "Evander." Even with the space between us, I felt August stiffen behind me. The two didn't acknowledge each other.

Evander smiled down at me. "Your sister mentioned that you had a favorite place in the gardens. I was hoping you could show me. She said it was spectacular."

"She did, did she?" I chanced a glance at Misha over his shoulder. She was looking at Gemma and Julian, pretending to be immersed in their conversation.

"Yes. But of course if it's too late, I suppose I could see it another time." Evander continued.

"No, now is the perfect time. The place is best seen at night."

Evander held out his arm for me to take. Before we walked away, he inclined his head, "August."

"Evander." August's tone was cold, and I felt it down my spine. I didn't offer him any departing words as we walked toward the descending steps.

"You know, you could call me Van. My family does." Evander said as we started down the path to our left, winding through the fragrant lilac and foxtails.

"Van," I said, trying it out.

Evander smiled at the word, then inclined his head. "I apologize for interrupting you two just now."

"You didn't interrupt. If anything, I was relieved by the intrusion."

"Good, I'm glad," he said as I led him down another corner. The path was darker here, though we could still see well thanks to the full moon. The night turned the lush garden into colors of deep teal, navy, and purple—equally as beautiful as during the day.

"I'd never met August Warin before these events. I can't say I was particularly looking forward to it." He admitted.

"And why is that?" I asked, and Evander's mouth hardened. I could see on his face that he felt as if he'd said too much. "What is it?"

"It's just...there have been rumors on my travels."

My curiosity piqued. "What kind of rumors?"

Evander exhaled. "I feel like I shouldn't say...that I shouldn't even entertain such talk about another of the four kingdom's rulers."

"Van, now you have to tell me." I chuckled, squeezing his arm.

Evander's mouth tightened, conflicted about repeating whatever he'd heard. "I've heard from the merchants that have traveled to Montevalle there may be reason to suspect that Josiah Warin didn't die of natural causes like we were all told."

"What do you mean?" My brow furrowed in confusion. "He didn't die from a blood disease?"

"Maybe, but there are some that believe—" he let out another sigh "—they believe that August murdered him. For the crown—for power."

I gasped. "That can't be true. Surely someone would have known about it. I also can't imagine someone as kind hearted as Julian defending such a thing, and he and August clearly have a good relationship." I didn't mention that he and Misha had been writing and were friends for many years now. Julian surely would have let something about it slip in all that time.

"Julian was a child, only nine years old at the time of Josiah's death. Maybe he doesn't know."

"Maybe...but Josiah was horrible right? You'd met him. Alé and Eve, my parents, even yours all despised the man."

"Josiah was definitely...unpalatable at times." Evander cringed. "But still, to be capable of that, of murdering your family? I fear Josiah may have died only to be replaced by worse."

I remained silent as I processed this. It seemed too wild a story to be true. And I couldn't discuss it with Misha, she had never been good at keeping secrets, especially juicy ones like this. She would ask Julian about it immediately who would surely tell August.

By this time, we'd reached the small pond in the northeast corner of the gardens. In the breeze the branches of the large weeping willow swept against its surface, creating gentle ripples and making the water lilies dance.

"No more morbid talk of rumors and murder. Not here. This place is sacred." I said with mock seriousness.

Evander laughed in response, the sound carefree. "Deal. This area is lovely, Nic. So peaceful," he said as he looked around. The moonlight on the water was a brilliant silver. A nightingale nearby sang her melancholy song.

"But that's not the best part." I tugged on his arm to bring him closer to the water's edge.

Using my magic, I stirred the water along the bottom. Slowly, tiny flickering lights floated to the surface, then brushed the edges of the pond in the small waves I created. Unlike the gold of the faerie lights that were cast around the castle, these shone in varying shades of blue, purple, and silver.

The water now mimicked the night sky, with hundreds of thousands of tiny dots like stars glowing upon its surface, churning with the water I controlled.

"What is this?" he whispered, his face slackened with awe.

"Bioluminescent algae. Misha grew it. When stirred, it glows."

"Magnificent. In all my travels, I've never seen anything like it." He knelt down and reached for the surface of the water. The glow coated his fingertips as he rubbed them together, still smiling softly in wonder.

Evander turned to me as he stood, that look of amazement still lighting up his face. I was unable to keep myself from smiling as well, his being too infectious. His arm encircled my waist, drawing me closer to him.

"Would it be okay if I kissed you?" He asked quietly, his other hand cupped my chin. My heart fluttered in my chest.

"Yes," I breathed, enraptured by his warm hazel eyes as he leaned in.

Evander's lips brushed mine, softly. Then he pulled back, looking at me with as much wonder as he had the bioluminescence. He smiled as his lips met mine again, harder this time. My hands wound around his neck, pulling him closer, loving the way our mouths met in perfect synchrony. In this moment I was lost with him, in the best way.

Lost in a sea of stars.

CHAPTER 14
Nic

H ow was the Star Pond?" Misha asked as we dressed the next morning, an impish grin on her face.

Evander and I had stayed awhile, talking, kissing, and laughing between the stars in the sky above and those in the water below. I'd floated back to my room in the early hours of the morning, high on the magic of the night. I woke to my mother's dress slung over the nearest chair and my dagger earrings left on the nightstand.

"Good." I turned away, sorting through my earrings. I chose a matching silver set, one sparkling star and moon.

"Oh, don't you dare be coy now, sister." She leaned around me, reaching for pearl studs. "Spill." She pointed an accusing finger at me.

I moved away from her to the mirror as I donned the earrings. "We kissed."

Misha broke into a wide grin, smiling back at my reflection in the mirror, practically bouncing with excitement. "And how was it?"

My cheeks warmed, "Good."

Misha let out a high-toned screech and threw out her arms, embracing me in a hug—still bouncing. "Ah, I knew it! I'm so happy for you, Nicky."

"Get off me, you big goof." I laughed but didn't shake her off as she crushed my arms into my ribs.

"No, Nicky. I need *details*. Tell me more."

"No," I shook my head. "We need to head down, I'm sure everyone is waiting for us." It was mid-morning already. We'd both taken breakfast in our own rooms, too tired to join the others in the dining room.

"Okay then." Misha let go of me. "I'll play it cool and try not to swoon over you both too hard."

We made our way down to the West Wing terrace, just below our chambers, where we would be meeting with the others that wished to visit the beach. It was no surprise to see Eve and Alesia already waiting, leaning against one of the stone walls. Lorraine and Gemma sat on a peony-covered outcropping, Evander standing over them.

Warmth rose to my face as I thought of what had transpired between us last night. Evander gave me a lingering hug and smiled as he took me in, and I was sure my cheeks turned even more pink under his gaze. I turned to my aunts for some relief. "We aren't late, are we?"

"No, Nicky." Eve smiled, her hand threaded through Alé's. "We're just waiting on the last two."

A few moments later, Julian and August appeared. Misha's face lit up as she glided over to him, wrapping her arms around his waist and pressing her face into his neck. He beamed equally, planting a kiss on her golden hair.

"That's everyone," Alesia said, watching them with a hint of wariness.

"Your parents won't be joining us?" I asked Evander as we stood, walking toward the doors.

"No, I believe they wanted to stay behind to keep Adrienne and Alexander company." He said.

They certainly wouldn't join us then. The Deimos rarely deigned to leave the comfort of the palace, I rarely saw Adrienne near the forest or even so far as the lake.

The mid-morning sun was bright overhead, so we chose to walk to the beach instead of the more expedient winnowing.

"There won't be any sirens in the water?" Lorraine asked Alesia, walking in front of us, her face edging on concern.

My aunt turned her head back to answer. "No, Lorraine. They stay on the outside of the barrier reef, over three miles away. They have never been spotted any closer."

Lorraine nodded but didn't seem assuaged in her fear, her eyes filled with some emotion, though Evander relaxed a bit with my aunt's reassurance. Then Gemma quickened her pace to walk beside our aunts, looping her arm through Eve's. "Can you tell me more about them—the sirens?"

Alesia, smiling softly, indulged her. "The sirens are different from the other water-bound faeries, the nymphs, and sprites. They are descended from an ancient tribe of High Fae, water elementals. They were a matriarchal society, powerful and self-sufficient without the need for males to continue their way of life."

"Sounds like a dream," Misha whispered into my ear from behind, causing me to stifle a laugh. At her side, Julian scoffed in mock outrage. She stepped back to take his hand and brought it to her lips. "Except you, love. You are allowed."

"Perfect." He pulled her into his side. "Then we'll have all daughters and daughters-in-law and I'll never have to worry about them being hurt by any males."

Misha grinned widely at this, thrilled that Julian hinted at a future together.

Alesia briefly looked back to silence them and returned to her story. "They eventually were attacked by males, jealous of their prosperity, their lands. The females' food was poisoned with a concoction of rowan ash, tasteless and unde-tectable, and then they were attacked in the night, making it impossible to fight back effectively. Many of the females were beaten, raped, and tossed into the sea for dead, their young daughters taken to be slaves."

"Now you see why they make prey of predatory males?" Misha said to Julian, her eyebrows raised.

"I do, and good for them." His face was solemn.

"Shh," Eve turned back, shushing them playfully as her mate went on.

"The Son saw what happened, heard their prayers. He is a kind god and took pity. He healed the females, transforming them into the beings they are today, so that they may live peacefully in the oceanic depths, safe from their attackers. But it was the Mother who was truly outraged. It was she who gifted them their songs to seek vengeance against their attackers—as well as fangs and talons to tear them apart. Their animosity is said to be only reserved for males that resemble those that assaulted their ancestors so long ago."

At this point, we reached the coast. We stood to overlook the seemingly neverending sea before making the climb down the stone steps.

"How do you know so much about the sirens' history?" Gemma asked Alesia. Lorraine on her other side looked wistfully at the waves, arms wrapped around her core, likely from the cold breeze coming off the water.

"Diana and I were infatuated with stories of the water-blessed faeries, particularly sirens. Their story resonated with her. I think she admired their resilience—their strength." Her lips formed a sad smile as she thought of her sister.

I looked over the edge and pictured those females, the horror they'd gone through. My pale mauve dress fluttered around my legs as I wondered whether it was a blessing or a curse that they were to live a life only under the waves, to never again set foot on the land that was once theirs. As with most things in life, it was likely both.

We made our way down the staircase in the cliffside hewn from the rock by our father. He created this particular beach and small alcove for our mother. When the weather was amenable, it was her favorite place to come. Misha and I loved to explore here, swimming through the reefs in the bay and diving off the tall cliffs nearby for the thrill of the free fall. If only the gods had blessed us with wings like some of the other faeries, I doubted we'd ever be on the ground for long at all.

As our feet touched the sand, Evander returned to my side. "I know nothing else has been formally planned for today to prepare for the Summer Solstice, your birthday, but if you don't have any other plans I was hoping to steal you away for a bit this afternoon."

"And what for?" My eyes narrowed playfully.

"*That* is a secret," Evander said as his face broke into his crooked grin.

I couldn't help but smile back. "I think I can possibly find some time for you."

He and I lingered by a tide pool, taking in the little anemones, coral, and starfish. Evander and I took turns pointing out different things we'd spotted to each other. Then I heard a hum off the water, an odd sound—almost like a beckoning.

Misha turned to me from across the beach, about thirty yards away where she was standing with Julian and August. She mouthed, "Do you hear that?"

I replied with a quick nod.

Her brow furrowed as her lips moved again. "What is it?"

I shrugged back. *I don't know.*

Only Alesia seemed to have noticed it as well. She waved to us that it was probably nothing but kept a closer watch on the surf, nonetheless.

I stood, walking over to a rock that jutted further out into the sea. The shape of the alcove calmed the water on our beach so it broke in gentle waves around the stone. I looked back toward Evander, but he was still on the sand, crouching over a tide pool. His eyes were lifted, watching me. I motioned for him to join.

He shook his head, declining. "You go ahead. Something about the sea unsettles me."

"Oh, come on," I shouted back to him. "Doesn't your role as Desdemon's ambassador require you to travel often by ship?"

"Occasionally, but I much prefer land. The sea has too many secrets." He smiled, but the emotion no longer reached his eyes.

I playfully rolled my eyes at him and knelt down, overlooking the surface of the clear blue water two feet beneath my perch. Below the rock fell into a steep decline, dropping to the ocean floor over sixty feet down. My eyes skimmed the fish that fluttered around the colorful corals and sea plants attached to the rock, like living jewels in a sea of sapphire. I felt a tug in my chest that nudged me closer, to look harder.

I reached my hand into the water.

The power of the water flitted through my fingers, the fish pausing before resuming their swimming and searching for food. The pull traveled down—down to the sandy bottom. Her eyes were what I saw first.

Large and cat-like, they were more hauntingly beautiful than the stories portrayed. I'd only ever seen them once before, when our father and aunts had taken us out to the barrier reefs as children. But then it was from a great distance. Now—

She shot upward. The siren grabbed my outstretched hand, pulling me off the rock and into the sea.

The water thrashed from my magic though it was ineffective against her, she wielded it with more skill than I could. Water was my gift, but this was her home. She'd been born in it, and I couldn't beat her here. But that didn't mean I wouldn't try. I kicked and scratched, anything to escape her hold, but nothing loosened her grip.

My knees hit the sandy bottom. The siren knelt in front of me, grasping my head with her palms. She had pale green skin, long dark green hair, and a scaled tail that caught the light like emeralds. Two other sirens hid behind a bit of reef, watching. Hardly visible against the reef in their shades of blue and purple. The siren's elongated nails, talons, and webbed fingers held my skull—not hurting, just holding me still.

"Sister," she said in our common faerie language. Her voice was melodic, akin to a whale's song. As she spoke, her pointed teeth became visible, along with the fangs she used to tear apart her victims. Though now I felt no fear.

She hadn't done this to harm me, but for another purpose. Even as I thought how crazy it would make me seem—I relaxed.

The siren brought her forehead to mine. The act paralyzed me, and I was caught in a vision. Dark scenes flashed before my eyes.

Whispers and shadows, bells ringing at midnight, sheep becoming wolves, blood on fingertips—I was running through a dark wood, the thorns and vines tearing at me, catching my skin and hair. Mirrors and reflections that didn't match. Then I was choking, drowning, falling away from the water's surface into icy darkness.

My blood turned to ice. The siren was showing me visions of things not yet passed, horrible things—a warning.

Almost as quickly as it began, I felt myself being jerked away from her. With our broken connection the vision ceased, and I was dragged back to the surface, solid arms grasping me around my waist.

The siren reached for me as I was pulled from her, and I reached back, struggling against the arm that held me. I wanted to know more—had to know why she was showing me these things, but she didn't follow. She and her companions remained still, not acknowledging whoever was pulling me away. Before I broke past the surface, the siren waved goodbye and said in her own melodic language, *"Resurge et ardere."*

Then I was out of the water and back on the sand.

Everyone was crowding around me as I laid there, coughing, not quite comprehending what had just happened. I couldn't hear their words or feel their touches, still in shock.

I could only see silver.

August's hands were on my face. He was saying something. I tried to make out the words but everything was still a blur.

"Where are you hurt?" He was nearly shouting.

"She didn't hurt me." I finally rasped, my throat sore from the shouting and saltwater when I'd first been pulled under. Relief washed over his features, his hands lingering before he stepped back to give us room.

"What happened?" Alesia was at my back, her arms around me, as I turned to face her. "The sirens have never attacked a female before. What did she do?" Her eyes were panicked as she looked me over, checking for any injuries.

"It wasn't an attack I...I can't explain it." I said, holding my tongue.

My aunt hesitated, reading in my eyes there was more I didn't want the others to overhear. "Eve and I are winnowing her back to the palace. I suggest the rest of you follow unless you want to end up as the sirens' lunch. Misha winnow the others back." She said as she took one arm, Eve the other. They looked at each other for a brief moment, then we were pulled through that pocket of space, landing directly in their chamber's bathroom. As part of the royal family, the winnowing wards wouldn't block us like the others. Misha would have to take them through the ward barrier herself.

Alesia set me on a plush settee in the center. "What really happened, Nic?"

Eve skimmed my body for wounds, her hands glowing with her healing gift, not trusting that the siren had left me unharmed.

"She showed me a vision. Did you know sirens can have the Sight?"

Alesia shook her head as she stood over us. "No, I didn't. But the High Fae have always been too self-important to realize that other beings may possess such power. The siren may have been drawn to you because of your water gift, and the fact that your mother was a seer."

Eve finished looking me over, finally content that I was unharmed, nodding to Alesia who let out a sigh of relief. "What did she show you, Nic?" Eve asked softly, coming to sit by my side.

I explained the vision to them both, the horrible darkness I felt from it. "It was vague, but it felt like a warning." I finished.

Misha then barged into my aunt's chambers, the doors loudly flying open, as she called our names.

"We're in here," Alesia shouted back.

My sister's eyes were misty with tears as she rounded the corner into the bathing room. "I'm so sorry, Nic. I should have been paying closer attention.

We just saw your splash and before Julian or I could process that you hadn't intentionally jumped in, you were already being brought up."

"It's okay Misha, really. I'm not hurt." I reassured her.

"But you could have been! And Evander just stood there gaping like a damned fish." Misha fumed.

My heart sank. "He...he didn't—"

"He didn't do a *thing*. He didn't even yell for anyone, the fucking coward. I could kick him straight in the balls." She turned as if she would leave and do just that before Alesia set a hand on her shoulder, stopping her. But my aunt's eyes blazed. She agreed with my sister. Eve's silence indicated she did too.

Swallowing, I said, "You can't blame a male for not jumping into the water with sirens. It would be suicide." My words defended him, even as my chest constricted.

"*Yes,* I can," Misha seethed. "August did."

I blinked. "He what?"

"August went in after you. He didn't even hesitate."

"No, it was Alesia," I countered, confused. I looked to my aunt but she shook her head in denial.

But she'd been there on the sand, had been at my back with her arms around me....but she'd been dry, and she wasn't the first thing I saw.

Misha went on, "August was in the water before anyone else could even see what had happened."

"August saved me?" I reeled, my mind refusing to comprehend what they said happened. It wasn't logical that August would've jumped in the water for me, not after what he'd said that first night. *Him* and not Evander, who'd shown me so much admiration thus far.

"Yes, Nic. That's what I said," my sister snapped. "Eve, check her again. She must have a concussion."

CHAPTER 15
Nic

S he'd warned me.

The siren had risked much in coming to the shore to give me that vision, the message. It wasn't for nothing.

After I'd gotten out of my now dry but still salt-covered dress, I changed into fresh linen pants, a sleeveless shirt, and flat silk slippers. Then I headed to the library in search of past prophecies, the siren's language, or anything else remotely related to what had just happened to me on the beach.

I stood in a semi-private alcove in front of a large table covered in books the librarian, Marle, a tiny pixie with a brilliant mind for remembering what each of the thousands of tomes contained, and I had pulled from the shelves that might give me the information I sought. They were haphazardly lying open with notes scrawled in my hasty handwriting tucked into pages with passages I thought might be useful. I'd spent two hours pouring over the text with little headway.

Some of the books on the stars and their visions past gave me clues as to the images' meaning. Whispers and shadows were commonly thought to portray the plotting of others. Sheep becoming wolves was easy—friends turning to foe. I assumed the mirrors and their mismatched reflections meant something similar, someone was misrepresenting themselves and their intentions.

The blood on fingertips could mean many things: a horrible choice and a sacrifice made, or red blood for new life, dark blood for loss of life—a miscarriage perhaps. But what I'd seen had been somewhere in between.

Then the running, the thorns...what was I running from? I couldn't make out the drowning either, the text differed in its meaning. It could mean something as simple as feeling overwhelmed or foreseeing an actual death. Was it real or an analogy?

That was the trick of the stars, the visions could be metaphorical or literal...you could never be sure until it played out.

Resurge et ardere.

The siren's words repeated over again in my mind, and I wondered if they tied into her warning, some key I needed. I hadn't yet found a text that could translate it and was growing increasingly frustrated.

And what of Evander?

He'd done nothing, had let me be dragged into the sea without so much as a flinch to stop it. My thoughts circled around what it could mean. For him, for us.

But August came for me.

He hadn't hesitated, diving in after someone that had shown him nothing but disdain since we'd met.

I remembered what Evander had said last night, what he'd accused August of. How could the same male that was accused of murdering his father for power, have done such a thing for me? The pieces didn't fit, and August had been so elusive the past hundred years, no one here would be able to speak truly to his character.

Proud and unreasonably arrogant. Any interest I find in her will pass.

I bristled. The male was an paradox of conflicting words and actions.

Footsteps approached from behind as I kept my gaze on the books scattered before me. I began to wonder if he could read my thoughts—they seemed to summon him.

"Nicole."

"August." I acknowledged as he came to stand beside me at the table. "Are you here to ask how I am feeling?" I kept my gaze on the pages before me. The book that currently held my attention was particularly promising on the siren's language, though I hadn't found the words I was searching for.

"No, Snowflake. I would think it would take more than that to truly rattle you."

That stupid nickname. I felt my lips wanting to turn, whether into a scowl or a smile I didn't know, but I still didn't look up to face him.

August went on, "Though with sneaking into town and causing fights, public disputes with your stepmother, then being taken underwater by a siren—you are single-handedly providing all the entertainment for this Treaty gathering."

"Not all. You forget the Hunt fiasco. I had nothing to do with that." I countered dryly.

"Ah, no. But your twin sister did. You two have a flair for the dramatic."

"If not to inquire as to how I am, why are you here? It can't be to chat about Misha's and my *dramatics*." I leaned my hip against the table, finally lifting my head to him.

"The siren didn't harm you at all, but she did tell you something. I want to know what it was, and because the Sancristas are so fond of the water-blessed faeries, easily winning their allyship in the war, Hahnaley's library contains the most information on them. More than anywhere else on the continent. But it appears as if I've been beaten to all the relevant books."

"Too bad."

August ignored my retort. "I also suspect that she was showing you something, a vision perhaps—call me intrigued."

"Even if she had, why would I share that with you?"

"Are you not the sharing type?" August cocked an eyebrow, already knowing how I would answer.

"Not with you."

"Ouch." He brought his hand to his chest in feigned heartache. "Here I am, thirsting for knowledge you could easily give me. You alone hold the key to putting me out of my misery."

"I hope the lack of such keeps you up at night, tossing and turning over what it could possibly mean with no hope of an answer."

"Still wishing such atrocities on me, sweetheart? Even after this morning?" August said, his face teasing, though I detected a hint of something else in his tone.

I clicked my tongue in exasperation, returning to the books as I tried to regain my place in the book.

"If you truly wish me gone, I—"

"Do you see me kicking you out?" I cut him off, my eyes not leaving the page as my finger slid down the lines of text.

Without another word he remained, turning toward the table to face the other books lying open. His attention went to one on the elemental lineages I'd had yet to peruse.

August reached for it, and almost out of nowhere, Marle zoomed in front of him on hummingbird-fast wings, slapping his hand away. "You must wash first." Her tiny brown hand, no larger than a copper, pointed to a nearby basin. I bit my lip to keep from laughing.

August held his hands up, backing away from the pixie staring him down with such ferocity, before inclining his head with something like reverence. "Of course. Please forgive my horrible manners."

Marle's round cheeks blushed rose to match her pink hair, all forgiven, before she flew away again.

I rolled my eyes. August's charm was becoming ridiculous.

After he washed his hands, ensuring none of his skin's oils would mar the delicate pages, August returned to my side and began flipping through the book.

We stood this way for several minutes in silence, though I was having trouble focusing on the words. I needed to get the weight off my chest. I mulled over what I would say, working to force the phrase from my tongue. It would be my only concession to him.

"Thank you." The words were no louder than a whisper.

I turned my head as our gazes met again, each of us leaning over different books. August's silver eyes darkened as they met mine. "I—"

"Here you are, I've been looking for you."

Evander rounded the corner into the alcove. My posture stiffened as he came to stand beside me, putting a hand to my waist in greeting, in possession, as he joined August and me.

"Hi, Van." I went still to keep from recoiling.

Though I hadn't seen it with my eyes, my mind couldn't help but picture what he'd looked like, standing there, as I was taken into the water. Useless and gaping.

If August Warin, infuriating male that he was, could dive in the water with sirens to save a female he thought barely interesting, why the hell couldn't Evander go after the same one he'd kissed late into the night?

"How are you feeling?" Evander's hand tightened on my waist, pulling me into him so that my body was against his. Concern etched his hazel eyes.

"I'm fine. I wasn't hurt." I answered, pulling back an inch. Evander didn't catch my irritation—but August did. The male's eyes flickered in acknowledgment.

"Thank the gods. I don't know what I would have done if you had been hurt—or worse." Evander drew me in for a kiss, but I turned so his lips landed on my cheek. I could feel his confusion, but he didn't remark upon my rejection. His posture stiffened as he turned his attention to the other male.

"August."

"Van." August mocked my use of his nickname. His lips were turned up in a smirk as he basked in my irritation. My eyes cast daggers back at him.

"Thank you for today. I greatly appreciate what you did for Nic."

August gave a slight bow of the head to Evander. "It was nothing, any valiant male would have done it."

Part of me wanted to defend the male at my side, only because it was August that insulted him. Another part of me wanted him to feel the affront, to regret not having acted quickly himself. The former was fighting a losing battle.

"May we have a moment?" Evander said to August. I silently fumed at the notion that he would ask for my time from another male instead of me directly.

August's knowing eyes sang as he dipped his head and sauntered off. As he turned the corner, he gave me a look that said he still wanted the information in those books. I gave a quick nod of acquiescence before he disappeared.

Evander watched him go, then turned back to me. "What happened with the siren, Nic?"

My low back dug into the table as I pressed against it. "It's hard to know. It was all a blur." I lied, waving my hand toward my head. He easily accepted my words, not reading into them any further. He simply nodded his head in acceptance.

"And all the books?" He turned to the ones I had laid out before me, reaching for the nearest.

"Hands!" Marle returned, faster than lightning, slapping his hand away.

Evander stood stunned, momentarily confused.

"Marle is our librarian," I clarified. "She keeps these books in such pristine condition because of her strict rules on temperature, humidity, and, of course, hand hygiene." The pixie nodded firmly in confirmation of my words.

"Ah, I will keep my hands to myself then," he said, tucking them behind his back.

Marle eyed him skeptically before giving me a look. *I won't let him touch them,* my eyes spoke back to her. Satisfied, she returned to her own restorations.

Evander watched her fly away, curious, before settling his gaze back on me, waiting for my response to his earlier question.

"I'm trying to understand what happened." I shrugged. "I wasn't hurt, but it was still the first time a siren has approached a female that we know of. I thought the books might hold some answers."

"Well, if you could take a break from this," he said, waving a hand over the table, "I had something set up for us this afternoon. I planned it yesterday before…everything. I was hoping you still felt well enough to enjoy it."

I hesitated, my mind warring. I felt how much he wanted me to say yes. Part of me wanted to agree, the part of me that remembered how happy I'd been being held by him last night. But now—

"Sure, just let me take these up to my room." I let the earlier part of myself win, the hopeful part. So though I was still angry with Evander for not coming to my aid, for standing by, I would give him another chance.

Evander broke into a smile that lit up his handsome face before pressing his lips to my temple. I attempted a smile back before I pulled away to gather the books, making sure that certain pages were marked for later with my notes.

"I will meet you in the gardens." He said as he turned to leave.

After I took the books up to my room, leaving them towering on my desk, I came back downstairs and exited the terrace. The palace staff directed me to the southeastern portion, past the daffodils and irises, where Evander stood waiting near the towering sunflowers.

"You look lovely, Nic, even in such plain clothing you continue to be striking"

My stomach tightened at the less than stellar compliment. "Yes well, I am pleased that you can see through such *plainness*."

"Of course," he smiled brightly, missing my meaning, as he pulled a chair out for me from the table set with various foods and a bottle of wine.

I sat, taking in everything before me. "This looks lovely, Evander."

He poured me a glass of white wine, a honeysuckle-based variety I discovered as the flavor hit my tongue. I held back a grimace, the sweetness turning my stomach.

"Do you like it? Misha told me it was your favorite." Evander raised his glass, clinking it with mine.

"Did she?" I was going to have words with her for this.

During the dinner, Evander talked, and I ate. He regaled me with tales of his travels all over the continent, telling me of the beauty he'd seen and people he'd encountered while I sat quietly, letting him speak. He was passionate about his stories, even if he never noticed I had little to say in return.

As the palace staff cleared our plates, Evander continued to talk, and I quietly thanked them. They brought us dessert in turn, a chocolate ganache. I lifted my dessert fork toward the plate set before me.

"No, let me." He said, putting a hand on mine until I placed the silverware back on the table. I gave him a confused look as he held out his fork to me. Then I realized he intended to feed me himself.

"Oh, no Evander. Really it's okay." I chuckled awkwardly, moving to pull my hand away. He could not be serious.

Evander nodded his head. He was indeed serious.

I considered outright refusing, I couldn't imagine he truly thought it would be enjoyable to be fed like a small child. But as he waited I gave in, wanting to avoid the awkwardness that would follow my rejection. I took the bite from his spoon and he beamed at me, even if I felt ridiculous in doing so.

After I leaned back in my seat, lifting my own fork again so that he couldn't reach me, and finished the dessert on my own. Evander seemed disappointed at my moving away, but I could only sacrifice my pride so much.

As the sun slowly began to set, our dessert finished, we stood. "I chose this spot because the sunflowers remind me of you, of your radiance—like the sun," Evander said as we faced the tall blooms.

I hesitated, wondering how wholly vain it would be of me to hate such a thing. It wasn't that the sunflowers weren't lovely, but looking at their golden shade against my pale skin—it seems almost sickly in their presence. I forced a smile but could think of no words to say in response to his comparison.

"And Nic, I know I said it earlier, but I really am so relieved that you are unaffected from this morning. I don't know how I could have stood it if you were hurt." With these words, Evander pulled me into him. One hand came to my low back, the other gently lifting my chin, as he lowered his lips to mine, a second passing before I broke away.

"I will see you tomorrow then, at the ball?" I said as I stepped back, putting space between us.

Disappointment flooded his eyes once more, but he did not reach for me again. "Yes, the Summer Solstice. I'm sure it will be lovely, Nic."

I gave him a quick smile before turning away, escaping back up the path to the palace. As I walked, I mused over the day's events, over how I'd felt with Evander just now.

When his lips were on mine, I realized—I felt nothing.

CHAPTER 16
Misha

I walked out onto the western terrace and found Julian and August there, seated and leaning toward each other in deep discussion. Julian faced away from me and did not appear to hear my approach. I held a finger to my lips as August's eyes flicked to me. He kept his face neutral, humoring me.

Coming up behind Julian on silent, cat-soft feet, I covered his eyes as I spoke into his ear. He jumped in surprise. "Hello, gorgeous. Sitting alone with just your brother for company? I'd have thought a handsome male like you would be flocked by hordes of adoring females." I whispered in his ear, so low August couldn't hear.

He settled in recognition of my voice, his cheeks rising in a smile beneath my hands. "That is because I am spoken for. I diligently await my love's return."

"Ah, I see. She must be an extraordinarily remarkable female to have caught and kept *you*." I teased.

"She is indeed...beautiful and intelligent and cunning and compassionate. She is divine—a goddess in the flesh," Julian said as he indulged my ruse.

I couldn't help my wide smile as I took my hands away and Julian looked up at me, standing just behind his chair. My hands came down to rest on his chest.

He broke into an even larger grin and reached for my hand, his fingers intertwining with mine. "Ah, there she is." Julian's eyes raked over me. "How is your sister feeling, love?"

"Nic is fine. She was physically unharmed and refused to let us dote on her. I don't know if she is as truly unaffected as she's acting, but the best course is usually to let her work it out for herself." I said, then focused my attention on August. "Thank you for going after Nic. She and my aunts, they are...well, I couldn't imagine if anything had happened to her. I would have gone in myself if you hadn't reacted so swiftly."

"Yes, you would have. Then my brother would have gone after you, and we would have been in a real mess. I would have ended up in the water, regardless. So no apologies are necessary. I was creating less trouble for myself," August said, though it didn't seem to be the entirety of it.

"Regardless, I appreciate it more than you can imagine." He nodded in acceptance of my gratitude. "Would you mind if I stole your brother away for a bit?"

"I don't need his permission, love." Julian lifted his eyes from our intertwined fingers back up to my face.

"One of us has to be polite," I snapped at him playfully.

Julian smiled crookedly at me, making my heart flutter, then turned back to August. "Brother, I will see you later then?"

August nodded, then returned to his reading. A book on the elemental lineages. Julian stood, keeping our hands intertwined as we walked.

"And August—" I turned back. He glanced up. "If my sister finds out you nicked that book, she's going to hunt you down. They're like children to her."

It wasn't an exaggeration. It didn't matter how often she'd read them, Nic kept all of her books in pristine condition. Once I'd borrowed a novel from her room—possibly without permission—and when it finally was returned to her with dog-eared pages and a worn spine, she nearly lost it. It was a good thing she loved me. But August...he wouldn't be so lucky.

August's lips lifted in one corner as if he wouldn't mind that one bit.

"Tell me about Montevalle." I walked alongside Julian, hand in hand, down the gravel path shrouded with green leaves, lit up brilliantly in the afternoon sun.

"I've already told you, dozens of times now in my letters, love."

My heart squeezed at his term of endearment. "But I didn't see your face when you said it, and I never get sick of hearing about your home."

Julian smiled, then indulged me. "My home, our capital city of Ankaa, is in a valley deep in the Mountains of Rei. The mountain's jagged slopes and our family's wards protect the city. It is newer, post-war, and its exact location is a secret to all that aren't our citizens. Foreign trade persons have to be winnowed in, then our Ambassador of Trade wipes their mind of it."

"They're a mindcaster?" Julian nodded his head in confirmation. "And it would be a secret to me as well? Even now?"

"What do you mean *even now*? Has something changed between us, love?" Julian cocked a brow, teasing me.

"Julian Ororo Warin." I lightly punched his arm.

Julian stumbled back, grasping his muscle in mock outrage. My hand tightened on his to pull him back to me.

"Don't worry, love." He hugged me to him, pressing a kiss to my hair. "I formally extend you an invitation to Montevalle. Then you can see all our secrets for yourself."

"Do I get a personal tour, from the prince himself?" I wagged my eyebrows suggestively.

He chuckled again, "Yes. We can start in Haldrin, a town near the border—one of our outposts. I can introduce you to part of my brother's council that lives there. You would love them, and I have no doubt they would adore you." His gray eyes seemed to spark as he spoke of his friends.

I pinched his side. "Everyone adores me."

Julian shook his head and laughed. "Oh gods, the trouble you and Damian would get into together." One of his best friends and only a few years apart in age, he had mentioned the male to me before in his letters. Julian continued, "Then we'll go north into the mountains, and after two weeks' time we'll reach Ankaa. We could winnow there much faster, but I suspect you'll want to see all of the landscape and nature along the way."

"You would be correct." I nodded, eager to see all of what his country had to offer. All the new flora to admire and discover.

He looked around, his arm wrapping around my shoulder. "Speaking of tours, where are you leading me now, love?"

"It's a surprise." I grinned. At this point we'd walked far enough to pass the wards surrounding the palace, passing through the barrier that would allow us to winnow the rest of the way. "Hold on tight," I squeezed his waist then winnowed.

We landed in a denser part of the forest, the trees angling overhead to block out the sunlight. After a few more meters through the brush, we emerged past the wards, in front of the abandoned castle.

Julian whistled in appreciation as he took in the aged walls and gothic arches, crumbling away in some parts. Vines, moss, ferns, and other flowering plants covered much of the dark stone, a favorite hideaway for deer, smaller animals, and birds to make their nests.

"What is this place?"

"One of the former High King's summer castles." I pointed to the scorch marks along the walls. "It looks like it was destroyed in the war by lightning strikes and dragon fire."

"My brother's work then," Julian said simply. "And this is the hideaway you spoke of? Where you and your sister would sneak off to as children—where you wrote some of your letters to me?"

"It is. My favorite place in the world. There is something peaceful about it—I feel safe here, and now that my favorite person is here too, it's perfect." I pulled at his hand, urging him to walk toward it with me.

I'd imagined for years what it would be like to have him here with me. To have it become more than just hopes and dreams...there were no words for the feelings that cascaded through my heart.

Seeming to read my thoughts, Julian smiled and pulled me closer, planting a soft kiss on my lips. I could have burst with happiness.

We continued on the path and passed through the ornate stone archway in the surrounding wall, coming into the courtyard. The space was overgrown with wildflowers, ivy, small trees, and other greenery. I drifted my hand along the one wall, casting vines of climbing roses as I went, adding to the charm. The birds sang to us in greeting.

The grand doors of the entrance had long been broken down, and we carefully stepped over them into the throne room. Julian and I navigated the large flat stones of the bubbling stream, our sure footing allowing us to do so without getting our boots wet, making our way toward the large stone seat of the High King was still intact after all this time.

As we approached the dais I paused, turning to face him. "So, let's track back to when you are taking me to Montevalle."

"Yes, love?" Julian wrapped one hand around the base of my neck, the other coming up to toy with a wayward strand of hair.

"What else are we going to do there?"

"I have many, many things in mind." Julian smiled, his eyes teasing as his fingers twirled around that strand he held captive.

"Like?" I persisted, bumping my shoulder into his playfully.

"They are *secrets*. And I know how you love surprises, Misha. I wouldn't dare ruin it for you."

My mouth opened to protest, but his lips captured mine in a soft kiss, his teeth coming to nip at my bottom lip.

I pulled back, "You think you can distract me with kisses?"

"Yes—is it working, love?" He said as he leaned in again.

I laughed, "Maybe."

We met in another kiss, and I opened my mouth for him, letting his tongue meet mine in soft strokes. Our kisses grew more passionate, more breathless as we began to lose ourselves in one another.

Julian lifted me so that I was sitting on the raised dais. As we kissed, he began to lay me back, soft moss sprouting beneath us like the earthy bed of a princess in all those old faerie tales.

He deepened the kiss, and I hooked my legs around his, pulling him in closer. Eventually, he pulled back, planting kisses along my jaw, then my neck. I arched into his touch as he removed my shirt, then the undergarments beneath. His hands came up to touch my breasts, to pinch and tease. I groaned at the sensation, begging for more.

"Did you think about me, love—" Julian's lips grazed along my ear, "Before now—did you picture that we would be together in this way?" His words shot sparks through me.

"Yes," the words came out breathlessly.

"Good, because I thought about you too. What you'd feel like, the sounds you would make. And I have to say, love, you are so much better than I could have ever imagined."

Julian slid a hand along the band of my pants, teasing. I whimpered at the contact before he slowly unbuttoned them.

"Show me...show me what you did when you thought about us," he whispered against my lips, then sat up, kneeling between my thighs. Julian removed my boots, then peeled my pants slowly off me, leaving me bare to his sight.

I hesitated, knowing what he was asking for and a shyness came over me, I hadn't yet been with anyone in this way. But this was Julian...and everything was different now.

"You don't have to, love. I don't want you to ever do anything you are uncomfortable with. Just tell me—talk to me." He leaned down and planted a kiss atop my knee.

"No, I want to." I let my hand slowly drift down. From my breast to my stomach, then lower, between my thighs. Julian's eyes were entranced, watching my every movement.

"I thought about you so often these past years," I said breathlessly as I slowly moved my hand, heightening my pleasure, but not enough pressure to make me finish. No, I wanted to wait until he joined me. "Especially these last few months, when I knew I'd see you again. I couldn't stop myself. I thought about you every night like this. Wondered what it would be like."

"Fuck, Misha." He groaned. Then Julian shifted himself back and knelt before me. He took my hands in his, moving them, placing them back up onto my own breasts.

"You are so exquisitely beautiful, love." He whispered against me, his breath hot as his fingers parted me, making me squirm in anticipation.

The first sweep of his tongue made my back arch. He moaned in approval of my reaction, of my taste. Julian licked and kissed, focusing on my clit as he used one, then two fingers to enter me. As he curled them, I saw stars and broke apart, my climax shattering me across the soft ground.

Julian rose up as he looked down at me, then leaned forward kissing me, open and deep. I tasted myself on him and groaned in pleasure again, to know that I'd claimed him. That this wonderfully perfect male, my friend for so long, was *mine.*

He reached down a hand to line himself up, nudging me at my entrance.

"I love you," he whispered to me with heartbreaking softness as he slid in. I could only whimper in response to everything I was feeling, at how much I knew I loved him then.

"I know, love. I know." Julian said with his eyes locked on mine as he began to move, then leaned to press kisses down my throat.

My best friend in my darkest times, always there for me through distance and time—as he always would be. His gray eyes shone back, storm clouds whirling within them, and I knew he felt this love just as deeply and irrevocably as I did.

Julian. His name was a brand on my heart.

It would never be anyone else, could never be anyone else for me.

"My beautiful mate," Julian whispered, speaking aloud my same thoughts, as he kissed my temple, his hand gripping the moss beneath us as he began to move faster. I moved my hips in time with his, unable to get enough of him, as our lips and tongues met again and again.

"Mate." I repeated against his throat, feeling the pulse beneath my lips, pressing my lips to it. I put my hand on his heart as well, feeling it pound in time with mine. Mirrored, our souls each made for the other.

Julian let out a low growl of satisfaction, then moved faster, deeper. Each of us became more frantic as we chased our release. We shattered together and at that moment, in every moment from now on, I was his and he was mine.

There was no beginning and end. Only us.

Our eyes met again as we caught our breath. Julian touched my face. Softly. Reverently. I smiled up at him. Radiantly. Fervently.

The world ceased around us. There was only him and me.

Forever. Always.

"Let's do it again." I pushed him over, flipping us. Julian choked out a laugh as I pinned him beneath me.

"Whatever you want, love."

CHAPTER 17
Misha

W hen we snuck back into the palace it was well past dark.

Julian and I parted in the central stairway. He headed east to the guest quarters, and I went west back to my rooms. But before we split we'd shared a few more kisses, more whispered *I love you's* as we did so. They were three words I would never tire of hearing from his lips.

I entered the West Wing, walking down the halls as silently as possible, coming to a stop as I noticed the light streaming from under Nic's doorway. Slowing my steps, I neared the door, then ran thorn-tipped fingernails along the panes of the wood there, the sound eerie in the silence and echo of the hall.

"Meesh. I know it's you."

Gods damn her.

"You ruin all my fun," I whined as I pulled at the handle, then leaned against the open door frame. Nic was sitting up in her bed with only the bedside lamp on, her favorite book in her lap, and Ras purring at her feet.

I gasped, "Traitor!" The giant jaguar rolled onto his back unapologetically, beckoning me for a belly rub. I laid next to him on Nic's bed and obliged, sprawling out on my side.

"You can't expect to run out until all hours of the night and not think he'll search for affection elsewhere," Nic teased as I rubbed my hand up and down his fur. Rasalas purred contentedly as I scratched him on his furry chest.

"What are you doing up?" I said. "Aren't we training in the morning before the Summer Solstice celebrations?"

"I could ask the same of you, clearly sneaking in at this late hour," Nic cocked an eyebrow. "I couldn't sleep. My mind won't settle." My sister waved a hand to her temple, her mind seeming to slip elsewhere for a moment. Before I could ask about it, she deflected. "How was Julian?"

"Perfect." I couldn't help the smile and flush that crept onto my cheeks. I had never thought it was possible to be this blissfully happy. Nic smiled back at me, just as pleased for me as I was for myself.

"Hey, you know what I'm thinking?" I rolled onto my stomach, resting my chin on my fist.

My sister caught on, her eyebrows raising. "You want to sneak into our aunts' room?"

I nodded. "It's been a while. We'll be twenty-two tomorrow, and on our next birthday, we will be crowned with a million more responsibilities. Let's pretend we're children again."

"Fine, but if Alé is grumpy and kicks us out, this was all your idea," Nic said as she set the book on her nightstand on top of the stack of others. Some new novels, some her old favorites.

"Let me change." I squealed in excitement, then bounced up and dashed into my room across the hall, quickly bathing then changing into my nightclothes and slippers before I met Nic outside my door.

We silently made our way just down the hall to Alesia and Eve's chambers. Light spilled from under their door indicating they were still awake at this late hour too.

"Okay Nicky, you knock."

"Me? It was your idea. You knock."

"No, I can't. What if they get mad at us for disturbing them? You knock, you're the oldest."

"By *two* minutes," Nic hissed.

"Girls, we can hear you," Alesia called out as Eve giggled.

Nic rolled her eyes at me, then reached for the door handle. I smiled innocently as the door swung open, peeking around the frame. "We couldn't sleep."

Alé laughed, "Well come on then, we'll make room."

I pranced to the bed, jumping right in the middle of them onto the lilac-colored duvet. Both were in long sleeved night clothes, Alesia's a deep blue, Eve's a pink with florals that matched the silk bonnet that kept her tightly-wound curls from frizzing. I put my back to Eve as I leaned into her embrace, and she chuckled at my exuberance. Nic walked over at a slower pace and sat at the edge of the bed, pulling a pillow into her lap.

"How was your night with Julian, Misha?" Eve asked as her hand went to my hair, gently combing through the blonde strands with her fingers. My aunt brushing through my hair was my favorite thing as a child. I nearly purred in contentment.

"It was good," I blushed.

Eve's hands paused. "That's it? That's all we get? You're not usually so coy, my love,"

"I told him I loved him." I smiled shyly, taking Eve's hands to cover my face.

"And he felt the same?" Nic's eyes were probing—protective. I knew she liked Julian, but she would always be hesitant when it came to matters of the heart. My sister never wanted to see me hurt.

"Yes, he said it too, and when we were together, it was—it felt different. Maybe it's because we've known each other for so long, because he's been my closest friend but it felt like more. Like he is everything." I admitted, playing with Eve's mating band on her left hand. The gold glinted in the light, catching on the inscription there, the one that matched Alé's.

Eve rested her cheek on my head. "We can see that, darling. Since he's been here, Julian has only shown you devotion. It's plain as day how he regards you." My heart swelled at her words, for seeing him as I did.

"Oh, mija," Alé said, her eyes uncharacteristically glassy. "That's all we could ever want for you, such happiness."

"Enough about me," I said as I wiped the dampness from my eyes with Eve's sleeve. "How did it go with Evander, Nicky?" I turned to my sister, deflecting the attention to her, my eyebrows raising. He'd come to me earlier wanting to know Nic's favorite wine and foods. I'd been honest with him—mostly.

"The wine was horrible," she cut me a sharp look "—but the rest was fine."

"Oh come on Nicky, I only lied about the wine. He told me all about his comparison of you to spring daisies and sunflowers, he picked that spot all on his own."

Nic fit much better among the calla lilies and night-blooming jasmine—all of which surrounded the Star Pond they'd gone to if he'd taken the time to notice.

"And you did nothing to discourage him?" Nic's eyes narrowed.

"Why would I? The poor male was so proud of himself and the date he'd planned, I wasn't going to ruin it for him."

"Oh please, Meesh, don't act like you did it out of the kindness of your heart." Eve chided.

I shrugged, not denying her words as Alesia chuckled, taking a sip of the wine she'd set on her bedside, the bottle she and Eve had been enjoying before we'd taken over their night. Nic caught the movement and with a flick of her wrist winnowed a matching wine glass into her hand, looking at Alé expectantly. Our aunt clicked her tongue but poured her some without hesitation.

"What else did he do?" I said. My sister was much too quiet—leaving something out.

Nic leaned back onto one arm as she stretched out her legs before her. "Who says he did anything?"

"We know something is up, love." Eve chimed in, fingers running through my hair again. She knew Nic's evasive ways as well as I did. We three looked at her expectantly, she couldn't lie to us.

"Ugh, fine. You know he set up dinner for us in the gardens near the sunflowers, saying they reminded him of me. It looked like he put a lot of effort into it, even if Misha tried to sabotage him."

I threw up my hands. "If he had paid any attention to you at all at dinner or the first ball he would have known you hate sweet wines and wouldn't have needed my advice."

"Well, it's thought that counts—"

"What *thought*?" I scoffed. "That could have been a date for anyone. He didn't consider *you* at all."

"Shh, darling." Eve chided. "But what? It sounds lovely, Nic." She urged my sister on.

Alesia balked. "A lovely date for whom? It sounds like he hasn't even met Nic. He compared her to *sunflowers*." She snorted. "Complete and utter horse shi—"

"Alé!" Eve cut her off, then laughed. Alesia and I along with her. Even Nic's sour mood cracked as she smiled.

Alesia spoke nothing but truth. Evander would have been better off asking her to sit on the palace roof with a bottle of wine, anything dry, and pondering the existential meaning of the stars, the gods...anything really. Nic just wanted what anyone did—someone to see her for who she was.

"You can't expect all males to pick up on such things as wine or date preference, their gender is typically lacking in such observations. At least he put in some effort at all." My sister defended, though weakly.

"But if it was so *considerate*, Nic, what turned you off to him so much?" I wanted to get her back to talking about what had happened. She was still leaving something out.

"I started thinking about what happened this morning and how he didn't even attempt to come after me. It just kept plaguing my mind, the picture of him standing there, useless. And—"

"*And.*" I sat up, tired of her dancing around the subject.

"Well, he wanted to...feed me."

"Feed you?" Eve's face pinched.

Alesia roared with laughter. "Himself? What—with his hands?"

"No, thank the gods for that, but off his fork like I was a baby bird. It was terrible." Nic shuddered and the three of us rolled with laughter.

"It's not funny" Nic grabbed a pillow, hitting Alé and me in the chest, then chunking it at Eve, all of us still giggling uncontrollably.

"Oh no—no, you're right. It's not funny. How dare he? Oh gods, how will poor Evander ever recover?" I said, causing renewed laughter from the three of us. I was thrilled that she was no longer interested in him, but the reasoning was so ludicrous, I couldn't help but tease her. "You would have forgiven him for not jumping in after you, but you aren't willing to overlook *that*?" I gasped between laughs.

"You're telling me you'd be okay with Julian hand-feeding you? That you wouldn't be disgusted by it?" Nic accused, even though she was now smiling along with us.

"Of course. That male can feed me anything he wants. Including that big, hard—"

"No—" Eve said as she covered my mouth to finish what I was going to say, pulling me back into her. "My poor ears can't hear those words from my sweet, little niece."

Nic and Alesia laughed along with us before my sister grew serious again. "No but really, it was something about our conversations—not that he let me get a word in." Nic's eyes flashed with irritation, then grew soft. "It's as if he has built up this idea of me that is not at all accurate."

"Oh mija, you can't be worried about that forever," Alesia said as she hugged Nic to her, her arms wrapping around my sister the same way that Eve's were around me.

Eve pressed her hand to my sister's cheek. "You have to be vulnerable some-time, Nic. If you keep being so closed off, darling, no one will ever get to see the beautiful soul that we do. And that would be such a tragedy."

"The real tragedy is Evander's courting, with those damned horrible feeding habits." I quipped, and Nic's lips lifted.

"Fine, I'll work on it." My sister relented.

"Okay, great. Now let's all talk again about how beautiful and flawless Julian is." I said as we began giggling again, all four of us.

CHAPTER 18
Nic

M isha, Alesia, Eve, and I stayed up late into the night gossiping about the events thus far in the Blood Treaty celebrations as well as reminiscing on old stories that were favorites of ours.

Alesia and Eve told us more tales of our parents from before we'd been born. I wondered what it would have been like for them to be here with us for this. To hear Misha talk about Julian, and me about Evander. What would have been their takes on everything that had happened in the past few days?

Even in my melancholy musings of what could never be, my heart was full as we all laid down to sleep, still crammed together in their bed—nestled between the aunts and sister I loved more than life itself.

As I laid there, I couldn't keep my mind from wandering back to the previous day. It seemed like more than just hours had passed since I'd been pulled into the sea by the siren, when she'd shared that vision. Her warning.

Who among us were wolves pretending to be sheep? Wearing a fake mask for all? The siren had risked much in coming so close to shore and taking me, her message had to be dire. And yet I still hadn't interpreted it fully.

The easy assumption was Adrienne, she'd already misrepresented the social program's status and funding, hiding her spending from us. But was that it, or was she ambitious for more? Would she truly step down from her role as Queen in one year's time, allowing my sister and I to take our rightful place in our parents' stead...or would she attempt a coup?

She had to know she wouldn't win, not with only the support of her brother.

As I reflected on this, the siren's prophecy and all its possible meanings, I drifted off into sleep. Into a dream worse than a nightmare.

A memory.

I awoke in my bed, alone. The spot beside me was cold, indicating that it had been that way for quite some time now.

My gut sank. Where had he gone?

Sitting up, I told myself that he must have had a reason to leave without waking me, even if it had been our first night together—the only night I had ever spent with someone in that way.

Callum was the son of one of the females on the royal council and as we were the same age, he was often at the castle with Misha and me for events and tutoring. We were friends though he always flirted with me in a way that indicated he wanted more. After months of his courting, I finally gave in, sharing kisses and stolen moments in the palace, the gardens, the woods.

I was infatuated and liked the attention, even if I wasn't sure if it was love. Something always held me back from reaching that point.

I rose from the bed to dress and make my way down for breakfast. The Summer Solstice, and our eighteenth birthday, was approaching and many of the council were present in the palace for the celebrations. Today there was a large luncheon for the council members and their families.

When I arrived in the large dining room, I didn't see Callum there at first, just his mother. Adrienne walked in after me and was seated at the head of the table, my aunts already present and busy engaging with our many guests. I found my sister and sat with her as we were greeted as well.

We were seated around the table when Callum finally arrived, sitting by his mother. I looked at him with a small smile, remembering the night before, but he didn't return my glance. He didn't look my way for the entirety of the meal.

We had kept our relationship a secret in respect for my privacy as one of the heirs, but this felt different. He seemed colder, more detached than he had ever been.

My gut twisted.

Misha knew about us, but I hadn't yet told her about last night, though I could tell she sensed something was off as she looked back and forth between us. Concern edged in her eyes.

Afterward, I left, hoping to find solace in my sister's gardens, the place she'd made for me with my favorite flowers, calla lilies, red roses, and the algae that shone like stars. I needed a moment to think, to breathe after being stuck in that stifling room with Callum's indifference. I couldn't make sense of the sudden change in him.

I stopped suddenly before rounding a corner, recognizing the voices coming from the alcove. They hadn't heard me approach, my ever-silent footsteps hid me from their fae ears. I stood behind the lilac shrub, concealing myself as I listened.

"I can't believe I lost." Resa, a councilman's daughter, whined.

"Yes, she held out longer than we thought. Looks like Kalina won. She guessed it would take six months." Garreck, the son of a governor of one of the coastal cities, said.

"I knew she couldn't be as prudish as she looked and would give in, eventually." Kalina, Garreck's sister, gloated.

Logic told me they could have been talking about anything, anyone.

But in my gut I knew—I knew.

Then I heard it, that laugh. The laugh I'd heard so much over the past months as he joked with me.

"No, a prude she most definitely is not—at least not anymore," Callum said as the others snickered.

My chest imploded. Me—they had bet on me. *On how long it would take Callum to seduce me—to be with me. It was all a long running joke, and I had been too naïve and blind to see it.*

I couldn't breathe.

"I can't believe you spent so much time with her for this. She's so quiet and stuck up." Resa noted.

"Yes, her twin definitely got all the personality of those two," Garreck added. "I mean, she's beautiful, don't get me wrong. But it had to be ridiculously dull courting her."

"Yes, she's shy, but she did open up after a time. It turned out to be a bit fun even." Callum said almost regretfully—almost. "Though she's not interesting enough to want to continue."

I had always been quieter than my sister, more reserved. Misha lit up every room she entered, drew every eye to her without trying. I never resented her for it—and never would. But hearing them talk about me in this way...having all my worst fears about what people might say about me brought to fruition? I was a joke, just a fucking joke to them—to him.

My eyes misted—my chest felt like it was going to crack wide open. I started to back away before I did something stupid.

I stepped back, bumping into someone. Turning, I looked straight into her blue eyes. I was so in my own head, lost in listening that I hadn't even heard her follow me. The rage on her face was like nothing I'd ever seen. She'd heard everything too.

"Move, Nicky," Misha whispered in a low voice.

I couldn't. My self-directed rage and embarrassment rooted me to the spot.

My twin stepped around me, the four going silent as they saw her, quickly changing the subject.

"Princess," Kalina jumped. "So happy you're here with us. Care to give your insight on who will win the Hunt this year?" She giggled nervously.

Misha didn't answer. With a wave of her hand she transformed them all—stinkweed, mountain ash, corpse flower, and a venus fly trap.

"Now you all smell like the rotting words coming out of your festering mouths," she snarled.

"Kalina! Garreck!" Their mother, Louisa, wailed as she rounded the corner and saw what Misha had done to them.

I wiped my face, gritting my teeth as I stepped around the corner as well, ready to stand between her and my sister that had only reacted in defense of me.

"Change them back. Change them back now!" She was howling at my twin like she had forgotten she was speaking to the crown princess. "You spoiled girl! You can't just change people into plants at your whim."

"Your children are hateful little shits. They will serve much better in the dirt." Misha snarled, not backing down an inch.

"Governor Louisa," Adrienne said, coming around me before I could speak to defend my sister. When had she gotten here? My heart plummeted for Misha—caught in this situation because of me.

"Your majesty. Please, make her change them back. The princess has gone mad!" Louisa begged.

"Misha, if you will, please return them to their fae forms," Adrienne said with a calm, but unyielding, voice. "Governor, you will bring these four and their parents to my throne room. Now. We can handle this misunderstanding there."

Misha looked ready to argue, but she held her tongue and did as our stepmother asked.

"Girls," Adrienne nodded to my sister and me. "My chambers, first."

I turned and walked back up the path, grabbing my sister's hand, avoiding the others. My gaze averted from hers as well, from the pity I knew would be there on my behalf. I kept my chin high, though I wanted nothing more than to lock myself in my room and never emerge, never have to face any of them again.

We went into the study near the throne room. Adrienne sat behind a large, ornate desk before she spoke. "Why don't you two tell me what happened?"

I told our stepmother everything, needing to take the blame from Misha. I told her about Callum and my secret courtship, about what transpired last night. Then what Misha and I overheard this morning in the garden. I kept my story concise but truthful, my voice unwavering, refusing to break in front of her.

"Misha was only defending me. She is not to blame. I am." I finished.

Adrienne sat still for a few moments, unspeaking. Then said quietly, "Thank you for telling me, Nicole. Now, let us see to the others."

We followed Adrienne into the throne room, sitting on our thrones as she took hers, our father's, in the center.

"It has come to my attention what was the cause of my stepdaughter's sudden outburst this morning," she addressed Resa, Garreck, Kalina, and Callum, as well as their parents, the courtiers who had also arrived.

"My son told me as well," Evangeline, Callum's mother, replied. "And I am so sorry for what transpired. My son and his friends meant no harm—"

Adrienne cut her off with a laugh, a deep cruel thing that had no trace of humor in it. "No harm? Oh, surely you can't believe that?"

"My son swore to me that he never meant to offend, he does truly care for the princess. Though I know the situation she is in now." Evangeline continued. Misha gave a disbelieving snort. Callum just stared at the ground, unable to meet my gaze. Coward.

Adrienne's pale blue eyes assessed the courtier. "And what situation is that?"

"Well...now that the princess's virtue is—well, my son knows what this means for her, for someone of her stature and her potential of marrying one day, and he will graciously extend his hand to her, so that they may be married."

My stomach turned to ice. I would rather rot in hell than be bound in marriage to him.

"Her virtue? Was your son not present as well? Can only one person commit the act? What of his virtue as you say?" Adrienne said, her voice still and quiet. Only a fool wouldn't detect the violence in it.

"Well...no, but the connotations are often different for females—"

"So because my stepdaughter has 'lost her virtue' as you say, she is not worthy of marrying in the future? That she will not make a great Queen—"

"No your majesty, I didn't mean—I didn't intend to imply that—"

"You all will leave my court. Today. Now. You all will be stripped of your titles and will never return again so long as I am Queen."

"But your majesty—" Resa's father sputtered.

"Surely there has to be another solution." Louisa interrupted.

"We can't just be stripped of our titles for our children's disagreements," Evangeline said, shocked.

"You can, and you will. There are ethics clauses in all of your appointments. Maybe if you had taught your children those same ethics, they would not have put you in the position you are in now. So I'll say again: leave and do not return to this court. Do not make me repeat myself a third time." Adrienne stood from her throne, her posture rigid and commanding. She would not back down from her decision. I could understand now why so many people had feared her during the war.

They all left the throne room without another word, escorted out by the royal guard.

Only then did my eyes grow misty once more, still locked on the door they had all walked through. Callum, the male that had spent so many months pretending to care for me, didn't look back.

"Nicole," Adrienne said, and I finally turned to her.

"Only you decide what hurts you, what defines you." She put a steadying hand on my shoulder, then walked from the room as well.

I kept my face blank, my head high until she left. With only Misha there to witness, I fell to my knees and finally let the tears erupt from me, and my sister held me as I broke apart.

I awoke coated in a cold sweat at the memory.

The morning dawn streamed through the windows. Misha and Alesia were cuddled together. Eve and I were the same, her arms wrapped around me. I desperately hoped that I hadn't moved in my sleep as I'd been prone to do when I was younger. The thrashing I'd done when dreaming of our father's loss.

I snuggled into her and before I drifted back into sleep, I remembered what I had promised myself so long ago—what I'd sworn then. That I would never let anyone else hurt me like he had. The female Callum had manipulated was dead and gone. Her naivete, her weaknesses—I'd buried them long ago.

For as long as I lived, I would never be anyone's joke again.

CHAPTER 19
Misha

We woke early the next morning to the smell of bacon, eggs, and pancakes from the breakfast our aunts had delivered to their room. All of us ate in their large bed, still in our night clothes. Then they surprised us with our birthday gifts. Little pendants hung on bracelets, silver for Nic and gold for me, each containing a tiny moonstone orb.

"It's so lovely," I gasped, admiring the way the light caught on the orb inside its cage of gold, no bigger than the tip of my index finger.

"We had them made early this spring, when we'd gone to visit the Priests of Oscuri." Eve said.

The Priests of Oscuri were High Fae, all with the gift of mindcasting. They lived secluded on an island off the coast of Desdemon, near Eve's birthplace. Their High Priestess, Katarina, was a particular friend of our family.

"So that's where you and Alé snuck off to for two weeks. I'd just thought you were visiting your birthplace in the East, an extended mates' getaway." Nic said as she admired hers, letting it dangle from her wrist and catching the morning light.

"We couldn't ruin the surprise," Alesia said, sipping from her ginger tea.

"Why did you visit the Priests to have them made?" I extended my wrist to Eve, and she helped me clasp the bracelet.

"If you turn the orb thrice, you will see." Eve beamed.

Nic and I each did so. As the little orb spun around a third time, we were caught in a vision, a memory. The four of us this time last year doing nearly the same thing, cuddled in our aunts' bed and sharing breakfast, Nic, Alesia, and Eve laughing at some joke I'd made. The vision lasted for nearly a minute. When we came out of it, Nic's and my eyes were both misty with unshed tears.

The little orbs contained a vision of our family—of a moment of pure happiness.

"Thank you," Nic whispered softly. I nodded in agreement, my throat still tight from what our aunts had given us.

"The priestesses were able to siphon from each of our memories of that morning to give a full picture of the moment." Alesia said, her eyes damp.

Eve was fully crying, tears streaking down her lovely face, but still, she smiled. "There are other memories too, girls. One of you with your father when you were young, and another of your mother when she carried you. So you will always have a piece of each of us with you, no matter where you go."

I turned the orb again as I saw my mother, Diana, sitting in a large chair gazing lovingly down at her expanded belly, singing us a lullaby in her native tongue, our father standing over her as he planted a kiss softly on her head. Turning it again I saw him years later, sprouting flowers for my sister and me, pink roses and white lilies, as we squealed in delight.

When I came out of the visions, I saw that Nic had done the same, her eyes unseeing as she was still absorbed in the memories. Then I launched myself at my aunts, squeezing them into tight hugs.

"They're perfect," I whispered to each of them. Alesia pressed a kiss to my cheek, and Eve still cried her silent tears of happiness. Once Nic was done she did the same, hugging each of them as she whispered her thanks.

"Of course. Just know that we love you, that your parents loved you, and they still do from where they rest among the stars." Alesia said as tears began to streak down her face. Then we were all crying as we held one another.

Our little family, both complete and incomplete, but my heart had never felt more full.

After we'd gotten ourselves and our emotions in check, Nic and I left our aunts' chambers and snuck back to our own before we were caught meandering about in our robes and slippers.

Once we'd changed into more appropriate clothing, we met Alesia and Eve in our hidden training clearing in the northern woods.

"Don't worry, girls, I promise to take it easy on you," Alesia smirked at us.

"I still can't believe you're having us train on our birthday," I whined, albeit halfheartedly. I already knew what she'd planned for today, and it was one of her more fun training exercises. Power sharing.

The High Fae could very rarely open themselves up and share from that core of magic within them. Usually only with their family, close friend, or spouse—someone they trusted implicitly.

The magic residing in our hearts felt like a well, still and deep, though at times it felt more like a beast sleeping with one eye open, waiting for its moment of release, for the tether that kept it in check to snap. It could become overwhelming if left restless for too long. To keep the beast sated, we siphoned off some of the power with the more ordinary displays of magic that Nic and I could conjure, much like what we'd done the night of the dinner party. But if released all at once, it did have a bottom, a limit to what we could expel. That was where power sharing came in.

My sister and I together could fuse our wells of power, double our reserves by combining. This wouldn't change the element we could cast, sharing with Nic did not mean I could pull water from my fingertips, but it did mean that I could cast greater, stronger earth magic for longer durations.

Power called to power, and mine purred in my sister's presence, eager to be joined. Together we were stronger, fiercer—unbeatable and unbreakable.

"No whining, Meesh," Eve crooned, taking her mate's hand. "We'll go first. Then you and your sister."

As our aunts locked hands, their power flowed seamlessly through them. Because Alesia had the more demonstrative power, she was the one that led the casting. During the war it had often been the opposite, Alesia had the greater reservoir of magic and would return from battle to assist Eve, supplying her mate with more power so she could continue to heal the fallen rebels.

Alesia cast animals of water from her hands. Birds, horses, and great cats prowled along the clearing.

After a few moments, she nodded to us to begin. Nic and I smiled as we joined hands. She nudged me to go first.

I let down my shields as Nic's power joined with mine, thrumming in my veins. I cast great writhing vines from the ground as well as the shifting of the soil and rock itself. My earthen beasts competed with Alesia's, locked in a small-scale battle. Rocks and earthy masses floated above us, crashing into the creatures she'd made. Hers in turn became ice and sliced through my vines and plants.

My blood hummed with the energy pulled from my sister. Alike and not alike my own. So much depth, so much power. With this much, I could be unstoppable, un—

"That's enough Misha." Alesia's voice rang out, breaking through my trance.

Such was the problem with so much power. It could be seductive, taking over so that only it remained and your own conscious will and desire faded. The sleeping beast asleep no more. You became a vessel to only the magic and its own desire to ravage and conquer. That was the reason we trained in this way, to resist its lure.

I yanked on the magic's reins, reminding it that I was in control. I was its master and bearer.

"Good, Misha." Alesia applauded my ability to regain control.

"My turn," Nic smiled.

We continued in this way for another hour, working on the ebb and flow between my sister and me.

As much as the power enthralled me, it was always harder for Nic to pull back, to keep from taking and expelling too much. Much like her quick temper, she needed to learn to control her more volatile tendencies, but today we had done equally well.

Once finished with training, Alesia and Eve winnowed back to the palace, wanting to assist the royal staff in some of the final set up for tonight. Nic and I decided to walk back, enjoying the summer morning that had not yet grown too warm.

A few minutes into our walk we met both Warins on the path.

"What are you doing out here?" I asked them, going straight to Julian.

"The Sun herself, on her birthday no less." He beamed, tucking me into his side and planting a kiss to the top of my head. "We were feeling a bit restless and decided to take a walk around the grounds."

My eyes went to his clothing. I'd only seen him dressed so casually once, when we all wore riding leathers for the Hunt. The way the supple leather fitted his form suited him. The way it clung to his lean muscles gave me flashbacks to the night before, and I considered how appropriate it would be to drag him into the woods for another round.

"We were just heading back," Nic added, breaking me from my heated thoughts.

"As were we." Julian nodded to my sister then turned his eyes back to me. The flash in them told me he'd been thinking the same thing.

I grinned. "Would you two mind if I showed Julian something nearby? It's a favorite place of mine in the woods."

Nic's eyes narrowed either at my lie or that I was leaving her to walk back with August, who had been quiet thus far in our meeting.

Julian was quickly winning my family's approval, but would I have August's? By his unreadable expression, it was hard to tell. My heart constricted in my chest.

My sister's eyes shifted to him too. The hard look in them told me Nic was wondering the same, if the King of Montevalle hadn't quite decided if he approved of this match between his brother and me.

"We wouldn't mind at all. Would we, August?" Nic's gaze was challenging, daring him to disagree.

His eyes met hers with equal intensity, the same unyieldingness. I prayed to the gods if they ever had it out I was present. I wasn't quite sure who would emerge victorious in that fight of wills, but it would be extremely entertaining.

"Of course not." August agreed, but neither his nor my sister's eyes softened.

"Sister," I said, snapping her from her stare off. "I will see you later."

Taking Julian's hand in mine, we turned back up the path, heading further into the forest, leaving Nic and August behind. Before long he tugged at my hand, then backed me into one of the towering oaks.

"Happy birthday, love," Julian whispered before he kissed me. I sighed into it, into him, my body going molten and tense all at once.

"What was it you wanted to show me?" Julian said as he continued kissing me, down my jaw to my neck.

"I think you know."

CHAPTER 20
Nic

O ut with it."

"Out with what, Nicole?" August turned to me, his gaze breaking from where our siblings had disappeared.

"That look. You're contemplating something, and I want to know what it is," I said as he began walking silently up the path. I followed, quickening my stride until we were in step.

"Do you disapprove?" I pressed and was met with more silence, but his eyes sparked.

"Why?" I said, coming to stand in front of him, planting my feet so he had to stop short. "In what way is my sister unworthy of your brother?"

August sighed, looking down at me. "I did not say that, Nicole."

"You might not have, but your face says you are less than happy with those two running off the way they have been these past few days. So tell me. What are your reservations?"

"Julian is my brother, my only remaining family. Can I not be worried about him as a brother is?"

"Worried about what?" I pushed. August was out of his mind if he thought I would let this go.

He hesitated as if seeking the right words. "Your sister may not be taking this as seriously as he is."

"And whatever gave you that impression?" He couldn't be serious.

"Misha is lovely. Kind and affectionate with everyone she meets. Those are not negative qualities by any means, but...she is used to being the center of attention. My worry is that she seeks Julian's affection for the sake of having it, not for the commitment my brother is hoping to secure with her."

August's observations of my twin's personality weren't wrong, but his assessment of her character was. Misha would never lead someone on like that. He truly had no idea how in love with Julian she was. That he would dismiss her attention to his brother as so trivial was insulting.

And if it was as Evander had suspected, that August had killed his father for power—to become King—what would he resort to if he believed his brother needed protecting? Even if the only suffering was a broken heart, what lengths would he go to shield him from my sister?

What lengths would I go to keep Misha from the same fate?

Endless—there were no bounds to what I would do for her.

"So you have observed my sister a few times and now think you know her? You know exactly what she is thinking?"

August shook his head. "No, that's not—"

"My sister is gregarious and playful, yes, and it may often be misconstrued as carelessness, but Misha has the purest of hearts and is unmatched in the lengths she will go to for her family. She loves those close to her with everything she has, and she has been in love with your brother for *ten years*. Julian should consider himself the luckiest male in the world that she has chosen him—that she *loves him*."

August's mouth opened, as if he were going to refute me, but I cut him off again as I stepped closer.

"I swear to the gods, August, if you come in between them and my sister gets her heart broken, I will personally hunt you down. I don't care if it means another war." I snarled as I turned on my heel and stormed away.

I didn't care how old and powerful he was, how many dragons he'd slain. I refused to be cowed by him.

"Nicole—" August started after me.

Without looking back, I rooted his legs up to the knees in ice and slicked the path after me for good measure.

A moment later I heard him break through the ice with a strike of his lightning, but he wisely didn't follow.

I returned to the palace grounds, cutting through the gardens. My blood still boiled from that interaction with August.

If Misha and Julian wanted to be together, that should have been the end of it, but he had to insert himself into their relationship, into what was clearly none of his business. If he got in Julian's ear and made him question, made him break my sister's heart, treaty or not I would tear him apart.

I briefly wondered if he could have been the sheep turned wolf in the siren's vision but quickly thought better of it.

August was all wolf.

I made my way past the ranunculus to the stargazer lilies when I turned to see Evander walking toward me, his face lit up in a smile. "Nic."

"Hi Evander," I said, not quite able to return his enthusiasm.

"I knew we planned to see each other at the ball later, but I am so glad I found you early. There is something I wanted to give you before tonight." He pulled out a flat, blue velvet box from his jacket pocket and handed it to me.

"That's really sweet, but you know you didn't have to get me anything for my birthday," I said, hesitating before opening it.

"Oh, your birthday—yes, of course." His bright smile faltered just a moment before recovering. "I thought it would fit you perfectly. Go ahead and open it."

I slowly flipped open the lid. Resting on the dark velvet was a necklace. The chain was made up of small round diamonds set in gold. In the center sat a large yellow diamond pendant. It was beautiful...and *huge*.

I shook my head. "Evander, it's stunning, but I can't possibly accept this."

"Please, let me give you this Nic, as a token of my feelings."

His feelings? We'd only been spending time together for a few days. Panic began to rattle in my chest.

"Watching you being taken by that siren in the water—" he continued, shaking his head. "It made me realize how easily everything can be taken away from us."

The water you watched me get dragged under? While you stood there and did nothing?

"So, I remembered our family had this and immediately thought of you, of the sunflowers yesterday. It radiates with a beautiful golden light, just as you do." He smiled, gazing back up at me.

Wrong—his entire assessment of me was wrong. Misha was the golden one, I was her shadow.

"Let me put it on you," Evander said as he lifted the necklace from the box, inclining it toward me.

"Okay," I conceded, though my mind was still racing with doubt. He linked the thick chain at the back of my neck, the pendant weighing heavily on my chest.

Even as royalty, the necklace seemed too much. The center stone itself was the size of a quail egg.

Evander grinned as he stood back to admire it, then leaned in to press his lips to mine, lingering for a moment. "Happy Birthday, Nic." He whispered as he pulled back. "I'll see you later tonight, lovely. And maybe we can meet after too?"

"Sure." If he heard my hesitance, he didn't show it.

"Save a few dances for me." Evander smiled, then turned to head back into the palace, leaving me there alone.

Facing the lilies I reached up, unclasping the necklace before I placed it back in its box. I took a deep breath, but it wasn't enough to expel the dread that had begun to take root in my chest.

CHAPTER 21
Nic

Walking up the palace steps, I realized it was past noon, and I was starving. I headed to the kitchens and there found Alesia standing over a pot of soup.

"Oh, that smells amazing Alé." I leaned over the pot to breathe in the heady scent.

"Back up, scavenger, it's not ready yet." She playfully pushed me away. "I thought you and your sister would like one of your mother's favorites before the final ball tonight."

She was absolutely right. This soup was composed of small pan-fried noodles with crushed tomatoes, onion, garlic, shredded chicken, zucchini, chili powder, and other spices. My mouth began to water.

"What do you have there?" Alesia motioned to the box holding Evander's necklace as she stirred.

"Evander got me a gift."

"Hmm," she mused, unimpressed. "Well let's see it, don't keep me in suspense." She set down her wooden spoon, wiping her hands on a towel.

I handed Alesia the velvet box, and she flipped open the lid.

"Oh my gods, Nicole, that thing is huge." Her eyes went wide. "He really gave this to you?".

"It's wild right? I mean it is beautiful, but what on earth could I ever wear it to?"

"It sure is...something," Alesia said with her eyebrows high on her forehead. "I guess you could wear it tonight? I'm sure he's expecting you to."

I shrugged, taking back the box and shutting the lid as I set it down. "You don't feel this gift is too much too soon?"

She paused for a moment, analyzing my tone and expression. "Oh mija, this isn't about the necklace at all is it?"

"No." I sighed, drawing out a stool from the table behind her before taking a seat.

"Well you know how I feel about what happened at the beach, and we already discussed your date. But I know you, Nic—you love a challenge. You hate to be told no, but love overcoming it. Evander has been fawning over you since he arrived. It's been too easy."

As much as I wanted to deny it, she wasn't far off the mark.

"But isn't it wrong to feel that way?" I lifted my elbow to rest on the table, my head leaning on my hand. "Shouldn't courtship be easy if it's with the right person?"

"Eve and I weren't easy. We hated each other at first." Alesia smirked as she returned to her stirring.

"What?" I couldn't fathom how two people that loved each other as much as they did could've had any moment in time where that wasn't the case.

"It's true." She shrugged. "I thought she was a self-righteous pacifist, and she thought I was nothing more than a warrior brute. We couldn't stand each other for at least six months."

"When did it change?"

"I was hurt on the front lines, badly. Eve saved me, she even killed a few of the High King's soldiers defending me. I saw her differently after that. Afterward I needed time to heal, and she helped me—came by to check on me every day. Slowly, she started to see me differently too." Alesia's eyes gleamed with love for her mate. As different as they were, they were matched in their passion for each other.

"And your mother must have had something to do with it as well," she continued. "Eve and I were always somehow stationed near each other. I think she could see what we couldn't. Diana always was the perceptive one, seer or no."

Alesia lifted the ladle to scoop soup into bowls for each of us, then handed me the sliced avocado to add along with the flat bread to dip into it. I placed some in my spoon and blew on it to cool. Once I was satisfied I wouldn't burn my tongue, I sipped. Perfection.

"Where did your sister run off to?" She sat next to me with her own bowl, thankfully changing the subject.

"She left with Julian after training," I said, and she gave me a knowing look. I chuckled, we both knew what they were likely off doing.

"Do you think they are suited for each other? That they could be mates?" I asked. If Alé had any reservations remaining about Julian, I hoped she would share them, so I could ease any concerns she had.

"At first I was wary of course, because of his father, but they are very good together, and the way those two look at each other reminds me of Dom and Diana. Utterly hopeless." Alesia said with a melancholic smile.

"So you approve, even with him being a Warin?"

"You and your sister know how your parents, Eve, and I felt about Josiah. But just because a parent is one way doesn't necessarily mean the son will be the same. Besides, Josiah died when Julian was young, he likely didn't have a very strong influence on him. I won't let my opinion of the father cloud my judgment of the son."

I considered what she said. At the mention of Josiah's name, my thoughts circled back to what Evander had told me the night of the dinner on the terrace. Of the suspicions that Josiah had been murdered, and that August had done it for the crown. I didn't know if I believed it, but wasn't sure if I completely doubted it either.

I stared into the soup as I dipped my bread and took another bite.

"What are you keeping from me, Nicky?" My eyes snapped up to hers. For Alesia saying she wasn't the perceptive sister, I could get nothing past her.

"Something Evander told me. After the dinner in the gardens."

"*And?*"

I set down my spoon, turning to face her more fully. "He said he had heard rumors. That Josiah didn't die from the blood disease like we were all told."

Her brow scrunched together. "Did he say what he heard happened?"

"He thinks—" I sighed. "—well, he'd heard from other merchants that August did it. He killed his father for the crown, to take power."

Alesia shook her head. "That makes no sense, Nic."

"How so? None of us knows August that well. This is the first time any of you have seen him in one hundred years. We have no idea what he is capable of."

"You're right, we don't. But I do know what I heard and saw during the war in our short time together during those last days. August Warin was merciless, but not in the way his father was. Josiah was cruel to all. August was only to those that truly deserved it, the war criminals. He spared and protected the innocent where he could unlike his father and the Deimos. Not to mention he mostly raised Julian, and does that male seem like he fears for his life around his brother? That he suspects he killed his father?"

"No." My lips tightened.

"Also, we've all been here together for days, Nic. Do you think I would accept anyone into our home, around you and your sister, without keeping an eye on them to ensure your safety? Besides, August cares nothing for the usual royal pomp and circumstance. He's never even attended any events until now and has never flaunted his crown. I can't say the same for the rest of the royals, including you and Misha."

"Damn, Alé." I sat back in my chair.

"That's not a bad thing, Nic." She laughed. "You two were raised in this. I love that you both are so confident in your titles and who you are. You should be, but why would August kill his father for his crown, then avoid all the pleasures that come with it, all the power and recognition?"

Alesia grew more serious again. "What you really need to ask yourself, Nic, is why you are so quick to believe the worst about him. Sure, you two got off to a rocky start," she chucked, "but your prejudice blinds you."

She of course didn't know what I overhead in the gardens later that night, and I wasn't about to tell her about it now. "Fine, I see your point. But rumors don't come from nowhere." I stabbed my spoon back into the bowl, the liquid splashing.

Alesia laughed, "Cálmate, mija." I lifted my eyes. I was calm. "That may be so, and there could be some truth to it. Let me see what our spies know, what they've heard. But regardless, from what I remember of the war, if August ended Josiah the male likely deserved his fate."

I nodded, going back to my soup before changing the subject. "Speaking of royal activities, does Adrienne have any more extravagances planned?"

"Who knows with her?" Alesia exhaled. "I can't imagine she'll let you and your sister's stunt with the thrones go lightly."

"Well, the funding is squared away with Niall," I said. "He assured me it would be righted, even telling me he would attribute more to the social programs to make up for their deficits in the past few months. So anything she does will have to come from her personal coffers."

"We should have never let her have so much time with the council unchecked this last year." Alesia seethed. "Eve and I should have been there, but instead I prioritized your training, readying you for coming into the height of your magic following this birthday."

"You can't blame yourself for that, Alé. You prioritized what you thought was most vital. And it's been sorted out for now. When the council reconvenes next week, we'll be there."

"Still," she shook her head. "Adrienne Deimos is a snake. I should have known better."

Prior to this week, Adrienne, Misha, and I were typically on good terms. Eve was always friendly, but Alesia seemed to hate her with every fiber of her being, though it wasn't always outright. Alé usually expressed more of a cold detachment to those she disliked versus outright animosity.

"Where did your issue with her start, anyway? During the war?" I asked.

"Yes," she exhaled. "I'd never met her before then, but Adrienne and Alexander may have been the only two people guilty of more war crimes than Josiah, though they hid it much better."

"What do you mean?"

Alesia pressed her mouth in a firm line, rethinking if she wanted to share what she knew, but she did so anyway. "You and your sister were always too young to know what the war was truly like, I didn't want to put those horrors on you two when you were so young, so Eve and I haven't shared everything. And then when Adrienne became your stepmother, I didn't want you girls to have negative connotations of her. Your father thought she was redeemed, so I tried to give her the benefit of the doubt as well, but some things just can't be forgiven. I guess now you're old enough to hear it."

She went on, "The Deimos are mindcasters. While that magic alone doesn't make them sinister, look at the Priests of Oscuri and all the good they've done, the way those two used it in the war does. They didn't just shatter their enemies' minds, they made them suffer. It was like their very worst fears consumed them slowly, ripping their soul apart. You could see it in the corpses' faces. The agony they expressed was disturbing." Alesia shuddered slightly. "They were our enemies and fought for the High King, for the oppression of faeries and human alike, but they were living beings too. The fact that Adrienne and Alexander could have killed them easily with no suffering at all, but to choose that method instead didn't sit right with me. I'm not sure anyone deserves that kind of end, not even the High King himself."

My blood went cold as I pictured it, the horror Alesia must have seen to have shaken her so thoroughly.

"Did our parents know?" I couldn't fathom how my father could have witnessed that and still thought Adrienne was someone he could marry.

"They did, but Adrienne's charm hides her callousness well, though Diana and I saw her more for what she is. Adrienne was always dismissive of us, of our opinions due to being half-human, always slightly attacking in her tone to your mother and me. I'm surprised she even fought on our side with her haughtiness, though I'm sure Adrienne will always choose the side with the most power. She loves power more than anything else and won't enjoy giving up the throne to you and your sister in the next year."

My gut tightened as I thought of the siren and her warning.

Whispers and shadows, bells ringing at midnight, sheep becoming wolves, blood on fingertips—I was running through a dark wood, the thorns and vines tearing at me, catching my skin and hair. Mirrors and reflections that didn't match. Then I was choking, drowning, falling away from the water's surface into icy darkness.

I looked around, confirming there was no one in the kitchen except Alesia and me before I whispered, "You think she's the sheep?"

Alesia sat silently for a minute, considering. "Possibly, but she's more fox than wolf. Her brother too. But have you considered..." she paused, her mind appearing to drift, making some connection.

"What is it?"

"Orelia and Cedric have been spending a lot of time with the Deimos, no? Sitting near them at every breakfast and dinner, foregoing the Hunt."

The breath stilled in my lungs. "It couldn't be. They were Mother and Father's closest allies—their best friends. They couldn't be the ones waiting to betray us."

Orelia and my father had centuries of history. They'd been friends long before the war and had formed the rebel resistance themselves. I couldn't fathom her and Cedric betraying all of that and for what? To support Adrienne? It didn't make sense. Of course, there could be pieces Alesia and I were missing.

Alesia tilted her head. "I don't want to think that of them either, mija. But they are the only ones that could pull off such a thing with the siren's warning. They may choose to support Adrienne if she decides to bid to keep your throne. It is better to be cautious in these instances, to consider every possibility."

Even so, as I pictured Orelia's warmth, Cedric's kind smile, and I couldn't fathom such a betrayal from them.

"And you think Adrienne won't give up the throne?"

"Possibly. She has made no qualms about how much she enjoys it. But even if she tries, Adrienne is no match for you girls, especially with the power you will come into this year." What my aunt said was true, though dread still coiled deep in my stomach.

"If Adrienne is that way, then why did my father marry her?"

"Your father was always so kind—too kind, too quick to forgive and forget the sins of others. It was his strength but also his downfall." Alesia sighed, her face conflicted. "I loved your father, he was like a brother to me, and he adored Diana. She was his perfect match, his everything." Her eyes went glassy—her sister had once been her everything too, as Misha was to me.

"Dominic and I were both stubborn and passionate, so we disagreed often, but I could always understand his side—except in his marriage to Adrienne. I can rationalize that the alliance strengthens our kingdom, but that was the purpose of the Blood Treaty. And Diana was his mate, he could never love another like that again." Being mated herself, Alesia couldn't fathom loving another after Eve—couldn't dream it possible.

Alesia shook her head. "I knew him for over a century, but in those last three years of his life he was more withdrawn—different. Yes, he'd lost his mate, a pain worse than death, but he had you girls. You were his entire reason for existing. I'll never understand what happened."

I'd never heard Alesia speak so candidly about our father, about his choice to marry Adrienne. It stirred something deep within me. Why *had* Father chosen to remarry? And why Adrienne?

Alesia stood then, gathering our empty bowls. "Enough speculating. If Adrienne comes for your throne, she'll not only have you and your sister but me to contend with. And she well remembers from the war just how easily I can best her." My aunt said with an almost feral smile.

"And you need to go get ready." She ushered me up. "Later we can sort the sheep from the foxes and the wolves."

I smiled back at her, planting a kiss on her cheek. "What are foxes and wolves to a lion like you?"

CHAPTER 22
Nic

I pulled on the dress of deep red, the straps and edges embellished with tiny sparkling rubies. The color perfectly matched the red I'd painted onto my lips, of my mother's ruby necklace that hung from my throat.

Today was Misha's and my birthday, but also twenty-two years since our mother's death and over nine years since we lost our father. I wondered what they would say to Misha and me if they were here at this moment, on this pivotal birthday.

Alesia entered the dressing room then, coming up behind me as I stared at myself in the mirror. "Oh mija, you look so beautiful—just like Diana."

So much like Alesia too. The twins had resembled each other closely, much more so than Misha and me.

"Thank you Alé."

My aunt pulled my wavy hair back behind my shoulders as she stood by me in the mirror, adjusting the chain of my necklace before she pressed her cheek to mine. Our resemblance was undeniable.

"You know your mother never told us—about the prophecy," Alesia said wistfully.

"What prophecy?" She'd never mentioned anything like that before.

"The visions Diana had just before you were born. Your mother knew she would die during your and your sister's birth—she hid it from Dominic and me. She left us a note we found only after. Diana knew Dom and I would look for any way to change it, but her fate was already sealed, and she didn't want that time wasted by sorrow."

I clutched the skirt of my dress to still the shaking in my hands. Our mother had known she wouldn't survive our birth and had loved us—believed in us enough that she had given up her life, anyway. How could I ever live up to that?

Alesia uncurled my fingers, taking my hands in her own as she turned me to her. "I know what you are thinking, mija, but don't. Diana would have given her life for you girls over and over again if it meant you'd become who you are today—your father too. They would be so very proud of you."

Tears streamed down my cheeks. "Our parents did so much for us, for the people...what if we mess it all up?" I whispered, letting my fear show. Only to her, only to my family.

"You won't, Nic. You or Misha. You two are strong, kind, everything your parents would have wanted you to be." Alesia's hand came up to cup my cheek. "Do not doubt yourself. To protect your family, the people, you won't give in. I've never known you to back down from anything. Even when you were a child, even when you were scared, you would give it everything you had. That fire has always been inside you, and when you let it out—gods help anyone in your path. Your sister's too."

I rested my hand atop hers on my cheek. "Alé, you know that Misha and I are the way we are because of you too, don't you? You and Eve were the perfect mothers to us. We couldn't have been raised by better parents." Hugging her to me, I pressed my face into her shoulder, breathing in her scent of sea salt and jasmine.

She squeezed me tightly. "Oh Nic, we couldn't have asked for better daughters. You are our lives, you and your sister."

When I pulled back, I saw tears streaming down her face as well. Not from sadness, but from love so unconditional her dark eyes couldn't contain it all.

"Now stop crying on your birthday." She used her thumbs to wipe away any black smudges to my eye makeup, even as she sniffled herself.

I handed her a tissue, and she fixed her own in the mirror before facing me again. "Let's go find that sister of yours before she runs off with Julian again and skips the ball completely."

Alesia and I chuckled as I took her hand, leaving the mirror behind. We would indeed have to keep an eye on my twin or one half of the guests of honor would be sure to go missing within minutes of the ball.

She and I crossed the hall into my sister's chambers together, the train of her plum gown trailing behind her. We found Eve already there, helping my sister finish the last of the tiny buttons coming up the back of her dress.

Misha wore a gown of gauzy turquoise. Everything about it, from the heart-shaped neckline to the slightly sheer skirt, was woven with intricate crystals and pearls like foam on the sea, also adorned with tiny lotus blossoms cast from her power. The effect was dreamlike, an ode to our mother's water element, mixed with the earth magic she and our father shared. In the Summer Solstice tradition of wearing crowns of flowers, Misha had already cast a tiara of little pink lotus flowers to sit atop her golden head, as well as two rose gold combs adorned with diamonds and pearls tucked back the sides of her hair.

"Sister," Misha said in greeting as she stepped off the small raised platform in front of her large mirror. Then she cast a crown of roses on my head, a dark red to complement my gown. I cast frost over the petals, the crystals flickering in the faerie lights of her room, making it my own.

"You two look beautiful," Eve said, hugging Misha and then me.

My godmother looked radiant in a silk gown of champagne gold, the color matching the beaded embellishments on Alesia's. Misha cast similar crowns in each of our aunts' hair, stargazer lilies for Alesia, and cream peonies for Eve.

"Thank you, *mi vida*." Alesia smiled endearingly at my sister, her fingertips grazing the soft petals on her head.

Together the four of us left my sister's chambers, connecting arm in arm in the hallway, and made our way to the final night of festivities. Misha and I entered the ballroom side by side, hand in hand, as we came down the steps.

Summer Solstice, the longest day of the year, was a celebration of life, growth, and harvest. A luminescent sun swirled in the center of the ballroom ceiling, the constellations flickering beside it. The five stars of cancer glowed especially bright—the constellation currently ruling in the sun. Below the tables were draped in white silk, flowers of every type and color overflowing on them.

As we reached the foot of the stairs, Julian reached for Misha. The smiles on each of their faces were devastating. No, I was definitely not going to have much sister time tonight. So long as August heeded my warning and let them be.

Julian pulled Misha into a dance as both my aunts turned and headed toward the tables for food and wine. As I watched them go, a broad arm wrapped around my waist.

"Hello, little dove," a voice whispered in my ear, and a flash of annoyance coursed through me, not just at the absurd term of endearment. I'd never enjoyed being touched by surprise like that—at least not by someone that wasn't my family.

I turned to face Evander, stepping back slightly, as his eyes traveled to my neck. His mouth hardened faintly, the expression gone in a flash and his usual grin back in its place.

"You're not wearing the necklace."

I stepped back. "Oh, it just didn't quite fit with the dress. It's my mother's and I had been planning to wear it to honor her tonight."

"I wish I had known." His eyes crumpled in disappointment as they lowered, taking in the gown. "I could have gotten you another one that would have matched perfectly, one that you would have no problem wearing."

I frowned. He'd said the necklace had reminded him of me, not that he'd wanted me to wear it tonight. "Oh no Evander, it's beautiful. It is just that yellow diamonds would clash with the rubies in the gown. I'm sure there will be plenty of other events I can wear it for."

"But you're not wearing it tonight." He said obstinately, his mouth falling into a hardened line. "And I really hoped you would."

"I didn't mean to upset you." Even if it wasn't my intention, I refused to apologize. Not for this.

"Of course, Nic." Evander nodded, a softness returning to his gaze before he kissed my cheek. "You look beautiful regardless. Let me grab you a drink," he said as he turned away.

Evander quickly returned with the glass of champagne which I took but didn't drink, still unsettled by his reaction. I'd begun to feel an itching, a burning under the surface of my skin. Gods, the male was going to make me break out in hives.

I turned to watch Misha and Julian followed by Alesia and Eve glide past us on the dance floor during a waltz. So happy each of them was, lost in the eyes of their partners. I knew then that I would never look at Evander that way, my eyes would never shine for him like that.

Setting my glass down on a nearby table, I excused myself with a lie about spotting a courtier I wanted to greet across the room. Evander once again looked disappointed as I parted, which only made the sinking feeling in my stomach grow.

Distracted by my thoughts, I nearly bumped into Adrienne.

"There you are, dear." She smiled, offering me the glass of untouched wine in her hand, a deep red instead of her usual honeyed white. I shook my head, declining.

"Adrienne." I inclined my head to my stepmother, clothed in an elegant white gown embroidered completely with crystals and diamonds. Tiny purple belladonna flowers threaded through her hair, braided in a coronet atop her head. She looked like a fallen star.

"Having a nice time?" She eyed Evander over my shoulder before taking a strand of my dark hair between her fingers.

We stood eye to eye as I straightened. "I am. It has been an intriguing last few days, to be sure."

What a contrasting pair we made, her light to my dark. Blood red and glimmering white.

"Yes well, now that all that silly funding business seems to have been settled, I'm sure you can truly enjoy yourself." She twirled that strand of my hair, wrapping it around her finger.

"Indeed," I said, wondering why she suddenly seemed so blasé about the very topic that had been such a point of contention between us since that day I'd snuck into the city. "Niall and I decided it would be best discussed at the Council meeting tomorrow night. Just to be sure nothing like that happens again."

"Yes, tomorrow...of course." Her mouth pulled into a feline grin before she dropped that strand of hair. "We will all make sure it is settled then. Enjoy your night, Nic." Adrienne said before turning away, making to sweep about the room and greet the other guests.

My eyes followed her back, her pale gown shimmering out behind her. Our interaction further unsettled me, the burning I felt in my veins growing more prominent.

I slipped out a side door, returning to my original mission as I made my way back upstairs to find Evander's necklace. To decide what I wanted to say when I returned it—when I broke my feelings to him.

CHAPTER 23
Misha

Gemma and I had just finished a dance together, a lively one in which everyone stood in lines and there were many partner switches and turns. I was just catching my breath when Nic came sauntering up from out of nowhere. I'd only been able to catch glimpses of her the past hour between the dancing and birthday wishes from guests.

"Where have you been, Nicky? Poor Evander has been moping around most of the night looking for you." I teased, falling easily into Alesia's native language. The few times I'd caught sight of her tonight was when she was either dancing with Evander or seemed to be avoiding him.

"He's upset that I didn't wear the necklace he'd given me, and he's been acting strange and clingy ever since. I've already danced with him four times but it doesn't seem like enough. He's having a hard time understanding that I don't intend to be by his side all night."

Nic had shown me the necklace earlier before we'd dressed, a monster of a thing. Gorgeous, but it didn't suit my sister's tastes at all. It was much too ostentatious for her.

"So you're saying you *don't* want to be showered in gifts and praise. What if he hand fed you the hors d'oeuvres? Would that do it for you, Nicky?"

Nic scowled and I laughed, throwing my head back.

"Misha, I'm serious. I can't take it anymore. Not to mention I feel like I'm going to burst through my skin any second—maybe I'm getting sick and that's why I'm so irritable."

I brushed my hand against her forehead. Warm, but not enough to worry about. "Nicky, you aren't sick. You're frustrated and dramatic—" My sister gave me another scathing look at that, "—but what do you think is really up with him? Do you think he's making up for his inaction on the beach?" I asked her, more seriously this time. It was a plausible conclusion. Though if so, it was backfiring horribly.

"Who knows...but the way he is behaving, the necklace, it's all too much." My sister sighed.

Nic had a tendency to push away any males that pursued her—justifiably or not—as a protective mechanism from what had happened with Callum. No one could blame her for such a reaction after what'd happened.

"Well heads up, because lover boy is back," I whispered as I looked over Nic's shoulder. Evander was approaching from behind, looking like he wanted to pull her into their fifth dance.

Nic's eyes screamed, *help me,* and I was feeling charitable so I decided to save my poor sister.

"August, Nic needs a dance partner."

If looks could kill, my sister's eyes would have been daggers. I suppressed my smile as my hand reached back for his arm. Nic must have been really irritated by Evander not to notice him standing right behind us with Julian, but I cherished the rare opportunity to surprise her. August and Julian both turned to face us.

"I would be honored, Nicole." August seemed to be also hiding some amusement behind those gray eyes. I wondered if he'd somehow understood our conversation.

Nic hesitated as she appeared to be having an inner debate over which male was the worse choice. The one that seemed to infuriate her at every opportunity, or the one currently annoying the hell out of her. She was going to have to choose fast.

"There you are, dove. Would you like this dance?" Evander said as he sidled up next to Nic, his hand coming onto her low back, fingers flexing around her waist possessively.

My sister's eyes flashed, either at the touch or the name. I was working doubly hard to suppress my grin, my lips twitching. *Dove.* Nic was more akin to a hawk at this moment, looking as if she wanted to rip into someone with her talons.

"Sorry, but I've just promised this one to August." Nic gritted out, giving him a small, forced smile.

Evander watched as she took the arm August offered her and they headed toward the other dancers. His eyes slightly hardened with an extra sting of rejection.

I enjoyed the entire interaction thoroughly. Evander Shaw could stay upset for all I cared. Even as close as we were to their family, I would wish my sister with no male that wouldn't risk his life for hers.

"Misha. Julian." He turned to us with a stiff incline of his head before making his own way through the crowds, to ask Lorraine for this dance by the looks of it.

Julian and I watched him go for the next several moments, each keeping our composure—until we turned to face each other. We lost it at the sight of the other trying to hide in their laughter, so it ripped out of us like a tidal wave. I clung to him by his arms as I laughed, his hand holding me steady at my waist.

"What are you two going on about?" Eve smiled as she and Alesia approached.

I turned to my aunts as I brushed the wetness from my eyes before it could ruin my makeup. "Oh, us? We're just having a bit of fun, Auntie." I smiled sweetly.

"I'm sure, Misha." Alesia frowned at us disapprovingly, but her eyes sparkled with amusement all the same.

"Commander Sancrista, may I have the honor?" Julian inclined his head to my aunt formally into a bow as an invitation to dance.

"Yes of course. But call me Alesia—unless of course we ever go to war." She said with a wink. My heart warmed with the casualness with which she regarded him, hoping that it meant she was beginning to approve of us.

"Then you can call her your worst nightmare." I quipped, pinching his arm.

"Surely if another such atrocity occurred that would bring us back into war, Hahnaley and Montevalle would be allies. Then I may call you our salvation." Julian said of Alesia.

"Quick with the praise, this one is. A smart, smart male." Eve said approvingly as she took me by the arm so they could dance. "Come Misha and show me the desserts."

CHAPTER 24
Nic

August took my hand in his, his other arm circling around my waist, as we made it to the middle of the floor.

I avoided eye contact with him. He was the better choice to Evander, but still...I was going to kill my sister.

The dance itself was a waltz with a series of spinning couples, each intermittently changing partners with those nearby, as the song called for it, then returning back to your primary. The song crooned of lost memories you can almost remember, glowing embers, and silver storms—fitting, I thought as I remembered our brief clash of ice and lightning this afternoon.

I was still furious about what he'd said, how he'd questioned my sister. Even if guilt sank into my gut that my reaction might have further negatively influenced his approval of her.

"Nicole," August broke the silence first, but I spun away, into the arms of another male as opposed to answering. After several turns, I spun back toward August, continuing to ignore him.

"Nicole," he said my name again. There was something pleading in his voice, and I couldn't help but wonder what his eyes would say if I met them.

"I wanted to apologize."

My eyes finally lifted to his, the silver there gleaming. Had he ever apologized for anything before? The way the words sounded like acid on his tongue, I doubted it.

"So the King in the North can admit he is wrong?" I said, wanting to see just how far I could push him.

"You are protective of Misha and the rest of your family, are you not? If you weren't convinced of Julian returning her feelings, would you not have responded in the same way?" August challenged.

I didn't answer immediately, my lips settling into a hard line, as the song called for another partner change. I savored the moment away from him to think.

August was right, of course. I would have behaved exactly in the same way if I thought for a second that Julian's feelings weren't as strong or genuine as my sister's.

He read my face, seeing the confirmation there, as he reached for my hand, drawing me back to him as we whirled together once more. "Of course, you would. So while yes, I can admit when I am wrong, however rare that may be, you cannot criticize me for being protective as well. I care more for my brother's well-being than my own." The resolution in his words struck me, how adamantly he'd meant every word.

I spun away again, changing partners for the final time. The male was a courtier from one of the other kingdoms based on his finery, but I couldn't focus enough on him to determine which one even as he smiled at me, his hand gripping my waist a bit too tightly.

My lip lifted in a snarl as I went to remove said hand when August reached for me early, pulling me from the courtier before the song called for it. I could see the male about to protest before he saw the look in August's eyes. He wisely let me go.

"Thank you," I whispered to August without meeting his eyes. I didn't know if it was for pulling me from the too bold male or the concession he'd made in his apology. Likely both.

A moment later, the song came to a close, ending in a final spin as I finally lifted my gaze to his and saw the summer storm raging in his eyes. The music transitioned into the next and we dropped our arms, no longer touching, but we still faced each other—unyielding ice and stone.

Something simmered in the air and, not knowing what to make of this charge between us, I pulled back and stepped off the dance floor, leaving him behind, then made my way toward the doors for some much needed air. As I went, my skin was humming from where he'd held me. I could still feel every place his hands had been.

I hurried across the room, but before I reached the doors, I saw them and paused.

Alesia and Julian finished a dance of their own, greeting Eve and Misha. I saw the way his eyes shone when he returned to my sister, at the way Alesia and Eve's did the same when they saw what I had.

Before I walked outside, I spared one last glance behind me to where August still stood. He was watching them too, something yearning and sorrowful in his silver eyes. He slowly moved his gaze from them to me.

I tore my eyes away, turned, and walked out into the night alone.

CHAPTER 25
Misha

After scanning the ballroom and coming up empty, I stepped out on the terrace in my search for Julian. After he and Alesia had danced, winning my aunt's approval with whatever they'd discussed, he'd excused himself, and I hadn't seen him since.

My eyes didn't spot him out here either, but I did see August and another male talking, one I hadn't noticed before. Judging by the way they leaned toward each other, he and August were close, but I didn't think anyone else had come from Montevalle except for him and his brother.

The male was tall, though not as much as August, with tanned skin and eyes so dark they were nearly black. I thought he might be from the south. His hair color was a similar enough shade of white to Adrienne's that it wouldn't be an outlandish assumption. As I observed them, the male's eyes met mine. *Shit.*

"Good evening," I said, feeling awkward as I approached them. "Have you seen Julian by chance? I thought he might be out here."

August and I hadn't interacted much without anyone else around, mostly because the Northern King could be intimidating. I was a bit in awe of Nic that she sparred with him so easily, without batting an eyelash. Nic would go toe to toe with anyone; she'd even broken his nose, for the gods' sake. It was one of my favorite things about her, second only to the huge heart she hid from anyone that wasn't her family.

"I haven't. I'd assumed he snuck off with you, though I'm sure now that he may have just stepped away for a moment. Even the life of the festivities such as yourselves needs a moment of fresh air, I'm sure." August said reassuringly.

"Yes, surely he will turn up, eventually." My fingers played with the emerald necklace at my throat.

He inclined his head. "For you, I am sure of it."

I blushed slightly. It was one thing to have my sister comment on our relationship, but Julian's brother was different. I couldn't help but wonder how he felt about it, about us. And now I had to know.

"Ah Misha, excuse my rudeness," August stood straighter, then motioned toward the male beside him. "This is Shai. He is from the north as well. Part of my council."

"It is an honor, Misha," Shai said, moving into a small bow. "I have been told great things about you by Julian and based on what I've heard, he is truly enamored by you."

My blush deepened at his words and my heart quickened its pace. The feeling was mutual, but it was odd to have it commented on by someone I'd just met.

"But if you two would excuse me," Shai said. He gave August an incline of the head in farewell, though his eyes flashed—so briefly I might have imagined it. It was as if they were silently communicating something. Then he bowed to me again and unhurriedly made his way into the ballroom.

"Would you mind if I stay out here with you while I wait for Julian? I have to admit that I'm growing rather tired of the party." A lie, but I was hit with the sudden urge to better get to know the male that could very well be my family via Julian. At least, I hoped so.

"Of course, Misha."

I came to stand by him at the railing overlooking the gardens, my arms resting on the cool stone next to his as we faced outward.

After a moment, I decided to break the silence. "How old are you?"

August let out a small chuckle before answering. "282 years."

He was older than Alesia, older than my mother would have been if she were still alive, though not nearly as old as my father. He'd been over four hundred when he'd met my mother. Sometimes the way the Fae aged compared to the humans still amazed me. August didn't look more than a few years older than Julian, but he had over two and a half centuries on him. No wonder he saw August as closer to a father figure than a brother.

My curiosity got the better of me. "And in all that time you've never married?" August's eyebrows rose slightly in response to my question. "Sorry, you don't have to answer that. Nic always says that I am way too nosy for my own good."

August chuckled, "Really it's fine, Misha. No offense taken."

"I just would think that as King it would be expected for you to marry at some point, to have a Queen." I turned toward him. He seemed somehow less intense in this light, the soft glow of the moon caressing his features, making them softer somehow.

"I'm sure my kingdom would like the solidarity that both a king and queen would provide." He said, surprising me with his candidness.

"So you've never met someone in all your years you thought suitable? None that you could see yourself with?"

"While I have met many intriguing persons, none were what I would consider to be my equal. I won't settle for anything less than my mate, my match in all ways. Much like your parents and aunts were suited for each other." He reached a hand down, brushing the single white petal of a calla lily below us.

August didn't use his father and mother as that example, nor his father and Julian's. I suddenly realized I may have taken for granted the healthy relationships I'd been raised with.

"Do you think—" I started, looking down at my fingers, fiddling with the bracelet my aunts had given me that morning. My nerves wouldn't let me finish the sentence.

"Do I think that you and Julian are such a match?" August continued for me.

I looked up at him shyly. "You know him better than anyone, and I know your opinion means a lot to him."

August looked away, his gaze falling out onto the gardens, taking a moment to ponder my question as my heart hammered in my chest. Not butterflies. No, it was more like eagles flew around within my ribs as I waited. Julian had mentioned before that he didn't require his brother's approval of me for us to be together, but no matter what he said, I knew he hoped for it.

"I have to be honest...I had my reservations at first," he sighed before facing me again. My heart stopped beating all together. "But knowing your history with each other, and seeing you two together this week...I could not imagine my brother being happier with anyone else."

For a moment I thought my chest might burst, setting those dragons free, and before I could stop myself, I flung my arms around his waist in a hug.

August was frozen, initially shocked by my exuberance.

Did they not hug in the north?

After a moment he relaxed, briefly returning my hug before I stepped away from him again. My cheeks turned pink in embarrassment at his obvious awkwardness to my outburst.

"Thank you," I whispered, my voice hoarse.

"Of course, little one. I could not have hoped for better for him." He said, his face lighting into a warm smile, the motion transforming his face.

"I guess I should go find him then," I smiled back before turning to walk away.

"And August?" I paused after a step. He pressed his back to the stone railing to face me again.

No one could have missed the way August had looked at my sister tonight, the yearning in his eyes, except for Nic herself—blinded by whatever grudge she'd decided to latch onto where he was concerned.

"I know that my sister can come off as rather...distant, and her pride gets the better of her more often than not, but she has the biggest heart of anyone I've ever known." He went utterly still at my mention of her.

I kept going, "Evander has been plying her with pretty words and gifts since he arrived, yet she cares nothing for him. Because none of those things mean anything to her. Because he's already failed her when she needed him most."

He seemed to mull over the words I'd said and the ones I hadn't, then nodded and turned back to face the gardens.

I left then, walking back into the ballroom, not waiting to see how he would be affected, if he would be affected, by what I'd said.

Nic would kill me if she knew I'd told August that, but I couldn't understand why she was still so angry with him. Sure, they hadn't met in an ideal way, but the animosity she had toward him seemed to only grow worse. She really needed to get over herself and let it go. Evander was kind, but he was weak where it counted. Nic could never be happy with him. But August...

"There you are, love." The words were whispered in my ear just as I turned the corner through the doors. Muscular arms snaked around my waist from behind. I leaned back into the familiar smell of rain, petrichor, and moss—into Julian's chest.

"There you are, you sneak." I lifted my head to see those gray eyes, churning like clouds just before a summer rain.

"I had something to attend to. Would you like another dance, or are you ready to get out of here?" He planted a kiss on my temple.

"Hmmm, tough choice." I hesitated, wanting him to squirm a bit, already knowing what he was hoping I would say. Julian clicked his tongue in impatience, then nipped my ear with his teeth, and I squealed.

"Let's get out of here."

His face broke into that beautiful grin I loved so much, both dimples on display. "You don't have to tell me twice."

CHAPTER 26
Nic

I walked out of the large glass doors and onto the vine and rose covered terrace. The cool night breeze hit my skin, but did nothing to calm the heat in my blood. The night was quiet with not a single cloud to block the shimmering sky above. Walking down into the gardens, I headed for the stone bridge that crossed part of the lake. I stopped in the center of its arch and stared down at the water, making ice crystals dance on the surface in an ever-changing kaleidoscope.

I heard footsteps coming up the path to me and stilled.

"Nic," I heard from behind me. I didn't bother to raise my head.

"Evander."

He came to stand at my side, overlooking the railing to the ice I'd created. "I've been looking for you. I didn't realize you'd left."

"I just needed a break—some air."

"It is a beautiful night out." He gave me that stunning smile, the one that had made my heart flutter only a few days ago. "May I join you?"

I hesitated, wanting to deny him, but there were things that needed to be said between us. "Sure."

His hand came to my low back. I stepped back before he could pull me into him. "Evander, I—"

Evander's smile vanished as he read my expression. "What's happened, Nic? It felt like you were avoiding me earlier."

"I wasn't avoiding you." A lie.

"But you danced with August instead of me." Evander's brow furrowed.

Before the hurt in his expression would have inspired empathy. Now I just felt tired. "I'd promised that dance to him. I couldn't very well go back on my word."

"I just thought, well, since you and I had been spending so much time together—"

"That what?" I sighed. "That I would only speak to you tonight? That I wouldn't dance with anyone else? That isn't avoiding you, Evander." I said. Though the look on his face told me he had thought exactly so. "You can't be serious." I laughed, the sound humorless, as I looked back at the water. My crystals had gone still.

"Nic, I am. I have developed very strong feelings toward you the past few days and I was hoping—"

Shit.

I cut him off before he could continue. "I am very happy for the time we have spent together these past few days, Evander. I really am. You are a great male, but I just don't think we are a match in that way."

He stepped closer, his face a frown that was completely unbecoming. "You don't mean that, Nic."

"Yes, I do." My spine straightened. I wouldn't budge on this.

Evander grabbed my forearm, his grip tight. "You don't. You're being rash, we can—" I hissed as I pulled back. Luckily for him, he let go. "I'm sorry, Nic. I just—please, let's talk this through."

"No. I am leaving now, and I think it is best if you did not follow." I said as I reached into the hidden pocket of my dress. I handed him back the necklace he'd given me earlier. He almost dropped it from the force I used to push it into his palm. Fuming, I pushed past him, making my way back up the path to the palace.

"Nic—" he called after me, but I ignored him. I didn't even spare a glance back.

Driven by the need to put distance between us I walked through the gardens, hoping he didn't decide to follow. My skin flushed, getting hotter by the minute, worsened by what had just happened.

I heard more footsteps as I approached a bend in the path, and cursed under my breath. But it couldn't be Evander. The steps were coming from in front of me, not behind. Then I saw him.

August.

Not now. I couldn't do this with him now—not after that disaster of an encounter with Evander.

"Nicole, I was looking for you."

I froze. "Why? Has something happened?" There could have been no other reason for him to seek me out.

"No, of course not, but—" August's eyes darkened as he took me in. "What happened?"

Why do you care? I wanted to shout.

August Warin had sworn he didn't care for me, then risked his life saving me from the siren. He was accused of his father's murder, but also played the doting brother. He'd judged my sister's intentions, then apologized. It was senseless, all of it.

"Nothing that concerns you." I began walking again, moving to go around him.

"Nicole, wait." August sidestepped, cutting me off. "I was looking for you because—there were things I wanted to say to you before we left tomorrow." His silver eyes were piercing.

"I'm sure that cannot come soon enough for you." I knew the words came out harsh, but though he'd apologized for his misjudgment of Misha, there were still some things I couldn't let go. Maybe he had been right that first night—pride was my greatest flaw.

"What would make you think that?" August's brow furrowed as he looked down at me in what appeared to be genuine confusion.

My chin lifted. "Your interest in anything here surely has passed, and you're ready to return to the North."

Realization flooded those stormy eyes. After a few heavy heartbeats, he said, his voice no more than a whisper. "You heard."

He was quick. I would give him that.

I stepped closer to him. "You mean I heard you insult my family's influence? And that you were surprised I had *spark* after hearing how cold I am? About how I am so proud and unreasonably arrogant?"

"Nic—"

"Don't." I spat, cutting off whatever meaningless excuse or story he was about to weave for me. "I am no one's entertainment or plaything or joke. So when you leave, you can take your teasing and flirting and nicknames back with you to the North."

I stood tall as I said it, but I could feel my eyes begin to grow glassy, remembering how I had very much been someone's joke once. I looked to the lavender surrounding us as I forced myself back into that cold calm I'd perfected in the years since.

August stepped even closer to me, only a hand's width away as he slowly, tentatively, reached up a hand to my arm. "Nicole."

The way he said my name, always my full name, sounded too shattering, too devastating. Like he'd been born to say it—like it had been chosen to come from his lips, roll off his tongue.

I flinched. "Don't say that—don't say my name like that."

I hadn't meant to. I'd meant to steel myself into an immovable, unbreakable wall. The flash that crossed those silver eyes told me he'd seen it. He lowered his hand back down to his side.

August let out a long exhale. "What you heard was what I thought to be true—what I had hoped to be true at the time." He stepped back, giving me space. The air charged in the silence that passed between us for a few moments. Then August said softly, just hardly loud enough to hear, "—but it wasn't. It was all untrue."

He turned and walked away, leaving before I could respond.

It was good, I told myself. I didn't want to process what he'd said, didn't want to think about it, didn't want to let go of my anger and consider if I'd overreacted. After a moment, I began to walk, taking a different path back to the palace, praying I wouldn't meet anyone else out here.

Untrue. He'd said it was all untrue.

I knew I had been too unforgiving—too unyielding, but I couldn't stop myself. It was how I'd protected myself all these years.

Don't think about it. Don't wonder what he could have meant.

I again forced myself not to mull over what August had said—to ignore the words. Forget them.

Untrue.

I reentered the ballroom minutes later to find Alesia standing with Eve.

"Nic, what's going on? Are you well?" Alesia asked as she saw my face.

"It's nothing." I huffed. Both aunts saw straight through the lie. "It's just been a strange night. I'll tell you both about it tomorrow. Can you tell Misha I've retired for the night?"

Eve snickered. "Of course, though I think she's beaten you to it, Nicky. She and Julian wandered off some time ago and we haven't seen them since. But Evander was looking for you earlier, lovesick little thing. Do you want us to say anything to him?"

"No. That won't be necessary. We've already talked," I said, my spine going rigid.

Eve raised her eyebrows at my tone. "Then we shall not." She wasn't going to let me keep our confrontation from her for too long.

Alesia added, "Another matter you should be aware of, mija, the guards told us that skinwalkers were spotted in the forest, just outside the town to the north. There have been multiple reports from humans over the past week who said they were attempting to lure children into the woods. There is to be a scouting party in the morning. At first light."

"Gods, those things are vile." I crossed my arms as a chill snaked down my back. "Assuming you're both going, I'll join."

"No, Nicky." Alesia shook her head. "It's your birthday, sleep in a bit before the farewell luncheon. There is no need to trouble yourself with this. We'll handle it."

"I know you will—but regardless, I'm going. You know I can't pass up a good hunt, Alé." I smiled with little humor. The distraction would be good for me. I could continue to push back all the thoughts I would rather ignore indefinitely.

"No one ever could talk you out of something once you set your mind on it, Nic." Eve chuckled. "Go get some rest then. We will relay your message to Misha if we see her."

I smiled at her, more genuinely this time. "I'll see you in the morning." I gave Eve a quick hug and kiss on the cheek, then did the same with Alesia.

Then I snuck out a side door, wanting to avoid anyone else that might keep me from escaping this night.

CHAPTER 27
Misha

Holding Julian's hand, I led the way through the vines and the rubble into the abandoned castle. As we walked through the arches toward the throne room, Julian cast faerie lights to illuminate our way, even though we saw fairly well in the dark without them.

I cast my magic as well—pink roses of various shades bloomed around us, adding to the romantic feel of being here with him. Our eyes met as I squeezed his hand, his face breaking out into that breath-stealing smile.

My core tightened as I remembered how we'd spent that first night here, how it had felt to finally show him just how much my heart wanted him.

"Misha..." Julian whispered as his eyes lifted from mine. "Look."

I followed his gaze. All around us were fireflies. They were everywhere—above near the arched ceiling, below on the moss and rocks, coming in through the windows with the streaming moonlight.

We took a moment to exhilarate in it, in this moment—together.

Julian suddenly whisked me up. I squealed at the motion, clinging to his neck, as he sat us on the stone dais. I remained perched on his lap.

"Happy birthday, love." Julian whispered as he kissed my temple, my cheek, then his lips finally met mine.

I smiled as I pulled away. "This might be my best yet. All my wishes came true," I whispered to him.

"Oh yeah, and what were they?" His lips trailed down my neck.

"That you'd be here. With me." My words came out breathlessly. I felt Julian smile against my skin, pausing before his lips continued their assault, trailing down to my exposed shoulder.

"I got you a gift, love," he said, pulling back as he began to reach into his pocket.

"Oh, another one?" I beamed, bursting with excitement. Call me shallow, but who didn't love being showered with gifts by handsome males?

Julian hesitated, his head tilting. "Another one?"

"The one you left for me? On my bed?" His brows knitted together, confused. "The rose gold combs, I wore them in my hair tonight." I clarified for him.

Julian went still. "Misha, I didn't get you those." My heart dropped into my stomach.

"But then, who were they from? It wasn't Nic, Alesia, or Eve..." I said as I went to reach for one of them to show him. As I pulled a comb out of my hair, it caught, one of the points nicking the skin beneath my hair. I hadn't realized they were so sharp.

"*Fuck*." I reached for the cut.

"What is it, Misha?" Julian reached for my head as well, then looked at the comb.

I brought my hand between us. Two drops of red blood sat on my fingertips. "It cut me."

"Misha, this doesn't feel right." His face was grave while he examined my head, then the comb. "It looks like—" All of a sudden his words became blurry.

"What?" I slurred. When had my tongue gotten so heavy?

"Misha?" Julian looked back up at my face. Then he reached for me again, holding me up. I was falling.

"Misha!" Julian's voice was panicked now. My hands grasped onto his arms, my fingers not quite able to find purchase, as he held my head in his hands. Terror—I'd never seen such terror on his face, on anyone's. But I couldn't keep my eyes open to see him clearly.

The comb. The blood. The siren's words to Nic rushed back to me.

Whispers and shadows, bells ringing at midnight, sheep becoming wolves, drops of poison and blood on fingertips.

Poison.

I'd been poisoned. The siren had seen this and tried to warn us. But there was more to the vision. More that I couldn't recall at this moment.

Nic.

My sister—where was my sister? What if whoever had poisoned me had gotten to her, too? Oh gods.

I felt myself losing control. I reached for my magic—I tried to winnow us, but the abandoned castle was warded against it. Nic and I had cast them so long ago so that no one else might stumble upon what we'd found, on what we had claimed for just us. We hadn't thought to make them impermeable to ourselves.

"Julian," I rasped, forcing my eyes back open. He was hysterical, tears streaming down his face as he carried me. He wouldn't be fast enough to get me back to Eve.

Then something changed. I felt the earth, the life all around me, my magic acting almost of its own accord. I felt a burst of power flow from the earth, the air itself, surrounding us and the ruins.

As I looked at Julian, his beautiful gray eyes began to change—to shift.

Then he stumbled. He cried out, gasping for air, as we each tumbled to the soft ground just outside the ruined archway.

Julian—no.

I tried to reach for him but couldn't—couldn't move, couldn't stand, couldn't do anything at all but stare from where I lay paralyzed. I was frozen, strewn out on the ground as I watched him and the earth around us. Vines and thorns and blooms and—

What was happening to him?

I didn't have to wonder long, as I saw what he became in my final moments of consciousness.

Oh gods—

Then everything went black.

CHAPTER 28
Nic

I awoke in a sweat.

Tossing and turning most of the night, I'd only been able to sleep intermittently in those few short hours until dawn broke. The humming under my skin had only gotten worse, making me restless. I was glad we were going into the forest this morning. I needed to work last night from my system.

Untrue.

My mind whirled as I forced the thoughts away again.

Standing from my bed, I made my way to the bathing chamber. The cold water I splashed on my face only helped somewhat, my skin still felt like it was burning.

I changed into plain black fighting leathers and braided my hair in a simple plait down my back. I strapped the Galorian silver dagger to my thigh, placed two more daggers inside the shaft of my boots, and buckled a belt with throwing knives at my waist. I sheathed a short, curved sword on my back for easy access.

Once dressed, I went across the hall to see Misha. I didn't have long before I needed to meet Alesia and Eve, but I wanted to know how last night went with her and Julian. Forgoing a knock, I opened her door. She slept like the dead and wouldn't hear it, anyway.

"Meesh?"

Her bed was still made, unslept in. I didn't see her dress, shoes, or any of her jewelry, nothing to suggest she'd returned last night. Even Rasalas wasn't there.

I smirked. She must have stayed with Julian in his chambers. My twin deserved nothing but the best happiness, and I knew without a doubt that Julian would give her everything she ever wanted.

In the stables, Alesia and Eve were already dressed and waiting, sitting on a bale of hay. Eve's head rested on her mate's shoulder. It looked like three guards would be joining us, but not the usual hunting party.

"Where are Santiago and Fitz?" I asked the guard nearest me. Iago, I thought his name was. I'd rarely interacted with him as he was usually with Adrienne's guard. He was just a few inches taller than I was, with black curly hair that reached his shoulders and dark brown eyes.

"Oh, Princess," he said, somewhat startled. "We were not expecting you to join us after the revelry last night."

"That's not an answer." I looked back at him and the other two guards. I'd never seen them before.

"The others have been given the day off in celebration. The Queen ordered we assist the Commander in assessing the threat of the skinwalkers."

Our guards all deserved rest and were given ample time for the holiday, but also I knew that San and Fitz were typically the first to volunteer for such ventures, no matter the circumstance. They were the most skilled in facing this type of situation, and I didn't want to worry about watching the new guards' backs as well as my own.

I pinched the bridge of my nose as I let out a long breath. "Have you three dealt with skinwalkers before?"

Alesia snorted. She'd apparently given them the same round of questioning before I'd arrived, just as unenthused by their joining us. But with these creatures, there was safety in numbers.

"Yes, Your Highness, but it has been quite some time. They tend to avoid the more populated areas." He said.

I nodded my head in assent. "We should be on our way then. Can you introduce me to the other guards? I don't believe I've had the pleasure of meeting them."

"Of course," Iago said as he indicated the other two. "This is Peter and Cayne. Aircasters that have recently joined us. They're new and need to get a feel for the excursions." Both men were blonde with tan skin and brown eyes, brothers mostly likely.

"Shall we be going then?" Alesia stood, clearly done with waiting around. She handed me a quiver and bow in addition to the sword strapped across my back. The arrows were of rowan wood.

"The walkers were spotted near the northern woods, near the cherry orchards. We should look there first to see if we can spot any trails." Alesia said as she joined hands with Eve, meaning to winnow the two of them together. I would go on my own. One of the new guards, Peter, would winnow himself and the other two.

Everyone nodded their heads in agreement, then we all winnowed at once.

We reconvened in the orchard. Cherries were in season, the rows of trees heavy with the fruit still covered in morning dew as the sun broke on the horizon. The sickly sweet smell of the rotten ones fallen to the ground surrounded us.

"Let's head inside the tree line to see if we spot any unusual tracks. From there we can move inward." Alesia instructed. Eve and I nodded, and the guards followed, letting us take the lead.

"Remember if you hear anything, keep your eyes down. You don't want to lock your gaze with one. Rowan arrows ready and be sure to hit the heart." Alesia warned.

I pulled an arrow from my back and loaded it into the bow, ready for whatever may come.

There were many different creatures that inhabited the forests of our continent, but skinwalkers were one of the worst. They were animals, sometimes humans, inhabited by the passed spirits of fae and mortals. To end up with such a fate after death, you would have had to do something truly abhorrent in your lifetime, such as murdering a close relative, child, or lover. Someone who trusted you completely, and you betrayed them.

The skinwalkers often possessed predatory animals such as wolves, foxes, cougars, and bears; but they could take the body of any living thing to carry out their sinister purposes. They could even possess a human or faerie. They passed into you if you locked eyes with them, and once they inhabited you, they could speak through your mouth, move through your limbs. Your body no longer belonged to you, your soul trapped until they abandoned the body or someone killed the creature and set you free. The only way to kill them was burning them or rowan wood or Galorian silver through the heart.

Because the spirits were not meant to remain on this plane, they slowly killed their host from within. This made them a walking, rotting corpse. These were the tracks we looked for. The tracks of animals that weren't quite right. Dragging and shuffling. Then we would know skinwalkers were in our midst.

The soft early morning light filtered through the leaves as we walked, the birds singing and chirping.

"So tell me what happened last night, darling." Eve moved beside me. We didn't try to keep our voices down. If anything our normal conversation would draw the skinwalkers to us.

"Not much to tell," I responded, still not wanting to talk about it—what had happened with either male.

Eve rolled her eyes and elbowed me gently, arrows still at the ready and our gazes trained downward. "That's not what I saw. I spied two very handsome males pining over you all night."

Now I rolled my eyes. "One definitely was, way too much, but I don't know what you mean about the second." I evaded, my eyes sifting through the forest floor for any sign of disturbance.

"Oh, come on, Nicky, don't play dense. August Warin was looking at you like you're water, and he's been stuck in the sandy deserts of Reyna for a very, *very* long time. I also could have sworn I saw him following you into the gardens last night."

I clicked my tongue, "You're being ridiculous, Auntie."

"Whatever you say, Nicky." Eve's smirk was all mischief. "But what about Evander? What happened there?"

I sighed. "We were...I don't know. He has been a lot the past couple of days, it was too much, too soon. Then he gave me that necklace but afterward I felt like he was trying to manipulate me into feeling bad for not wearing it. So I returned his gift and ended it."

Eve furrowed her brow. "Yes, well, none of us are surprised by that. We adore him and his family, but that male wasn't made for you. You need someone more strong-willed, my fierce heart." She teased lovingly.

Eve never failed to make me smile. "Sure, Auntie." She gave me a wink before walking back toward Alesia.

I moved ahead with my gaze down, still searching for tracks. So far there had been nothing, no muddled prints or broken branches. We were spread out as we continued to make our way deeper into the woods. At this point, the five of us had been searching for close to half an hour, surely we would have seen something by now.

As I paused to look closer at a track, the wind picked up. Something floated down from the trees, a soft power that fell like snow. The substance made me cough, my aunts as well.

Rowan wood ash.

What the fuck, I thought as my magic drained away with the heavy dose, much more than we'd ever used in practice.

An arrow fired.

"No!" someone screamed. I turned, my own bow ready to fire, just as the arrow found its mark—but not quite. Because Alesia hadn't been standing there before, she'd been over a dozen meters away.

The arrow protruded from her chest, going straight through her ribcage. Her heart. As she stood in front of me, her face was frozen in terror that wasn't for herself. Because the arrow had been destined for me, and she'd winnowed into its path instead.

I screamed.

Alesia's knees buckled, and I dropped my bow to catch her before she hit the ground. I sank to my knees in an attempt to hold her up.

Eve's wail of agony rang out. She moved toward us, but she was slow, as full High Fae the ash had affected her completely. In her own horror and diluted senses, she hadn't seen the guard take a knife—hadn't heard him come up behind her.

"No—" I gasped, trying to warn her but the words were too slow from my mouth. I tried to stop him, but I couldn't move fast enough—not with Alesia in my lap.

The guard slit her throat.

Eve was standing so close to me her blood splattered across my face. Because of the ash, she couldn't heal herself and bled out almost instantly as she dropped to the ground beside me. Her dark eyes unseeing.

No.

The three guards' weapons were trained on me but based on the surprise coating their faces, they hadn't expected Alesia to still be able to winnow after being ashed. It made them hesitate for one second too long.

With a scream of horror, of agony, of pure *rage*—I exploded.

The burning hum I'd felt since yesterday, which had been steadily growing worse over the morning, erupted from my skin. As I knelt on the ground, my arms holding Alesia as she lay dying, fire poured out around us.

The flames incinerated everything save for my aunts and me. The trees nearest us burned, casting a thick black smoke into the air. One guard was hit fully, engulfed in flames as he fell to the ground screaming, writhing until death claimed him. The other tried to throw up a weak air shield, but the fire blasted right through it. He was covered in burns on his arms, chest, and face. Brutalized but still alive. Iago, the farthest away, turned from the blast just before it hit his entire right side and back, sparing his face.

I set Alesia down gently in the grass, her breath still coming in short pants, and stood. A cold kind of shock came over me. Resolve hardened in my veins.

I'd once asked Alesia how difficult war had been, how it was to take another life. Now I thought it would be rather easy.

The two remaining guards stumbled in an attempt to flee, but the first was ended by my thrown dagger as it embedded itself in the back of his neck. His body crashed to the ground as he choked on his own blood. Then I'd regained some control of myself and encased Iago in ice. I needed to keep him alive to question him, to know why they'd done this to us.

I went back to Alesia, lying on the hard ground. She was still alive, but barely. I left the arrow where it was, removing it would only make it worse, and applied pressure to the wound around it to try to staunch the bleeding.

Tears streamed down my face. "No, please Alé. You're going to be okay. We can fix this, I can get you home—" My voice broke on the word.

Except I couldn't winnow that far. I didn't have enough magic left after that attack, not to carry us both back to the palace. Not after being hit with that much ash. The realization devastated me. I choked on another sob.

"Nic," she reached for my face. I held her hand to my cheek, tears steadily streaming down my face.

I couldn't save her. She'd already known that, but I was just now comprehending.

"You have to—" she whispered, her words cut off by coughs of blood.

"No. No, please. You can't die. You can't." I cried, but we both knew it was too late.

"I love you, Nicky." Her fingers brushed my tears. "My whole life," she whispered. My tears only fell harder.

"You have to go." She rasped out. "Now. Go—*run*" Her hand gently squeezed mine, then pushed it away. In the next moment, her eyes went glassy—blank. Gone.

My aunt was with me no more, her soul joining her mate's, headed toward the stars. My mother, my father, now Alesia and Eve.

Dead, like I now felt inside.

They'd raised me, taught me everything I knew, laughed with me, held me when I'd cried, protected me. The only maternal figures we'd ever known—gone. Now the only family I had left was my sister.

Misha.

My broken heart shuddered in fear for my twin—my sister that hadn't been in her room.

I swept my hands over my face. Now was not the time for falling apart. Not until this was dealt with.

Swallowing, I stood and walked to Iago. I put on that cold, hard mask to face him. I unfroze his head so he could speak.

"Why." My words cut low and deadly.

"I swear, Your Highness, she made us do it. She threatened us, we had no choice." His face was pale, not just from the cold.

"Who." I snarled.

Iago paused, unable to decide if it was worth my wrath to say more. "I can't say, she'd kill me. Please, it wasn't our fault. Please—" The coward was crying now. I stepped closer until my face was only a foot from his.

"You think I won't?" I grasped his throat in one hand. With the other, I drew one of my daggers along his cheek, the thin line leaving a trail of blood. At this moment I was no longer the princess, I was the warrior my aunt had raised me to be.

"Please, mercy," he begged. "Your parents were kind. You are kind. You can grant me mercy."

Mercy.

Mercy after he and the other guards killed Alesia and Eve without any hint of remorse. Now that death was staring him in the face, all his bravado was gone.

"You just killed the only kindness left in me." My grip tightened on his throat until he choked. "Tell me now. Or I will drown you from the inside out—but not kill you. Not until you tell me what I need to know. You know your ash didn't work, you saw what I can still do to you." To prove how serious I was, I made good on my threat.

I filled his lungs with water until he choked on the endless stream erupting from his mouth. After nearly a minute, when his lips began to turn blue, I let his lungs clear.

"The Queen," he sputtered when he regained his breath.

Tomorrow...of course. Adrienne's words from last night clanged through me. She'd said that knowing what she planned to do, and had *smiled*.

My gods-damned stepmother. That lying, conniving *bitch*.

I sneered, my lip curling back in a snarl. "What did she tell you to do?"

"The Queen wanted the Commander and her mate dead. She also wants your heart," he gasped, still coughing up water. "She told us to kill you and them. To get it in any way necessary, and we would be rewarded."

Icy rage tore through me. "You did this for *money?*"

"Yes—no." He rasped, barely able to speak with my frost-tipped nails digging into his throat. "She threatened to kill us if we didn't succeed. Please, it was a mistake—" he continued with incoherent begging.

The magic of all Fae originated from the heart. That was why it could fluctuate with our emotions, especially children as they are more ruled by their feelings. If Adrienne wanted my heart then she planned to steal my magic, my mother's magic, for herself. I didn't know it was possible, but she must have discovered a way.

Adrienne couldn't have only wanted mine.

"Where is Misha?"

"The Queen doesn't have her yet. We were supposed to find her after the ball, take her heart as well, but no one knows where she is. Her or the Warins."

I stepped back, releasing him with my hand, though my ice still held him in place. My head swam with everything he'd said. Iago continued to beg, but the sound was muffled as if I were underwater.

I didn't know if I could trust his claim, if I could trust anyone in the palace anymore. Adrienne may have been able to coerce the guards against us, the Council too. If not with her magic then with her charm and manipulation. Who knew how long she'd been planning this—had been planting the seeds of this coup? The only thing I was sure of was that my home wasn't safe any longer...and that my twin was still alive. I could feel it in the bond between us. We were two halves of the same whole, our souls bound to each other. More than just sisters. I would have known if she were dead—her heart taken.

Adrienne couldn't have her. Not yet.

Where was she?

Misha was last with Julian, never returning to her chambers after the ball. She had to still be with him. Iago said they didn't know where the Warins were either. They had to have gotten out—had some warning early this morning before everything went to hell. I could only hope that they'd gone north and were safely there.

Somehow, the Warins alone had become the only ones I could trust. So I would run north and seek them out.

The border was nearly three hundred miles from Sanserria. It would take almost two weeks to reach on foot, though significantly shorter once I regained my magic and the ability to winnow. But that would be days from now, and Adrienne was expecting my heart. If she didn't get it soon she would know that her plan had gone awry, and I needed to buy myself more time to get there.

If a heart was what she wanted, a heart she would get.

I turned back to face Iago. "I've decided to spare you."

"Wh-what?" He sputtered, confusion followed by relief flaring in his eyes.

"You get to cut out your friend's heart." I nodded to the less charred corpse, my dagger still lodged in his neck. I stood, walking over to retrieve it. "Take it to Adrienne and tell her it's mine."

His eyes widened. "I can't. She'll know the difference. Please—"

"Will she?" I cocked my head. "That sounds like your problem."

I began to let him thaw, his limbs stiff and immobile from the cold. Before he could move I took his pouch of rowan ash and dumped it over his head. Then I took the dagger, plunging it into his stomach. A fatal wound unless he found a healer, but it wouldn't kill him quickly. He had a couple of hours at least.

"Now if I were you, I would get to work cutting out that heart with the dagger I've so graciously left you." I twisted it, causing him to cry out. His blood poured over my hand. "Or you will bleed out before a healer can save you. Better get to it. It's a long walk back to the city." I snarled as I backed away.

Iago only hesitated a moment, then began to crawl toward his fellow traitor.

My aunts still lay nearby, fallen as if they were still reaching for each other, even in death. Adrienne wanted my heart, but I couldn't let her discover my aunts' bodies and take theirs either. There wasn't time for the proper goodbyes they deserved, but I couldn't leave them like this.

I went to them, kissing each of my aunts on the forehead in one last goodbye, my hands shaking as I slid their gold mating bands from their still warm fingers and tucked them into the pocket over my shattered heart. I took the sword from Alesia's side, the Iradelmar forged from Galorian silver, and placed it across the other on my back. Then I dropped my plain elm wood bow, replacing it with Eve's of bronze, adorned with the language and markings of her homeland. These were the only pieces of them I could take with me now.

Swallowing my heartache, my regret, I engulfed them in flames with the last dregs of my magic until there were only cinders left. The breeze picked up, and what was left of the only mothers I'd ever known, soared away together in the wind.

The worst moment of my life began and ended in ash.

I prayed they reached the sea Alesia had loved so much. A final tear slid down my cheek as I stepped away from the blood-soaked earth and turned toward the forest.

Then I ran.

CHAPTER 29
Adrienne

B ring her to me."

Something happened to the palace this morning. No one could enter the throne room, library, gallery, or the entire West Wing. All were sealed off by magic. I had my guards and council working to break the wards, but there'd been no luck so far. So here I sat on the northern terrace.

"Your Majesty, Robyn, the Royal Steward." A guard brought the middle-aged human woman before me with her dingy brown hair and skin cracked with age. Gods, those Briars loved to put mortals in positions of power they didn't deserve. I couldn't deign to understand how one of them would be able to help me solve my ward problem when humans knew nothing of magic, but I was out of other options.

The High Fae were immortal, descended directly from the gods themselves. It was their power that flowed through our veins. Humans had none of this, their bodies much too fragile to handle the volatility of magic, but Dominic Briar and Diana Sancrista had still insisted we were all equals. The thought was absurd.

"Your Highness," the human acknowledged but didn't bow.

The disrespect grated on me. I had the urge to break into her fragile mental shields and force her to do it, but I took a deep breath to let it pass. I still needed her mind intact. "The castle seems to have sealed itself off in the early morning. Can you tell me why?"

The human was unphased. She'd anticipated my reason for calling her here. "The palace was built from the ground up by King Dominic and Queen Diana's magic. They set protections within the walls tied to their bloodlines."

"They are both gone. Their power no longer has life here," I said.

"But it does," the steward contradicted, "in their daughters. Through the princesses the magic thrums through the grounds, giving it life. They are why the plants bloom, and the water flows. As long as a Briar lives, the palace lives. And as long as a Briar reigns, the palace remains unsealed."

"Steward," I clicked my tongue. "In case you haven't noticed, I am the Queen, and I am a Briar."

"Indeed. You married a Briar, but the magic recognizes the daughters alone as the true heirs, and there are rumors that something has happened to them. None of my staff have seen Princess Misha since last night. Princess Nicole, the Commander, and the High Healer left this morning at dawn and have yet to return."

"Are you suggesting something?" The years of practice kept my lips from parting in a sneer.

The mortal lifted her chin in defiance. "All I am saying is that none of them have been seen, and now the palace is locked in wards."

I kept my composure still as I looked down at the human. Denying her words would only make her believe them more. And while it was true, I needed the country to believe a different narrative—one I'd spent so long crafting.

"My Queen," a Reynian guard interrupted.

"What?" I snapped, turning to him.

"Iago is returned. He has what you seek. The others have taken him to the infirmary. The General will meet you at your chambers with it." The words were music to my ears. At least this one thing had gone right.

I turned back to the human. "Steward, see yourself out. Your position in this castle is revoked." I no longer had to keep any humans here to appease the Briars. I considered killing her for her insolence but was in too great a rush to get to my chambers. Besides, it would make a mess.

"Um, your majesty..." the guard interjected as I stood.

"Yes," I said sharply, irritated that he would keep me here a moment longer.

The guard flinched. "The Steward is the only one with relationships to our suppliers, many of the vendors. If she is dismissed, it will take some time to set up new ones."

"How much time?" I bared my teeth just slightly. The guard looked ready to wet himself. Pathetic. I'd need to better screen the next batch of guards that swore fealty to me.

"For some of the more specialty vendors, the luxury ones...weeks, maybe even months, m-my lady."

I held back a curse, turning back to the human who appeared to be completely at ease. Braver than my own guard. "Fine, Steward. You may stay, but make sure you nor any other human or lesser faerie shows their face in the royal areas again—work areas and servant's quarters only. You are dismissed." I stood before she could give a response and left the terrace, my guards following.

I'd tasked Iago with ensuring that I would be rid of Alesia and Eve and to bring me the heart of the Briar once he'd notified me that she was joining them. It was supposed to be mine last night, but both she and that sister had gone off earlier than I'd anticipated.

Alesia Sancrista was a self-righteous thorn in my side. I knew she would be a problem I had to rid myself of if I was going to make my play for the Hahnaleyan throne. Thankfully, that part of my planning had gone well. She and Diana had never trusted me in the war, and she didn't trust me now. Even after I'd won over Dominic.

Well, not so much won over but outmaneuvered. Dom was ever the idealist, always hoping to see the best in others, including my brother and me. Dominic's kind heart made him love a half-breed and be convinced by her to care for the worthless humans. It made him soft, made him *weak*.

So when we invited him to Reyna for trade talks, he obliged. And when I'd slipped him my newest development, a tasteless and odorless neurosuppressant, I gave him just enough to weaken his mental shields so I could move past them without his notice, planting the seed for our alliance—our marriage. It was convincing enough that he would think it was his own idea. How beautifully it all came to fruition.

Diana's death was a gift from the gods that allowed all of this to be set into motion. It gave me such a beautiful opening to take everything she had taken from me.

It was too bad that Alesia had the entire palace staff trained against mindcaster influence before I'd arrived, and Eve Kamati had become a master in poisons. She could sense them by sight alone. They were a stalemate in my plans, but I'd found other methods to meet my ends.

This overthrow had been a long time coming and had taken years to perfect. The Briars, Warins, and Shaws claimed the best of the continent for themselves after the war, leaving my brother and me with their scraps. Sure, the South had beautiful white sand beaches and turquoise waters, but what can you grow or mine from *sand*? The sun was blistering and rain almost never fell. The land was beautiful but empty. The East had lush rolling landscapes of fertile soil and farmland, supplying much of the continent with food. The North had mountain peaks full of clear glacial springs, rich minerals, and metal ores. The West had *everything*. And now one of the heir's hearts would soon be in my possession, as would her magic.

The princess with an affinity for water. The daughter of the greatest known Seer. But Diana hadn't been powerful enough to see this, to prevent even her own death. She and Alesia thought themselves so great because of their gifts, and their affinity for combat and strategy in the war. They thought their human blood was a strength. It nauseated me how none of the others saw them for what they were.

Impure abominations.

All the humans did was take. They used up so many resources with their short lives and rapidly growing populace but contained no magic or real talent to give back to the High Fae.

Nic and Misha were growing too bold, too defiant. That night on the terrace only confirmed what they'd soon become, and the twins grew more powerful by the day. My window to be rid of them was shrinking. But soon I would hold Nicole's heart in my hand.

General Lachlan, who arrived from Reyna just this morning, stood outside the doors to my rooms holding an obsidian box, adorned with a golden heart pierced by a silver sword. He knelt before me, dropping into a low bow.

The reverence in the motion brought a smile to my lips. "Lachlan, make an announcement that Nicole Briar, Alesia Sancrista, Eve Kamati, and Cedric and Orelia Shaw are slain. All committed by August Warin of Montevalle, and Misha Briar kidnapped by his brother, Julian Warin. Their atrocities are an act of war. Reyna, Desdemon, and Hahnaley will retaliate. I want every eye searching for the lost princess, to bring my stepdaughter home to be under my protection."

"As you wish, my Queen." From where he knelt he offered up the box holding Nicole Briar's heart of ice.

I accepted it, and before he rose I said, "Lachlan, announce yourself the new Commander of Hahnaley's armies now that Alesia Sancrista is dead."

The male's face shone with only devotion as my fingers grazed his chin. My most loyal General since the Great War. There were rewards for such allegiance.

Leaving him, I pushed open the door to my chambers and entered alone. No one had yet located the other Briar princess, but it was only a matter of time. Everyone would be on the lookout for her and the young Warin prince after that announcement, and pinning the murder of the others on him and August had been crucial.

This morning I'd hoped to trap them both, the King and Prince of Montevalle, but they'd slipped out with the dawn and were nowhere to be found. If everything had gone to plan, I would already have each of the princesses' hearts and both Warins locked away to face trial for their murder, but they'd somehow evaded my carefully laid trap. An inconvenient snag, but one I would soon overcome.

The Shaws hadn't originally been a part of my scheme, but Cedric and Orelia had ended up needing to be put down. They spent too much time sniffing around my brother and me, we hadn't been able to shake them all week. They sensed something was off, and being too smart for their own good, discovered our plans late last night.

But we'd gotten to them first, before they could reach Alesia, with the one weapon they never thought to protect themselves from.

I walked into my closet and approached the floor length mirror at the end of the long room. Placing my palm flat on its surface, its reflection rippled, and I was able to step through into my private chamber. The one no one knew of save for me.

The room was small and dark, offering no light except the few faerie lights I cast around the edges of the room. In it seven mirrors were housed—my most precious possessions.

I approached the largest in the center. Eight feet tall and nearly as wide, the frame crafted from obsidian. All of the constellations were carved along its edges, inlaid with moonstones and stardust. A single large glittering crystal sat at its peak, a piece of a star itself taken from a long forgotten tomb. A gift for a promise.

Looking at my reflection, my fingers went to the edge of my scalp, slowly pulling off the stolen faerie skin attached to my forehead. a necessity to cover the red mark of betrayal permanently inked there. Stripping the skin of another faerie, enchanting, and binding it to myself was a small price to pay to hide the mark after what I'd done to Dominic nine years ago. Though this piece would need replacing soon.

I was ever thankful that the others agreed this would be enough punishment for breaking the Blood Treaty—the Mark of the Traitor. Before long I would no longer need to cover it, wouldn't care who saw the mark. It would be a Mark of the Traitor no longer, but the Sign of the Conqueror. Until then I needed to maintain a certain image, one of victim instead of victor.

I shook my platinum hair free before I reached for the lid of the box. My fingers grazed over the heart. It was still warm, still thrumming with the magic encased there, less than I'd expected. Of course, the princess wasn't nearly as powerful as she'd thought herself.

Lifting the heart into my hand, I spoke into the obsidian mirror. "Mirror of Sight, tell me what you see in my future."

"There are many possible paths, but they are unchanged my Queen." A deep voice echoed.

"How is that possible? I hold the heart of a Briar." I snarled into the shimmering reflection, my fingers tightening on the heart as blood snaked down my forearm.

"The path remains, my Queen. *Take the hearts of the rising after the sun sets on the longest day. To claim their magic for your own is to claim the continent. But fail to end just one before the longest night, and you will never rule as High Queen.*"

I turned to my left. An oval mirror with a simple silver rim, boasting no other embellishments or adornment. Plain. Honest.

"Mirror of Truth. Whose heart am I holding?"

The reflective surface spoke in its melodic voice, "You hold the heart of a loyal guard, my Queen. An aircaster. His name was Cayne."

I screamed in fury and crushed the useless organ in my fist, throwing the trodden remnants to the ground. I turned back to the Mirror of Sight.

"What is the future of Nicole Briar? Where did she go?" I demanded. Those imbecile guards were unsuccessful, then *lied* about it. I had been too elated to have the heart, too hasty in telling the guards to announce Nicole's death.

I needed to find her, or she would ruin *everything*.

The Mirror of Sight spoke again, "The descendants of Diana are shielded, they evade my sight. I only see how they affect others' futures. There are still many possible paths."

I turned to a large mirror on the right. A horizontal oval with a black frame. Two identical gold serpents wound around its edges, a reflection of their open mouths meeting at the top. In its glass, I could see out into all other mirrors and reflections.

"Mirror to Spy, call to your sisters. Show me Nicole Briar."

"My Queen," the reverent voice came out in a hiss. "The descendants of Diana hide from my sisters. Their reflections I cannot contain, but I hear whispers of their names. Others search for the sisters that were promised."

"Who?" I demanded.

'We cannot show you their faces. They have yet to reveal themselves. Though not all are of this plane." The mirror crooned.

Infuriated by the revelations and riddles, I turned from my mirrors, walking back out of the portal. Outside my chamber doors, my personal guards stood waiting for me. "Pull Iago from his sick bed and have him brought to me."

"Where, your majesty?" the startled guard asked, his face pale.

"The gardens."

"Guard, you lied to your Queen."

The blood withdrew from Iago's face. "I didn't, not entirely" he sputtered from where he knelt on the ground before me. "The Commander and her mate are dead."

"I don't give a fuck about the Commander. It was the *heart* I needed." I snarled in his face, my blood boiling with rage. She'd been so *close*.

The guard flinched. "I'm sorry, my Queen, the princess made me do it. The ash didn't work. We planted it in the trees, just like you told us. But when the

Commander and Healer went down she just...*erupted*. She cast fire and burned the others alive. We didn't know she would be capable of that."

Fire.

On the Summer Solstice, her twenty-second birthday, Nicole Briar had not only begun to grow into her full power of water, but now she'd revealed an affinity for fire.

The fire elementals had been too powerful—too threatening to be allowed to continue. I only wished I'd had my talents of stripping and containing magic then as I did now. Then I wouldn't have had to convince the High King of their threat, wouldn't have needed to persuade him that they needed to be wiped from existence. The magic would not have gone to such waste.

For Nicole to hold two elements, it was unheard of. Not once had I seen it in all my centuries. Although Diana had two gifts, Sight and water....but this was different—two *elements*.

The reemergence of fire, such a turn of events. The heart, the power it would bring me—

"Did you at least weaken her?" I asked, basking in my sudden delight.

"Yes, I think so, your majesty. She didn't winnow away, she ran. North, I think. The ash must have affected her more than she let on." Iago said, his face regaining some color.

I smiled brightly. "Show me."

Iago brought the memories into his mind, and I watched the images unfold with my gift. Nic and Alesia retained their magic, even after the ash. Interesting, no wonder the guards were caught unaware. It was commonly believed that the ash rendered all faeries mortal, though no one ever gave much thought to the half-breeds.

I would need to spend time deciphering what had gone wrong and how they were able to resist it, then develop something that would render her truly vulnerable.

"Thank you for that, Iago. I appreciate your one instance of honesty. You are dismissed." I smiled as my magic shredded through his mind.

Iago's face was frozen in agony, mouth open in a soundless scream as blood ran down from his sockets. His eyes sank into his now empty skull.

Clasping my hands together, I turned to my commander. "Lachlan, gather twenty of your best guards on horseback and have them travel north into the Redwood. Split them into three groups to cover more ground. Nicole Briar must be found. She will be weak but do not underestimate her."

"Yes, my Queen." My Commander responded. His demeanor was only resolute obedience, though the other guards' faces had fallen pale at the display of what happened to those who disobeyed me. Fear would keep them in line well enough.

"And if you do not find her, remember what your fate will be."

CHAPTER 30
Nic

The branches and bristles of the forest sliced through me as I ran, marring my leathers and exposed skin in scrapes and cuts.

Alesia had known this day would come, that Misha or I would be attacked with rowan ash and need to fight or escape. She'd trained me for this, for this exact moment. Had she known she wouldn't be here to protect us?

Agony sliced through my heart, but I couldn't stop.

...running through a dark wood, the thorns and vines tearing at me, catching my skin and hair...

She had known. The siren had seen it all. The vision hadn't been a metaphor at all—it was my future, plain and clear.

Hours later my muscles began to give way to fatigue, and my knee buckled. I hit the ground hard—then stood again and kept running, ignoring the sharp pain that shot through my thigh. I couldn't stop, couldn't break down. Not yet—not here where I was still vulnerable. It was only a matter of time before Adrienne realized what happened and sent her huntsmen for me.

I ran until my legs gave out once more from exhaustion, my muscles failing before my will. My hands flew out to keep myself from crashing face first as I hit the dirt. The breath was knocked from me with the impact.

As I lay prone on the ground, I was swarmed by the image of Eve with her throat slit, lying in the dirt just like this—her brown eyes devoid of all their light and warmth. Looking toward her mate, but seeing nothing. Alesia with an arrow through her chest.

I pushed myself up just before I vomited the contents of my stomach onto the ground. I continued to heave even when nothing came up, sobs wracking my body.

Gone.

Alesia. Eve. My father. My mother—all dead.

A scream wailed out of me, the sound so forceful the trees shook. Birds scattered.

Their blood still coated my face and hands. I retched again.

No no no no no.

My hands dug into the dirt as I sat hunched over my knees. I forcibly swallowed down my grief, choking it back down deep inside me.

Misha—I still had my sister.

My twin needed me, and I couldn't break now.

I pushed away from the mess to lean against a tree, the steady trunk holding me up as I gulped down air. My hands tangled into my hair, loosening it from its braid. I tried to get my shaking under control as more sobs threatened to consume me.

My aunts were dead, and in reaction I'd...

Fire—I'd exploded into *fire*.

My hands shook as I peered down at them. I could still feel a ghost of the flame flickering beneath my skin.

This was the year in which my sister and I would complete the ascent into the full potential of our magic. My *water* magic...the ice. No High Fae ever manifested a second element, not in millennia.

The burning I'd begun to feel under my skin last night, what I thought had come from irritation, was the flames. A flicker of them licked along my veins even now. It was nothing like the magic I'd come accustomed to. Water flowed, sometimes serenely, other times thrashing like the sea. Ice was cold, calculated, and piercing.

This element was more volatile, savage—angry.

The firecasters had been deemed too dangerous by the High King and marked for death. As I remembered the way I'd exploded, I thought he might have had a point. A good portion of the forest could be left in cinders if I didn't tread lightly. But I would master it— this brutal, burning gift. The gift I'd used to save my life but had also taken others. Our family trained us to fight and defend for as long as I could remember, but I had never taken a life before today. I swallowed, my mouth dry and foul from being sick.

I refused to feel one ounce of remorse for what I had done to those guards. They could rot in hell for all I was concerned, and I was glad it had been me to send them there after what they'd done to my family. They and soon to be Adrienne. I was going to burn her and everything she loved to ash for this betrayal.

A whisper of a breeze grazed my skin, the air cool on my damp forehead and hair. I looked down at my hands again. Covered in so much blood.

Would seeking her death, as well as anyone else that threatened my family, and finding satisfaction in it make me as callous and horrible as Adrienne herself? Would I become everything Alesia hated about the Deimos in the war, the cruelty and brutality?

"Know this, Nicole. If anyone ever puts a blade to your throat, your family's, an innocent's—you do not hesitate. They made their choice of violence—you give it to them."

No, it was not the same.

The thoughts of finding my sister and seeking vengeance were the only things that slowed my breathing. They were what kept me from shattering into a thousand tiny pieces.

The bubbling sounds of a nearby river called to me. I forced myself to stand, my muscles already aching with soreness and fatigue from running for so long. Slowly I walked toward it, my mind still racing.

North. Misha had to be there. She had to be headed to Montevalle with Julian.

The border would be either heavily guarded or warded making it difficult to cross into, but also the safest place my sister could be. August would shield her because of what she was to Julian. At least, this was my hope. We shared in the protectiveness of our siblings. If I found him and Julian, I would surely find her.

Though this meant traveling through the Redwood, the ancient forest that made up most of the border between Hahnaley and Montevalle. There were stories of how it got its name, from the soil so supposedly inundated with spilled blood that the trees' bark grew with a faintly reddish tint. Considering I was alone with limited weapons and severely depleted magic, this was especially risky, but any other path would take too long.

The border was approximately midway through the forest. I should have gained enough strength back for winnowing the remaining distance in four or five days as the ash wore off—if I didn't have to use any significant amount on threats until then.

My feet sank into the soft soil as I reached saw the small river. Clear rapids flowed over large rocks. I walked along it until I found a deeper, calmer portion, its banks teeming with witch hazel, crested iris, and mountain laurel.

Kneeling in the mud of the riverbank, I cupped my hands to bring water to my face. I filled my mouth with the cool water, rinsed, and spit, trying to rid it of the taste of my own vomit. Once it was gone I swallowed several handfuls, then I used the water to scrub the blood from my face, hair, and hands.

My aunts' blood. The traitors' blood.

I choked back a sob at the red blooming in the water.

My skin was raw and pink by the time I finished. The small cuts on my face, hands, and arms stung. My hands still contained a small tremor.

As I washed, I hadn't noticed the three naiads emerge from the water near the opposite bank, approximately thirty meters away. When I lifted my head, I saw their large gray eyes, like river stones, were locked on mine.

Naiads were one of the many water-blessed nymphs, but unlike the sirens, they were more water than a corporeal body. They were notoriously temperamental with a history of drowning faerie and human alike that impinged upon their territory, especially if they damaged their beloved habitat. I didn't know how they felt about me rinsing myself in their water when I was covered in blood and vomit, and the last thing I wanted was to incite them when I was already so weak.

Still on my hands and knees, I carefully began to back away.

When I moved, one of them sank below the water. A second later she emerged before me, faster than I'd thought possible, using her slender arms and webbed fingers to pull herself up the bank. I froze.

Her pale blue skin simmered in the sunlight, her silvery hair tucked back behind her pointed ears. "Daughter of water and fire," she said in her light, fluid voice, akin to the river rushing over smooth stones.

I blinked. *How could she know about the fire?*

She smiled, the action terrifying though she clearly meant it to be soothing. Her lips pulled back to reveal small pointed teeth—poisonous. "The forest and wind whisper of fire's rebirth, but this is not why I come to you. Be wary, daughter of Sancrista. The shadows, they follow you. The reflections, they watch you."

"You mean Adrienne?" I said, still wary of startling her.

At the sound of her name, the naiad's features twisted. Her eyes turned pitch black, her mouth widening into a horrific slash across her face like a gruesome smile, her fangs emerging. It took everything in me not to flinch, not let my distress show on my face. The motion may have offended her, something I could not afford if I wanted her information.

"The false one defies nature, the magical balance. Abomination." The naiad's soft voice twisted into a terrifying hiss. "Yes, it is she who hunts for you...among others."

"What has she done?" I whispered, very thankful that the naiad's wrath wasn't aimed at me.

"*Thief*," she spat. "She takes what does not belong to her. She twists it, maims it, so it is no longer natural. The beings of earth, air, and water won't stand for it." The naiad's magic churned the water around her, her slender legs kicking restlessly.

Naiads and other nymphs were faeries of nature, born from it and more in tune with any disruptions in its natural order than any other. This was why Adrienne nearly always remained within the palace grounds, forgoing the forest and the sea. If this was how the naiad reacted to just her name, I couldn't imagine what the other nymphs would have done to her in the flesh.

"How is she watching me?" I asked, returning to the naiad's initial statement. If my stepmother was tracking me somehow, I needed to find a way to evade it.

"Of that we are unsure." Her face slowly returned to its delicate features as she looked pensively at the surface of the still water, once again glassy as she calmed. "But we sense her. The false one's darkness reaches out, searching, feeling. Be aware of your surroundings. Look for what is not natural. Nature rejects the false one."

I knew it couldn't be that easy, but I would stay alert, nonetheless. "Thank you."

"Do not thank me. *Remember*," she said forcefully, gray eyes flashing.

My eyes hardened as I nodded. I would not forget her words.

"Farewell. *Resurge et ardere*," The naiad said before slipping under the surface to rejoin her sisters.

"Wait—what does that mean?" I leaned over the water, but she was already gone. Her sisters disappeared as well.

Resurge et ardere.

Words I did not understand from the siren and now the naiad...another warning?

I stood and walked back toward the forest. The ground near the river was too uncovered, too soft. It would make me easy to track. So I returned to the dense darkness of the woods, thankful for the refuge it provided.

It wouldn't be long now until I was fully in the Redwood.

CHAPTER 31
Nic

T he trees grew taller, their trunks wider. There was a primordial stillness in this place, somehow untouched by time. Even the most powerful fae knew it was foolish to travel in these woods alone. If I'd had any other choice, I wouldn't have been. My only hope was that its reputation would dissuade my trackers from following me here.

The light began to change, becoming the golden hues of the last hour of sunlight. I needed to find shelter. Soon.

The ancient beings that lived here, both animal and faerie, were of story and legend. I wasn't sure how effective my weapons would be against them, but at least the arrows were rowan wood. Better than nothing.

The light continued to fade as I came upon an unusual tree. It was larger than the others, one of the roots lifted, the space just large enough for me to fit through. After checking for animals, satisfied that none called this place home, I crawled inside.

Once in the little cave, I cast a silencing ward around the space as well as a trigger at the entrance, just in case anything did decide to come in here as I slept. This depleted some of the magic I'd gained back since this morning, a necessary expenditure, but I would recover more in the night if I was able to sleep securely. I slowly laid on my side, bringing my knees up and using my arm to support my head. Due to it being summer, the night would be chilly but not so cold as needing to risk a fire for warmth. A blessing. Fires and smoke were too easy to track.

My mind reeled in the stillness. A lone tear streamed down my face.

Lock it down. Don't break. Not now.

Eventually, sleep found me.

It didn't take long for the nightmares to come.

I awoke with a start.

The image of Alesia and Eve lying still on the ground burned into my mind, my eyes. In my nightmares, I relived all the horrors from yesterday, saw them die in front of me again. I was shaking as I pushed myself up from the ground, my arms wrapping around my knees.

The first light of dawn streamed through the cave's entrance as I crawled out, my arms weak and shaky. Tracks of beasts that had roamed the forest last night covered the forest floor. Large prints with scrapes from talons, others looked as if something was dragged. I shuddered before walking toward the river.

When I was done refilling my water I continued walking north in the woods, never veering too far from the river's edge, gathering blueberries, wild leeks, and hazelnuts as I went. Even with my stomach still sour, I would do myself a disservice by not at least trying to eat, to regain my strength faster.

I felt the familiar hum of my magic returning to my veins, but it came back slowly. Not nearly enough to winnow to the border, to the place we'd visited with our father when we were on a tour of the kingdom years ago. Located near one of the few roads that crossed the Redwood, it sat exactly between the border of Montevalle and Hahnaley.

The rest of the day and the night passed the same.

I scrounged for food and shelter, successfully keeping down everything I'd eaten, and fell asleep in another small hideaway only to wake to nightmares hours later.

On the third night in the Redwood, I found no cave, climbing high into a tree instead. There I would be safe from whatever lurked along the forest floor, but I would need to be aware of the winged and slithering predators.

Once I awoke to golden-slitted eyes peering at me from the canopy, assessing me.

I only stared back.

Try it, my eyes pleaded with the creature, eager for the fight, for some way to take out my rage and grief. I would not back away, would not cower before it.

The creature didn't move to attack, content to observe. After a few moments, it slunk away, back into the dark. They would not test death tonight.

There would be no sleeping after that, but still nightmares danced before my eyes. Horrors I would never unsee. My family's faces as they were ripped away from me, and I was unable to protect them.

Even the pale light of dawn, the golden sun rising in the East, could not make that darkness abate.

CHAPTER 32
Nic

C limbing down from my tree, I felt the return of my magic thrumming in my veins. The most substantial it had been since the attack. I relished in it, playing with frost at my fingertips as I upped my pace. I needed to winnow to the border before nightfall.

After an hour I heard a noise, the footsteps of something swiftly coming toward me. I froze, listening. My feet planted.

Only prey ran.

The birds still sang, the forest did not still. The creatures that lived here did not fear whatever was approaching.

I stepped between the nearest tree's large roots and knelt behind an elderberry bush, concealing myself from view as I drew an arrow, drawing it into Eve's bow, then sat quietly and listened.

"Nic!" My sister's voice shouted frantically. "Nicky!" She continued yelling my name, growing more desperate with each call.

I slowly crept out from my hiding spot as her footsteps neared. As I came around the tree, I saw her. Her golden hair was tied back in a braid, the style she'd always used for hunting, wearing her favorite warm brown leathers. Even our mother's golden bow was slung across her back.

She turned to me then. "Nic!" she exclaimed, her face breaking into relief, a mixture of a smile and a sob, and ran toward me. But before she could reach me, I cast ice up her legs and feet, rooting her in place a few meters away.

"Nicky?" she said, confused. Her expression was pitiful, her eyes watering as she looked over me. "What are you doing? I've been looking everywhere for you."

"You can stop pretending to be my sister now," I said as I trained my arrow on the selkie.

It was a perfect likeness, taken from my mind as the creature sensed me near the river, seeking to lure me out with what was most precious to me. The selkies could peer into faerie and human minds, but not in the way Adrienne and the other mindcasters did. Their power was limited, they only saw what their prey cared about most. It made them nearly impossible to keep out. Then they donned said appearance, a true transformation they would shed later, unlike the illusions the mindcasters often crafted.

"Nicky, it's me. I've been searching for you. I was so scared that something terrible had happened." The selkie whimpered.

"Stop speaking with *her* voice." I snarled. "My sister is a trained hunter. She would have never given her position away with shouting as you've done, not with so many other predators nearby. Not to mention the ridiculously loud steps you were taking."

The selkie stood taller, all emotion wiped from its face. "Your worry and grief were so tempting, almost as lovely as your sister's face. It would have been so delicious to feast upon." It said in its true voice with a rasp like gravel, completely different from the naiad.

"Do you even know whose face you donned when you slithered out of the water and took this form? Are you brave or foolish, selkie, to have donned the face of a Briar?" I said, replacing the bow to draw the Iradelmar from my back. The selkie's eyes went wide as if it had finally realized who it had mistaken for prey.

"*Sancrista*." Its voice hissed my mother's and aunt's surname as it cowered, still rooted to the spot by my ice.

"I will free you, selkie, only because your blood will draw worse beings, but do not follow, or I will trap you here so far from your precious water to slowly dry out and die." The selkie still shrunk back from me in my sister's form. It nodded hastily, eager to be free.

"And *never* impersonate a Briar again," I growled as I called back my magic, freeing its feet.

The selkie immediately slunk onto all fours, moving grotesquely in my sister's form. It kept its eyes on me as it crept back into the woods from whence it came.

I stood there watching, listening for several more moments. When I was sure I was alone again, I continued walking, my ears open for the selkie or anything else that might be stalking after me.

The selkie had meant to lure me with my sister's likeness and failed. But seeing her face, even falsely, renewed my sense of urgency and I quickened my pace northward. The sooner I crossed the border, the sooner I would find help for Misha.

Soon, sister.

CHAPTER 33
Nic

B y midday, the sky had grown cloudy, heavy with rain from a summer storm that was sure to unleash itself soon.

The soft clop of hooves against the forest floor was accompanied by muted voices. From the sound of it, there were at least six of them. None of the voices I immediately recognized.

I quickly ducked into the nearby brush, leaning into where the foliage was thickest to camouflage myself. Through the dense leaves, I watched them as they passed.

The riders each wore purple uniforms with white detailing, the colors of Reyna. Adrienne had replaced the green and gold guard uniforms of my family's house with her own. That certainly hadn't taken long.

With a significant amount of my power returned, I should have winnowed away before they found me, but I was determined to overhear their conversation, desperate to see if they knew anything of Misha. I needed to be sure that Adrienne didn't have her.

The group slowed. "Should we rest? It's past noon," one of the guards inquired to whoever was their leader.

"Sure. Take the horses to the river. We are only stopping for a half hour then continuing north. If the Briar girl makes it to the border before we reach her, the Queen will be displeased." He wore the same patch on his arm my aunt had once worn—Commander. My nails dug into my palms.

"Displeased?" Another whispered to one of his comrades. "I heard what she did to Iago."

"Gruesome, it was," his friend replied. "If we don't find the princess, we may as well never return."

"Do you intend to abandon your Queen?" The Commander snapped. "What you speak of is treason."

"Um, no sire...I did not mean—" the second one sputtered in response.

"Good." The commander cut him off. "Because if you were intent on betraying our Queen or your duty, it would be *my* duty to hang you," he threatened, his voice like cold steel, as the others went silent. Their conversation temporarily ceased as they rode toward the river.

When their horses' steps became distant, I soundlessly followed, remaining hidden in the shadows of the forest.

They made a small camp on the river bank, pulling out food and canteens from the saddle bags. There were eight guards in total, all armed with rowan wood arrows and I assumed the ash as well. Though by now I was sure they would be well aware that it was not fully effective against me. Iago without a doubt gave them that information before his death.

Once eating, the two nearest me continued conversing. The cowardly one that had spoken earlier, a male with light brown hair and tan skin, and another guard with similar features. The commander sat the furthest away with his nearly white hair. Definitely born of Reyna. His second in command sat with him, another male with dark skin and black hair.

"What about the other Briar—the golden one? Any word on her capture?" the nearest whispered to his friend.

"Nothing, they haven't been able to locate her since the ball. The guards are guessing she left with the Warin prince. He may have taken her with him to the North when everything happened. Which would be a shame—hard to get to her if she's there. The Queen wants her just as much as the other."

Iago had spoken true. Adrienne *didn't* have Misha. My heart swelled with hope.

"Such a shame, a fine piece of ass like that getting away. Hopefully, they find her too." The guard wagged his eyebrows suggestively. "Or maybe we'll find her. Take the long way back. Have a bit of fun first."

I went utterly still, a deadly sort of rage filling me.

His friend laughed in agreement. "What happens in the forest stays between us." The rest of the guards overhead them. Some snickered. All smiled—every single one of them.

The two nearest me continued mocking my sister and me, saying all the vile things they would do if they were the ones to find and capture us. The others intermittently chimed in as well, their suggestions growing more despicable by the minute.

My hands grew hot. Flames threatened to erupt from them, but I pushed down my anger, holding back the fire. I'd planned to slink away after I'd gotten information about Misha and continue northward on a different path. But now? I wasn't going anywhere—not while they still breathed.

It was still over a hundred miles to Montevalle's border. The jump would take nearly every drop of magic I'd gained back since being ashed.

Silently, I removed Eve's bow and quiver from my back, tucking it into the shadows to retrieve later. Then pulled the Galorian silver dagger from its sheath at my thigh, my thumb running along that swan's wing hilt.

I was Alesia Sancrista's protégé. I didn't need magic.

The dagger's glint seemed to darkly agree with my need for vengeance as I patiently waited. One of them would wander off alone soon.

The two continued in their disgusting conversation, their words only growing worse as they remarked on their past exploits. I said a prayer to the Mother for every female that had ever been victimized by them and vowed retribution. Males like this didn't turn into monsters overnight. These thoughts were nurtured, reinforced...acted upon.

Minutes later, the guard stood to relieve himself in the woods, walking to a tree out of sight of the others. I crept after him. My dagger was at his throat before he realized he wasn't alone.

Grabbing his hair in one hand, I sliced until I hit bone.

The guard died quickly and silently as I caught him, his unseeing eyes still wide with surprise. I slowed his fall to the ground to prevent too much noise.

One down. Seven to go.

"Ames?" the guard called, his footsteps rapidly approaching. I hid crouched among the brush again, the soft leaves caressing my face. Their shadows concealed me.

The male, the vilest of them, saw his friend and hesitated, disbelieving of his own eyes. I was at his back before he could call for help.

"I heard you're looking for some *fun*." I crooned into his ear as I reached my arm around and slid the dagger into the space just to the left of his sternum and between his ribs, piercing his heart. He fell to the ground with a thump.

This one the others heard.

The Commander and his second came running as I took cover. "Ames! Wickam!" They called, just before they saw the bodies.

"Shit. Something out here got them. One of the monsters the stories talk about." The second looked around frantically, every shadow seeming to make him jump.

The Commander crouched over the body. "No, it wasn't. Look at their injuries. These were done with a weapon, a small blade I imagine. Which means we have company." The two drew their weapons. The second already had his bow in hand as he reached for an arrow, rowan wood of course. The Commander pulled his sword from its sheath. Ornate Galorian silver.

"Come out. We know you're here." He sounded almost bored.

The other four joined them in the small clearing across from me, no farther than fifteen meters away. Six guards remained.

The thick clouds above finally opened up, warm summer rain pouring from the sky as I remained crouched, hidden. I couldn't have asked for better timing as the rain and mist would help me hide from their view.

My disadvantage was that I didn't know these males—didn't know what their abilities were. If they were elementals or could winnow was a mystery to me, though at least one had to be a healer, it would have been foolish to travel without one. But I did know Adrienne. Because of her love of power, the Commander would be the strongest magically. Ideally, I would kill him first and hope the others fell apart without their leader.

The males kept their eyes on the woods, weapons raised as they scoured the area, searching for me in vain. After a few minutes, the second in command walked past my hiding spot, his back to me.

Beggars couldn't be choosers.

If he turned, he would see me. I didn't give him the chance as I sprinted forward.

As soon as he heard my steps, he turned and released his arrow. I dropped down to the mud in a slide, the shot missing my head by a foot. I hit his shins with my boot, taking his legs out from under him, too fast for him to avoid. Before he hit the ground I was on him, Galorian dagger through the heart.

"Cute trick, little Briar." The Commander condescended, still somehow unbothered. He hadn't even raised his sword in a defensive position, but his mind prodded at mine, testing my shields with his mindcasting ability. His stone composure cracked to reveal a hint of irritation when he found no weaknesses. "Come now. The Queen is waiting."

I didn't move, rain splattering around me. I sized up the other four while they did the same to me. Two guards with a sword and shield apiece, one with two swords, and one with a bow drawn. No magic revealed—I would take the bet in assuming they had no elemental gifts or they'd have displayed them by now.

I sheathed the Galorian dagger in favor of two throwing knives from my belt.

The commander let out a cruel laugh. "Come now, Princess, you cannot escape us. You will only get hurt trying, and your filthy half-breed aunt will be so disappointed—would have been disappointed. I misspoke. The dead cannot *will* anything."

Before he said his last hateful word, I struck.

I turned on the guard with the bow, dodging his shot as I threw the knives in my hand—one hit its mark in his shooting arm, the other went straight through his eye. He dropped to the forest floor before he'd finished his scream of pain.

The next two came for me at once. On the offensive, I ran for them as I drew the Iradelmar and short sword from across my back. We were a flurry of blades, strikes, and blocks. But I was too fast and had been trained too well. A strike of the Iradalmar through the chest ended one. The other's head rolled to the forest floor.

The last remaining guard turned to run. I spared a drop of my magic for him as rainwater tunneled into his lungs, filling them and cutting off his breath. With half a thought the water became ice, shattering him from within. His body dropped with a thump.

The commander was no longer laughing, no longer sneering, when I faced him again.

"Alesia Sancrista made sure no one could ever hurt me. Today..." I stalked toward him. "She *is* proud."

Thunder shook the sky overhead as my blood thrummed with power that begged to be released, for me to end him. But in the next second, he was gone—winnowed away. *Fuck.*

He would be back.

I sheathed the short sword across my back, trading it for a knife from my belt. My other hand still held the Iradelmar. I took a deep breath. I had trained for this too.

Just before someone, or something, materialized from the fold in space we used to winnow, there was a crack. A silent spark in the air that could alert you to their arrival if you were aware enough to feel it. Alé made us practice this over and over. She must have knocked me to the ground hundreds of times before I was quick enough to catch her. And this asshole wasn't even a tenth as skilled as she was. After a few moments I felt it, the ripple just by my left flank. I turned and threw the knife toward that crackle in the air.

The Commander roared in pain as he materialized, my knife buried in his shoulder. Then I swung the Iradelmar. He jumped back just in time. I only gave him a shallow wound across the stomach.

"*Bitch*," he spat as he pulled out the dagger, blood pouring from the wound. Furious, the Commander lunged for me.

I rolled to the side, ducking under his swinging sword and using his own momentum against him. Alesia's blade cut across his back, but not deep enough to kill, as the sword snagged on his armor.

He laughed humorlessly at my failed blow, throwing my dagger back at me.

Dodging it, I grabbed another knife from my belt and hurled it at him. This throw's aim was far better than the first. The blade buried into the forearm holding his sword, severing important nerves and tendons as he screamed and the blade fell from his grasp.

The Commander dove for his sword with his opposite hand as I sheathed the Iradelmar across my back and ran for him again. He grabbed his blade from the ground and swung it toward me with his uninjured hand. His non-dominant, less-practiced hand.

I swerved and leaped, using the nearest tree as a backboard for my foot. I hit it and rebounded. As I sailed through the air, I took the last knife from my belt and with it struck the soft part of his flesh between his shoulder and neck. I landed in a crouch, pulling the Galorian dagger from my sheath and sliced it into the upper part of his thigh, striking true.

Between the spewing blood from the artery and the rowan ash bonded to the blade, the wound would not heal before he bled out. And I'd already killed his healer.

The force of the impact knocked the Commander onto his hands and knees. He pushed up from the ground, lips unfurling into a roar, blood covering his teeth. I sheathed the knife and pulled the short sword from my back, then I swung for his head.

The Commander turned his sword to the side in a last second block, the force of our collision reverberating through my body.

I moved quickly, reaching up with my left hand to grab his blade, the sharp edge cutting into my palm. Using my own sword, I hooked my blade into his hilt and twisted, retching his sword down from his hand and into mine, disarming him again.

He reached for his sheath then his boot but came up empty. The Commander had no other weapons. His eyes lost that arrogance as they met mine. He was beaten, and he knew it.

I stalked toward him as he stood, ready to deliver the killing blow. Before I could reach him, the Commander was struck from the left—a blur of black that knocked him to the ground.

A gaping maw with long, edged teeth ripped out his throat.

Shadowhound.

The creatures were similar to the hounds the fae often used for hunting but—wrong. These beings were nothing but darkness and bloodthirstiness given form. The shadowhounds were supposed to only hunt at night, they couldn't bear direct sunlight, but today—thick clouds obscured the sun as the rain continued to pour. The spilled blood, the stench of death, had attracted it here.

I should have winnowed away then, but...Eve's bow. I didn't trust I could find this place again if I jumped, and I couldn't leave without it—I wouldn't leave one of the few remaining pieces of her behind.

The beast lifted its eyes to me. It was larger than the palace hounds but smaller and leaner than Rasalas. Sleek black fur, mouth with too long teeth like the serrated edges of hunting knives, pointed ears pinned back, and a long, lean body that allowed it to run as swiftly as the High Fae. The forest went still as its eyes locked onto mine. Its lips pulled back in a snarl as it assessed me. A low rumble came from its chest, but the terrible beast in front of me wasn't what scared me, wasn't what made my heart hammer in my chest.

It was that I hadn't seen its pack—yet.

The bushes to my left thrashed apart as another shadowhound crashed through them, its jaws aiming for my head. I thrust my sword up, piercing the beast in the chest as it came over me, then rolling away on the ground as it fell beside me, dead.

I only had time to rip my blade free from its chest and stand before the first was charging me, that one killed with a strike through its neck with the sword I'd taken from the now fallen Commander.

Another attacked. Then another and another.

I was covered in their black blood as I fought to reach the base of the tree where Eve's bow was hidden. One of the swords slipped from my grip in the gore, then the other became lodged between one of the shadowhound's ribs. And for just one moment, I wasn't fast enough.

My hand still on that sword, one of the shadowhounds latched its jaws around my forearm. With its bite, I heard the sickening crunch of bone, and I screamed out in agony. With the Galorian dagger in my other hand, I pierced the beast through the eye.

The shadowhound's bite was venomous, a paralytic that slowly worked its way to your heart. I had half an hour at most to find the antidote or someone that knew of it, a rare flower that grew in the Redwood.

Another hound flew for me. I didn't have time to draw the Iradelmar from my back. I sheathed the dagger and called on my magic. A blade of diamond-hard ice formed in my hand instead, though it would cost me some of the power to winnow. I prepared to defend myself when another creature tackled the beast before it reached me.

A lion as large as a horse.

The golden creature lifted the hound by its neck, then tossed it to the side like it was nothing more than a doll. The hound was dead instantly, its throat crushed by the great cat's jaws. Then the lion turned its attention to me.

The Nemean lions were legend, seen so rarely that most doubted their existence. They refuted that it had to have been a normal lion that others had exaggerated the size of in fear, but I couldn't doubt what was right in front of me.

Its golden-brown eyes pierced mine, something uncannily familiar in them. They spoke to me—they told me to *run*.

Another of the shadowhounds jumped on its back, teeth aiming for the skin over its neck. The lion roared loud enough to shake the trees as it shook the beast off, evading its bite, then tore through its chest with one swipe of a great paw. More hounds turned their attention to the lion, and I was forgotten. The great cat tore through them easily.

I didn't waste the opportunity the lion had given me. I turned and sprinted to retrieve Eve's bow from where I'd hidden it. Slinging it over my shoulder, I ran as hard as I could through the still pouring rain and mud.

The venom was spreading, searing through my veins. If it reached my heart, I would be dead.

I pictured my destination in my mind to winnow. I'd planned to jump to the border tonight. Even then it would have been the farthest I'd ever gone at once. I prayed that in doing so now I would stand some chance of finding help in breaking the border wards.

I pulled on all of my magic's strength, nearly draining what I had left to tear through that pocket of space. The darkness squeezed and pulled at me as it sucked the air from my lungs. I willed myself to push through, to reach farther.

My arm seared in pain as I landed, bracing myself on the ground—the kind of pain so severe it froze your lungs, rendering you unable to scream.

I'd made it to the northern border, to the tree I remembered from the travels around the country with our father. Its barren branches reached up to the sky, its bark bleached white by the sun after hundreds of years. The Death Tree stood out starkly against the lush summer forest surrounding it.

As the ability to stand evaded me, I gritted my teeth, using the last of my strength to drag myself over the border the tree demarcated. When I crossed, it felt like I'd torn through some magical barrier.

Someone knew I was here. Gods bless the North and their wards.

The pain in my arm spread with each movement, my breath growing shallow and frantic. With desperate hope, I prayed to the Mother that whoever found me would help me, that they would recognize my bite and have the antivenom I so desperately needed.

Just past the tree, lying face down in a meadow of wildflowers, the exhaustion took over, and I blacked out.

I woke to more pain, worse than before.

It was darker, the surface beneath me hard. Outside of the blinding pain, my brain couldn't comprehend much more than that. It seared through my body, spreading.

A scream erupted from my throat as I writhed. I reached for my arm to scrape and tear my burning skin off, anything to escape this pain, but my arms were bound as well as my legs. I pulled against the restraints as hard as I could.

"Celeste, secure her!" A female shouted, her voice commanding. Someone's hands came over my arms, holding me down. I kept fighting against them and my restraints, still screaming.

"I need her still to apply the antivenom or she won't make it." The same voice shouted. More hands held me still. I begged them to let me go, the words incoherent.

Someone applied a salve to my arm. It burned, worse than the bite. Another set of hands came over my head, a female voice whispering words I couldn't make out as I tried to fight her off.

As she spoke, everything started to go numb, my vision blurring as I fell into a dream.

CHAPTER 34
Nic

G olden light streamed through the glassless windows in the abandoned castle, the place I loved to play as a child. Dust motes danced and floated in their wake. I lay on a bed of soft moss, the pain in my arm dull, tolerable enough to ignore.

I stood, wandering to the hall. As I walked, I admired the climbing vines and the pink roses with their lovely yellow centers.

Roses, I thought fondly as I touched my fingers to the petals, avoiding the sharp thorns.

During play, we would imagine we were sirens in the sea, but instead, we would save the sailors from drowning instead of killing them. Next, we were dragons, soaring high above the clouds where no one could touch us.

Us.

Misha.

"Sister?" I called, my voice echoing in the cavernous space. My twin. The other half of my being. My only remaining family.

"Misha!" I shouted as I searched for her, frantic now as I ran down the corridors and up the stairs to the tower.

My sister. She was in danger. She *needed* me, but I couldn't find her, no matter how hard I searched.

Useless—I was utterly and completely useless.

"*Misha!*"

My heart pounded against my chest as I awoke from the nightmare and froze. It took me a moment to remember what happened and where I was.

The guards and the shadowhounds.

The soft light of morning bled through the curtains of the only window. The guards had stumbled upon me midday, and I'd winnowed not long after. I didn't know if my extended sleep had been from my exhaustion or induced when I'd been healed of the shadowhound venom. The pain of the bite was dull now, a mere fraction of what it had been before.

My hands were strung up behind my head, but I could feel my left palm was healed as well, only a small raised line remained from where I grabbed the commander's sword. Both my wrists were bound with cuffs of rowan wood to a bar on the headboard. My captors might have saved me, and I was deeply thankful they had, but they certainly didn't trust me. Which was fair, considering how I must have looked. Injured and covered in blood, not all my own, and armed to the teeth—all of which were gone. Even my feet were bare, the knives in the soles of my boots out of reach.

I looked down and didn't recognize my shirt. It was white and loose, not the leathers I'd been traveling in. I vaguely remembered being held on the table while someone applied the antivenom to my arm. They must have cut the leathers off with their long sleeves to get to the wound faster, it was what Eve always told us to do in an emergency, to not waste valuable time caring about clothing.

Eve. The rings.

My aunts' mating bands had been in the breast pocket of my leathers. It took everything in me to keep still. To keep from thrashing when I realized they were gone. Alesia's sword and Eve's bow as well.

Those things were all I had left of them. I had to get them back.

I could still feel my mother's ruby pendant resting on my chest under the shirt and the weight of the bracelet on my wrist. I was thankful neither had been harmed in the fray.

Voices began in the next room, four distinct ones. They spoke softly, but if I craned my neck just right, I could listen.

"She's been traveling for a while, likely alone but we can't be sure. If she was with someone they are either now dead or abandoned her." The voice was female, the tone warm even in her hushed whisper. I thought she was the one that had been shouting as she applied the antivenom salve.

The next voice was also female but slightly deeper with an accent similar to Eve's. "My guess is alone. She's dressed like an assassin, must be one of Adrienne's. That bitch queen already killed Cedric and Orelia Shaw, Hahnaley's Army Commander and High Healer, as well as the icecasting Briar. Adrienne will stop at nothing until all the other royals are murdered and she and her brother can take over as high rulers." Footsteps as she paced. "That female was probably sent here to finish the job. We should have left her there to die."

The Shaws were dead.

Guilt flooded through me. Alesia and I had considered the possibility of their betrayal when in truth they were targets like the rest of us. I added Orelia and Cedric's names to the list of those I'd avenge when I saw Adrienne again and prayed to the gods I wouldn't have to add more.

My captors hadn't recognized me, their thinking I was dead surely helped with that, and seemed to be no fans of Adrienne's. I could use that to my advantage, convince them to let me go so I could continue to Montevalle's capital.

I maneuvered so my hands reached the back of my head to my braid, where I had small pins tucked into my hair. Grabbing one, I began using it to pick the lock in the cuffs, another skill Alesia had taught me. She'd escaped many handcuffs this way when caught stealing as an adolescent. As I worked the pin into the wooden lock, I continued listening.

The third voice that spoke was light and airy, another female. "If we had left her there, we would get no answers. She will talk easily enough when the others return." A chair squeaked as she either stood up or sat down. "And I agree, an assassin is likely. She even had throwing knives hidden in the soles of her boots. Who does that? I mean it's kind of cool though. Do you think she'll tell me who made them?"

"She's more likely to kill you first," the second female snickered.

A male, the fourth voice, spoke next in a low whisper, "The room is too quiet. She's awake."

I frantically finished picking the lock, wedging it open just as their footsteps neared the door. I put the pin back in my hair and leaned my head on my hands to conceal what I'd done.

A female entered first. She had long, curly black hair, dark tan skin, a curvy figure, and was slightly taller than me. Beautiful, her features softer than the ones that followed. My eyes caught on her ears. Round. Human.

The male came in just behind her. She went to lean on the dresser across from me while he walked to the chair in the corner. He had lighter tan skin with dark brown hair and eyes set in a kind face, even if it was currently devoid of any telling emotion. His ears were pointed. High Fae.

He sat down on the arm like he didn't have a care in the world, but he was too stiff in his pose, his nonchalance forced. He may have looked relaxed, but he could and would spring into action quickly if necessary. I noted the matching gold bands around their third fingers and could smell their entwined scents. *Mates*—very interesting. High Fae and human liaisons were rare enough, marriages even more still. But mating bonds? I didn't think it was possible. o

The last two followed and stood near the couple. A petite faerie with pale skin, tinged a soft green, and short golden blonde hair like the sun's rays—like Misha's, I thought with a clench in my gut. Like her voice, her features were delicate. She perched herself on the dresser, feet swinging carelessly. Her eyes were large and round, a brilliant blue-green color. She was not High Fae but a nymph. As she was here, I quickly ruled out the water bound. The faerie also seemed much too grounded to be air blessed—leaving only earth as a possibility.

The last to enter was a female about my height and build with dark brown skin and black hair that reached her low back, fashioned into many small braids adorned with rings of gold. Her dark eyes were assessing, they seemed to miss nothing. She was the first to speak. "Who are you?"

I matched her voice with the second female that had assumed I was an assassin. Her posture, her voice, everything about her was intense—calculating.

"No, *Hello, how are you?* Is this how everyone welcomes guests in the North?" I said with a groan.

"This is how we welcome *trespassers*." The human woman responded. She was the first voice, the one with the antivenom. A healer of some sort.

"You're human?" I asked her, redirecting.

The male at her side responded, "Yes, but thinking she is the weakest because of it would be a mistake." The protective, devoted fae mate.

"I can't read you at all anymore." The petite one pondered in her light voice from the dresser perch. "Most fae still wouldn't be able to keep up such strong mental shields after being poisoned like that. Even after the antivenom and the healing—not so quickly."

Great, the tiny one was a mindcaster. Part nymph and High Fae. "Good to know," I rasped.

I mentally berated myself that she'd been able to affect me with her mindcasting earlier when the pain made me vulnerable. Though she couldn't have seen much if she was in here questioning me, which meant she'd only been able to use her gifts to render me unconscious.

The intense one stepped closer. "I asked you a question. Who are you?"

"Isn't the better question, *why are you here?* Because I think we can help each other." I countered.

"Not necessary. How much help can we possibly get from a Fae that lets herself get nearly killed by a shadowhound?" She mocked me.

"Look, it's been a rough last few days" I said sharply. "I'm no threat to you or anyone in Montevalle. I just need to keep traveling—I've got places to be. So kindly let me go, and I will be on my way. I mean no one here any harm."

"You certainly meant *someone* harm," the petite one muttered, her eyes going to my still blood-spattered pants.

"To where?" the human woman asked.

I took a deep breath. It couldn't hurt to be honest. "I need to get to the capital."

They all went still. "Why?"

"*That* is between me and whom I seek. Help me get there and I'm sure I can figure out some reward."

"You travel alone with no money and a cache of weapons, needing to get into the capital. It all seems a bit...suspicious." The intense female raised an eyebrow. "Were you sent by the Queen?"

My lip curled back in a snarl. "That *traitor* is no queen."

The human and the intense female remained expressionless, not giving anything away. But my response got a swift upward lift from the corners of the mouths of the nymph and the male before they hid it. Their reaction was promising.

"Last chance, *who* are you?" The intense one grew impatient with me. She stepped closer.

"I am from the West. I am loyal to the Briars. That is all you need to know. I told you, we can help each other. I am no threat to you," I said, hoping it would pacify her but knew it likely wouldn't.

"You really expect us to believe that?" she sneered. "We know you were listening. You know how we feel about Adrienne. You could very easily be lying, and the second we let you go you will stab us all in the back. Not that you would be successful," she said, breaking into a cruel smile.

I took a deep breath. So much for getting them to trust me. "I am not with Adrienne. I told you I'm loyal to the Briar crown. I don't know how you expect me to prove it."

The nymph shrugged like I had a point. I couldn't tell if any of the others were buying what I was saying.

"I guess you can't." The intense one said. "But all we know is that one Briar princess is dead, their aunts and the Shaws too. And here you are, an assassin on the run. Have anything to do with any of those?"

"No." She needed to be very careful with what she said next.

"We found you covered in enough blood, shadowhound and fae. It didn't all smell like yours. You sure you didn't murder them then travel north to finish the job, assassinating the last ruler that isn't a Deimos?"

Her accusation pushed my anger over the edge. Insinuating that I'd murdered my family, even if they had no idea who I was, was something I could not let stand. They should have ashed me when I was out.

I quickly pivoted my wrist and slid my hands free from the cuffs. Then I launched myself at her.

As I flew from the bed, I hit a wall of solid air and crashed to the ground. They'd warded me in. The female didn't even flinch.

"You did that on purpose," I hissed. She'd goaded me into attacking, knowing she was safe behind the invisible barrier. I should have reached my magic out, felt for one earlier. It was a mistake that wouldn't happen again.

"I had a feeling those cuffs wouldn't last very long." She smiled tauntingly and shrugged. "We'll get the truth when the others return. They won't be long now. We'd been hoping to capture a spy from the West to get answers from." She waved a dismissive hand before turning to leave. The others stood with her.

I snarled my frustration, my palms heating as I hit my fist against the ward. The barrier shook, the power of my hit cracking the magic.

I'd nearly broken it.

The intense one spun back around, eyes flickering with uncertainty—no longer confident that the ward would hold me.

I smiled, taunting her as she'd taunted me, then raised my arms to hit it again when the human woman doused me in rowan ash from the right. Not as much as Adrienne's guards had used, but enough to subdue most fae. My hit landed weakly, and the ward didn't shake this time. The petite one let out a breath of relief.

Then all four exited the room wordlessly, this time closing the door behind them.

Now that I was awake, I was sure they would also put up silencing wards to keep me from eavesdropping again. They wouldn't be repeating the same mistakes either.

Pacing the floor, I got a feel for my invisible cage, how much space I had before I felt the hard barrier. I placed my hand on it again and smiled, genuinely this time.

They'd ashed me, unaware it wouldn't have a full effect.

And I remembered what August had said at the dinner on the terrace. *It was thought that a firecaster's flame could burn through almost anything, even shields and wards.*

My smile grew. They weren't the only ones that could play games.

CHAPTER 35
Nic

I gave it half an hour. Enough time for the four to lull themselves back into the comfort of believing that I was securely confined behind their magical barricade.

It was quiet all around me indicating the silencing wards were indeed up. I could only hope that they were confident enough in their magic and the ash that they weren't keeping a close watch on where they had me kept. Though I didn't know where I was. All I saw through the window was more forest and late afternoon light, but there had to be a town nearby. I could determine my location from there easily enough then head to the capital to find Julian and August, to Misha hopefully with them.

I stood and approached the ward.

The last time I was ashed I was still able to produce quite a bit of flame, though it was remarkably volatile—much like my emotions in the moments after we'd been attacked. I knew I could produce the force that would be necessary to burn a hole in the ward, but I also knew that I couldn't control it, at least not well.

But I had to try. I couldn't stay locked up in here for another minute. Not when I so desperately needed to know if my sister was safe with Julian. Placing my hand on the ward, I tried to conjure flame.

Nothing happened.

I groaned internally. I didn't expect it would be as easy as water or ice, but it was still frustrating. Earlier when I'd cast the fire I was emotional, in a rage. I remembered that night of the Summer Solstice.

Tomorrow...of course.

Adrienne's grin as she said it, knowing what she planned to do, as she toyed with that strand of my hair. Winding it around and around and around her finger.

The flame under my skin roiled. My palm heated, and a small burst of flames erupted. The ward disintegrated, cracking apart in streaks of glowing embers and falling away like ash.

Listening for any indication they'd heard or sensed the ward break, I stepped past where the barrier had been on my bare feet. I heard no noise from the outside as I made my way to the door.

Once out of the room I emerged in a short hallway with two other doors, the end opening up into what looked like a great room. This was someone's home.

There was no one in my line of sight as I stepped into the hall. It might have been foolish, but I wouldn't leave without my aunts' rings and weapons. I tried the door across from mine. As it quietly swung open, I recognized it as the room I'd been healed in...and there in the corner, lying discarded from where they'd taken them off me, Eve's bronze bow, the Iradelmar, and my leathers resting on the floor.

The pocket in the leathers didn't take long to find, the rings still safely tucked away. I placed one on each of my ring fingers then tucked the sword into the belt at my side. I slung Eve's bow and quiver across my back.

I looked around—no boots. Instead of wasting more precious seconds looking for them, I decided I could make it through the woods without them for now and steal some off someone's porch the first chance I got.

Reentering the hallway, I still didn't see anyone as I crept toward the great room. There was a door directly across, the window next to it indicating it led outside. I backed up a step and came onto my toes. It was now or never.

I took off in a sprint from the hall, running for the door.

"*Oh shit*—" the male cursed as my hand hit the handle, blessedly unlocked, and wretched the door open.

A chair crashed to the floor. Footsteps pounded behind me, but they wouldn't be fast enough to catch me before I was outside. I was slower than normal with the ash, but still faster than most thanks to all the sprints I'd run in training under its influence. Winnowing wards were up, but I could beat the four to their edge.

My feet hit the wood of the porch. I leaped from its edge, jumping the stairs completely. I landed in a stride as I ran for the tree line.

The first trees were only feet away when someone tackled me from my left. The force of our combined momentum caused us to lose balance, and we began to fall. Before I could faceplant into the dirt we spun. Instead of crashing into the ground, I landed on a hard chest with arms like vices of iron locked around me. The air seemed to crackle with the force of us.

"Ni—"

I threw an elbow back, connecting with my captor's jaw as he grunted in pain. Then I kicked my legs over my head, rolling out of his grip. I pivoted away, turning back toward the forest.

A large hand grasped my ankle out from under me, knocking me back to the dirt. I kicked my other foot as I fell, connecting with a crunch that made my opponent swear. But the hand wouldn't let go of my leg, it hadn't yielded one bit.

I went to kick again, but he grasped the other ankle and pulled me, flipped me onto my back, and was on top of me again in an instant. He pinned me in the dirt with his hands on my wrists, legs straddling mine as I continued to fight like hell to get free.

Until I saw him, those silver eyes, and froze.

"*Nicole,*" rasped that deep, familiar voice.

August.

Relief fell over me like a cool wave.

Blood was running from his nose, I'd likely broken it again, and a whelp was already forming on his jaw. But he was here, which meant—

"*Julian.*"

"Misha!" I shouted this time, looking around for his brother and my sister. August was here. They had to be with him.

He only held me tightly as I thrashed. He shook his head. "They're not here." The words were forced—pained.

My heart thudded to a stop in my chest. "No—no, they have to be. He has to be with you. *She* has to be with you." I rasped and continued struggling against his hold. My breath grew frantic, erratic.

"We couldn't find them." His voice cracked with the words.

I thrashed against him, his arms unbreakable stone. Julian had to be here. Misha had to be here. Because if they weren't with August that meant—

August shifted so his hands were grasping my face as he crouched over me. I could see myself in his eyes—panicked, feral.

"I swear on my life, I will find them—*we* will find them."

The ferocity in his gaze called to me, and my breathing slowed. I didn't know if it was his words, his promise, or that his eyes held that same fierce desperation, rage, and fear...but I believed him.

I stopped fighting.

August. I'd found him—or he'd found me. Regardless, he was here, and he was my best option to find Misha. I could see it in his eyes, had seen it the entire past week, the love for his brother that was shown there. He would tear apart the continent to find Julian, just as I would do for Misha.

"You two know each other?" the intense female from inside interrupted.

Still on the ground, August moved off of me. I sat up, turning toward the four from inside that were now watching us. Three others stood nearby that must have arrived with August. He answered the female but his eyes never left my face.

"Nicole, these are the Seven. Seven, meet Princess Nicole Briar of Hahnaley."

CHAPTER 36
Nic

I thought she was dead." The male from inside murmured to his mate. Some emotion filled her eyes, shock and something else—a realization. The others stood wide-eyed in front of the large wrap-around porch of a large cabin.

August finally released me. As he stood he reached a hand down to assist me up. I took it and could have sworn that surprise flickered on his face. "The Seven are my closest council and advisors. This is my nearest outpost to Hahnaley. We've gathered here as we search for information on where our siblings may be."

I kept my eyes on the four I'd already met but trained a part of my awareness on the three behind me, the ones that had come with August. If they shifted even a fraction, I would know. I sensed they watched me just as closely.

"How did you break the ward? We just ashed you." The intense female questioned, clearly irritated.

"Isn't it clear?" The human woman responded. "The Briar princesses are part human. She goaded us into ashing her to let our guard down, then broke the ward after we left. Though the exact how is still a question...but I doubt she will tell us."

"Not to be underestimated indeed," I said, mirroring her mate's words from earlier. The woman smiled at me, the motion warming her face.

My own resolve softened as I felt a tie, a kinship to her. She seemed someone I could be friends with in different circumstances, even as concern bloomed in my stomach from her suspicions as to how I'd broken the ward. The fire was a secret I'd prefer to keep hidden for now, it made me too much of a threat. Though I was particularly worried the nymph would discover it. The naiad had known, had heard of my power spoken on the wind and between the trees.

August nodded toward the human. "That is Miranda. A Seer like your mother, but she is also the rare human born with magic—a witch. Most adept in poisons and potions."

I studied her. Her strong posture, her seeming unwillingness to yield even surrounded by the stronger, faster High Fae. I admired it and her.

"Beside her is her mate Damian, a healer." August continued. That was why I had healed so quickly. Miranda had created the antivenom for the shadowhound's bite, and once it was out of my system, Damian was able to heal me.

"He fixed your nose." I assumed, remembering August and my initial meeting in that alley. "...the first time."

"Looks like I'll have to do it again," Damian sighed.

August's mouth hinted at a flicker of a smile before he continued. "This is Celeste," he indicated the intense female. A large golden eagle swooped in to perch next to her on the porch railing. She absentmindedly stroked the large bird's feathers.

"Animaglia," I said, and she nodded in confirmation. A High Fae with control over animals, like the infamous High King.

"I'm Teale," the nymph introduced herself. "My gift is mindcasting but I'm sure you already guessed that. My specialty is illusions. I would show you except I still can't manage to penetrate your shield, even after the ash."

"Impressive," August murmured. "Teale is even more gifted than the Deimos." I tensed at the name.

"And much less sadistic," she added, frowning at him.

As I looked at the four, I began to feel less wary of them, a calmness coming over me. I felt more at ease like I could trust—

My head snapped to the fae out of my line of sight. Specifically, a male. He was tall, with tan skin and white hair, his eyes so dark they were nearly black.

A low, rumbling snarl broke from my lips. "What are you doing?"

The male was a mindcaster as well, and he'd just been attempting to manipulate my emotions, trying to slip under my shields—no, *blend* with them in an effort to bring down my guard. It was a tactic that was difficult to perceive, to notice in its subtlety. I'd only felt it once before.

The bone white hair, tan skin, mindcasting. It was much too similar to—a double-bladed sword of diamond-hard ice formed in my hand.

"Shai, stand down now," August said firmly as his eyes remained on me.

"Why did we even bother with the ash?" Damian whispered to Miranda, who snorted.

My eyes were still on the male, on Shai. I was blind to anything else except the person who was so remarkably similar to Adrienne. The blistering rage I felt toward her rose up. Rage for what she'd ordered done to my family, to me—my body pulsed with the need to attack.

I sensed August shift ever so slightly to come between us. "He is not a Deimos. Yes, he is from the same region but he has no relation to them, no allegiance."

My body still thrummed with my remaining power, but my tension eased somewhat at his voice.

Shai's voice was like his power, cool and calming. "I meant no harm, Princess. I was merely trying to diffuse your wariness. You appeared to be relaxed but were not. An adder that feigns sleep." His tone was soft but not contrite, no apology there.

I stood more erect, relaxing my posture to demonstrate I was no longer going to attack, but my eyes never left the male.

August was still facing me, his body angled between us. "How did you sense that?" He said quietly.

"Do you really believe my aunts would allow my sister and me to be within miles of Adrienne and Alexander without adequate training?" I snapped, finally pulling my gaze from Shai to look up at him. My hand tightened on that weapon of ice.

"Never. But Shai's gifts are different. His methods allow him to mimic an individual's mental shields, to slip through them undetected. I've never seen anyone but another mindcaster sense it until now."

"My training was very good," I said simply, then turned back to the male, Shai.

"Do not ever try that on me again, mindcaster. Because every time you will find that though I am immune to your gifts, you are not immune to *mine*." I let the warning hang in the air as the weapon of ice slowly shrank back into my palm, but I kept a coating of frost over my hand. A reminder of the deadly cold that crept beneath my skin. The male nodded in understanding. He would heed my warning, but I knew he would keep a close eye on me, regardless.

I finally pulled my gaze from him to take in the other two more closely. Another male and a female with white feathered wings. *Seraph.*

The Seraphim were winged faeries that hailed from the northernmost mountains. Built similarly to the High Fae, they were renowned warriors and experts in battle strategy. Their people split and fought with both the rebels and loyalists in the Great War, leading to catastrophic casualties on each side. Because of this, there weren't many of their kind left.

August noticed my gaze on her. "Jophiel, the Commander of my armies."

The female was tall, nearly as tall as August. Muscular, powerful, with pale skin and short blonde hair. With the fighting leathers and wings, she looked formidable. I wouldn't have liked my chances against her magicless, though even if I was at full capacity it would still be a challenge. The Seraphim were truly a warrior race not unlike the Khutulun.

The male she stood next to was her same height. He had dark skin and short black hair, almost like a halo that framed his face. His dark brown eyes were warm, ears rounded like Miranda's. He appeared to be somewhere in his fourth decade. August nodded to him, "Simon, my third behind Julian."

"Another human?" I turned to face August again.

"Yes, head of my council and spymaster. He and Shai work closely together." His eyebrows raised. "You sound surprised for a princess with humans on her own council."

"I just didn't expect you to be so...equitable."

Simon spoke then. "As far as the kingdoms have progressed since the war, there are still those that see humans as no better than the animals, meant only to serve. It makes spying that much easier when those we are surrounded by act as if we don't exist. Although the Briars were always more than fair to humans in their realm." He said his words with a warm smile. His voice was elegant, thoughtful. Simon's words warmed me to him, complimenting my parents was always a good way to ensure that. Regardless, he led Montevalle's spies, and I knew I couldn't allow myself to be lulled into complacency around him.

Damian spoke up then. "Sorry about the constraints we had to place on you, Princess. Considering where you came from and all that has happened, we really couldn't be too careful." He said, a bit sheepish. A full turn from Shai, I could feel that Damian genuinely felt bad. Though he shouldn't have, I would've done the same.

"Understandable, and you can stop calling me Princess. My name is Nic. I should also thank you for healing me, for finding me when you had." There was no doubt I wouldn't have survived the shadowhound's venom if they hadn't gotten to me so quickly.

August's head whipped back to me. "What happened?" His silver eyes grew cold as he looked at me more closely, assessing for injuries.

"It's nothing, August. I'm fine now—clearly."

"What. Happened." He repeated, less a question than a command.

I rolled my eyes. "Adrienne's guards caught up to me in the Redwood. We fought. The blood must have attracted shadowhounds and I was bitten. I landed at the border and crossed the wards. They—" I indicated the four, "—found me, gave me the antivenom, healed me, locked me up. I escaped, you caught me, and here we are. That's it." I left out the Nemean lion that had saved me. It was a piece I couldn't understand, why the great cat would have bothered risking his life for mine.

August's eyes were still hard as they caught on the freshly healed bite on my forearm then quickly to the line of pink flesh on my other palm. I crossed my arms to hide it from his sight.

He grabbed it, yanking my arm away from my torso and turning over my palm. "What is this?"

"You're fussier than a mother hen, you know that?" I snapped as I tried to pull my hand back, irritated, but August's hold wouldn't give. I sighed. "I grabbed the blade of one of the guard's swords to disarm him."

"Were you successful?" He drew a finger across the pink scar, so softly I hardly felt it.

"Of course I was." I yanked my hand back, successfully this time. Damian suppressed his cough that sounded suspiciously like a laugh.

"So the Briars can fight. How exciting." Teale whispered to someone, amused.

"Of course, they can," Celeste murmured back. "Think of who raised them."

"Why didn't you just winnow away when the guards found you? Why did you fight?" August asked.

"I stayed hoping I would overhear news of what was happening at the palace or anything about Misha, the guards said they thought she had escaped with your brother, but then they began to...insinuate things. Things they would do if they found her."

August nodded in understanding. "Did any of them follow you?"

"No."

"Are you sure?"

"Yes," I hissed.

"How can you be certain?" He pressed.

"Because that blood your councilors found me covered in? It wasn't all mine."

His eyes flickered with relief. "How many were there?"

"Four." I lied.

August smiled appreciatively as he motioned toward the cabin. "Come. Let's go inside. There is much more to discuss."

CHAPTER 37
Nic

I took note of the cabin's furnishings as we re-entered through the door I'd burst out of only a handful of minutes ago. The dark wooden walls were covered in colorful art, varied rugs scattered across the hardwood floors, and the space was filled comfortable furniture that at once did not match and yet fit together seamlessly.

"Who lives here?"

"Miranda and Damian permanently," August answered, wiping the now dried blood from his face with a damp towel that had come from Miranda. "This is Montevalle's southwestern border outpost, one of the locations where my council and I can meet to strategize privately, especially if there was to be a threat from Hahnaley. Which there now is."

Everyone walked to the large dining table to the right of the great room. I removed Eve's bow from my back, setting it on the table before me with the

Iradelmar as I sat in a chair near the right corner. Jophiel glanced at the sword, recognition alighting in her eyes.

August sat at the head of the table on my right. Damian quickly reset his nose with a crack, and a second later it was healed with the golden magic cast from his hands.

The chair on my left scraped across the floor as Celeste pulled it out and took a seat.

"The Seven are my most trusted council, and we will be working from here while the situation with Adrienne is assessed." August wiped away the fresh blood that had come from resetting his nose, then set the towel down. "The cabin is heavily warded. We can sense any movement at the perimeter located in a hundred meter radius around us, and there is no winnowing in or out of it except those with express permission. Which is only those you see here as well as Julian and my stepmother, Sena."

"Do I get that privilege?" I asked, already knowing what his answer would be.

"Not yet. Not until I am sure you won't leave impulsively." August said like I hadn't just agreed to stay. I quite literally had nowhere else to go.

"Speaking of, how did you break down that ward after we ashed you?" Celeste inquired, her eyes hard as her fingers thrummed against the table.

"Brute force." I gave her an icy smile in return. Her fingers stilled.

August's brows raised, an unreadable thought swirling in his eyes. "The force of what?"

"My hands—don't look so surprised."

"I am not, only..." His gaze traveled down to appraise them. "Intrigued."

I crossed my arms, tucking my hands underneath so he would stop looking at them.

A smile flickered on his lips before he became more solemn. "We need you to tell us what you know, Nic—" August's words stopped short. "Nic. Anything you saw or can remember, even from the celebrations or before could be useful."

I stared down at my hands as I spoke, telling them about how Alesia and Eve were given false information about the skinwalkers the morning after the ball—a ruse to draw them into the woods. How they'd attacked my aunts and me with the ash, how they'd killed them. I didn't mention how Alesia had chosen to sacrifice herself.

August's eyes never left my face. When I finished, he said with a deep exhale. "I am so sorry. I know how much your aunts cared for you and your sister."

With a curt nod, my eyes met his. I saw the sincerity in them but would say no more about it. Not now, possibly not ever.

He quickly continued, "Did the guards say what they were sent to do? To kill you or take you hostage?"

"I killed two immediately and kept one alive to question. He said that Adrienne ordered them killed, and she wanted me brought to her—that she wanted my heart. I suspect she wanted to pull my magic from it, but I didn't know such a thing was possible."

"Unfortunately it is." Miranda sat across from me, leaning forward onto her elbows. "It is very old, very dark magic. Something that hasn't been used in a very long time. Killing a faerie to steal their magic will strengthen the murderer, but it can only be held in a vessel. Otherwise, the magic would work against them, tearing them apart from the inside. Adrienne wouldn't be able to wield it without binding it to such an object."

Thief, the naiad had called her, and I knew I wasn't the first Adrienne had hoped to steal from. How many others had she already killed in her quest for power?

"I am surprised my father never attempted it." August sneered, distaste in his eyes.

"He may have considered it, but it takes great skill to transfer the essence successfully. Not to mention the dark magic stains you. The more you use, the less your soul remains intact. There is always a great cost to such actions." Miranda explained. "Even he had the sense to fear such consequences."

August nodded then looked to me to continue with what I knew.

"After the guard told me everything, I ran north. Adrienne's guards caught up to me yesterday as you heard outside. As for Julian and Misha, I haven't seen them since the night of the ball." I finished.

August let out a breath, leaning back in his chair. "I haven't seen them since then either. They left together, but after the ball, Julian never returned to his quarters, I assumed he was with your sister. In the early hours of the morning, Miranda had a vision that something horrible was going to happen after sunrise. We searched, Shai and I, but couldn't find Julian anywhere, so we were forced to leave without him. According to Miranda's vision, to have any chance of finding him I needed to leave and return here." August explained.

His knuckles had gone white from where he was gripping the arms of his chair. Though it had been his only choice, I knew it tore at him. It was the same way I felt about leaving without Misha.

"I tried to find you, but you and your family had already gone," August went on. "I didn't know where." Something like pain flashed in his eyes.

He'd looked for me.

I pushed the feeling down, turning from him to Miranda. "The visions—what did they say of Julian? Of my sister?"

"That was the strange thing." She shook her head. "I only saw August in my visions, not Julian. He was suddenly hidden from me when he never had been before. Not until that night."

"Miranda has been scrying for Julian using my blood," August said. "We can sense that he lives, but we don't know where. The crystal refuses to land. He and Misha could be hiding behind wards, but Miranda has always been able to find people in those situations. She could not search for Misha as we had no personal effects of hers, though with you here we may be able to."

"Though I don't know how successful I will be." Miranda crossed her arms. "I have never seen you or your twin with the Sight before. Adrienne either. It's like you are all shielded somehow."

"How is that possible?" I leaned forward, nearer to the witch.

"I have no idea," Miranda answered honestly.

"But we can try? To look for Misha?" I tried not to hope, especially as Miranda wasn't able to see us in her visions, but I had to attempt it, even if August had not been able to find Julian's location with the scrying. Misha and I were twins, they were half brothers...maybe it would be different

As Miranda nodded, August waved his hand. A map of the continent unfolded before us. The witch took a crystal from her pocket, amethyst on a chain of silver, and a tiny knife of Galorian silver.

"Your hand," She said, reaching for mine. I placed it in hers, palm up. She took the small knife and nicked the pad of my middle finger. Taking it in hers she squeezed, letting the blood drip over the amethyst. As she released me, Miranda began chanting words in a language I'd never heard, the crystal twirling around the map as she spoke. All of our eyes were glued to it. The amethyst spun and spun for a long minute, but never landed.

Miranda sighed. Disappointment flooded her eyes as she looked up at me, a silent apology. "The magic is unable to track her. Even with your blood, Nic."

I nodded. She'd tried. It was the most I could ask of her. "What about the Shaws?" I sighed, changing the subject. "Gemma, Lorraine, and Evander?"

Simon spoke up on Miranda's other side, "We are unsure, though it is likely they are still in Sanserria. They have not returned to Desdemon, we know that for sure."

My heart panged. Though things had ended poorly between Evander and me, I still cared for him, for Gemma—even Lorraine. I knew what they must have been feeling with the loss of both parents.

I turned back to August. "What will happen now that the treaty has been broken? Adrienne attacked my family and murdered Orelia and Cedric. She's betrayed us all." He, Adrienne, and Alexander were now the only living forgers of the Blood Treaty.

"The blood pact was made to ensure peace, that no one would betray the others. If one of the royal bloodlines attacked another, they would be marked by a red mark on the forehead. The Mark of the Traitor." August drew out the symbol with his finger on the wood. A Scythe tilted on its side.

"That's it?" I gaped. "They won't lose their magic or be cursed or *anything*?" It seemed like a lot of build-up around the blood pact just to be marked on the forehead.

"Oh, it was discussed." August hissed, equally frustrated. "Your parents in particular pushed for the stripping of magic in the case of betrayal, and I agreed. Unfortunately, we were outnumbered by my father, both Deimos and Shaws. I think my father and the Deimos were already planning to break it. The Shaws were too trusting and thought that such harsh punishment meant that we didn't trust our newfound peace. But the red mark will have more of an impact than you think. Adrienne will be branded a traitor, marked forever by what she has done." He finished as I fumed. Of course, Adrienne and her brother pushed for no real punishment.

Simon leaned forward, his hands clasped together. "Adrienne must already be marked though no one has seen her to confirm. Her new Commander addressed the people of Hahnaley claiming August attacked and killed you and the others, and Julian kidnapped Misha against her will. Adrienne did not appear herself as she is said to be in mourning for you all."

A low hiss broke from my throat. "She claims to mourn the murders she ordered herself?" Adrienne was despicable.

"Yes," Simon nodded. "And she's using the Warins as the scapegoat for her betrayal."

"I wonder how long that story will hold up now that the princess is indeed alive," Jophiel added from the opposite end of the table. Adrienne did prematurely announce my death, too confident she already possessed my heart. And with Misha missing, I was the only one that could speak out against her version of the events, the only one that could clear the Warins' name.

"No one is going to know she is alive, not yet," August said.

"Why not? We need to expose her lies as soon as possible." I turned back to him, disbelief written on my face as well as the other's.

August didn't back down. "Adrienne wants you. Badly. We are not going to announce to everyone where you are so she can find you faster. You will remain in hiding until we can ensure your safety, until we can find our siblings."

"And how do you suppose we do that? I am not hiding here like some coward—not while Misha is still missing," I seethed.

"I never said you were." August's eyes softened just a fraction. "But we need to remain close to the West and as hidden as possible while we search for Julian and Misha. This cabin and the town nearby are heavily warded, but would be vulnerable in an attack from any army Adrienne would march here to collect you, and I cannot mobilize my own armies here as that would be a giveaway as to my own location. Adrienne knows you were traveling north and is clever enough to recognize your plans. She has to know you've crossed the border and are in Montevalle by now—that you've sought me out for help."

August made valid points. "So what do you suggest we do?" I leaned back.

"We stay here and keep searching covertly, keep meeting with the spies for any information. Once we have them safely returned, we can go to our capital. Even if Adrienne brings the might of all three kingdoms, she won't be able to breach our walls. Then both you and Misha can dismiss her lies as we plan the counterattack—maybe even sway the Hahnaleyan and Desdemonan armies to our side."

I frowned. It was a good plan.

"But everyone is going to think the North is responsible until then," Jophiel said, making another good point. I couldn't have August and Julian take the fall for the betrayal, and let everyone believe they were the traitors, even if only temporarily.

August answered. "It won't be for long, Jophiel. The other kingdoms already fear me—feared my father. That is why it was so easy for Adrienne to sell her story. Getting them to believe otherwise would take more time than we have. They'd sooner believe I'd kidnapped and subdued Nic with my own mindcasters than think we are united. So right now, the only priority is finding Julian and

Misha and keeping her," his eyes flicked to me, "hidden. It is our only focus. Nothing else matters."

August was willing to take the fall to help find Julian and my sister, image and pride be damned. He may have been a better male than I'd given him credit for until now.

I turned to Simon. "Spymaster, you brought up your resources earlier, that you are hoping to hear from them." He nodded slowly, tensing. "How long has Montevalle had spies in Hahnaley? In my home?"

"Nic—" August started.

I cut my gaze to him. "*How. Long.*"

He still leaned toward me, unflinching. "Since Adrienne arrived. Ten years ago."

"And they so willingly turned on my family? Changed in their allegiance?" I spat, calling back the heat that had once again risen in my hands. We'd treated our guards and staff like equals and provided for them handsomely. Some were like family to Misha and me.

"No, they were very hard to persuade, but the palace staff and guards that eventually agreed to share information with us were never disloyal to you or your family." August clarified. "The opposite is true. They never once shared information about you, your sister, father, or aunts. You all were kept out of this. We only received information about Adrienne, of her movements, her conversations—her guards'. The spies we had in your palace cared for your family. They never betrayed you—only her. It appeared that the more loyal to your family they were, the more they were willing to turn on Adrienne."

"And in all that time, they heard nothing, saw *nothing* that could have prevented this?" I said incredulously.

"No," he shook his head. "Adrienne hid her plans too well. Her personal guards were impossible to infiltrate. The only warnings we had were Miranda's visions of something happening at the Blood Treaty celebrations—visions of conflict, a surge in power on the Solstice. But even those were vague and unclear." August sighed, his displeasure evident. We'd both missed the signs of what was to come.

I mulled over his words. *A surge in power.* That could have been Adrienne—or me.

"And you are not worried that Adrienne may look into the spies' minds? That she might see that their loyalty is not to her? She could have them killed or, if she's smart, begin to feed you false information." I inclined my head to Simon.

The spymaster shook his head. "The spies know the danger of their work, but it is very unlikely that Adrienne will be able to read them. Alesia," a stab went through my heart at her name, "had all of the staff trained in mental shield work. Not as impenetrable as yours, but Adrienne would spend very little time in a mind that she believes so far beneath her. They show her what she wants to see, dutiful thoughtless servants, and she moves on. Besides, Shai can confirm their honesty. That is something they do not have the skill to shield from."

I let out a breath, appeased for now.

"I think that's enough for today. We can rest and reconvene in the morning." August said as he pushed back from the table.

I wanted to disagree, to continue strategizing on how to find my sister, but my eyelids felt like lead, exhausted after not having slept properly in days—not to mention filthy.

"I can show you to your room." Teale leaned around from Celeste's other side. "It won't be the same one, I promise." Such a bright personality made it easy to warm to her. It reminded me of Misha. Though I had to remember hers and Shai's skill set.

I nodded to her before standing to follow.

"It's on the third floor, where the only unoccupied room is now that everyone has returned," Teale explained as we climbed the stairs. The place was even more spacious than I'd thought. The trees must've obscured portions of it from the outside. "You will have a lovely view up here though the room is small, but there is an attached bathing chamber. I'm sure it's not what you are used to," she said with a small apologetic smile.

"I'm sure it will be great. Thank you for accommodating me." I tried to return her smile but faltered. I hoped she didn't take it as a grimace.

On the third floor a door sat straight ahead and another around the stair railing to the left. Teale opened the one nearest us.

It was a small room with a moderately-sized bed, a three-drawer dresser with an oval mirror hanging over it on one side, a small end table, and chair on the other. Near us sat an armoire for clothing and weapons. The walls were a soft white with dark wood molding around the ceiling and a large window on the opposite wall. From it, the roof extended covered in cedar tiles and the lush forest was visible.

"We can borrow some clothes from Celeste until someone has the chance to go into the village to get more, you look to be about the same size. Through there is the bathing room." She indicated a door to my left.

Teale walked toward it, opening the door as she beckoned me inside. I ran my fingers over the wooden vanity, noting the intricately-patterned blue and white tile floor.

"Here are the linens," Teale said as she reached into a small cabinet. "The water is always hot or cold to your liking in either the shower or the bath." She nodded to a clawfoot tub. "The magic ensures they never run out." She handed me a towel and soft linen robe in dark green. "I can leave you now to get washed up, but don't hesitate to let any of us know if you need anything, Nicole."

I wouldn't be going to Shai or Celeste after our rough start, and Jophiel was much too intimidating to approach for anything trivial like clothing or linens. But my gut told me I could trust Teale. Miranda, Damian, and Simon as well.

"Nic, you can call me Nic. Everyone else does."

Teale smiled warmly in response, then closed the door behind her as she left, giving me privacy.

I chose to take a shower first, then a bath. I needed to wash all the grime from my body and hair, to free it of the dirt and blood that still coated it.

Afterward, I ran a bath with scalding water, bubbles, and a jasmine scented oil from a basket near the tub. I took a brush and scrubbed at my skin until I was pink all over. No amount of bathing could erase the image of my aunts' blood on my hands, though I'd nearly scoured myself raw in trying.

When I finished I sat still for a moment, staring blankly at the ceiling, then cast a silencing ward around the room. After it was in place, I sank below the surface of the water and finally let it pour out of me, the sorrow and pain and grief. I let out all the tears and sobs I'd been holding in since my aunts' deaths. The water churned, my control of the element allowing me to stay under for longer than most.

Something about going underwater made it feel less real, like the past few days hadn't happened, and I would emerge on the surface at home in my own chambers. Alesia, Eve, and Misha waiting for me just down the hall.

After what felt like an eternity, I rose to the surface for air.

I wasn't home. I was in the North. Everyone I loved was gone, and I was still wrecked. The pieces of my heart only held together by the sheer force of will that kept me from splitting open completely. The only thing that would keep me going was that Misha was somewhere out there, alive, waiting for me to find her.

Slowly I rose and stepped out of the tub to dry myself with one of the towels laid out by Teale, then donned the dark green robe. It was much too big, but the linen was soft against my raw skin.

I walked back into the bedroom and to the small dresser near the bed. There I placed the Iradelmar and Eve's yew bow. I knew that the armoire was the more appropriate place to store them, but I didn't think I could stand to be so far from my aunt's belongings.

I needed to see them.

Spinning one of my aunt's mating bands around my finger, unable to tell the plain rings apart, I looked down at the weapons, fighting to keep from falling into more tears.

Then I laid on the bed, climbing under the dark blue duvet and ivory sheets. I submerged myself in the pillows and plush bedding, as I shut my eyes and drifted off into oblivion.

CHAPTER 38
Nic

W hen I awoke, my face was wet from the tears streaming down my face. I looked around the room as I returned to the realization of where I was.

Dark blue bedding, wood furniture. The golden light of late afternoon streamed in from the window. I was in Montevalle, in an outpost with August and seven others. I was safe...for now.

But Alesia and Eve were dead. And Misha was still missing.

My hand reached for the orb that hung on the bracelet at my wrist, but I stopped myself. I couldn't touch it, couldn't stand to see the memories of all the family I'd lost—not yet.

I wiped away the residual tears and sleep from my eyes as I pushed back the covers. Based on the sun, it looked as if I had slept a few hours, but I still felt exhausted—and starving. I saw that the clothes I arrived in were washed and folded on the dresser. A small note sat on top.

We found clothes for you. They are in the armoire. – Teale

Pulling open the carved wooden doors, I found several pairs of pants, shirts, and training leathers. Even boots and socks.

I reached for a pair of black loose-fitting pants and a pale green sleeveless shirt. The clothes fit just slightly too large due to my lack of substantial food during my time in the woods, but they were comfortable and easy to move in. I tucked my mother's ruby pendant under the collar, hesitating on its touch. I left my hair long and loose in waves down my back, too lazy to braid it back. My stomach rumbled as I turned away from the mirror to make my way downstairs in search of food.

Miranda and Damian were cooking together in the kitchen. He looked up from chopping vegetables and quickly planted a kiss on the side of her head atop her thick, curled hair. She smiled at him, her dark eyes shining. My heart stuttered. They looked at each other like Alesia and Eve had.

Shai leaned over a map of the continent on the main table, this one with more landmarks of Montevalle than any other map I'd seen. He slowly began to roll it up as I approached. I couldn't blame him.

"She awakens," Damian said chipperly, just noticing my presence.

Miranda paused from mixing the stir fry. "How are you feeling?"

"I'm still tired, but better now that I've slept for a few hours."

They gave each other a look. "Nic, you've been asleep for more than a day," Miranda said, concern in her eyes.

I shouldn't have been surprised by that, even if I still felt exhausted. "Any news?" I pulled out a stool from the large island and sat.

"Not that I know of. We'll know more when the others return," Miranda said

"Where did they go?" I said a bit too quickly. I would be furious if they'd gone off on some tip of Misha and Julian's whereabouts and no one had woken me to join.

Miranda noted my concern. "They just went to the border." Then she returned to her cooking.

"And get ready for when Teale gets back." Damian said, looking up. "Now that you've rested, she wants to know where she can get boots like yours, with the knives in the soles." I remembered her saying that when I was eavesdropping.

"What are they doing at the border? Did something happen?"

"No," Shai answered from his new spot leaning against the kitchen island opposite me. "August wanted to make sure no one tried to follow after you, scout the area. They should be back within the hour."

"Yes, it won't be long now." Miranda came to sit beside me. "How is your magic doing?"

"I'm at about half of my normal capacity. Two more days and I should be at full strength again." I said. The sleep and the food had helped. I was regaining it much faster than I had in the Redwood.

Miranda seemed surprised by this. My confusion to her reaction must have been evident on my face as she said, "I hit you with enough ash to keep most fae down for a week."

"Demi-fae, remember?" I pulled my hair back behind one ear. "My mother and aunt are half—were half human."

"I knew you would be less hindered by it, but still to be able to recover so quickly is surprising...we definitely didn't hit you with enough," she said with a hint of humor.

I tried to give her a quick smile, though it didn't quite reach my eyes. We all fell into silence as Damian finished preparing the meal.

"Is there anything I can help with?" I offered, restless as I sat there watching.

"You can help us set the table," Damian said. "The plates are in the cabinet here," he pointed to a cabinet on his left, "and the silverware is in the drawer below."

I walked to where he'd indicated, hesitating as I opened the door. "Everyone is coming?" I asked, unsure of how many plates to grab.

"Yes, everyone will be back," Miranda answered. That made nine plates for the Seven, August, and me.

I took the plates and silverware over to the large dining table and began setting them out. I was so used to casual dinners with my own family, Alesia and Eve cooking for my sister and me, that it took me a moment to realize there were no staff here. The cabin only housed August and his council. I wondered why. If it was for secrecy or if it was as Alé had deduced, that August Warin cared nothing for the finery that came with being king of one of the four kingdoms. I was still laying out silverware and mulling over this as the others returned.

The Seven greeted each other and then began talking about the scouting trip. Keeping my gaze down as I listened, I gleaned that there was nothing of note at the border. They didn't believe I was followed, an unnecessary precaution since I'd killed all the guards, but I could understand why they'd want to be sure. I stopped eavesdropping as they transitioned into small talk and returned my focus back on my task of table setting.

I felt footsteps coming toward me and knew who it would be without having to look up.

"Whose idea was it to let you hold so many knives?" August asked from where he stood behind me.

I flipped one in my palm before setting it down next to a plate. "Is the great King in the North afraid of an ashed demi-fae with some butter knives?"

"*You* don't require fancy weapons or magic to be lethal."

I snorted at his assessment, but he wasn't wrong.

"How are you feeling?" he said, his voice softer as he came to stand at my side. Shrugging, I didn't look up and continued to the next place setting.

"Nic," he pushed. I finally looked up at him. His silver eyes churned with a concern I didn't want to think too deeply about.

"I'm fine, August." I sighed, then looked back to what I'd been doing. I felt August's continued gaze on me, assessing. Thankfully, he didn't push me on it.

I'd noticed everyone else had gone silent during our interaction. I looked up at them, and they were all suddenly very interested in helping to bring the food to the table.

I sat in the same seat I had yesterday, but today Miranda sat at the head to my right and Teale took the chair to my left. Damian sat across from me at Miranda's right hand, August on his other side. Simon, Celeste, Shai, and Jophiel sat at the other end.

I wondered if it was a coincidence or if they were strategically surrounding me with those of the Seven I seemed to be most comfortable around.

As we began eating, everyone spoke of theories of where Julian and Misha might be, where they might have gone and why no one was able to contact the Prince, why I hadn't heard from Misha. I kept quiet as I listened, but in their conversation, it was clear that it was all speculation.

Nothing was new, nothing had changed.

I had no idea where Misha could be if not held captive, no clue where she would have run to except North. I'd never before fathomed that we would be separated—could be separated in this way. If she were able to reach out, if it didn't jeopardize her, I knew she would try. There was no possibility that she wasn't as equally desperate to find me as I was her. But if Adrienne didn't have her...what held her back?

I looked up at Miranda. "It was mentioned yesterday that you had visions of the treaty celebrations, of something happening." She nodded. "What did you see?"

She hesitated and I didn't miss the quick glance she threw to August before speaking. "It was more of a collection of vague images than a true picture of the future," she said. "I saw whispers of shadow, clocks striking midnight, sheep becoming wolves, and writhing, twisting vines careening from the earth. But mostly I saw power. It had no form or identity. It just *was*, and it was more than I'd ever felt before."

Similar to what the siren had seen then.

August spoke again, "We thought it would be you and your sister as you came into your twenty-second birthday on the Solstice. Misha particularly with the earth. Though with recent events—it is possible that the power seen was Adrienne."

"Is that why you came to the celebrations early?" I leaned forward. "Why you were in the city that morning?"

August nodded. "Simon, Shai, and I were to meet with one of the spies to get any knowledge on if things were shifting in the palace, with you and your sister's power especially, but the spy wouldn't tell us. They only shared Adrienne's increasing secrecy. They believed that she was planning something." August said.

I took a breath, "There was a siren, also a Seer. She showed me images like the ones you described."

"That was why she took you," August murmured, understanding alighting in his eyes. I nodded, then explained to Miranda what she'd shown me. The similarities and the differences.

"What kind of power is she playing with then?" Jophiel said from the other end, leaning toward us. "For you," she inclined her head to Miranda, "and a siren to see such visions? To deem them so important?"

"Unfortunately as she is somehow shielded, only time will tell," the witch answered.

August nodded to the Seraph. "You and I will go to the capital at some point, ready the armies. It can't hurt to have them on standby until we know Adrienne's next move."

I wondered—"Adrienne wanted to steal my magic by taking my heart. Do you think it's possible that I was not her first target? That she's stolen others' to give herself the power you described in the vision?"

"I don't think it's only possible," August said. "I think it is very, very likely."

Shai added, "Adrienne only had her own power during the war, the mind-casting. If she has begun to covet and steal power from other High Fae, this is a relatively new development."

"She's always been a schemer—untrustworthy," August scowled. I remembered how he'd rarely spoken to her in our time during the celebrations. The one time I saw them interact he was cold and reticent. His eyes softened with something like regret as he leaned toward me. "If I'd had any idea of what she planned to do, Nic, I would have tried to stop it. I would have gone to Alesia immediately."

My throat constricted. I couldn't move for the pain that filled my chest at her name, couldn't take the way they were all looking at me now. Finally moving, I shifted in my seat, turning to Teale on my left. "You are like me, not fully High Fae."

"I am not," Teale said, the corners of her mouth lifting. "I am dryad on my Mother's side."

"It's what makes her hair so cool," Celeste said, before taking another bike of food.

"What happens to your hair?" It was short, not coming past her ears, curly, and a brilliant shade of gold. Beautiful though not uncommon.

"It shifts with the seasons," Teale shrugged, tearing apart a roll. "Gold in the summer, red in autumn, a pale blue in the winter, and pink in spring. I have wings too."

My eyebrows raised. I hadn't noticed that she had any, not like I had Jophiel. The Seraph ruffled her feathers subconsciously.

Teale lifted the sleeve of her shirt. "They're similar to gossamer. They cling to my skin when not in use. Down my back and along my arms. I can unfurl them when necessary." Sure enough, there was gold veining laced down her arms, not unlike a dragonfly's wings.

"With you being dryad, would you be able to sense Adrienne's magic if she neared, the stolen aspects at least, as it doesn't conform to nature?" I asked, remembering the naiad's words.

Teale pondered this. "Yes, I think I could. Nature despises the unnatural. Though as I am not fully dryad it may be more difficult. I could ask the trees, though they don't always share with me."

My brow pinched. "Why not?"

"I am only half dryad and have lived most of my life with the High Fae. My mother gave me up when I was young. I couldn't become a wisp of the trees as she could, and a fully corporeal faeling was too difficult for her to care for, so I lived with my father. Hence the nymphs are more reluctant to share their secrets with me. Though with the increasing threat, they may be more open to it. I have heard the wind and trees whispering more than normal lately."

I nodded. It gave me some relief she had not heard of my emergence of fire, that I could keep to myself for now. At least until I saw Adrienne again—then I would blow her to hell.

Teale took her opportunity to ask a more probing question as I'd warmed to her. "How did you withstand mine and Shai's mindcasting? I mean no offense, of course. It is just that Shai is over two hundred years old, and I am 133 this year. We've been at this for three centuries between us. As young as you are, it fascinates me how talented you are in keeping us out."

"The High Priestess of Oscuri trained us." The conversations at the other end of the table quieted at my statement.

Jophiel dropped a fork. "Katarina trained you? Herself?"

I nodded.

"How?" Shai leaned forward on the seraph's right, more intrigued by this than anything else I'd said thus far. "Once the Oscuri take their oaths, they do not leave their home. The war was the only exception."

"My aunt, Eve, saved the High Priestess's life in the war and she pledged a favor in return. Over that time, Katarina became friends with her and Alé. When our father announced he was to marry Adrienne, Eve asked her—begged her to come, to train us all in shielding. She and her three strongest mindcasters came in secret to Hahnaley, and we trained directly with them for three months before Adrienne's arrival. Alé hid the lessons even from my father." I touched the bracelet on my wrist but not twirling it to keep the memories locked away.

"That makes sense then, how you were able to sense my magic," Shai said. "Katarina taught me that method during the war as a way to feel out other's intentions."

Teale chimed in, "Even during the healing, the day we found you, I could only get through enough to make you sleep. I couldn't see anything else, couldn't influence you. But even then it felt like your mind was open to it, like it was seeking the darkness—the oblivion."

I was sure that I had been not just seeking solace from the physical pain, but the agony of the loss of my family.

Looking around the table, there were too many eyes on me. Too much interest in my direction. "I'm going to call it a night," I said to no one in particular as I pushed back from the table. I'd eaten plenty in order to keep my strength, and now just wanted to return to my solitude.

"We will train tomorrow. All of us," August said. "Unless there is any new information."

I dipped my head in acknowledgment as I took my plate and silverware back to the kitchen. The others stood from the table as well, each of us clearing our plates. Simon was on wash duty, one of the other Seven announced.

While everyone else stayed to talk and strategize below, I trudged up the stairs alone. After I reached my room, I ran another bath and drifted below the water.

Then I let myself once again drown in my agony.

CHAPTER 39
Nic

T he next morning, the rest of the house seemed to be still asleep as I made my way to the kitchen in search of tea, still in my nightclothes and the overly large green robe. As I reached the bottom of the steps, I hesitated.

August stood in the kitchen, his back to me as a kettle heated on the stove. He was dressed in training leathers already. My breath stilled, and I began to retreat, unsure if I was ready to be in his company alone—not after the way we'd left things on the Solstice.

"Good morning." August turned from the window to face me.

I frowned and gave up on my escape. How was it I was able to sneak past everyone except him? Well...except that first night.

The kettle whistled as I sat at the island. August moved quietly and efficiently, taking a mug and gently dumping a tea bag in the water. I looked out the window as I sat, waiting for him to finish as I watched a blue jay flitting between the trees and the posts of the porch.

August set down the mug before me. I frowned. "I could have made my own."

"You can drink it, it isn't poisoned." He said and I glared back at him.

Making tea was something I always did very particularly. Misha had often teased me about it, my rigidity. But he'd already made it, and if I didn't take it now I would be a jerk. I took a sip, and it was exactly as I made it for myself. Not too light, not too strong, just enough sugar so that it wasn't bitter. My frown grew as I stared down at the cup.

August sighed, "What's wrong with it?"

I looked back up at him from under my lashes, my mouth set in a hard line. "Nothing."

"So, then what's the problem?"

"Nothing." I snapped. He gave me an exasperated look in response. "You made it right." I gave in.

August's mouth pulled into a soft smile. My eyes narrowed before I took another sip.

"What's with all the grouchiness this morning?" Damian yawned as he came into the kitchen. "I had to put silencing wards up around Miranda to keep out the sound of you two. She would curse you both into next week if you woke her up so early with your grumbling."

I stood up quickly. "I'm going outside," I said, pushing away from the island.

Pulling open the door to the porch, I paused, turning. "Thank you for the tea," I murmured softly, but I knew August could hear me. I walked out before he could respond.

The words he'd said that night in the gardens rang unwilled in my head. *Untrue.*

Later that morning I stood in front of the targets, a birch arrow positioned in Eve's bow.

We each trained as a way to release our restlessness as we waited for any news from Simon's spies. To remain ready to go to them at a moment's notice.

The bow snapped as I released the arrow, striking the tiny discoloration I'd spotted four inches from the center. I hadn't missed yet, though a stationary target was no real challenge.

"No bullseyes?" August commented as he sidled up next to me.

"The ash affects my eyesight and therefore my aim," I lied.

"Does it?" he asked with an arched brow.

"You can see that it has." I snapped, hoping he assumed my irritation was from my aim being questioned.

"Hmm." August mused before walking away.

I continued to practice for another half hour, enjoying my solitary training and focusing on my breathing, until my fingers were raw. Only then did I walk back toward the others.

Celeste leaned against a table while she rested, escaping the bright sun in the shadow of a tree. "Let's spar, Princess. Let's see how Western training compares to the North."

"Maybe another time."

"It is okay to be scared. With the remaining Seraphim loyal to Montevalle, we can't expect the other countries to be so well versed in the combat arts," Celeste mocked. I stiffened.

"Cel—" Miranda started.

"No," I held up a hand, cutting her off. "She's right. I'm sure I could learn a lot from this." I painted a soft, non-threatening smile on my face as I sat Eve's bow on a rack where it wouldn't be disturbed. "Sparring only, no magic."

"No magic. No weapons." Celeste confirmed. Then we stepped into the ring, her brown eyes gleaming with excitement. "First to yield loses."

She struck first and I blocked her easily. We went on like this for a minute with a series of well timed hits and blocks. Celeste even threw in a few kicks that I dodged easily. She was fast. Good—very good.

Against my instincts I dropped my arm, leaving myself open as I let myself miss the block as Celeste's fist connected with my jaw. This kind of pain I could take, but the agony I couldn't escape since I'd watched my aunts—

Celeste struck harder than I'd anticipated, and it knocked me to a knee. No sound came from me as I took the hit, but the coppery tang of blood filled my mouth.

"Well, that was quick." She taunted me, thinking I would yield. I spat the blood onto the dirt next to my hand. I was done with this. No more pulling hits.

I quickly stood and swung my right hand in a cross—a distraction. She blocked my blow just as my other hand collided with her lower ribs, the ones she'd been neglecting to protect all morning. Celeste hissed in pain. Then I struck with a kick and spun into her, as I did so I connected the sharp point of my elbow with her nose. She stumbled again, her foot catching over mine where I'd planted it next to hers. She hit the ground hard as I stood over her.

"Yield," she said, knowing I had her. "That was a dirty move."

"Must be my Western training." I held my hand out to her.

Celeste took it. I kept hold of it as she stood, drawing her close to me. "That was me holding back. That was me holding back at *half* capacity from the ash. Don't ever disrespect my family's training again." I hissed.

When I pulled back I expected to see fury or anger, something I would have felt if I'd been in her place, but instead she...smiled. Not mocking or teasing, but knowing. "Good." She wiped away the blood from her nose that had begun to run down her chin. "Damian, my nose needs a mend," she shouted as she walked away.

Afterward, I went to one of the tables where carafes of water sat under the shade of a large oak. As I drank, I overheard Simon and August talking.

"It is inadvisable. We are having a hard time getting to our contacts there. Several of them have fled to the borders. The ones that remain are unable to reach out without putting them in danger of being discovered." Simon said.

"Regardless, we need information. Any information. We'll go tomorrow." August replied.

"Go where?" I walked over to them. Simon nodded to me in greeting before he stood to join Teale, who had just motioned that she wanted to speak to him.

I stood over August as answered me. "Now that you are more recovered, Jophiel, Shai, Simon, and I are going scouting. Trying to see if we can reach any of our contacts in Sanserria through our network."

"Were you not going to mention this?" I hissed.

"I just did," August said as he leaned back in his seat.

"I'm going." I crossed my arms.

"No, you aren't."

"Yes, I am." I snarled, leaning forward. "I decided to stay here so we could find them. *Together*. You can't expect me to wait around while Misha is the gods only know where."

August's jaw clenched. "Adrienne is hunting for you. It's too dangerous for you to be in Hahnaley where anyone could easily recognize you. Besides, we don't know what we could be walking into. My spies are hard to reach right now, so I know nothing of her plans or how many guards Adrienne has out patrolling in case you return."

"I snuck out into the city before with no issues, and I can handle her and any of her guards."

"You think the guards don't know to be looking for cloaked females with their faces covered? In the dead of summer?" My stomach tightened. He might have had a point. August continued, "Besides, Celeste just nearly had you on your ass."

"I can beat anyone here," I snarled, my pride getting the better of me.

August paused, contemplating as he read my face. Then he leaned forward, bracing himself on his knees. "Prove it. Let's make a deal. If you can beat each of the Seven and me, with no magic—you can go."

"Well I just beat Celeste and I've already beaten you so that's two down."

"You may have gotten the better of me in that room, but I wasn't really trying, Nic. And if memory serves me right, I got the better of you two days ago." August said as we both remembered how he'd caught me in my escape attempt from the cabin.

"I was ashed," I scowled.

"Yes, ashed but still capable of producing enough force to take down a trapping ward," August mused. My face heated as I fumed.

I considered sneaking out on my own to try to find information on Misha, though I had no idea where to even begin looking for my sister. Not to mention it would be difficult to try to do it on my own with little to no resources. I needed August's help, his spies, his information, even if I hated to admit it. The look on his face told me he knew it too.

"Fine." I hissed. "Damian—" He was seated nearby, just finishing healing Celeste's nose and ribs from where I'd struck her. "Can we spar? With swords?"

August's eyebrows shot up. "Going again so soon? That might not be wise."

"If I wanted your opinion, August, I would ask for it." I turned and walked back toward the ring. Someone, Shai from the sound of it, chuckled under his breath.

Damian smiled and joined me as I took a short sword from the rack. As he did the same, I wondered if there was anything that could ever ruin his lighthearted demeanor.

We stepped into the dirt ring and circled each other. I attacked first this time, now more eager to win, as I swiped my blade low at his core. Damian had anticipated the move and easily blocked it.

A second later he struck, swiping his sword down and across. I dropped my chest, spinning beneath his blade. I led with my outer elbow, moving faster than any ashed fae should have been able to.

I wasn't holding back now, no longer caring if I showed my hand. If I had to beat all of them into the dirt to convince August it was safe for me to join, so be it. If I couldn't hide the threat I was, I would make myself so threatening that no one dared challenge me.

When I came around, the sword in my right hand was blocking his—the dagger I'd hidden in the sleeve of my left forearm at his throat. The sparring match hadn't lasted more than a few seconds.

To Damian's credit, he only smiled and was unperturbed by the loss. His good-naturedness rivaled Misha and Gemma's. "Am I that easy to read?"

"Just before you strike, you shrug that shoulder up." I dropped the dagger, stepping back.

"And you caught that just this morning?"

Shai, who'd been quiet nearly all training, spoke then. "Diana and Alesia Sancrista spent over a hundred years living on the streets, where noticing the smallest of details meant eating or starving, living or dying. The princess is their protégé."

I blinked. I hadn't fully considered that others here besides August might have fought with them, might have known them. I wondered how well.

"No wonder you fight so dirty." Celeste snickered, her nose once again straight and free of blood.

"You do indeed move like your aunt," Jophiel said from where she stood watching us, leaning against a near tree. My heart squeezed painfully as I gave a curt nod, not wanting to talk about my family. "But you also move like Daiyu. You trained with her as well," the Seraph said appreciatively.

Daiyu was the Chief of the Khutulun Tribe we'd trained with. Undoubtedly the two warrior females had crossed paths once if not many times.

"In case you haven't noticed, Jo knows everyone. It's what happens when you're older than some of the peaks in the Mountains of Rei." Celeste teased, flitting a dagger back and forth between her fingers.

"I do not," Jophiel said flatly, her wings rustling. "I have no memory for the mediocre." Celeste snorted a laugh at this.

I turned back to August. "Two down."

"Three down." Simon joined us. "I know when I am at a loss. Not to mention that Teale just shared some interesting news with me."

August's eyebrows raised and I went still, wary of whatever he'd learned.

"She was finally able to connect mind to mind with one of our guards in Adrienne's personal forces." We all moved closer to Simon as he spoke. "The Shaws, Evander, Lorraine, and Gemma, remain in Sanserria with Adrienne. They do not appear to be aware of who actually orchestrated their parents' deaths as they remain guests in the palace."

"And they are unharmed?" I said, dread settling in my gut.

"Yes," Simon reassured me. "Adrienne needs them to control Desdemon. Evander has been named King following their parents' loss."

I breathed a sigh of relief. Gemma had shown great promise in her aircasting abilities. She was predicted to be the Heir after she came into her full power in two years' time. But as she was still young, still growing into her magic, Evander was the only one with enough power and experience to fill that role now.

Simon went on, "Adrienne needs the Shaws to believe that their parents' death was orchestrated by August to keep their armies on her side. If they continue to believe her lies, she has no reason to harm them."

I slid a glance at August. His face showed no change as if he was used to everyone believing the worst about him. I couldn't stand the feeling that boiled in my chest at the sight, hating that he had to accept the blame for their murder. That he would take the accusations without question, just to keep me hidden.

"Can we get them out?" I couldn't let my friends remain there with her, their parents' murderer.

August shook his head. "Not without significant risk. We can't prioritize it until we've found our siblings, until we can refute Adrienne's claims. Even if we showed up with you telling them otherwise, I won't risk them not believing us and alerting Adrienne. She won't hurt them, Nic," he reassured. "She needs the East as allies too badly."

I nodded, letting it go. Even if it made me horrible, Misha was my priority. I would find her, then we could free the Shaws together.

"That is only one part of the news Teale shared." Simon let out a breath, shifting uncomfortably. "It also seems that one of Adrienne's hunting parties went missing in the Redwood, over a hundred miles from our border. They were discovered yesterday—all eight found dead. A pack of shadowhounds nearby had also been slaughtered."

Everyone's eyes turned to me then. August's voice lowered as he spoke, "I do recall you saying four guards found you, Nic."

My face remained carefully blank. "I might have miscounted."

Damian snorted, "You think?"

"Technically I only killed seven, a shadowhound stole the eighth's final blow from me."

"How many shadowhounds?" Jophiel turned to Simon.

"Fourteen."

"You killed *eight* guards and a pack of *fourteen* shadowhounds." Celeste's said incredulously.

I shrugged. I hadn't been counting how many of the hounds I'd killed in the sheer chaos of it all, but I knew the lion had contributed greatly to that number. Relief went through me as there was no mention of his body with the others.

"Nic wields water and is on path to be more powerful than either of her parents after this year. It is not inconceivable," August said.

Teale coughed. "The wounds on each of the bodies, guard and shadowhound, suggested they were all killed by metal blades. All except one guard—his lungs were indeed shattered and filled with water."

"You *were* holding back with me." Celeste accused but her eyes were alight with something like admiration.

Simon turned back to August. "We could use Nic with some of our connections—our spies. They are loyal to the Briar crown. They will be honest with her if they know anything about Misha's whereabouts, more so than they would be with us."

August gave his spymaster a sharp look as he assessed his words. After a moment he said, "I will consider it. But I'm not risking it, not now. Not so close to the palace and Adrienne."

I took a deep breath in, then exhaled slowly. "Fine, but I'm going on the next excursion."

"We'll see."

That night after dinner, most of the Seven and August gathered in the main room again. They sprawled on the various couches and chairs, enjoying the fire that filled the hearth. In the north, even midsummer nights could become rather cold.

I turned away from them as I made my way silently up the stairs. On the landing halfway up, a small black cat blocked my path.

"That is Ker," Celeste said, not even gazing up from her book.

"Another of your pets?"

Celeste laughed, "Gods no. That monster belongs to Miranda."

I pondered how a little cat could possibly be considered a monster. "Did it piss on your pillow or something?"

Damian roared with laughter at my remark, throwing his head back on the couch. Miranda, chuckling as well, chimed in. "Ker is not an animal. She is a familiar."

Familiars, the creatures associated with witches. They took forms of ordinary animals, usually rats, owls, bats, ravens, or cats—hiding their true forms except when necessary to defend their liege. I thought they'd died out when the witches had, or so I'd been led to believe.

"You'd better hope you never see her true form, girl. It is the reincarnation of nightmares." Jophiel murmured from where she picked through a book from where she sat near the fire.

The little black cat came down the steps toward me, jumping onto the railing near my arm. It paused, sniffing as it assessed me. Then the familiar let out a contented purr, rubbing its head against the arm I hadn't moved from its place on the bannister.

I looked at the others' faces, all of them in some array of shock. "Don't look so surprised. I'm incredibly likable." I said flatly as I ran a hand down the familiar's back. The cat arched into the touch.

"I can't believe she just pet that thing like a housecat," Teale whispered, shuddering.

"You'd be less surprised if you saw the beast her sister calls a pet," August murmured from where he stood at the table with Shai, still looking over notes and maps.

My hand froze on the little cat. I hadn't thought about Rasalas, what might have happened to him in all the chaos. It might have seemed silly, but I couldn't stand the thought of Misha losing anything else she loved.

"The jaguar. I've heard." Celeste's eyes gleamed in delight.

"The Briars have an uncanny ability to tame what everyone else considers to be monsters," August said, his gaze lifting to mine.

I rolled my eyes as I continued walking up the stairs, little padded footsteps trailing behind.

CHAPTER 40
Nic

Two weeks passed this way with no new information, no new leads on where Misha and Julian might be. The cracks in my heart grew deeper with each one.

August and the others returned from scouting, and we heard from Simon's spies intermittently. The people of Hahnaley were in mourning for my aunts' death as well as mine but clung to the belief that Misha would be found soon. My sister gave them hope, but they hadn't rallied around Adrienne as I was sure she'd hoped they would. The traitor reportedly grew more determined to find us with each passing day as she still had neither Briar, all her bloodshed fruitless thus far. With her rising frustration, more staff and guards were being punished in cruel and unusual ways, an outlet for her vexation.

There was no way to help those I'd left behind. No way to help the staff that treated me like family, who were all now at the mercy of Adrienne's cruelty. I could do nothing to find Misha except continue to wait and rack my own mind for any possibility of where she might flee to. Every time I came up empty, I retracted further into my own hopelessness.

August did the same for his brother. He, Simon, and Shai kept reaching out to spies and pouring over maps, and discussing possible locations Julian might have fled to. We were both coming up empty.

Miranda sought guidance in her grimoires. She searched for any spell, potion, or item she might use to track or uncover the location of Misha and Julian. When I wasn't training, using the physical exertion to exhaust my body in the hopes that it would stave off the nightmares, I was helping her. Celeste and Damian too. August sometimes joined. She assigned us books and we searched, looking for anything that might help. Nothing ever did.

Jophiel traveled frequently back and forth to the capital, Ankaa. Disappearing for the day and returning late in the night, only to head back in the morning. She roused Montevalle's armies, readying them in case Adrienne decided to move on the North, for their own strike once Julian and Misha were found safe.

Teale was often in the Redwood convening with the nymphs. They too spoke of Adrienne's shadows, the unnaturalness that spread out around Sanserria. But none had seen the Golden Briar nor the Prince of Storms. Teale mentioned other vague hints of which the dryads spoke, of an awakening. According to the tree spirits, many long-closed eyes were opening deep in the woods, both benevolent and malicious. They watched—waited. They sensed the *Return*, she said. My pulse had stuttered at that, but she made no mention of fire. She said that they'd been vague and wary, though she would continue to seek them out for answers and hints. If Misha and Julian moved, the forest would know of it.

Since arriving I'd also beaten Teale and Shai in sparring. Teale was the smallest, but fastest of them. The only one that could match me for speed. With the ash completely gone from my system, we were a whirl of practice blades and shields though I'd eventually overpowered her. She might have been as fast as I was, but I was stronger.

It took some time to beat Shai. Withstanding his magic, he was remarkably gifted at reading those around him, using their subconscious habits and emotions to glean their intentions from them. I was forced to constantly change my approach to stand a chance against him. Eventually, I was successful, but only when I'd mastered leading him into a trap. I guided him with my false leads, subtle enough that he would think them natural. When he thought he'd had a match-ending opportunity and left himself vulnerable, I struck. Shai had only smiled softly when I'd finally bested him and bowed to me slightly in deference. Not for who I was, not for my royal title, but in the respect one warrior shows another. I liked him a bit better afterward.

In the two weeks here, I'd trained with the Seven and August, ate with them, searched for information with them—but I wasn't one of them. I didn't sit and talk with them at night, or joke with them as they did with each other in an attempt to diffuse the immense tension we all felt. At the end of each day, I returned to my room, alone, and let myself break apart where no one could see or hear.

We weren't friends, couldn't be friends. We were hastily made allies with the same goal—to find our loved ones.

The days began to blur.

All day I tried to drown myself in the training with the Seven and researching with Miranda, trying to distract myself from what had happened. All night the memories flooded back anyway.

The nightmares of Alesia and Eve's murders continued. Sometimes they were struck through the heart, then their throats were slit in horrific imitations of smiles. Sometimes they screamed at me to run, others they were dead at my feet before any words could escape from their lips at all.

The dreams came over and over, replaying the atrocity again and again in my mind—each time with some new sickening change.

Since I arrived I'd been casting silencing wards around my room before I laid in bed. There was no need to wake the rest of the cabin to my inevitable screams.

I wished the nightmares would stop. I also feared the day they did. These terrible dreams were one of the few ways I would ever see my aunts again. And

I was too much a coward to seek their faces through the memories held in my bracelet.

Every day I exhausted myself in training.

Every night I was out as my head landed on the pillow.

The deep exhaustion consumed me, sleep came so deep it was like being dropped in quicksand with a weight around my feet.

Heavy. Suffocating.

In the early morning glow, I walked through the woods, rowan wood arrow at the ready. I heard the snap of a branch at my back and spun, ready to take out the threat.

Alesia and Eve lay dead on the ground, hands still reaching for one another, hearts ripped from their chest. Kneeling between them was Misha—my sister in her gown of gauzy turquoise from the last time I'd seen her, a crown of pink roses with yellow centers on her head.

Adrienne stood behind her, a bejeweled dagger of Galorian silver at her throat.

"Give me your heart, Nicole. Or I'll take hers." She said, her mouth curling into a cruel smile.

She could have my heart, she could have anything, just let Misha go, I begged her.

Tears streamed from my sister's blue eyes, but no sobs came from her throat, no pleas on her own behalf. I could see in her eyes that she was terrified, but obstinate. She wouldn't allow me to save her, wouldn't let me take her place. My twin's lips mouthed to me to run.

"Please, I'll do anything, just don't hurt her—she's all I have left," I begged the female that had once been my stepmother, tears streaming down my own face. "Adrienne don't...you can have me, take me instead," I pleaded.

"Oh, I will, Nicole. But first..." Adrienne's lips curled into an even more vicious smile. "They say Misha is the golden one, with a heart to match. I think I will see for myself," she laughed as she sliced my sister's throat. Misha fell to the ground, gasping and choking on her own blood. Then Adrienne took the dagger and began to carve into my sister's chest.

I fell to my knees and screamed, screamed, screamed *until my vocal cords tore.*

I awoke to the sound of my own ragged screaming.

My hands were at my sides covered in jagged crystals of ice up to my forearms, as was every other inch of the room. The moonlight streamed through the window, making them glint like diamonds. The sheets were torn to shreds beneath me.

Because of the nightmares I'd been casting magic in my sleep, something I hadn't done since I was a child. It was common with the young fae before they learned control. I thanked the gods that was the ice and not fire, or the cabin would have been burned to a crisp.

I took a deep inhale. As I let it out, my breath came out as a fog in the chill of the room. I slowly let the ice fade away, pulling it back into my hands until it was gone.

The shredded sheets and tremors in my hands remained.

CHAPTER 41
Nic

"I met her, your sister."

I started at Shai's words, my warm up interrupted by his approach. "When?"

"We traveled with August and Julian to the Blood Treaty festivities, meeting with the spies and just...observing. The community, the people. When I met Misha it was the final night, the night of the Solstice ball. August already had an idea of how she and Julian felt about each other but he sought confirmation from my gifts."

"You went into her mind?" I stood from my stretch and turned on him.

"No," he shook his head, his eyes sincere. "I only sensed, or more so felt the emotion surrounding her. I did nothing but read what was already there, what she allowed to be seen—no manipulations." My expression must have cooled as Shai visibly relaxed. "I always sensed how much Julian cared for her, first as a friend and then more, but like August, I worried for him. Julian is so pure of heart, of spirit. To be so young and believe himself in that much love, it would be devastating if not returned. But then I met her. Misha is...I've never felt a kindness like hers, a warmth. Her heart and compassion are depthless. I could see it on her face as she searched the terrace for him. The way she loves Julian, the way he loves her—it could only be gods-blessed."

"I know," I said, my throat tight as I remembered the way her face lit up each time my sister received a letter from Julian, how they'd looked at each other in those few days.

"What I mean to say is that, though Julian is our family, we care about finding Misha as well, just as much. In the way they care for each other, she is already a part of our family." Shai's expression was open, genuine.

Only a brief moment, that's all it had taken for him to care for her—to see her as I did. He didn't need to use his gifts to make me believe he meant what he said, that he was devoted to finding her. A small thread of trust was built between us.

"Thank you," I whispered, my eyes glassing as I turned and walked away, his kindness overwhelming me. Right now I couldn't think too much about Misha and how each day without her was tearing me apart a little bit more.

As I walked to the rack of spelled practice weapons, my eyes landed on August as he worked through sword drills with Celeste. Not only practicing but teaching her.

I'd watched him train and spar before with the others. August moved like his magic, somehow both powerful and graceful—a hurricane made flesh. Though I'd seen only flickers of the storm, the lightning, I could sense the pure, unadulterated power there. My own perked up around his, like the cracking open of an eye deep in my chest where I kept it caged.

August's shirt pulled up as he moved, showing scars I'd never noticed. Some were thin bands, others large gashes that ran low on his back. Wounds on the fae had to be truly gruesome for them to not fully heal and leave a mark like that. Even ones made with rowan wood or Galorian silver would heal fully if treated appropriately by a healer. I wondered if he'd gained them in the war, from an enemy or dragon that had gotten too close, if the scars had set in the long battles while the healers tended to those with more life-threatening wounds.

August's eyes drifted to me, meeting mine as I watched. His gaze was always too probing, too piercing—like he was waiting for something. I quickly looked back to the weapons as I pulled a long sword and shield from the rack.

"Jophiel," I turned to the Seraph where she sat perched on one of the nearby tables. "Can we spar?"

The winged fae was the only one of the Seven I hadn't sparred with yet besides Miranda, who spent all her time still going through her grimoires. Jophiel had been hardened in battle over centuries. She would challenge me more than the others had, would give me the reprieve I needed to clear my mind.

Jophiel turned to me and nodded. Without another word, we entered the training ring. It grew quiet as the others stopped to watch.

She was taller, larger, and stronger—could take me out with one well-placed blow. My only advantage would be my speed and dexterity.

I struck first.

Jophiel turned her sword into a blocking position. My feet were already braced for the impact of steel on steel. A rattle went down my arm from the force.

We fell into a rhythm, a dance of blades, strikes, and blocks. My arms began to ache the more we parried. I blocked a particularly hard and well-timed strike with my shield, moving into position just in time and my arm shaking from the impact. It gave me some satisfaction to know that Jophiel wasn't holding back, that the Seraph respected me enough as an opponent to give her full effort.

But Jophiel was very close to wearing me down, and in a desperate attempt, I turned and spun. In the motion I let go of my shield, letting it fly toward her. It sliced through the air. When she blocked it with her own, I struck at her side, landing my first blow.

Jophiel hardly flinched as her sword flew toward me, toward my neck. I dodged, the momentum taking me to the ground as I rolled.

I regained my stance just in time to block another strike with my sword, but without the shield I was vulnerable. Jophiel's shield arm came up, her elbow striking me in my unprotected gut, knocking the breath from me. In the next second, she had me at the throat with her Seraph's shield, the edge that when prepared for battle would be as sharp as any blade.

"Yield," I relented, my breath heavy. I could already feel the bruises and welts forming on my body from the match.

"Not bad, Princess." Jophiel smiled as she pulled her shield back. Damian clapped from the edge of the ring.

"Not good enough to win," I said as we walked back to the weapons rack, setting them down for cleaning before returning them to their places. The others dispersed back into whatever activities they'd been doing before pausing to watch us.

Jophiel let out a short laugh. "You have the same Sancrista stubbornness. You were clearly trained very well by Alesia and the others she took you and your sister to. But you are still young—untested. I am sure in enough time, you will best us all, as she did."

"Alesia beat you in battle? During the war?" I asked, confused. I'd thought she and Jophiel would have been fighting on the same side.

"Let me clarify. We sparred together during a few of the stretches between battles, trained together many times—though she and your mother were already remarkably skilled. While they relied on their magic primarily, their power stronger and longer lasting than most High Fae, seemingly without an end, they didn't need it to win battles. Alesia once said that she wanted the humans to know they could face the Fae and win with sword and shield alone. She led by example—showed them how and trained many. Diana as well. That message has somehow become lost among many of the humans in the century since, that nearly as many of the King's High Fae soldiers fell at the hands of mortals as they did with the rebel-sided faeries. It is a shame."

Alesia and Eve told us stories of them when we were young, the humans that became heroes. Not all were warriors. Some were healers not gifted in magic but nonetheless saved many, skilled blacksmiths turned weapons makers, cooks that kept armies fed—our aunts told us all of their tales. Many fell in battle, but many also lived. Several of them were granted lordship under our parents, served in their councils, or remained generals under Alé. But the humans had not been granted a kingdom of their own as all four realms came to be ruled by fae. I couldn't help but feel that this was one of the many mistakes made in the aftermath of the war, that our continent could have used a fifth kingdom—would be better for it.

"My mother and Alé were raised in the slums, on the streets—self-taught out of necessity," I said. They'd been hardened by the worst of society, the worst of how High Fae treated the other faeries, demi-fae, and humans, which was undoubtedly how they could each hold their own against someone like Jophiel. "They were surrounded by more humans in their situation than fae. It is no wonder that they would wish for them to rise up, to find their strength."

"Yes. They had fighting experience already, with remarkably good skill for being solely self-taught, but they were each eager to learn more. During the war, the Sancristas took every opportunity to learn from all those that she could on the rebel side—fae, nymph, seraph, human, goblin—it didn't matter. If either saw a maneuver or technique that intrigued them, the sisters went to them, and asked the individual to teach them. Then they practiced until it was mastered. And years of war—it forges you. Not always for the better."

I nodded, contemplating as I focused on cleaning and sharpening the weapons I'd used.

Jophiel spoke again. "You yourself have never shed blood until recently. Even when it is for self-defense, even though justified, taking a life does not come without weight."

I slid a whetting stone down the steel blade. She waited for my response and wouldn't speak again until she'd gotten it. "I've trained all my life to defend myself, my family, our home. I knew I may need to take a life someday, but then when it did I…I didn't expect it to be that way. Yes, I feel some of the toll, but I thought I would feel more…regret?…guilt? Something. Alesia talked about the emotional toll of battle and that we needed to prepare ourselves for more than just physical wounds. But I don't feel remorse for them, for the guards that murdered my family, for the ones that spoke of such horrible plans for Misha. I still don't." I set the blade back on the rack and turned to her, "Does that make me like them?" She knew who I meant.

Jophiel's voice contained all the gravity and wisdom she'd accumulated in her centuries of experience in battle and ending lives. "In war it can be different, two sides fighting for what they each deem a noble cause. The emotional toll of that can indeed be taxing. Killing someone whose only crime is a difference in opinion is a mark on the soul that none of us can overcome, not entirely." Jophiel shook her head, "But that wasn't what happened to you. Those guards took your family from you and wanted to harm you as well. Those are not the same scenarios. You are not wrong in feeling no remorse for them. Tell me, do you regret what you did?"

I paused, considering, and could only speak my truth. "I only regret that they didn't suffer more."

CHAPTER 42
Nic

I 'd have thought you would have talked your way into joining the others by now." Miranda said as I came into her study.

The room was large with all of one wall and the ceiling made of glass, the space itself jutting out from the stone walls of the cabin. Another was covered from floor to ceiling with overflowing shelves. The books they held varied from grimoires to encyclopedias on plants and crystals, manuals for healing and anatomy, and almanacs of the tides and celestial events. They also contained jars filled with various ingredients, skulls and bones of several species, and an assortment of large and small crystals and powders.

Herbs and plants grew from hanging pots and trellises along the others. Benign things like thyme, rosemary, cilantro, hung there as well as the more malicious belladonna, foxglove, snakeroot, and more. Dispersed among them were eclectic frames filled with maps of the stars and currents, recipes, and one small oval mirror, its face warped and grayed with age.

August, Shai, Damian, and Celeste had left at dawn for Hahnaley. They headed for a hole in the wards that separated our countries near the coast, how they traveled to meet their spies in my home. We still hadn't heard any news of Misha and Julian, so they'd gone to the villages along the northern border to see if they could glean any information from whispers about them or Adrienne. They would return later tonight.

Jophiel was off flying—patrolling before the rain that was projected to come tonight. Teale was in the mountains reaching out to the Oreads, and Simon had gone into town for more food and supplies, leaving just the two of us here in the cabin. I'd given up on training, my muscles much too sore from the day before with Jophiel, and decided to join Miranda in her study rather than be left alone with my own thoughts.

I sighed as I sat next to her at one of two long tables that filled the space, one topped with several burners, flasks, other glassware, and molcajetes. Ours was covered in stacks of books and grimoires, one of which Miranda was pouring over as she sat in one of the many mismatched chairs.

"No, August is immune to logic. According to him, I still have to spar with and beat you, him, and Jophiel before I can join one of their outings."

Before he'd left early this morning, August had set a perfectly made cup of tea in front of me before walking out the door. In response, I'd whipped off my slipper and thrown it at his head. Unfortunately, August had learned from my affinity for hurling things at him and dodged it easily.

Miranda clicked her tongue without looking up. "I'm not sparring with you. I need to be here researching. There has to be a reason why Misha and Julian have not reached out, and I need to be able to quickly break whatever confinement they may be under when we discover them. And you are clearly more than capable of taking care of yourself." She clicked her tongue. "August's overprotectiveness blinds him."

I snorted, and Miranda shot me a glance. A quick upturn of her lips gave me the impression that I was missing something as she turned back to her grimoire.

"I haven't had the chance, but can I ask you something?" I said, changing the subject. Ker laid on the table before us atop an open book, her tail flicking contentedly. I stroked a hand down her spine.

"You *have* had the chance." Miranda countered as she flipped a page. "You just don't take the time to talk to anyone, to really get to know any of us—or let us get to know you"

Her unexpected words were direct but not harsh, and she wasn't wrong, I'd been very much keeping to myself since arriving as my grief over the loss of my family was barely contained. I wouldn't risk letting a group of strangers see how devastated I truly was.

"You're right," I swallowed. "It's nothing personal, it's just that I—" my words drifted off. I wasn't sure what to say or what excuse to give.

"Your mother, aunt, and I are from the same place," Miranda said in Alesia's native language, startling me.

"What?" I answered in the common faerie tongue. In my daze, I wasn't sure if I'd heard her correctly.

Miranda responded again in the language. "I grew up near Alara. My family moved Sanserria for business when I was nineteen, and I only immigrated to the Montevalle in my late twenties. I was ashamed I didn't recognize you immediately when we'd captured you, but you didn't look the way I'd expected. I hadn't seen you and your sister since you were fourteen, and I only ever saw you dressed up as a royal." I remembered that moment of realization when I'd arrived after August told them my identity. "In the cabin, you didn't behave at all in the way I'd expected a princess would, so the thought never even crossed my mind." She smiled as she said it, and I heard it, the accent. It was identical to Alesia's.

Miranda's eyes softened as she shifted on her seat, turning to me. "We've all tried very hard to make you feel welcome while respecting your space. None of us wants to impose on you, not with what you've so recently been through. But you can't keep going on in isolation forever, Nic, or you will continue to retreat into yourself and quickly become someone you don't even recognize."

Miranda went quiet while I decided on how I would answer. Maybe it was the familiarity in the language, the fact that she was from my home, or the truth in her words that let me answer as openly as I was able.

"The only people that have ever cared for me were my family. They were the only ones who could see me, all of me, even the worst parts, and still love me—and now they're all dead. All except my sister who is missing and I've been useless to find. They loved me unconditionally and I failed them—all of them." The words rushed out of me. "I can't let you be kind to me because I don't deserve it."

"That's not true. Everyone deserves it—well, mostly everyone. Your bitch of a stepmother doesn't." She said, and I choked out a laugh, thankful for the levity. "I would also bet you've never let anyone else see all of you except for your family—that you've never let your guard down for anyone else." She lifted an eyebrow.

I hesitated and she took my silence as an affirmation. It was true, even with Gemma, even with Callum, I had never fully been myself.

"You don't have to face this alone, Nic."

I kept silent for a few more moments. Lost in my thoughts as I considered her words.

Could I really trust these people I'd known for so little? They'd all made it clear that they were willing to do nearly anything to help find Julian as well as Misha. I'd had the most reservations about Shai, but after what he'd said yesterday—

"I think I could...try." I loosed a breath, not wanting to promise anything more than that.

"That is all I can ask," Miranda said, and I knew she wouldn't push me anymore on it. "So what were you going to ask me?"

"Can you tell me more about yourself? About the witches?"

Miranda rubbed a hand down her face. "Well if I had known you were going to ask me that, I wouldn't have jumped your ass for not getting to know any of us."

Her words loosened some of the tightness in my chest, my lips lifting in an almost smile.

"Firecasters are the best known example of the Etherii hunting down beings that threatened them, but they weren't the only ones. Long before they were targeted, over a millennia ago, they hunted the witches. Our kind used to be plentiful, at peace with the fae. But when our power grew to rival the High Fae's, we were sought out and slaughtered. Only very few remain and those of us that practice do so in secret, hiding from any High Fae that might choose to target us as well. Many more don't practice at all for fear of being caught or because they don't even know they possess the gift."

I thought over her words, so carefully chosen. "You said the High Fae, but not all faeries?"

"No," her eyes sharpened. "The other factions of faerie have no animosity toward the witches and have even helped shield us. I think it's because our magic is similar."

My curiosity piqued. "How does it work?"

"The High Fae, like yourself, have a core of magic within themselves, in the heart. While it can be substantial, it is limited to the well inside them and can be drained, as you know. In contrast, the various kinds of faerie including nymphs, sirens, and even goblins, draw their magic from the nature they are born of. Ours is similar. The witches' magic comes from drawing on the elements, weather patterns, nature, even constellations and solar events."

"So your magic cannot be depleted?" I thought of how that would feel, the depthless magic. Would it be a blessing or a curse?

"No, but whereas the strength of the High Fae is determined by the depth of their well, the witch's is determined by how much magic or energy they can channel."

"Like a conduit?" I shifted in my seat, propping my head in my hand.

Miranda nodded. "The strongest among us can channel quite a bit at once. The magic is theoretically endless as long as the witch has something to draw off of and her body can withstand it. Though even the strongest of us may not tolerate long periods of channeling so much energy. We are still only human."

"Are you limited in the type of magic you can control?"

"Yes. Most have an affinity for one of the four elements, sometimes two, as well as varying levels of adeptness in spell and ward casting. Others, like me, may also have the Sight."

"You channel the earth?" One glimpse at the room and the number of plants thriving in this space was evidence of that.

"Yes, but I also have an affinity for water." As she spoke, Miranda frosted the glass of water sitting nearby, ice crystals climbing up its sides.

"So you are one of the more powerful ones." I brushed my fingers against it, the magic feeling so similar to my own. Miranda smiled and shrugged—humble. "And is the witch gene, or genes, passed linearly?"

"Yes and no. Witches are only ever female. And while having a mother, grandmother, or another close relative that is a witch would predispose you to being one, it is not always the case. Witches can be born from a completely human lineage. Those are the ones most in danger of discovery. As children, they will exhibit some preternatural ability—a green thumb, an excellent swimmer without being taught, heightened senses, or an uncanny intuition. If their power is strong enough to be undeniable or passed off as normal human talent, the witchlings often go missing before they can be discovered by another witch and taught to keep their abilities hidden."

My blood chilled. I couldn't fathom it, targeting *children*. "Even in the last 100 years? Since the war?" Neither of my parents would have condoned any child or person being harmed for how they were born. My mother had faced enough persecution for that herself.

"It has been better, though some regions are safer than others. At their inception, Reyna was the most dangerous along with Montevalle. Desdemon was fairly safe. Hahnaley a haven. Because the humans were so protected, as were we—until eight years ago."

Within a year of our father's death. Bile rose in my throat, I was going to be sick.

Adrienne had done such terrible things and kept them hidden from us, utterly destroying everything my parents worked so hard to build. The worst was none of us had known, hadn't realized.

What horrible things was she planning to do now? And why keep silent these past two weeks? We hadn't heard a whisper of her movements or plans, which unsettled me more than anything else.

Miranda continued. "When August became King, Montevalle shifted. He tried to maintain the image his father cultivated, the image of fear and harsh rule as a precaution, but humans and witches talk. Our kind and theirs began to flock here under his rule."

"When did you come?" With Alara as her home, it couldn't have been easy to leave, to come here.

"Seven years ago, when I met Damian. He was with Simon as he met with spies. The spymaster can very well defend himself, but August always makes him take one of the fae in the Seven as a precaution when going to the other countries."

When she met her mate. My lips lifted in a ghost of a smile, their story seemed like it belonged in a novel. "How did you two meet?"

"You will have to ask Damian." Miranda's eyes shone when she talked about her mate. She twirled a lock of hair absentmindedly as she did so. "It's his favorite story to tell and he'll never forgive me for taking away an opportunity to tell it."

I nodded, sitting upright again. "Which of these do you need help going through?" I waved to the stack of books on the table in front of her.

Miranda contemplated for a moment then pulled one out from the center. A grimoire that focused on binding spells and sleeping curses. "I'm looking for any enchantment that could bind a High Fae for long periods of time and its counter-curse in the case that Misha and Julian are bound by one."

Such a curse would explain their silence. I took the book from her and began thrumming through the pages.

We stayed there for another few hours. I'd finished with the grimoire, notes tucked into pages with notable enchantments, then we'd moved on to what Miranda was studying. I knew much about herbs, medicines, and poisons from Eve, but the witches used them slightly differently.

As Miranda explained these variations I heard steps on the porch. "Sounds like Simon is back."

"Hopefully the more skilled herbalists went to market in Haldrin today," Miranda said as she stood and stretched, each of our bodies having gone stiff from so long sitting. "I'm running low on ingredients for my salves and haven't had any time to scour the woods for them myself."

Before we walked out, Miranda took my hand, wordlessly squeezing it in a comforting gesture, and I knew that my intuition when I awoke in the cabin that first day had been correct—she and I could be friends.

CHAPTER 43
Nic

The next night I sat in the large, cushioned chair nearest a large window with the curtains drawn. My feet were tucked beneath me, a book resting on my thigh that I hadn't paid any attention to for the past ten minutes.

One of the things that brought me solace, in the forest, especially during the summer, was listening to the song of the crickets and nightingales.

Tonight there were neither.

"Do you hear that?" I sat up in my chair, closing the book.

"I don't hear anything," Damian shrugged from where he stood in the kitchen, helping Miranda sort and hang the lavender, thyme, and other herms Simon had brought for her from town.

"Exactly," I said softly. "The woods are never quiet, especially not at night." I stood and cast water from my fingertips to put out the fire. Without the crackling embers, the silence surrounding us became deafening.

This got the others' attention, everyone going quiet at once.

Teale whispered, "Something is wrong. We are not alone." As if in affirmation, Ker hissed from her perch in one of the windows. Each of us sat unmoving, straining our ears, as we listened.

That's when we heard them—the whispers spoken from lips that were not their own.

"Little Briar all alone."

The voices were both old and young, beautiful and dreadful. Ice dripped down my spine.

"Skinwalkers." Jophiel mouthed silently from the table with Simon and August.

"How are they being so quiet?" Damian mouthed back. There hadn't been the rustle and dragging that typically accompanied the skinwalkers' movements.

Jophiel sniffed. Her eyes went cold. "High Fae. Fresh."

"Little Briar with hair like coal."

Skinwalkers were difficult enough to deal with when they inhabited the corpses of rotting animals and humans, but in the body of a High Fae, freshly killed—this was a nightmare.

"Little Briar with skin like snow."

I shuddered as they took turns calling for me.

"How many?" August's lips moved silently. Jophiel paused, listening. Then held up four fingers.

The others began to discuss a strategy to face them, mostly through Teale and Shai mind to mind with everyone's eyes intermittently flitting to theirs. I was left out of this as I'd kept that part of my mental shield up.

"Little Briar, covered in blood so red."

The cold spread, chilling my veins—until my fire rose up to meet it.

Very few things could dispel a skinwalker from its host. Rowan wood and Galorian silver imbued with the ash, both needing to strike through the heart. But also—

I shot water at August's chest to get his attention, interrupting whatever he and Teale were mentally discussing. His head snapped up. "Take down the winnowing wards." I mouthed to him.

He blinked, taken aback. "No." The others looked at me like I was insane.

"I have a plan." Maybe I was.

His face grew adamant. "No."

"Little Briar, tell us where your aunts lie." Another skinwalker crooned, taunting me—mocking Alé and Eve's deaths.

I looked to Shai, opening up my mind just a sliver so he could hear the thoughts I pushed toward him. "Relay this to him." I pointed to August. Shai nodded in response. "You know as well as I do that if we go out there blindly, even with the appropriate weapons, it is likely at least one of us will be skinned or killed. But I can end them, quickly and all at once, but it can only be me. I can't tell you how or why." I finished and Shai looked to August, both their eyes stilling as he conveyed my words.

When Shai finished, August looked furiously between us both. "No."

"We'll don their pretty faces..."

"Trust me." My lips moved, my eyes pleading. "Please." The word tasted like ash, but we were wasting valuable time. I'd already begun calling up my power, the magic humming beneath my skin, eager for release.

August evaluated my expression for a moment then closed his eyes, holding them shut for another long second. "Fine," He said silently, then nodded to Miranda. She immediately began silent chants that I knew would break the protective spells around us.

"Little Briar, no longer all alone."

"No matter what you hear, stay inside." I mouthed to the others, looking them each in the eye. I had a feeling they wouldn't if they sensed things had gone wrong, but they would let me attempt this mad plan for at least a minute—and that was all I needed.

I closed my eyes, listening, reaching for the dampness in the ground from our recent rain, feeling for where each skinwalker now stood. Two remained hidden in the tree line. Two were in the open, within twenty meters of the cabin and closing in from opposite ends. I would only get one shot at this.

I took a deep breath and winnowed into the training clearing.

"You want to know where my aunts lie?" I said, my voice loud and clear, my eyes shut tightly.

The skinwalkers were as fast as their hosts had been alive, not yet in the thick of decay. As their quick steps neared, I winnowed to my next location. They'd converged where I had been a moment before, their cold fingers reaching for nothing.

"They lie in perpetual dusk, beneath the starry night." More words, another jump. The skinwalkers were fast, but I was faster—winnowing too swiftly for them to catch me before I disappeared again.

"They fly on the wind that whips between mountains." Speak to draw them to me, then winnow. I taunted them as they had taunted me.

"They float—" The skinwalkers moved faster, growing more frantic. One reached out its arm, thinking it had me only to grasp empty air. The monster screeched in frustration. I only kept winnowing in my carefully planned pattern. "—on the cresting waves of the sea."

The skinwalkers grew silent. They were catching on now.

"They eternally dance—"

They'd solved it. All four skinwalkers had skipped chasing me to this location in favor of where I would undoubtedly appear next. Such horrible, clever creatures—but not clever enough.

I made my last jump.

"—in the *flame*."

I materialized coated in scorching fire as I let my power blast out around me, all four skinwalkers standing less than a meter from where I emerged.

The monsters screeched, wailing in agony as their corpses burned. I kept burning, singeing the trees and grass nearest to me, far enough away from the cabin that I wouldn't burn that down as well.

Only when their screams fell silent did I dare open my eyes. Nothing surrounded me but scorched earth and ash falling like snow.

My bare skin flickered with the deadly flame as I lacked the control to save my clothing. With the threat eliminated, I let go of the fire, replacing it from the neck down in opaque ice akin to armor.

When I was finished, I looked up to eight pairs of eyes on me. All had rushed to the clearing when they'd seen the light from the fire, smelled the burning corpses. The Seven's gazes were wide, disbelieving. I steeled myself, waiting for what they'd say, what they'd do now that they knew what I'd been hiding from them.

The return of fire.

One pair of eyes was unlike the rest. Silver—and gleaming.

"I knew it."

CHAPTER 44
Nic

S omeone has been keeping secrets," August said when we were back inside. Miranda had gotten a blanket for me to wrap around myself as we entered the cabin, even as I kept myself covered in frost. The cold soothed me after expelling that much flame at one.

"You didn't seem surprised," I replied. The nine of us sat around the large table, much like we had my first day here.

"Just because I had my suspicions, does not mean I am not astonished it turned out to be true."

Jophiel leaned forward, her great wings rustling. "How is it even possible? I've never heard of any fae having more than one element. Gifts sure—winnowing, the Sight, occasionally healing—but never this."

I shrugged my shoulders. As the oldest of us, she would know better than I did. The library in Sanserria was stocked with rare books with records of the elemental lineages. Many of them I'd pulled that day after the Siren had relayed her vision to me. Until I had access to them again, I would know nothing of why I'd been gifted with both water and fire.

"The *how* is something we will have to consider later, when our siblings are found and Adrienne is no longer such a threat," August interjected, his eyes focused back on me. "When did the fire emerge?"

There was no point to any evasiveness now. "The morning my aunts died," I said. Several of the Seven looked at me with empathy.

I sat up straighter, willing my spine into steel. "But I'd felt it building the day before." Though I meant the ordeal with Evander, I avoided August's gaze, also remembering the words I'd said to him. "When the guards did it—when they killed them—I erupted in fire. I couldn't have held it in if I wanted to."

August's eyes sparked as if I'd given him some piece to a puzzle. "I sensed the magic stirring that night. I thought it might have been Miranda's vision—some advancement in your water element to come. But when I'd heard that you'd broken through the imprisoning wards here, I began suspecting fire."

Miranda smirked. "I knew your escape couldn't have been so easily explained."

"Fire was the only magic that made sense, impossible as it seemed." August went on. "I'd hoped that in your frustration from being kept cooped up here that you'd eventually let it loose or give some sign. Your temper runs hot enough that I thought surely your control would slip in training, but it never did."

"*That's* why you said I couldn't join any of you? You were hoping I would get angry enough to lose control and expose myself?" I fumed, my hands white as they gripped the table—the conniving bastard.

"Once you begin scouting, lack of control over such an element can become dangerous quickly—not just to your enemies." He looked at my hands where they lay fisted on the table, scorch marks beneath them. I hadn't noticed, furthering his point. "You can't keep holding it in either. Such power has to be expelled intermittently or you will erupt again. That time might not be so beneficial."

My will kept me from flinching, but the sight of the black handprints rattled me. Sitting back in my chair, frost replaced the heat coating my palms as I brought them into my chest. He was right, I couldn't keep smothering the fire. The flames needed to breathe.

"Fine, I'll start working on it tomorrow," I conceded.

"Great, so glad we got that figured out." Damian butted in. "But *how* did the skinwalkers find us? Miranda and I've never dealt with such creatures in all the years we've lived here. Besides, aren't they more solitary? I've never heard of them ambushing in a pack before."

Softly, I said, "They came because Adrienne sent them. She knows I'm here."

Celeste looked skeptical. "How can she possibly know that?"

I shook my head. "I don't know for certain, but the skinwalkers called to me—only me. They taunted me with Alesia and Eve's deaths. How else would they know about that unless Adrienne sent them? How else would four very fresh High Fae walkers come here so soon after claiming their bodies? The only logical explanation was that they were made to track me here."

"But how?" Miranda leaned forward, bracing herself on her elbows. "Adrienne doesn't know this place. This outpost and the nearby town weren't formed until a few decades ago."

"A naiad spoke to me in the Redwood." Teale perked up at my words, and I turned to her. "I'm sorry I didn't tell you about it. I wanted to keep my fire a secret. You were all strangers, and I didn't know how you'd react. But since the naiad knew of it, I didn't want you making the connection too."

Teale gave me a smile that said she understood. "So you are what the nymphs whisper of. They speak of *the Return* but wouldn't give me any details. You have had all the forest in quite the tizzy."

I shrugged and I couldn't stop my lips from turning up to match hers. "I have to say I was most worried that you'd be the one to discover my secret first. Nymphs can be quite the gossips." At this Teale laughed, the sound high-pitched and lovely.

August cleared his throat, urging me to continue. I shot him a glare before I resumed. "The naiad warned me Adrienne had something watching—searching for me. She was unsure of how though, only that it was unnatural—would be rejected by nature, like the skinwalkers."

"The nymphs sense it too," Teale said. "They haven't elaborated to me either because they are unsure of the specifics or because they have yet to trust me with such information."

"The animals have been more restless as of late as well," Celeste added, her eyes going to the window. The sounds of the night had slowly returned, cicadas buzzing rhythmically outside.

"So that is how she found you—this unnatural magic?" Damian's eyebrows creased.

"That is my guess," I answered. "Though the how is still uncertain with us being so well warded and all, and I haven't left the ward's boundaries. Maybe the skinwalkers were able to pick up my scent from crossing and tracked me here. In that case, it's lucky I killed them all before they could give her our exact location."

"Miranda," August turned to the witch. "You and I will reset all the wards tonight and add more for good measure. Adrienne decided against sending her guard for some reason, and she won't risk coming here herself. She will likely continue to use beings like the skinwalkers to collect Nic, and we all know she will only get more desperate with time. It won't be long before she strikes again."

"I'll go too." Teale sat up. "My magic works differently. I can sense ways that other creatures, not just faeries, might get through like the skinwalkers did tonight."

August nodded and the three of them stood.

"Do I get to join now?" I said, my voice dripping in sarcasm as my eyes lifted to his.

"If you'd like, but you'll probably want to put on more than just that blanket." His eyes roamed down my body.

329

I frowned, wrapping the blanket a little tighter around myself as I stood with them.

Celeste scowled, noting the ash that still clung to parts of my hair. "You're going to owe me new clothes once this is settled, Princess."

I rolled my eyes. "I'll take you on a whole damn shopping spree if you wish." At this she smiled, walking toward the stairs to retire from this hellish night.

"You three better not leave without me." I looked back as I followed after her.

"And be turned to barbeque? No thanks." Teale deadpanned in a way that almost made me smile.

It was close to midnight before we'd finished resetting the wards. Following which, I scrubbed the grime and ash from my skin before I laid in bed, feeling more at ease than I had in weeks. Keeping back the secret of my power had been more exhausting than I'd realized, and since I'd stopped trying to hold it in, I felt alleviated from the strain of it.

Secrets could be binds, and tonight I'd been set free.

CHAPTER 45
Nic

T he next morning I went downstairs at dawn, hoping to eat breakfast then find a place in the woods with lots of rock and not much forest in case my fire got away from me. August, as always, was already in the kitchen.

"You don't think you are going alone do you?" He said as he looked up from the tea kettle. I'd been planning to do just that, not wanting to accidentally scorch any of the others.

August read my thoughts, always uncanny in the way he was able to do so. "Fire isn't like water or ice."

"You think I don't know that?" I said, not wanting to be lectured on my own magic.

"You need direction, and no one else here can build a shield strong enough to keep themselves from getting burned if you lose control."

I took the tea August offered me every morning, now our habit, the mug warming my hands. The darkness under his eyes seemed to have spread. He was sleeping just as horribly as I was then. "You said just last night I need to practice. How do you expect me to train then?"

"I said no one *else* can handle it, not that no one here could. You are training with me." He leaned back against the counter, bringing his own mug to his lips.

My heart stumbled a beat. It would be the first time we were alone since the Summer Solstice in the gardens. Our encounters in the cabin didn't count, there was always at least one of the Seven nearby. I couldn't help but remember what he and I had each said that night.

Don't say my name like that.

Untrue.

August went on, "Lightning and fire contain much of the same qualities, the erraticness and volatility. Not to mention that if you accidentally launch an inferno I can trap it with wind and extinguish it with rain." He went quiet, watching as I sipped my tea. I realized I still hadn't said anything.

His voice was soft as mist as he said, "Nic, if you're uncomfortable—"

"No," I said, cutting him off.

August had infuriated me, yes, but I'd never been uncomfortable in his presence, never felt unsafe. Even on that first day in the alley I'd known he wouldn't truly hurt me. Not physically at least.

"Okay. We leave in half an hour."

"Call the fire into your hand, just your hand." August stood with his arms crossed as he waited.

The small lake we'd winnowed to was perfect with its rocky shore and the trees set far enough away to be deemed safe. An environment that wouldn't easily burn.

I bristled at his command by instinct.

August noted the rigidity in my stance. "It's not a command, Nic, but we have to start somewhere. You've handled the fire only three times now, correct? With the guards and then the firewalkers you created blasts, but when you escaped your wards it had to have been more controlled considering I still have a cabin to return to. This is an easy starting point."

I closed my eyes to focus.

"Don't close your eyes."

I opened them to glare at him. "It helps me focus."

"You don't need to close them to call on water or ice. It's a bad habit to get into. We're breaking it now."

August was right, of course, but I still didn't like being called out on it. Though his pushing me made it easier for the flame to rise to my skin. I extended a hand toward him as fire erupted in my palm.

"Lovely," he said, coming closer. The flame reflected in his eyes, turning them molten. "Now practice a concentrated blast, over the water."

This took more concentration and energy, trying to tailor the power of the blast into stronger than what I could contain in my palm without losing control of it. Several of the boulders were scorched by the time I'd gotten it.

"You can make shields with water and ice, can you not?" August asked.

"Of course." They were one of the first skills learned, defense always came before offense in Alesia and my father's lessons.

"Make one with fire."

I paused. This task, to construct a wall of fire and hold it still would be much harder than simply letting it blast out around me and I'd only just mastered that.

August noted my hesitation. "You have superior control of water and ice, exert your will over the fire with the same precision."

"It's not that simple," I snapped. "They're different, feel different. Water is pliable, easy to manipulate. Ice is calculated, buildable. Fire is none of those things. It feels wild—untamable."

"Are you not those things?" A glint flashed in those silver eyes. "You may be well known for your icecasting, but you've always had a spirit akin to wildfire. The magic suits you. Let it."

"You said that fire and lightning are similar, that's why you came here with me." I crossed my arms, nodding to him. "Show me first, then I'll try."

August smiled, not one of teasing or mischief I saw so often on him, but genuine. He enjoyed casting his magic, setting the storm loose.

Lightning danced and flicked down both his arms, and I swore his eyes grew into a lighter, gleaming silver. With a simple raise of his hands, he constructed a wall of electricity between us. The light from which flickered and danced—beautiful.

"Test it."

Curious, I didn't hesitate. I cast a spear of ice into my hand and threw it at the wall. On impact, the spear bounced back. Unable to piece August's shield, but also unharmed by it—interesting.

"Not with ice," August shouted from the other side.

"What if I break through?" I hesitated.

"Your lack of confidence wounds me," August said, his voice laced with amusement. "Though if you do manage to burn me you have the ability to winnow me back to Damian. He and Miranda are stocked up on healing salves."

I called fire to my hands, letting it lick down my forearms as his lightning had, careful to not let it singe my shirt, glad I'd chosen not to wear sleeves. Then I pushed it out from myself, into a fire ball directly aimed at his shield.

Electricity and fire collided in brilliant white and gold sparks. August's shield held enough to keep him protected, but it had taken at least some effort for him to maintain it.

"Your turn." August dropped his shield, looking at me expectantly.

Like with the blasts, it took several tries to get enough control of the fire to hold it into a shield, and much more focus to maintain it as August began pummeling lightning strikes at it. Several times his bolts pierced through, lightly zapping me as they did so.

By noon, I'd cursed and called him every name under the sun thanks to the zing of his lightning every time my shield failed. But my power had progressed, though not without significant concentration. I knew it would take a lot more practice to get to the point of effortlessly producing them as it was with water and ice, but it was a start.

Afterward, we took a much needed break, sitting to quietly eat the food August had brought with us, knowing we wouldn't be done before lunch. Once rested, we began again.

"I want you to practice molding the fire further. Into shapes, weapons, whatever you wish." August said as he stood.

This task proved to be much more challenging. I had a difficult time shaping the fire outside of indistinct walls and balls of fire. The flames were difficult to grasp—they didn't wish to be held, to conform.

After an unsuccessful hour, August said, "Let's try power sharing."

"What?" I looked up at him from where I sat on the ground, catching my breath. I'd only ever shared power with my family, mostly Misha and occasionally Alesia and Eve. Our father had also done it with us as children when helping us learn to control our magic.

"We don't have to if you don't want to," August shrugged, setting down his water canteen. "But I think it will help. If we share power, I can help you guide your magic like I do the lightning."

Unease warped in my gut. "I'm not sure if I can." In power sharing you had to let down certain barriers, make yourself vulnerable. I didn't know if I was capable of that with him.

"We can try for a moment. If it doesn't work, it doesn't work." August said simply, his nonchalance easing something in me. Still, I hesitated.

His face softened. "You don't have—"

"No...let's do it." I reached for him, letting him pull me up, though my chest tightened.

August kept my hand in his as I stood, holding it firmly. I felt a flicker between us from what must have been the residual charge on his skin. Reaching through his hand to mine, his power felt like a mist tapping against my shields, seeking entrance.

I found my magic lifting its own head, curious—eager as it began to sense how much power was contained within August.

Dropping my barriers to let him in was easier than I'd thought, our magic colliding in a rush.

The feeling was heady, intense. It wasn't the same experience I'd felt when sharing with my sister or aunts, not uncomfortable per se but—different.

August had said all day that fire and electricity were similar, I didn't realize how true that was until right now. The magic hummed and burned as it coursed through me. It exhilarated me, even as I could see how easy it would be to lose control.

"Start with a sword," August instructed, his magic leading mine. It took a few tries but I finally crafted a single long sword from the flames. I let it slice through the air as I imagined fighting with this in one hand, the Iradelmar in the other. My grip tightened on his hand, his fingers laced through mine to steady our grip.

August led me through other weapons and shields. After I was successfully conjuring them we disconnected, and I attempted them on my own. The first few tries I fumbled without his guidance, but it was easier to master them in time, having already done it once.

"I want you to try bigger shapes, ones that move." August walked back toward me. "But this time your hands need to be free to better control the fire, and we still need skin to skin contact to maintain the power share."

My heartbeat picked up as he came to stand behind me. "Is this okay?" He said as he reached his hands toward my waist, pausing before he touched me. As I looked back at him, his eyes roamed my face, looking for any sign that it wasn't.

"Yes," I said hoarsely, giving him permission.

His hands, rough with the callouses that came with being a warrior, drifted beneath my shirt and came to rest on my bare skin, encircling my waist as we began to share our magic again. My skin sang beneath his palms. I couldn't tell if it was the power flowing between us or if it was just him—but I'd never had a reaction to anyone's touch quite like his.

It took some time, but with the help of his power, I cast waves of fire on the surface of the lake that rolled like the sea, as they crested the flames turned to galloping horses, then took flight into fiery birds.

August's power guided my own, it never wavered as he let me take more and more.

But as the magic swelled, it began to whisper to me, making me promises of power—revenge. It was all mine to take if only I gave myself over to it. And I wanted it—wanted it so badly. To use this power to defeat Adrienne, burn everything she ever cared about to ash. With power like this, I could burn the entire world—

A burst of winter-kissed wind whipped through my hair.

"*Nicole.*" A voice like thunder broke through my trance, pulling me back.

I yanked on the magic's leash—hard. It roared in defiance but then fell into line. I was in control again. Its master. Power like that was a curse. It had no thoughts for things like family—love. It didn't care if I got my sister back. It only cared to be used, to destroy.

During my trance, the magic had become a tornado dancing in the water. I slowly let it dissipate away into nothing.

"Good," August said from behind me. His grip had tightened on my waist, my back now flush with his chest. I felt his breaths rise and fall, too quickly, as if my pull on his power had overexerted him. The scent of rain and crackling embers surrounded me—my pulse slowed as I breathed it in.

"I think that's enough for one day." He whispered as he let me go, breaking our connection.

Facing him, I noted his silver eyes were more flat than usual—drained. "Did I take too much?"

"I have been much more depleted many times before." August assuaged me. "Though I might need to take some back to return us to the cabin." I held out my hand to him and he paused for a moment, staring down at it, before taking it in his. I wondered at the hesitation.

My magic purred at the renewed proximity to his, fluttering through my veins eagerly. I once again let down my barriers but kept tight control, not allowing myself to take from him again. The power initially protested, but then flowed into him willingly as he called to it.

When he'd taken enough we reconstructed those barriers between us—between the magic. Mine hissed inside my chest in displeasure. August's jaw clenched ever so slightly, and I wondered whether his was giving him as much trouble.

He squeezed my hand where ours were still joined. "Ready?"

"Yes," I said, the weariness from a full day of working with my magic catching up to me. "Let's go home."

Some emotion flashed in August's silver eyes, gone so fast I couldn't place it. He only said simply, "As you wish," and then we were gone.

CHAPTER 46
Nic

A week later, news finally came from Sanserria.

"From the palace, itself." Simon dropped a letter down on the table. August and I reached for it at once.

He pulled back his hand when he met the ferocity in my eyes. I wasn't above singeing his fingertips to look at it first. Not after the *you must train to scout* fiasco. The king threw his hands up in surrender as I pulled open the wax seal, hesitating briefly on the tree and river of the Briar crest.

The letter was written in an elegant scrawl, one I immediately recognized. Our Royal Steward, Robyn. My gut clenched. She'd been a part of my family's household since we were infants—before. She'd held Misha and me as newborns, helped rock us to sleep. Though I was grateful for this information—thankful she was even still alive—that she'd been one of August's spies stung.

I clenched my teeth, shaking off the feeling, and read.

The Sanserrian Palace had locked down on Adrienne, not allowing her or anyone loyal to her access to many of the rooms and chambers, including the throne room, the entire West Wing, and the vast armory. Infuriated, Adrienne was forced to have weapons and supplies brought over from Reyna by ship. They'd arrived only recently, the entire excursion taking several weeks.

Because I'd grown up there, the palace was all I had known. I'd almost forgotten the extent of the enchantments weaved into my home, its magic catering to nearly all of mine and Misha's whims. Part of such spells would lock down various, and very important, passages in the palace in the case of a hostile takeover.

I thought of Adrienne staring down the ice or thorn-covered doors, unwavering as they were blasted by the various elements of her guards, and smiled.

"No wonder Adrienne's made no major moves against us," I said as I handed the letter over to August, smiling like a cat. "She can't get to any of our resources."

The rest of the Seven looked confused, so I explained what I'd read as August looked over the letter for himself.

"But now she has what she needs from Reyna," Jophiel said solemnly as she sat across from me, at August's right hand. "Should we consider a strike imminent?"

"Adrienne can't move a large force without us knowing," August said, handing the letter back to Simon for a third perusal.

Armies needed time to mobilize, especially if they planned to come North. From Hahnaley, they'd either have to cross mountains, brave the Redwood, or sail. I didn't think Adrienne would take her chances on the water, not after the siren.

August went on, "Our forces are already on alert. There is nothing more we can do until we find Julian and Misha."

"What of a smaller attack?" Celeste leaned forward, bracing herself on her elbows.

August looked to me, then the rest of them—the staggering power in just this room. "I think we could handle one of those, don't you?"

Like her magic, Celeste's answering grin was feral.

Something else nagged at me about the letter. I thought it over again—of what hadn't been said.

The others chattered around me as I looked at the wood grain of the table, studying it, the way it seemed like tiny boats on an endless river, and tried not to hope. "What if they are still in the palace?"

The Seven went silent until I lifted my eyes. They'd all known who I meant.

"In one of the inaccessible chambers?" Jophiel said, her voice barely above a whisper. She was afraid to hope too.

I nodded. Once the thought had occurred to me, it seemed obvious. Just because they hadn't been in my sister's room, in Julian's, didn't mean they weren't elsewhere. August answered. "I would think that Misha would know which of the staff to trust, and Julian knows the spies' code phrases. They would have used one of them to get word to us, surely."

"What if they're incapacitated? Cursed somehow?" Miranda had already suspected as much. And I refused to believe them dead, to even entertain the thought. As did he.

August ran a hand through his black hair, considering. "It's possible. Though I have no idea how we would confirm their location without searching the palace ourselves."

"I could sneak in," Miranda spoke up. "I'm human. The spies can let me in, say I'm new staff. I doubt Adrienne spends any time looking at human faces enough to tell them apart. Once inside I can try to convene with the magic of the palace. If it can sense loyalties, I shouldn't have any issues."

"The human and faerie staff have indeed been told not to be seen by any High Fae while working," Simon said. "I could join her."

The Seven seemed to quiet at his suggestion, and I couldn't fathom why. While I wouldn't want either of them unnecessarily risking themselves, Simon was August's spymaster—had been for two decades.

"Are you sure you can take that risk?" August's eyes were unyielding on his friend. "Miranda can at least protect herself with magic, but you?" Simon was a skilled fighter from what I'd seen in training, but that would do him no good against Adrienne's High Fae guard if they discovered him and he was outnumbered.

Simon nodded. "I remember the day Julian was born. He is as precious to me as my own. I can do what needs to be done."

"And if you're caught?" August persisted.

Simon smiled, but the motion didn't quite reach his eyes. "Never once has anyone gotten close. This will not be the day they do."

August still looked intently at his spymaster, as if they were communicating wordlessly. Not mind to mind like Teale and Shai, but by the bond of two people that had known each other for decades.

"I can draw maps," I said, both turning to me. "If anything goes wrong, I can show you where to go and how to exit the palace through the tunnels that lead to the sea. The magic will protect you." It had to. If the palace's magic had the cognizance to lock out Adrienne, it should also help a friend.

Simon, though adamant he would go before, looked relieved at that.

"If we go, we also need to extract the Shaws," Jophiel said. "It is confirmed that Reyna has provided Adrienne support, but Desdemon could be just as easily sending supplies. We cannot allow Adrienne to have such power."

My heart fluttered at the hope of finding my sister and saving my friends, though freeing the Shaws would add another layer of difficulty in this mission, being as they likely all still believed that August murdered their parents. But Jophiel was right. From a pure tactical standpoint, the East had far too many resources to allow Adrienne to keep.

"And evacuate the staff," I said. If we were going to do this, then no one was getting left behind. "Simon can reach out to the spies beforehand so they'll be ready."

August and I shared a look. *I'm going, with or without you.* No longer could I sit here and wait for whispers and hints that may never come.

"Fine." He loosed a breath, eyes hardened with resolve. "We will plan it—then plan it again and again, accounting for everything that could possibly go awry. Then we will go."

The rest of the Seven seemed to hum with energy—eager. We'd all grown restless these weeks.

"But until then I want to account for every possible scenario in how it could all go wrong. I want no stone unturned, no possibility left undiscussed." It was the voice of the King and would not be contested.

The Seven nodded and even with no proof that Misha and Julian were there, it felt good to have a direction.

As the others left the table to prepare I hesitated, my mind drifting to all the places Misha and Julian could be hidden within the palace. There were many possibilities, and I would need to share plans to account for them all.

It was late into the night when I finished my drawings, accounting for every level and path through the palace and grounds. Known and secret alike.

Putting away my tools, the charcoal and parchment, my gaze snagged on August where he sat in a chair near the fire, staring into the dancing flames. Only he and I remained awake.

Though today had brought good news, he still had a weariness to his features, a darkness under his eyes that hadn't been present when we'd first met in that alley. The more time I spent with him in training, the more I saw it. I doubted he was sleeping much. Even as I looked at him now, the silver in his eyes had grown almost dull. And he never teased or smiled like he had before our siblings went missing.

As much as Misha's disappearance nagged at me every second of every day, I'd somehow forgotten Julian's was having the same effect on him, that he was suffering just as much.

Shame flooded me at the realization. I was the most selfish being on the continent...and I couldn't bear to see him like that.

Turning back, I went to the kitchen and poured two glasses of wine. I took them and a stack of cards someone had discarded in a drawer filled with the most unusual assortment of times. All things that seemed to be junk until you desperately needed them.

Walking to where August sat, I took the armchair opposite and turned it to face him. I pulled a low end table between us, setting the cards and wine down on its surface.

August cocked an eyebrow. "Done with your maps?"

I nodded, then pointed to the cards. "Which game?"

He studied me for a moment, at the setup I'd created, then said, "Your choice."

"Queen's card?" I suggested. A card and drinking game in one.

"Sure, I know that one."

"I'm sure you know plenty, as ancient as you are. You were probably there when they made it up."

August's lips twitched in the barest hint of the grin I'd once thought so insufferable. My heart leaped at the sight.

I gasped, "You *were*, weren't you?" His silence was all the confirmation I needed, I threw my head back and laughed.

"I believe it was Orelia that first came up with the concept in the war camps." August took the cards, shuffling, then began to deal them out. "It became very popular among the soldiers and spread quickly." He motioned to me to start as he took a sip of the wine.

"I meant that as a joke, but that it turned out to be true is wonderful," I said, still smiling.

August's eyes softened. "I can count on one hand the number of times you've smiled since being here," he said. "But never once have I heard you laugh."

Guilt settled into my stomach as I realized what I'd done. I was here, safe—laughing just one month after my aunts were murdered, my sister went missing and was still very much in danger.

"Don't do that." August interrupted my spiraling thoughts. "None of your family would want you to keep punishing yourself for things you couldn't control."

I tried to banish the feeling of guilt but—he was wrong. I did control what happened to me and my family. If I'd been more aware that night of the Summer Solstice, that morning in the forest...

Ker padded over, jumping into my lap and pawing at the blanket I'd set there as she made herself comfortable. August eyed the familiar. "Is there any monster that isn't in love with you or your sister?"

"The shadowhounds weren't particularly fond of me," I said, and considering Rasalas and the Nemean lion, I wondered if our affinity for creatures extended only to felines—or at least those that pretended to be. Ker arched into my hand as I stroked down her spine.

August smiled then, a true one. "Well, not many lived to tell the tale, did they?"

"No, they didn't, though one got in a lucky bite. I owe Damian, Miranda, Celeste, and Teale my life for finding me so quickly." I said as I focused back on our game, laying out another card. We took turns placing several down, his cards trumping mine more often than not. I scowled each time I was beaten and had to take a sip.

"Your mother saved my life once." August broke the silence.

"What?" I said, confused, as I looked from my cards to his face. I couldn't stop the pang I felt in my gut. I somehow always forgot he'd known my parents, my mother—he'd seen her, spoken with her. All moments we'd never gotten.

"We were in the final push, near the center of the continent where the capital once was. All of the civilians had been evacuated, a blessing as the ten day long battle turned the city to rubble. We were closing in on the High King's palace.

Victory so close we could taste it," he said as he laid out another card. Mine won this time.

"I'd just gotten word of my mother's death from one of my generals. I was devastated and blamed myself for not being with her." I'd read about her in our lessons on the war. Yuki Saito, the legendary stormcaster. Alesia had once said she was nearly as powerful as Josiah—their son more so than both.

August continued, "I was stationed with Dominic and Diana on the western front while my father, the Shaws, and Deimos attacked from the East. I was out for vengeance during the battle, reckless in my grief. I tried to take on one of the dragons on my own, the last remaining. She was the largest and eldest female, making her the most vicious. I was nearly drained before I began, then fought her for half an hour before I ran out of power. Standing before her, battered and bloody, I hoped the beast would end it quickly. But before she could douse me in her flames, the dragon began gasping for breath. Diana had filled the dragon's lungs with water, and I watched as she, with only a flick of her hand, turned the water to ice and shattered the beast from the inside. The icy spikes protruded from the dragon's chest as she died." My eyes glassed as I pictured it, her—my mother.

"Then Diana came to me and offered me her hand. We'd hardly spoken in those years, but I knew how she, her sister, and Dominic felt about my father. I'd been present in several of the meetings where they didn't try to hide their disdain. I was surprised she would help me, spare my life, knowing so little of who I was. I would've thought she'd been like most and assumed I was like him. But she said nothing and returned to the fighting. Eve found me shortly after and healed my wounds."

Eve, my heart ached for her—for her touch I would never feel again.

"Later, when it was over, I found Diana in one of the command tents, wanting to thank her for what she'd done. With her gift of Sight, she'd known why I'd come, and simply told me, '*There will come a time when you will repay the favor. I don't know how or why except it will be when snow falls in summer and you know nothing else.'* But the war was over then, and since nothing has come of her words."

"Seers do often say that the future is a fluid and difficult thing to read," I said. "The Fates speak in unpredictable riddles, even to the most skilled of them." Though I wondered what my mother could have meant, her predictions rarely did not come to pass.

"Maybe," he said simply, letting it drop as he placed another hand of cards down on the small table between us.

We played another few rounds, August winning most of them. I was a horrible loser, something that endlessly amused him. Though he equally hated being beaten in the few times he lost, scowling down at the cards as if they'd personally offended them.

"You should probably give it up. It's late," August said after I'd lost another round and cursed. "Accept defeat and call it a night, Nic—"

"Nicole," I said, laying my cards flat on the table. Done with the game as I leaned forward in my chair, reaching for my wine. "You once only ever called me by my full name. You rarely do so anymore."

August went still, even his breathing seemed to pause. "You asked me not to."

I hesitated, my heart pounding in my chest, before I said, "I may or may not have...overreacted. That night."

Something in his eyes caught fire, their silver blaze taking up all the air in the room. "Have you missed my names for you, sweetheart?" The way he said the last word made my heart stumble a beat.

"No." I denied. I didn't know what to do with my face, my hands, so I took another drink of wine. I hoped the flush in my cheeks could be blamed on the alcohol.

August leaned forward, his elbows coming to rest on his knees. His voice was a purr as he neared. "Are you sure, Snow—"

"Don't you *dare* finish that word." I pointed at him menacingly as I could manage, but the words came out breathlessly. The air caught in my lungs in his proximity.

A crooked grin, one I hadn't seen for weeks now, lit up his face. "As you wish...*Snow*."

I cleared my throat, backing away before I slowly stood. I'd begun to feel much too flushed by the wine and his closeness. "This may be the rare time that you are right, it is late. You did plan for us to train in the morning, yes?"

August leaned back, his eyes never leaving my face. "Yes, but we're staying here. You are in control enough now that we don't need to be away from the others."

Stepping around the chair, I paused before walking away. "Thank you for telling me—about my mother."

"Of course, Nicole." My name, my full name, called to me from his lips. The sound of it thrummed through my chest.

I left without another word, walking toward the stairs. Halfway up I looked back. August's posture was more relaxed. A small part of the lightness returned to his gaze.

The tightening in my chest at the sight was solely for his sake.

Untrue.

CHAPTER 47
Nic

Alesia's arms were wrapped around me as I awoke in my aunt's bed. Misha and Eve slept across from us, similarly cuddled. The morning of my and Misha's birthday.

Everything must have been a dream. A terrible nightmare. I breathed a deep sigh of relief as I turned into my aunt's embrace.

Her skin was clammy. Cold. Wrong.

I sat up as Alesia stirred, her eyes opening slowly. Black—the pitch black of darkness that swallows you whole, so endless no one would ever hear you scream.

"Nicole." Eve sat up as well, but the voice wasn't hers. Old and new, beautiful and dreadful.

Skinwalkers had taken over my aunts' bodies.

"Misha. Misha, wake up. We have to go. *Now.*" I pulled my sister to me, shaking her as tears streamed down my face. I had to get her out, get her to safety. My twin slowly opened her eyes.

Black.

I screamed.

"Shhh," the skinwalker in my sister's body stroked my face. "We're together again, Nicky."

I tried to push her away but she didn't budge. The monster with Misha's face only laughed.

Nicole.

The arms that weren't Alesia's came around me. No matter how I tried I couldn't break free of them. The skinwalker was much too strong.

Nicole, wake up.

All of them reached for me, grabbed for me, pinned me down. My hands were aflame as I tried to fight them off. My aunt's entire chambers were burning then.

I felt drops on my skin. Drops and drops of red—blood rain. I screamed again and again.

It's evaporating too quickly. If she doesn't wake up she's going to burn the entire place down.

The monsters hissed and screeched but they still held me, the arms around me never loosened as I fought against them.

Fill the tub. Freeze it now, Miranda.

The skinwalker in Eve's body held down my legs. "Remember to save the heart for the Queen," it said. The one in Misha's body was cutting me open, skinning me alive, readying me to be made like them.

Sweetheart, open your eyes.

I screamed, wailing as I thrashed and kicked. The skinwalkers only smiled and laughed.

OPEN YOUR EYES, NICOLE.

I lurched awake, arms like steel bands still wrapped around me. Tears were streaming down my face, sizzling as they met my cheeks. "

"*No*," I gasped. "Let go—" I struggled to break free but the arms that contained me didn't budge. "Let go. Please let me go." I sobbed, my throat raw from screaming.

"Nicole," The gentle voice came from behind me, from the arms that held me.

August.

I paused in my fighting and looked around, taking in where I was. I was no longer in my aunt's bed, no longer being held down and skinned alive by monsters with my family's faces. I was submerged in a large tub filled with icy water. August was in it with me in an attempt to hold me still, my back to his front with his arms around mine, locking them at my side. My skin still burned and hissed where the water met it.

Even with the realization that it had been only a dream, my tears wouldn't stop falling. I couldn't stop picturing my family like that—couldn't unsee the horrible images.

August's hold loosened as I stopped fighting him. I looked down and saw the burns on his arms. They were in the shape of handprints.

My chest constricted at the sight and I choked on a sob. "August."

"Hey," August spun me around. "It was a nightmare, Nicole. You're here—you're safe." There were burns on his chest too, straight through his shirt.

I clasped my hands in front of me and pulled them into my chest, not wanting to cause any more damage than I already had. "I'm sorry," I whispered. "I'm so sorry."

I clenched my teeth together in an effort to stop sobs from coming, so hard it felt as if they were close to cracking. All the pain I'd been hiding, which I only let out at night, came tearing out of me. None of my grief and rage had dissipated in the time I'd come here, not really, and I couldn't stop it from pouring out of me now that it was free.

"It's okay, sweetheart," August said as he held me, but he was wrong.

"No—nothing is okay. It's all my fault. Everything is my fault." I started to shake as my temperature cooled, though the once icy bathwater was lukewarm now. I couldn't stop the words from pouring out of me any more than I could my hands from shaking. "I should have known. I should have seen the signs...but I didn't. I didn't see it coming and I—I *challenged* her. I incited her and it's my fault she killed Alesia, that she killed Eve. They were our aunts—our godmothers, they raised us, and they're dead because I wasn't paying attention."

"Nicole, it wasn't because of you. You couldn't have known what Adrienne planned. You couldn't have stopped it," August said, but I couldn't hear it.

"Alesia dove in front of that arrow, the arrow meant for *me*. I became unfocused for one second and they both died because of it. I should be the one that's dead...I wish it had been." I choked on the last word.

I wasn't easy to love, and I pushed away anyone that might have tried. I was a coward, too scared of the vulnerability it would require. I'd always thought my family were the only ones I needed. They were the only people who had ever cared for me, truly. The only ones that could and would love me. But now they were all dead or missing, and it was my fault. All of the fight drained out of me as I began to implode in on myself.

"Don't you *ever* fucking say that."

The ferocity in his tone startled me.

August's eyes were furious, a lightning storm over a raging sea. His hands clasped my face. I didn't have the energy to stop him. He was the only thing holding me up at that moment. "Their deaths weren't your fault—*aren't* your fault. Alesia loved you and she sacrificed herself for you. Don't you dare dishonor her by wishing for that, for thinking it for even a moment."

He was right. Alesia and Eve would be furious with me for even having the thought. Yet here I was. Both parents—dead. The aunts that raised me—dead.

My twin was missing and still in danger. Each of us hunted by Adrienne for our hearts, our magic. And I was here...alone.

August followed my thoughts. "You're not alone, Nicole. There are people here that care very much about you. They won't leave you to face this alone if you'd just let them."

I looked around the room then. Seven pairs of eyes stared back at me. Concern and worry filled each of their gazes. I looked back down at the water, unable to make sense of it.

"Come on." August took me back into his arms then. I clung to him as he stood, lifting us out of the water.

He set my feet on the tile and handed me to Miranda. She took me alone into the large attached closet and stripped me of my burned and ruined night clothes. Then she wrapped me in a large towel I used to dry myself. When I was finished, she handed me a cotton robe that was much too big.

We exited back into the bathroom, her hand still on my arm to steady me. I'd never stopped shivering.

The rest of the Seven had gone elsewhere to give me privacy. Only Damian and August remained, the latter still soaked and in his scorched clothing.

"Damian, check her," August said. The male nodded in acquiescence before stepping toward me.

I stepped back. "I'm fine, but...I burned you. Damian needs to heal you first."

Damian himself looked torn at what to do. I felt fine, physically at least, but August, even with the expedited High Fae healing, was still covered in severe burns. Torn, Damian looked to August for guidance.

"Her first." August's tone was firm, a command not to be disobeyed. It was the only time I'd ever heard him speak to one of the Seven as their king and not a friend.

I rolled my eyes at his persistence, and though I tried to tell Damian I was fine, he still took his time examining me with the golden light of his magic.

When he was done, Miranda let me into the attached room

"August wasn't lying, you know. You scared the shit out of us tonight," Miranda said as she pulled back the soft black linens and duvet. I sat where she indicated. "And we were scared because we care." She handed me a mug that smelled of chamomile and lavender. "Drink this. It's a sedative tea and will help you sleep."

I shuddered.

"There won't be any nightmares, Nic, I promise. This will only give you rest." Nodding, I tentatively took a sip. "Sleep. It's been a long night," she said as she stood and walked for the door.

"Thank you." I meant the words for much more than the tea. "I don't deserve your concern, any of you. But thank you for it nonetheless."

Miranda paused, turning back to look at me from the doorway. "Yes, you do. But you aren't going to believe me until you start believing it about yourself," she said as she left.

I finished the tea as she'd instructed and crawled beneath the heavy blankets, comforted by the smell of rainstorms and embers as I quickly drifted into thoughtless sleep.

CHAPTER 48
Nic

The soft light of dawn streamed through the eastern facing window. I awoke in that same room, thankfully having no more dreams as Miranda promised.

The room was similar to mine in size and décor. The bed was slightly larger and there were more windows. August was seated in an armchair across from me. It was his room I realized then, the one adjacent to mine, to Julian's.

"How long have you had the dreams, Nicole?" he said softly. I looked him over before I answered. He was in fresh clothes and none of the burns on his arms from last night were present today. I breathed a sigh of relief. Then I closed my eyes to hide from his.

August nodded, taking my silence as confirmation. "I never heard any sounds from your room. It was unnaturally quiet, but I could feel your magic at the edges. You put up silencing wards."

I nodded. Every night I put them up in case the nightmares were bad enough, in case I screamed. After our interaction last night, I must have forgotten.

August went on, "I knew the grief you had to be feeling had to be extraordinary, but I didn't want to push you and told the others not to either. I wanted you to have time to grieve in your own way. But you weren't grieving were you?" His silver eyes pierced me through. "You've been blaming and berating yourself since that day."

I had no words. I couldn't deny it.

"I have similar dreams," he whispered. "What happened to my mother. That the same fate meets Julian or one of the Seven, their families, and I'm powerless to save them. That they die before I can get to them."

I saw the sincerity in August's eyes as he spoke. We were in the same situation, together. The ones we loved most—lost.

He understood.

"Miranda didn't listen." My voice came out in a harsh rasp, the vocal cords still sore and ravaged from the screams I'd let out in my sleep.

August gave me a smile that didn't quite reach his eyes. "No, she didn't, and thank the gods for that."

I took a second and studied his face before I answered. "Promise me we'll find them. Swear it." I kept picturing Misha that way, with those black eyes. We needed to find them—soon. Before my nightmares became reality, with my sister's heart in Adrienne's hands.

August reached for me and took one of my hands in his. He turned it over, studying it, his finger grazing along the lines of my palm. Then he clasped it between both of his.

"We will, Nicole—or I will tear apart the continent trying." The resolve in his voice soothed me. "You're still exhausted. You should sleep." He let go of my hand and stood.

"No," I said, sitting up. "I can't sleep anymore. I'm okay."

August looked as if he disagreed but didn't push me on it. "I will give you some privacy then. Though..." his voice drifted off.

"What?" I said as I stood.

"The fire. It was contained to your room but it destroyed nearly everything in it. Some of the clothes might be salvageable but you might need to see Celeste about borrowing some more."

I groaned. "She's not going to like that."

His lips turned up in the barest hint of a smile. "I'll be downstairs."

August had been right. There wasn't much left in the room that was salvageable.

The walls and floor were charred, some places worse than others. The ceiling blackened from the smoke. The bed had gotten the worst of it, halfway torn apart. The entire room had a damp smell to it from the rain August had cast to douse the flames. I pictured what it must have looked like and shuddered. August had walked into *this*.

I pulled open the armoire, the door snapping off in my hand before I chucked it to the ground. He was right, very few of the clothes I had survived the fire.

Thankfully my mother's ruby necklace, the memory bracelet, and my aunt's mating bands were still on me and unscathed by the flames. I was grateful they'd been made well enough to be resistant to high heat. Eve's bow and the Iradelmar were also unharmed as they'd been with the rest of the weapons.

Afterward, I came downstairs into the great room. The Seven were there with August, all eating breakfast quietly. There was no change in the way they looked at me, no pity in their eyes. No one asked or talked about what had happened last night. It was a kindness I would be eternally grateful for.

"You have absolutely lost your godsdamned mind," I shouted, furious as I paced before the fireplace.

"There is no other place for you to sleep, Nicole."

Just after dusk, August had informed me that we would be sharing a room now.

His room.

When he told me, any understanding or camaraderie I'd felt between us that morning vanished. To avoid regicide—his own—August had strategically informed me of this in front of witnesses. Miranda, Celeste, and Damian. The first two looked much too amused.

"There are plenty of other places in this cabin where I can sleep. This place is *huge*." I waved my arms toward the stairs.

August remained firm. "All of those rooms are filled with other people who are not equipped to disarm you should you burst into flames in your sleep again. I'm the only one that can."

"Miranda has an inclination for water. She made the ice last night." I looked at the female and she shook her head, dropping her gaze back onto her grimoire. *Don't drag me into this.*

Traitor. I shot her a daggered look before I turned to face off against August again.

August laughed humorlessly. "Good luck trying to separate a mated pair." I blanched, I hadn't thought about that. "Besides, Miranda can control water, change its state, but she can't cast it from nothing."

I hated to admit that he had a point, but I was still livid.

"This is going to be a disaster." I fumed as I turned and stomped up the stairs. I knew I looked like a petulant child having a temper tantrum, but I didn't care. August was lucky I hadn't burst into flames all over again. I heard his soft footsteps coming after me.

Julian's bathroom was still intact so I'd used it to shower and change into a pair of nightclothes from Jophiel which were much too large. The shirt reached my mid thigh and the pants dragged on the ground. Celeste had given me more training clothes but had refused anything else. She said she'd already given me enough—which was fair. I'd owe her a trunk full when this was over.

I hesitated in August's doorway.

The room was big but it wasn't *that* big. Definitely not large enough to fit a bed from one of the other rooms in here, not that there were any free, and I'd thoroughly destroyed mine.

Then the object of all my ire walked in from his own bathroom dressed in a plain cotton shirt and pants. He glanced at my stance in the doorway but didn't comment.

"We are *not* sharing the bed." I insisted as I crossed my arms over myself with the two extra pillows I carried. I suddenly felt too exposed even in the overly large nightclothes.

"I am not sleeping on the floor in my own room, Nicole." He didn't look up as he began to pull back the duvet.

"What happened to chivalry, August?" I walked to the opposite side to face him.

"When have I ever claimed to be a gentleman?" He smiled his usual feline grin.

I launched one of the pillows at him but he easily dodged, grabbing it out of the air. August threw it back at me with more force than I'd expected. I gaped.

"Don't throw things if you don't want them thrown back, sweetheart."

I was about to retaliate when a shout came from downstairs.

"Hey!" Damian shouted. "If you two don't shut it, Miranda is going to hex you so both your tongues fall out, and I am *not* healing them back."

I scowled as I claimed the side I stood on, the one nearest the window. August remained on the side nearest the door, as I began arranging the spare pillows I'd brought from the linen closet in the hallway.

"Are all of those pillows really necessary?"

"Yes," I grumbled as I fluffed them. Two beneath my head. One to keep between my knees, and two down the center of the bed.

"Is that supposed to separate us?" August laid with his hands behind his head, the picture of comfort and arrogance. I briefly considered hitting him with it on his unprotected stomach. His eyes read my thoughts as he grinned, daring me. I scowled.

"Yes." I finally laid on the bed, facing away from him as I got comfortable. I should have known better than to think that would be the last of the comments.

I felt him shift onto his side. "You do know that if I wanted to get to you, it would take more than linen and goose feathers to keep me away."

"And you know that if you tried it, I would scorch you to ash like I did that room next door," I hissed, keeping my back turned to him. I felt his low chuckle reverb from the other side of the bed.

"Do you always sleep straddling something?"

"I am *not*." My head whipped to him. "Sleeping with a pillow between your knees is better for your spine, old man. You should know, you're practically ancient." I considered coating the pillow in ice and thrashing him with it.

August held his hands up in mock surrender. "I'm done, sweetheart, I swear."

I shot him a look that conveyed if he said another word, it might indeed be his last before I turned back over and shut my eyes.

Even though I was exhausted, it took some time before I could unravel my mind enough to sleep.

In the small space, I could feel him, the heat coming from his body—it beckoned to me. It's what I'd been afraid of, why I was so adamant that we didn't end up in this exact situation.

I shoved the thought away as I hugged the pillow to my chest tighter.

CHAPTER 49

Nic

The next day, I hadn't spoken to August except to plan our mission to Sanserria, still fuming at our sleeping arrangements.

He didn't push me on it, giving me the space I needed to cool down, but the longer it went on a very small part of me began to wonder if I was avoiding the male not because I was angry, at least not anymore, but for another reason.

I refused to entertain the thought.

"Simon," I approached the male in a rare moment when he wasn't pouring over the maps I'd made.

His hands rubbed at his eyes, as if he could will the drowsiness from them. "Yes, Princess? Any more information to share?" Simon dropped his hands, looking up at me before I took the armchair next to his. The maps I'd drawn were laid out before him.

"No, but maybe you can share some with me." His eyebrow raised in curiosity, and I went on. "August doesn't want you to go, to be the one entering the palace in Sanserria." Not a question, but the insinuation was there. August hadn't been that way with Miranda's volunteering.

Simon let out a sigh, the lines on his face seemed to somehow deepen. "My husband and I have a daughter."

None of the other Seven had mentioned a child. But Simon had a daughter—a family. I understood August's hesitance now. "What's her name?"

"Jessa." He smiled, the motion somehow sad and blissful all at once.

The love that was shown in his eyes at her mention reminded me of my father. The memory was still melancholy, but less painful than it had once been. Time hadn't healed the wound of his loss for Misha and me, but it was more bearable.

Simon continued, "My daughter is not biologically mine nor my husband's. She will be thirteen this year—but she came to us only three years ago."

"Do you mind telling me the story?" I said, curling my legs beneath me in the chair. Alesia and Eve had adopted us as their own and with the fresh pain of their loss, I wanted to hear a story with a happy ending.

Simon smiled and obliged me. "Shai, Julian, and I were in Reyna for trade business, Malvada, one of the smaller seaside cities on the southern peninsula. We were all dressed in more common clothes to fit in, but this little girl, my Jessa, somehow noticed Julian's stance and walk as unique. She said later that he moves like a male that has never gone hungry," Simon chuckled.

"She pickpocketed him, a tiny ten-year-old girl that was half skin and bones with brown skin and a shock of curly brown hair. She was halfway across the market before Julian had realized, but Shai easily sensed her glee and we were able to follow her. We caught up to her in an alley and saw she'd been sleeping under a tarp near the back entrance of a seedy restaurant. But to keep her stolen prize, she was ready to face down two male fae, one nearly two hundred years old and the other a Prince. The gall and tenacity of her." Simon's face lit up with pride as he spoke.

"Shai used his gifts to calm her, and eventually she told us that her parents had died a few months before. She'd been living on the streets ever since. Reyna of course doesn't have charity for humans the way the other countries do, and she had run away from the orphanage that had beaten her on her first night when she'd cried too much for their liking."

My heart broke for her as he spoke. How many more human children were in her condition in Reyna? How many human children in Hahnaley since Adrienne had arrived that I'd been ignorant of?

Simon tugged at a woven bracelet on his wrist. I'd noticed it before but had never really looked until now. Three cords of burgundy, green, and pink weaved together. "The three of us couldn't leave her there, so we brought her back with us. It took quite a bit of convincing, but I promised her a room in the castle decorated entirely in pink along with dessert every day if she attended lessons.

His eyes peered up at me, laughter in them. "You should have seen my husband's face when we walked in the door. But I knew the moment I saw her that she was mine. Though when she tried to rob a Prince, I should have known then that she would have an eye for finery, but I would happily go bankrupt spoiling her if my husband would let me."

"She sounds incredible," I said, my voice thick. "Maybe I will get to meet her one day."

"Oh, she would be over the moon at that. They are covering the Great War in her history lectures. All the courtiers and staff's children attend schooling within the castle in Ankaa, and Jessa is enraptured by Diana and Alesia's stories." Simon's eyes softened as he looked at me, but my nod told him it was okay to talk about them, so he continued. "Because they grew up as she did, in the slums, and became two of the most powerful females on the continent. Though she is not faerie nor witch, she wants to be like them one day, the half-human Fae that led the charge against the High King. A warrior and also a healer. Her ambition knows no bounds." He smiled indulgently.

I smiled back, even if tears wanted to spill from my eyes. Reaching for his hand, I whispered, "Simon...you can't do this. The risk—"

"I know, Nic." His hand squeezed mine. "But Jessa cannot have a coward for a father. This is my duty. Not just to August and the crown, but to Julian. He has always been like a son to me...and his mother needs him to come home."

I didn't want any of them to come to harm, but after learning this— "Some-one else can go, Simon. Losing a father…" the words floated away from me. I hadn't realized for how long until Simon wiped away a tear.

Looking up at him, I could see it in his eyes. I was the daughter who had lost a father much too young, what Jessa might become if he were to not return. He loosed a ragged breath, "Shai—"

"Yes," the male answered from the table, where he'd been studying more of my maps before walking over. Simon seemed to silently ask him the question, either with Shai's thought-sharing ability or through their gaze.

Shai bowed his head in answer. "Yes, none of them will suspect a thing." With his Reynian features and ability to manipulate emotions, he wouldn't have any trouble entering the palace with Miranda, and his being High Fae gave him that much more leverage should it come to a fight.

"Thank you," I touched his arm, before rising to hug Simon. He stood, meeting the gesture. "I can't wait to meet her," I murmured, his arms hugging me tighter.

"Nothing would make me happier than for her to meet you both."

When Simon released me, off to tell August about the change in plans, Shai returned to his intense studying of the maps, and I joined him. An hour later, Miranda and Damian came to sit around the table as well. With them there, I pointed out any tricky parts and alleviated any confusion.

After our third perusal, everyone's eyes had gone bleary. In dire need of a break, I said. "I know Miranda's story, but did you two always serve the crown?"

Damian sat next to me, but Shai answered first, standing upright from his hunched position to stretch. "Yes and no. I volunteered to fight in the war and was assigned to one of August's legions at the start. It's how we met."

"I'm guessing your talents were particularly valuable in battle," I said, the words came out colder than I'd intended as I thought about how Adrienne and Alexander had used their mindcasting gifts.

"Yes, but not in the way you are thinking." He brushed it off easily. "I use my magic nothing like the Deimos do, it's why I refused participation in their guard though I am from Reyna. I used my gift to help our soldiers have courage, reduce their fear to a manageable amount, and generate bonding and camaraderie between them. This is why August's legions fought so well, even though he was more reserved, aloof at that age. While a brilliant war tactician, August didn't inspire allegiance quite like your parents did. After the war, I worked directly with August. He had spies even then, including Simon's great-great grandfather, separate from the crown. Josiah knew nothing of us."

I knew from Alesia and Eve that he and his father weren't close, but this was the first I'd had it confirmed by someone close to August himself. There must have been a substantial amount of distrust between them for him to hide such things.

"Speaking of the King, are you still icing him out?" Damian chuckled at his own play on words.

I rolled my eyes but couldn't help but smile back. The male's good humor was infectious. "I will ice him out as long as he continues to be an ass."

Miranda snorted. Ker, sleeping on a blank bit of parchment, jolted awake at the sound before settling her head back on her paws. "You still take the tea he makes you every morning."

"To not take it would be a waste of perfectly good tea." I countered though she had me with that one. "Damian, your turn." I changed the subject.

"Not always, I was too young until about thirteen years ago. I'm the youngest here besides Miranda." Damian grinned at her before turning back to me. "But I grew up in the castle. My parents served as royal healers, it's how they met. They were never directly on the King's Council though."

"Damian is a healing prodigy. Three times the talent of fae hundreds of years older." Miranda said of her mate. He blushed in response to her compliment.

"It was probably for the best that they weren't, I couldn't imagine Josiah listened to his council much," I said.

"Montevalle didn't have a royal council initially. Josiah believed himself so mighty that he did not have to answer to anyone for anything." Shai said, his tone even but with a hint of malice.

"Well that turned out to be very untrue, didn't—" Damian suddenly cut himself off. Miranda was looking at him intently and Shai had gone utterly still.

"Didn't what?" I asked but had a feeling I already knew.

"That isn't our story to tell," Shai said from where he stood. Damian looked sheepish for his slip.

I shrugged with disinterest, deciding not to dwell on the mention for Damian's sake, but I could put the pieces together—and I wouldn't forget it.

CHAPTER 50
Nic

Miranda, Damian, Shai, and I stayed up much too late. Finally, they each felt good enough about their knowledge of the palace to call it a night. With as many times as we'd discussed it, I was confident that all three could walk about the place blindfolded without missing a single step.

It was far past midnight when I finally crawled up the stairs and into bed, being as quiet as possible to not wake August. Luckily he didn't stir as I came in.

Not more than an hour later, I was awoken by the feeling of the sparks crackling over my skin.

Wiping the sleep from my eyes, I rolled onto my back, then sat up. The hair on my arms stood straight up, my nightclothes clinging to my body in the heavy static that filled the air. Even my long hair was affected and sticking out around me.

Another crack broke through the air, accompanied by a groan of pain coming from the only other person in the room. I turned in the bed to face him and saw electricity sparking over his skin.

"August," I said softly, but he didn't stir. I said his name again, louder this time, but he still didn't wake.

Shit.

I ripped the covers off of me and knelt next to him. He was sleeping on his side facing away from me. His shirt had pulled up as he slept. The scarring on his back was so much worse than I could have imagined from the glimpses I'd seen in training.

"*August.*" Still nothing.

I reached for his shoulder to shake him from his nightmare, stopping just before I touched his skin. I didn't know much electricity was he putting out right now, but it would hurt like hell to be zapped by that much power.

Reconsidering, I covered my hand in frost. My hand touched his skin, the ice protecting me from the bite of his magic. August thrashed at the touch, not waking but becoming even more distressed in his dream. With both frost-tipped hands, I rolled him to his back.

"*August,*" I yelled, but he still wasn't waking.

Covering myself in frost I leaned over him, my knees coming around his torso, my hands reaching for his face, more anguished than I'd ever seen it.

"August, *look* at me."

His eyes finally snapped open, their silver a raging storm, nearly white as they crackled with lightning. His hands came to my waist, covered in electricity, and ready to take out the threat from his dreams, but the power only grazed along my skin, it didn't shock or hurt me.

"It's me. It was a dream," I said, my voice soft so as not to rattle him further.

"Nicole," he finally whispered, his features softening, but I could feel his heart racing. His hands stayed where they were—still holding me, still sparking with the white glow of his magic.

I looked down at him as I moved my hands from his face to his chest. His skin was cold but covered in sweat. Through his white shirt, I could make out several scars across his stomach on the lower part of his ribs.

"The scars on your back aren't from the war," I said the obvious but needed confirmation.

"Some of them are." August's face flickered with emotion—pain. Though Misha and I both lacked the gift for healing, Eve had taught us extensively in battlefield medicine, in the different types of injuries, including lacerations, and how to quickly treat them on ourselves and others before reaching a healer. While a significant portion of the smaller scars did appear to be injuries sustained by sword, dagger, or claw—the largest of them could only have been made by a whip tipped in Galorian silver struck many times over.

My hands went to the hem of his shirt, needing to clarify what I thought I'd seen through the sweat-soaked cotton. My eyes asked for silent permission. The slight nod of his head was all I needed.

Lifting his shirt, I saw across his skin sprawled a word made of sharp slashes, cuts that must have been made then set with rowan ash to prevent them from healing completely.

Failure

Rage coursed through me, and I asked the question I already knew the answer to. "Who did this to you?"

August hesitated, his eyes bleak—haunted. "When I was a child, my father believed in a certain kind of training—a certain kind of punishment for not meeting his standards."

Bile rose in my throat. I'd been raised with the kindest, most gentle father in the world. Alesia could be tough in training, but she'd never hurt us, never caused us pain.

But this...

To have a parent, someone you were supposed to trust—supposed to protect you—become the thing you feared...I couldn't fathom it.

"That was done when I cried after one of his punishments—afterward, I didn't do so again." His fingers tightened on my waist at the words.

"How old were you?"

A heart-breaking second passed before... "Ten."

"How long?" My voice was so soft it was hardly audible. If I spoke any louder, I might have screamed.

"Only until he realized I could beat him. When he was no longer punishing someone weaker than him—someone defenseless."

"Is that what you dreamed of?" My fingertips traced the outline of one of the more prominent scars. His skin rippled under my touch, and the icy rage in my veins turned volatile—to flame. It worsened the longer I looked at them. If Josiah Warin wasn't already dead, I would have skinned him alive for what he'd done to his son.

I looked back to August's face before I got half a mind to find the bastard's grave and turn it to rubble and ash.

"No, Nicole. I haven't dreamt of that in a very long time. I dream of what you dream of."

"Julian?"

August nodded his head in affirmation.

A shiver came over me as I thought of all the nightmares I'd had since my aunts' death, my beloved godmothers I couldn't save, that now joined my parents among the stars. The nightmares since I was separated from Misha, who was still somewhere out there, unsafe and in danger. Just like Julian.

"Move," I said as I pushed against him. August looked at me with confusion as I moved off him, his hands reluctantly letting go. "You're huge—scooch over."

He obeyed, moving toward the middle of the bed, but remained confused as I laid next to him. Misha had severe night terrors after our father died and this was how I'd comforted her.

"What are you doing?"

"You're cold as ice. I'm warming you up." I told him, pressing my body into his side, my arm draping around him. His skin was still clammy but slowly warming. "But if you don't shut up, I won't."

August looked at me, dumbfounded at first, but then the corners of his mouth lifted.

"What?" I snapped.

"Who knew you could be so sweet?"

I rolled my eyes, resting my head on his chest, where his heart rate was beginning to slow. "If you tell anyone, I will deny it."

"It's a deal, Snow," August said as he wound an arm around me. I forced my lips together to keep from sighing at how good the weight of it felt. I told myself I would stay here just for a moment. Until August was warm and asleep, then I would put space between us again.

As I waited for that moment, I closed my eyes and thought of our siblings, of how we would find them and bring them home.

Then I realized I didn't know when this place had begun to feel like that—like home.

I woke slowly, surrounded by warmth. Much more comfortable than I had been in so long.

As I laid on my right side, my top leg was wrapped around the pillow I kept by me. My arms hugged another closer to my chest. I sighed as I snuggled into them, into their heat—

"Nicole," August's voice rasped with sleep.

I froze as last night came back to me. The nightmare. I'd only intended to stay like this for a few minutes, but I had fallen asleep first.

My eyes shot open, I wasn't wrapped around my pillows, I was wrapped around *him*—and he was looking down at me with his usual arrogance, all the vulnerability of the night before gone.

"If this is the way you wrap yourself around all those pillows of yours, I have half a mind to toss them in the fireplace."

I meant to come back with some scathing retort, but the words caught in my throat. And I was clinging to him like a snake on a vine...even my legs were tangled up with his.

"—except that you drool."

My mouth dropped open. "I do *not*." I gasped, although the evidence to the contrary was on my cheek and his shirt.

August laughed as I sat up and pushed away from him. "Sure, sweetheart. I'm just thrilled to know I now have proof that you do in fact, *salivate* over me."

"You are such an asshole," I hissed, wiping the proof from my face. "I do one nice thing—"

"—thank you" August quickly grabbed my hand as I knelt with one leg on the bed and the other reaching for the floor. "I don't want you to think that I don't appreciate what you did."

"Don't mention it. Seriously. Don't you dare tell a soul," I threatened, but nearly all my anger dissipated at his thanks.

August dropped my hand as I walked for the door. I needed to take a cold shower after I woke up with myself wrapped around him like that.

"My lips are sealed." He said from behind me. "Though, you really should work on closing yours."

I spun around. "The next time you have a nightmare, I'm not doing a thing to stop it. You can rot for all I care." I snarled, flipping him my middle finger before slamming the door. His booming laughter followed me into the hallway.

CHAPTER 51
Nic

A significant number of Adrienne's guards were missing.

We'd received news of it that morning, a raven flew the letter straight to Celeste as we ate breakfast scattered in the living room, not wanting to mar the maps still laid out over the large dining room table.

The guards' numbers had trickled down slowly over the past week. Our informant had no word on where they'd gone, if they were traveling here or elsewhere. August and Jophiel had assured us this changed nothing. Our plan to go to the palace was still in motion and Montevalle's armies were well prepared, as they had been since the Solstice. If Adrienne's guards turned up, we'd be ready.

After I did my part with the dishes, I walked back to the stairs, wanting to change into fighting leathers. I wanted one last sparring match with Jophiel before we went to Sanserria. As I went, my gaze landed on a very familiar book in the bookcase running under the steps. I checked the spine, to be sure.

"You *stole* this from me."

I snatched up the book on elemental lineages as I whipped back to face August still seated in an armchair, every account from the spies we'd received since coming here laid before him on the low coffee table.

"The correct term is *borrowed*. I had every intention of returning it...eventually."

I strode over to him, my hand coming to his chair's armrest to lean over him where he sat. The picture of relaxed, unapologetic ease. "I swear to the gods, August, if I find one crack in the spine or dog-eared page, Julian will have to be sworn in as King after we find him," I said as I waved the book in his face.

"As much as I'm sure you'd love to kill me, sweetheart, I think you would miss me more. Your magic certainly would." And as if it were its own living being, my magic purred at his mention of it.

"I don't care at all what happens to you," I denied, setting the book down on the table.

"Like you said you would leave me to rot this morning?"

"Yes."

August smiled and leaned forward, our faces only inches apart. "I never thought I would love to hear a lie so much until I heard them from your lips." His eyes roamed down to them. My heart thundered in my chest.

I refused to back up—to yield even an inch. Instead, I took my hand and placed it near the base of his neck, my fingers wreathed in fire. I let them lick at his shirt, his skin along the column of his throat, but not burn. Sweat built along his brow from the heat.

I lifted an eyebrow in a dare.

The air grew heavier, crackling in the space between us. August's silver eyes gleamed as he took in the flickering flames. He brushed the back of his hand up my other arm, leaving goosebumps in his wake.

He looked for all the world like he only wanted to move closer to my fire.

"You are insane." I meant to say it reproachingly, but the words came out like a caress. Nor could I stop the accompanying smile from forming on my lips. "Is there nothing I can do that would scare you?" I doubted it as I pictured how my room must have looked, up in these very flames, nearly a week ago. And like with the siren, I knew he hadn't hesitated.

August's eyes softened as he took a moment to answer, so long I wondered if I'd said the wrong thing. But then he whispered words I couldn't process until after he'd stood and walked away, leaving me breathless.

"The beach scared me."

The next night I awoke abruptly. Moonlight streamed through the window's glass.

Shaking—I couldn't stop shaking.

I wrapped my arms around myself as I sat at the edge of the bed, leaning forward over my legs in an attempt to hold myself together.

"Nicole." August's voice, raspy with sleep, reached for me.

I couldn't answer him. Because if I opened my mouth...I wasn't sure what would come out.

It hadn't even been a nightmare. It was a dream. A beautiful, wonderful dream. Misha and I were twelve years old. Our Father, Alé, and Eve all sat with us on our birthday. It was a day of presents and smiles and hugs and laughs. An obscenely perfect string of moments, like a perfectly crafted necklace of pearls—which my waking sent scattering across the ground.

I'd appreciated it then, had known how much they loved me, how much I loved them. But looking back from this perspective, who could have thought—predicted what would come?

It was the last birthday we'd had with our Father. And now they were all dead.

"Nicole—" August's hand rested on my back. I felt the shift as he sat up behind me. I tugged my arms tighter around myself. The tears wouldn't stop streaming down my face. "Shh, Nicole. It's okay, you're okay—"

"It's not okay. Nothing is okay," I nearly choked. Then I held my breath in an effort to lock the sobs deep within me, to not give them one chance to escape. My chest heaved with the effort.

August turned me to him, and I could do nothing to resist. His hand went to brush back the hair that had become stuck to my face with sweat and tears. "You can't hold this in, Nicole. Look at what happened with the fire, you will destroy yourself trying. I know, I've tried. When I lost my mother...in my grief, my denial—it only led to destructive behavior, inward and outward. Actions and words I wish I could take back, that still haunt me to this day. You can't keep this in. It has to come out, every ugly part of it—or you will slowly kill yourself from the inside out."

"I can't," I wheezed, a choking sob escaping with the words. "I feel like if I do, I'll fall apart into a thousand pieces, and I—I'll never be put back together again."

"Then let us hold you together, sweetheart. Everyone here knows and cares for you. You don't have to face this alone. Trust us—trust me. Trust that I won't let you fall apart completely."

I realized then that I did—I did trust him. To find our siblings, to share power. I cried and sobbed and shook as I leaned into him, letting him tuck me into his chest.

Then I touched the moonstone orb for the first time since we'd received them, the day before I'd lost everything, and saw their faces again—everyone I'd lost. August's arms came around me, and I broke apart. He held me tight as I was washed away in their memory.

And August's arms, his warmth, did what he'd promised. He held me together as I let so much of the grief and anguish pour out of me. The sorrow and heartache for all I'd lost, all I loved.

Until his chest, covered in the scars of his past, became covered in the tears of mine.

The next morning I awoke alone, my eyes still swollen from the night before. It was dawn, but the bed was cold. I lied to myself—told myself it didn't hurt something in me to find August absent.

I dressed and washed my face, the cold water reducing the swelling beneath my eyes. Then I went downstairs into the great room and kitchen. Miranda was the only one there. I looked around, confused.

"He's not here."

"Who's not?" I said, acting like I didn't know who she was referring to.

"August, Jophiel, and Simon had to winnow to the capital early this morning. Last minute check-in with the army before we go," she said, taking a sip of her coffee.

"Oh," I said casually, even as the feeling in my chest sank a bit. I went to the kettle and was going to refill it with water before I realized I had no idea how to work the stove.

August made tea for me every morning, sometimes night, since I'd come here. I frowned at the dials. Turning to Miranda, I opened my mouth to ask for help.

She was smiling like a cat.

"Don't worry," she said. "Your tea is right there. August made it extra hot early this morning so it would cool by the time you woke."

"I could have made my own," I said, even as my heart leaped.

Celeste and Teale came walking down the stairs and joined us, going for the kettle to make coffee and tea of their own.

"Oh, I don't think anyone doubts that," Miranda said as I reached for the mug.

After the night we'd played cards, August had taken to putting my tea in a holiday mug for the Winter Solstice, a pale blue with iridescent snowflakes spattered across it. A tribute to his nickname for me.

As I lifted the mug I saw the note placed beneath. My breath stilled.

I set down the tea in favor of the folded paper. It was enchanted and would only open at my touch—for only my eyes to see. I broke the magical seal he'd put on it as I unfolded it and read.

Nicole,

It was not my intention to leave before you woke. And though I am sure you will adamantly deny it, if you did wake and were disappointed to be alone, I sincerely apologize.

August

P.s. You are almost as beautiful when you sleep as when you are angry with me.

I only realized after reading it twice that I was smiling at a piece of paper. I bit my lip to rein myself in.

"Awfully thoughtful of him." Miranda interrupted my thoughts. I looked up. She, Celeste, and Teale had all been watching me.

I narrowed my eyes at her as I tucked the note in my pocket.

Miranda gave me a knowing look before mumbling something under her breath. Too low for even my ears to detect, but I swore I heard the word *denial.*

Celeste sitting next to her caught it and launched into a coughing fit, choking on the sip of coffee she'd taken, and Teale was trying very hard to keep her lips from turning up in a smile as she stirred honey into her tea with lemon.

They were wrong. I could admit that I felt some attraction for him, but I wasn't falling for August Warin.

I wasn't, I told myself again, willing it into being.

My heart whispered back.

Untrue.

CHAPTER 52
Nic

There were seventeen knots in the wooden beams lining the ceiling of this room. I'd counted them five times over now, hoping to distract my mind enough so that I could rest.

Anxiety filled me as our planning came to a close. In two days' time, we would begin the trek back to Sanserria to find Misha and Julian.

Hopefully.

As worry and concern knotted through my gut, I rolled over onto my side, facing the spot where August slept. The space now empty. We had become allies, friends even, but nothing more. I needed him to help find Misha and Julian and that was it.

These were all the things I told myself.

The stale air in the room turned stifling. I couldn't stand another minute, lying there tossing, and walked to the window.

When we were young, Misha and I would sometimes sneak out of her window to sit on the roof just above her bedroom to stare at the stars. There we felt on top of the world. High above anything that could hurt us. Untouchable.

I wrapped myself in an overly large sweater as I unlatched the window and pushed it open. Outside there was a bit of roof I could stand on before it slanted up toward the top. Easy enough to climb.

Stepping into the window frame, I made my way onto the shingles. With hesitant steps, I made my way up higher toward the peak of the cabin. Once I found a place I was happy with, I laid on my back, looking up at the stars.

The night was completely clear, the stars glittering like vast jewels on darkest velvet. I picked out the constellations my sister and I learned in our lessons as kids, slowly finding mine and her favorites. The longer I stayed there, I felt the chill of the night air. Even though it was late summer, the nights were colder here than in Sanserria.

Casting ice never made me feel cold, its chill was a part of me, but the cool air and night breeze coming off the mountains in the north was a different story. The control I had over my flame had grown exponentially in the past weeks, but I still didn't trust it enough to warm my skin with the fire. My nightmare made me hesitate, I might misjudge and burst into a living flame, burning even more of the cabin than I already had.

I sat up and drew my knees into my chest, wrapping my arms around them for warmth.

"You're cold."

I jumped, catching myself. A miracle I hadn't slid off the roof. August sat just above me, where the roof slanted away, hidden by the shadow of the chimney.

"Fucking *hell*, August." I hissed. "You can't just sneak up on people like that. I could have fallen to my death."

"I was up here first, so how could I possibly sneak up on you? It's not my fault you don't check your surroundings before making yourself comfortable."

I rolled my eyes as I turned my back on him. His comment flared the annoyance I already felt at myself.

"Nicole, you're shivering."

"I am *not*," I said even as the wind picked up, its chill deeper than before. I wouldn't be able to sit up here much longer.

"Are you so stubborn that you will sit there and freeze before admitting you're cold?"

"No," I snapped, willing myself into feeling warm to prove him wrong.

He might have had a point.

"Come on, sweetheart. I can hear your teeth chattering from here." They were, I realized. I ground my teeth together to get them to stop. "I have a blanket you can use."

"No, thanks. I'm okay." My muscles were tense now from holding back my shivering.

"Liar."

"Fine." I huffed, turning around and making my way to him.

As I carefully traipsed the transition in the slope, I told myself it was only because I don't want to go back inside yet, the stars too beautiful to miss.

August's lips lifted into that insufferable smile of his as I climbed up the roof toward him. I reached out for the blanket, but instead, he grabbed my hand and pulled me down.

"Hey—" my words were cut off by his tug. His hands easily guided me so I sat between his legs before he draped the blanket over me. Then he used his hands to rub up and down my arms, warming me further.

Even as irritated as I was, I leaned to press my back into his chest, my body seeking more of his heat. I sighed as I felt his warmth surround me.

"See, that wasn't so hard was it? You don't have to be so stubborn all the time, you know. You can accept help." He whispered to the top of my head which now rested against his shoulder. I tried not to think about how comfortable this was. How close we were, even as I could feel the hard planes of his chest through the blanket.

"I accept help...sometimes. Just not from you." Another lie and we both knew it.

August grazed his nose along my hair. My resulting shiver had nothing to do with the cold. "You wound me."

We sat in silence for a few minutes as his warmth coursed through me, the stars gleaming brighter than I'd ever seen them. The lack of light from the forest allowed them to be fully on display.

"Which is your favorite?" August asked, inclining his head toward the stars, the scattered constellations.

"Cygnus."

"The swan?" he said, intrigued. "Why that one?"

"It's a long story, are you sure you want to sit through it?"

"Nothing would make me happier, Snow." His words brought a flush to my cheeks I was glad he couldn't see from how we sat.

"When Misha and I were young, our father would tell us a story of a princess named Odette. She was gathering flowers, lilies, by a lake deep in the forest near her home when the sorcerer who owned the lake saw her. He became infatuated with her and begged her to stay with him, to be his bride. Odette, frightened by him, refused. When she turned to run, he cursed her, turning her into a swan. The sorcerer told her she could leave if she wanted, but Odette could only become a woman again at night under the light of the moon as it touched the water of that lake. So she stayed, tied to that place for many years. Each night the sorcerer would return and ask her to marry him, each night Odette would refuse and remain trapped as a swan.

"Then one evening the Prince from the neighboring kingdom was traveling home from war and stopped to make camp nearby. At midnight he went to the lake to bathe where he spotted the swans and paused, admiring their beauty. As the moon rose and its light hit the lake, Odette transformed. The Prince recognized her as the girl he had known since he was a child, the one he'd long been in love with. Odette had been missing and thought dead by everyone, even her own family."

August's hands dropped from my arms, tightening around me. "What relief the Prince must have felt, to find what he believed lost forever."

"Indeed," I said. "His relief overwhelmed him as he ran to her, then professed his love. A love she returned."

He let loose a breath. "And did they run away together then? Break the curse and seek her revenge?"

"Shh," I pinched his arm. "Let me tell it."

August chuckled, but said no more. So I went on, "But Odette knew the prince had to leave before the sorcerer saw them together, as he would kill him and her both in his jealousy. She then revealed to her Prince that the only way to break the curse was to find her one true love and seal their commitment to each other in a vow to the world. Because the Prince had already known and loved her for most of his life, he knew they were meant for each other and agreed. The next night there was to be a ball in his kingdom to welcome the Prince's return. Odette could leave the lake once the moon rose and attend. There, the Prince would announce his love for her and their vows would be sealed. Odette was filled with the hope she had long denied herself and agreed.

"Unbeknownst to them, the sorcerer overheard their conversation, hidden in the shadows of the nearby forest. He was as furious as Odette said he would be, but he was clever too. So he remained hidden, and the next night when Odette again became a woman, he chained her to the rocks beside the lake. The sorcerer then transformed a different swan into her likeness, taking her to the ball instead. There the Prince saw her and, thinking she was Odette, professed his vow and introduced her as his one true love. But when the Prince kissed her, he saw a vision of the weeping and chained Odette, and the woman in front of him turned back into a swan."

"Foolish." August rested his chin on my head.

"No more commentary," I scolded, though I could not keep the amusement from my voice. "Now aware of his tragic mistake, the Prince ran to the lake to find Odette and beg her forgiveness, telling her she was his mate and he could never love another. She was devastated but forgave him, knowing he spoke the truth and had been tricked by the sorcerer. Though now the curse could never be broken. Odette would be trapped at the lake as a swan forever. Then the sorcerer then returned to claim her, thinking she now had no choice but to marry him. But Odette resorted to her one last defiance and flung herself into the lake to drown. Her prince followed her and they both died, but in death their souls were free. They reunited in the stars, to be together and in love forever." I kept my eyes on the cluster of stars depicting the swan as I finished my story.

"A beautiful story but...tragic," August said quietly, his mouth close to my ear as I leaned into him.

"Is it? Odette broke the curse and freed herself. I would prefer the freedom of death to a prisoner. And now she lives among the stars."

"On that, we can agree," August said, taking my hands. He unfurled my fingers before pressing them between his, warming them.

We sat quietly for a few more moments as I worked up the courage to ask what I already knew, but needed to hear. "August, can I ask you something and you promise not to be mad?"

"Why sweetheart, are you worried about me being mad?" He teased.

"No, but it would take an awful lot of explaining to the others why we got into an argument and I kicked you off the roof."

August laughed. "That sharp tongue. Go ahead, Nicole."

"What happened to your father?"

August went still behind me, hesitating. His silence pressed in on me, and I opened my mouth to take it back. After the scars I'd seen across his back and chest, it didn't really matter how Josiah had died—just that he had.

He spoke before I could. "My father was a powerful but cruel man."

August let out a sigh, the sound weary, and went on, "I am sure you heard many stories from the war about his brutality, and all would be true. You saw the scars, Nicole. His cruelty wasn't just extended to his enemies, but also to his family. Particularly his wives and sons. My father tried his hardest to train me to be just as callous as he was, and in some ways, he succeeded. His favorite punishment was a whip, tipped with Galorian silver, the cuts set with the ash. My father told me the scars would remind me of my failures, remind me not to repeat them."

I shuddered but said nothing as he continued. "My mother had it worse. If she tried to protect me, she would receive the punishment instead as I watched." Rage bubbled in my throat at that horror. Not only the horrific treatment he'd received, but had watched thrust upon his mother.

"When I became old enough to step in, I did. I told my father that if he ever laid a hand on my mother again, I would end his life. She was also a powerful stormcaster, their combined gifts made me stronger than he was. My father knew my threat wasn't empty, that I could overpower him, so he heeded my warning. So instead she came to live with me here and my Council of Seven.

"During the war, my mother and I were separated, only for a few days, but in that short time, my mother died in battle. My father denied being there, but I knew in my gut that he'd been behind her death. I had no proof, just memories of how he treated her. The way he used to threaten her."

I remembered August saying over cards he blamed himself for his mother's death, for not being with her, and something within my heart broke for him.

"When the war was over and my father founded Montevalle, I continued to distance myself from him. For decades I didn't see or speak to him. Then twenty-five years ago I got word that he was to marry Sena, and I feared for her as I had my mother. I returned to the capital and warned him that if he ever touched Sena the way he did my mother, I would keep true to my promise and end him. Then I stayed, and he appointed me as Commander of his armies. Though still wary, I became more present in their lives, especially after Julian was born, to watch over the two of them and make sure my father kept to his word."

August stilled behind me, his voice dropping to nearly a whisper. "When Julian was nine, I returned home from a scouting trip along our southeastern border. As I embraced him, he winced from my touch. I demanded that he lift his shirt, and I saw the marks from the whip across his back, the same as my father had done to me. I sent him to the healers, Damian's parents, immediately before it could scar. Then I confronted my father. He didn't even try to deny that he was *training* Julian in the same way he had me, so I challenged him to a duel in front of the northern courtiers, knowing my father's ego would not let him refuse me in front of such a large audience. In front of them, I killed my father with a bolt of lightning straight through the chest. It was only afterward Sena told me she had lived in fear of my father since they were married, too scared to reach out because of his threats to Julian."

I turned to him then. August's jaw clenched, but I saw no regret on his face. "I only wish I had done it sooner, to save my stepmother and my brother from the same abuse that my mother and I had endured." He finished his story and went quiet, silently gauging my reaction.

I placed a hand on his chest, feeling where his heart beat wildly. "You should never feel regret or remorse for defending those you care about, August. Your father hurt not only them but you as well. You had to suffer decades of his abuse—and he can burn in hell for that."

August leaned in and planted his lips to my forehead, sending a spark through me. "Thank you, Nicole."

"For what?" I whispered, the sound breathless.

"For hearing my story, and not seeing a monster."

I shook my head. "We're all monsters in some way, but we get to decide which kind to be—what and who we would become the monster for. It's clear you are nothing like your father. I can see it in the way you are here with the others, in the way Julian loves you as you love him. But why do you let the other kingdoms think you're just like him?"

"I let them think what they want. If the other kingdoms fear me, they will think twice before they try to take or destroy what I have." I considered his words. In some ways he was right, there was something to be said of being feared as a means of protection. I had done the same for so long, letting my coldness form a wall between me and the world.

"But don't mistake me, Nicole. I am neither benevolent nor merciful. My family and my country are mine to defend. To those that would threaten them, I am the darkest of nightmares." He said adamantly, silver eyes glittering with violence. "Anyone that even thinks of it *should* fear me...except Adrienne."

"What?" I twisted in his arms to face him fully. Adrienne more than deserved his wrath. "What if she took Julian? You love him more than anything."

"But she also took Alesia, Eve, your home, and were it not for her Misha wouldn't be missing. I am not what she has to fear, Nicole, *you* are. I won't take your rightful vengeance from you," he smiled, a cruel and vicious thing. "I only ask that I be present when you destroy her."

His words thrummed through me, his declaration to support my need for vengeance. And the way he stared at me, starlight flickering in his silver eyes. Under them, I felt as if I might burn, catching fire every place they touched me.

"Look at you," August whispered. "Even your eyes spark like they're set aflame—an icecaster with a heart of dragon fire."

My lips turned up in a hint of a smile as I leaned closer, "Are you tempted to slay it, dragon killer?"

August paused, his eyes dropping to my mouth before slowly rising again. Heat scorched in his wake. "The dousing of your fire would be too great a tragedy to bear. Consider yourself safe from me, and..." he paused, taking a breath. "I'm sorry, Nicole."

"For what?" I might have forgiven anything he wanted then.

"For keeping you here, for telling you that you couldn't leave to scout with us at first."

"You *should* be sorry. That was one of your more prickish decisions." I teased, but August didn't smile.

"My reasoning wasn't a lie," he said, though he shook his head. "I *did* worry about Adrienne searching for you, and that you wouldn't be able to keep the fire in check. But—"

"*But*," I nudged him with my shoulder playfully, wanting to take that haunted look from his eyes.

"To me, you were dead, Nicole. For five days, I thought you were gone. And what I felt when I heard the news..." August took a breath, his chest seeming to heave at the memory. "When I saw you again, running out of *here* of all places,

I—I couldn't take it if you were put in harm's way again so soon. But even then I shouldn't have held you back, and for that I am sorry."

I studied his eyes, their storm-cloud silver churning with some emotion, begging my forgiveness. I hadn't thought—hadn't considered...

"Oh dear, I can't tease you for that," I said, the words barely a whisper as my heart pounded in my chest. Not like the butterflies so many spoke about feeling, more like dragons were beating their wings inside my ribs.

"I think it's time to call it a night," I said as I leaned away from him, breaking the spell he was putting me under.

August loosened his arms from around me. "Of course," he said, his voice hoarse. "I'll be there shortly. I just need a few more minutes."

Just before I crawled back through the window, I heard him murmur, "Sleep well, Snow."

I didn't look back, hiding my face as it warmed. The nickname had grown on me, but he didn't need to know that.

Closing the window, I left it unlatched before crawling back under the blankets and duvet. As I laid there, I still felt every place he'd held me. Still smelled his scent of embers and rain. A forest fire met by a thunderstorm.

I fell asleep telling myself I wasn't falling for him—that I hadn't fallen for him.

Untrue.

I drifted in and out of restless sleep, where dreams and reality seemed to merge, only soothed by the addition of warmth at my back. In the most fantastical of these were two voices, one a summer storm, the other a morning frost.

"August," the frost said.

"Yes," The storm answered.

"That day at the beach, you said it was to keep my sister and your brother from coming after me. Is that what scared you?"

Silence followed. Hesitation.

"No, Snow. It isn't."

I fell back into sleep, the warmth of the storm and mist wrapping around me as I reached for it. My mind fell empty, all except for a hand reaching for me in the water, pulling me out of the darkness.

CHAPTER 53
Nic

"Y ou absolutely will not." August clanged about in the kitchen the next
morning, irritated with me.

"If I draw Adrienne out, Miranda will be better able to search the palace and
Shai evacuate the Shaws," I argued from where I sat perched on the kitchen
island. With my mental shields, I was confident that I could easily face Adrienne
and win with either ice or fire, no matter how many guards she brought. "It will
give them more time."

August's sleeves were rolled up his forearms, the corded muscle flexing as he
made tea. I'd been fighting not to notice.

"You go in."

My eyes jerked up. "Go into the palace?"

He nodded, handing me the mug of tea, iridescent snowflakes glimmering.
"Miranda and Shai can go in one way, gather the staff for an evacuation while

you search. Even with all the maps, you still know the palace better than they do. If our siblings are there, you are best equipped to find them."

"Of course, I know it best. It's the getting in that's the problem. The winnowing wards have surely been reset and the guards know my face too well. They will have enchantments at every entrance that could warn them of my presence."

"So use one they don't know about." He leaned against the opposite counter, taking a drink of his own tea. "On the maps, there are underground tunnels leading from the palace to the beach yes?"

"Yes," my eyes narrowed, setting my cup beside me. "But we'd only ever been able to open them with Misha and my father's earth magic. The stone won't part for me."

"How do you it was their magic? That it wasn't opening for them because they were Briars?"

I went silent, unable to dispute his claim. We'd been banking on the fact that Shai and Miranda could get through the palace's enchantments because of their loyalty. If the stone opened because of our blood, and not Misha's magic as we'd always thought...it would be too easy.

"You don't think I should draw her out, but you're suggesting that I go straight into my palace she's taken for herself?" I cocked my head to the side. "And if Adrienne catches me?"

"She won't because *I* will draw her out," August said, a smirk lifting at the corner of his lips. "She wants you and your sister, but she also wants me as her prisoner. And you can't tell me she's not also tempted to steal storm magic." He lifted his palm, a tiny thundercloud forming above it. Sparks danced across the dark gray mist. "But don't worry, Snow. I will save her end for you."

"You think highly of yourself, dragon killer." I smiled and cast magic of my own. Little dragons of fire and ice. They flew around him, diving through his hand-held storm unscathed. Then they turned to swans, swooping, and landing on his shoulders, the ice one nipping at his ear just before disappearing. "You'd take credit for my murder to keep me safe, and now you want to be used as bait? Careful, August. People outside the north are going to think you care."

He set down his tea and came toward me, placing a hand on each side of where I sat so we were eye to eye. The air between us charged with some current, the kind that hadn't come from his magic.

"And if I do?" August reached up to push back the hair that had fallen into my face, his fingers hesitating before touching my skin, asking permission.

My breath caught as I remembered the first time he'd reached for me like that, the night of the Solstice ball, before everything went to hell. Then I'd flinched, not wanting him to touch me…but so much had changed since then.

When he reached for me this time, I leaned my head into his hand. His fingertips brushed my skin, a shiver running through me at the touch.

August looked as if he wanted to pull me in closer, to close this remaining gap between us. I realized I wanted him to, that I—

The door burst open.

I jumped off the counter, my bare toe hitting the cabinet as I cursed.

August's eyes could have been daggers for the look he was giving to whoever had come through the door just now.

Celeste raised her hands in alarm. "Whoa," she said, looking between us. "Didn't mean to interrupt, but we've got company at the border."

"The missing guards?" I said, straightening as I ignored the painful pulse in my foot.

She shook her head, eyes wide. Almost disbelieving the words as she spoke them.

"The Shaws."

CHAPTER 54
Nic

August and I winnowed to the Death Tree, where the break in the wards had been noted. Shai and Celeste joined us. Her eagle, Aetos, took off overhead to scout the area, to be sure the Shaws were the only ones that had come.

I looked around, desperate to spot them. In no time, wild red hair ran toward us.

"Nic!"

"Gemma!" I ran to her.

"You're alive." Tears streamed down her face from relief. "We've been in the Redwood for over a week trying to find our way. You cannot imagine how relieved I am to see you. We thought you were dead."

"Gemma, I'm so sorry. I heard about your parents," I said as we embraced. My chest filled with the guilt that I hadn't worried more for her in my grief and the desire to find Misha. But I was thankful she was here now, blessedly unharmed.

Gemma looked at my companions, her eyes widening as they landed on August and the others. She stiffened in my hold.

"No Gemma, it's okay. August didn't do it, Adrienne lied." I said, pushing her hair back from her face. She looked exhausted. Dark shadows pooled under her eyes, and her once soft curves had all but disappeared. Gaunt and frail.

"I know," she said, her eyes descending to the ground as we broke apart. "We discovered it some time ago but were just now able to escape."

"Nic," Evander said as he stepped out of the trees. His smile was wide but something was off about it, reminding me that the last time I'd seen him, he and I hadn't parted on good terms. His eyes darted from me to August, then Celeste and Shai, and back again. Whatever it was, he quickly brushed it off, his stance seeming to relax.

"And Lorraine?" I asked, an uncomfortable twinge in my gut.

Evander shook his head. "Lorraine remains in Sanserria. She could not escape. We barely made it out ourselves and weren't able to go back for her. We hope to make it back to Desdemon to gather our own forces, then return to liberate her."

"And your path eastward brought you north?" August said, his eyes trained on the male with a predatory sharpness.

"Yes," Evander answered, equally on guard. "We took a different path to avoid Adrienne's guard at the Eastern border, and as it would be unwise to pass through Reyna, we decided to go by way of Montevalle."

August's face remained devoid of reaction, but I could see the suspicion in his eyes. He inclined his head to me. "May we have a moment?"

"We'll be right back." I gave Gemma's hand a reassuring squeeze before we walked several meters away.

I cast a silencing ward around us so Gemma and Evander wouldn't overhear, turning my head so neither could read my words. "They have to come back to the cabin with us, August." I saw the *no* already forming on his lips. I spoke again before he could, "They are our allies."

"Hahnaley's. Not mine."

I clicked my tongue. "They can give us information on Adrienne, her plans, and if they have seen or heard anything of Misha and Julian."

August spoke through his teeth. "How can we trust that information? How do we know Adrienne didn't send them herself?" Even now he kept himself angled toward them, not allowing them from his sight.

"They know Adrienne killed their parents, they couldn't be working with her after learning that. Besides, I crossed here, happening upon the cabin and the Seven by accident, and you didn't accuse *me* of being manipulated by Adrienne."

He blinked, taken aback. "Of course, I knew you weren't working with Adrienne. I trusted you."

"You hardly knew me."

"I knew enough."

"*August*," I hissed, growing frustrated.

"*Nicole*," He said, equally exasperated. "I cannot allow them to know of the Seven or of the location of my outpost. It's too dangerous."

"We can't just leave them here either."

August studied my face, understanding I wouldn't let this go. "We'll talk to them first. See what they're willing to share. Shai will screen them before we go."

I considered a moment, not wanting to subject them to such a gross invasion of privacy, but I knew what the Seven meant to August—what they meant to me. We couldn't risk giving away their location and putting them in unnecessary danger.

"Okay," I said, conceding to this compromise.

I dismissed the silencing ward. As we walked back over to Gemma and Evander, August went quiet, sharing our conversation with the mindcaster as he stood back with Celeste.

Gemma and Evander still watched August—us—warily. To break the silence I asked, "Have you seen or heard of anything of Misha? Of Julian?"

"We were of the belief that Julian kidnapped her," Evander said, his eyes flicking to August who tensed at the words. Evander would be in a dire situation if he didn't watch his next words carefully.

"You had to know that wasn't true," I said, hoping to dissipate the tension, even as I angled myself between the two males.

"We didn't know what to believe, Nic." Evander's hazel eyes seemed to sharpen at the words. "Our parents were dead, we thought you were dead too until we saw you just now. Only when we learned of Adrienne's deceit in the death of our parents did we begin to question her other statements as well."

Gemma had seemed surprised to find me alive, but Evander...he'd seemed to almost expect us. I shook my head. "Julian is in love with my sister. He would never hurt her."

"Of course, Nic." Evander nodded his head, but it didn't feel as if he'd said the words because he believed them, but rather to placate me in the way one pacifies a child. I bristled.

August noticed and inched closer, his hand grazing my low back. The touch grounded me.

"Nic, may I have a word?" Evander's eyes moved between August and me. "With myself and Gemma—privately?"

"Nicole," August's silver eyes spoke to mine. *Don't go.*

I hesitated, considering as I looked up at him. "It will be just a moment. We won't go far."

After a few moments, August nodded. He wouldn't tell me no, but I swore I saw a flash of panic on his features.

Evander turned, Gemma and I following. We walked far enough into the trees to be out of sight of August to give us privacy. Being unable to see him made me uneasy, but if Adrienne could have somehow compelled the Shaws, and they weren't alone, Aetos would see the trap and notify Celeste.

Evander turned to face me in a small glade as he cast a silencing ward. "Nic, leave with us. You are not safe with him." He urged, reaching for my hand. Gemma nodded her head in agreement.

"What?" I pulled back before he could touch me.

Evander's tan face melded into hurt. "Come to Desdemon with us. We can sort everything out there. Help you find Misha."

"No. August has taken me in. He's helping me search for my sister. I'm not leaving him."

"Don't you trust me?" His eyes turned pleading.

I hesitated. I no longer knew the answer to that.

The hurt on his face hardened, turning into something else. "You don't, do you? Because now you trust *him*. He's a murderer, Nic." Evander snarled, stepping closer to me.

I steeled my spine, refusing to be intimidated. "You have no idea what you're talking about." My tone was low, sharp—a warning.

Evander put his hand on my shoulder, his face softening. A dizzying fluctuation of hurt and anger. "Nic, please—please come with us," he begged, but it did nothing to shake my resolve.

"No," I shook my head. "We still don't know where Misha and Julian are. Stay with us, Evander. We can find them and help you free Lorraine."

His hand slid up to my neck. I stiffened, but he either hadn't noticed or chose not to. Evander leaned in to kiss me, as he'd done before, but I turned away. I didn't feel that way for him anymore. I doubted if I ever really had.

Evander's lips missed their mark and landed on my cheek instead. My hands moved to his chest, to put space between us. "Evander, I—"

His grip tightened as his fingers dug in, the nails leaving little crescent moons on the skin of my neck. "It's not enough to show you love is it, Nic? To shower you with affection and gifts? To be generous and kind—you wouldn't even wear the necklace I gave you." He brought his other hand to my neck and squeezed.

My hands flew to where he held my throat. "What are you doing?" I gasped, trying to remove them, but his hold remained firm. His strength wasn't natural, even for the High Fae.

"If you won't come willingly, I can make you." The change in Evander was so abrupt it was startling. I'd never seen him act like this—had never heard him sound like this before.

"You're hurting me," I rasped. It was only for Gemma's sake, softly crying behind him, that I hadn't severed his hands from his wrists, but that sentiment wouldn't last much longer.

He needed to take his hands off me.

Now.

"Good." He grasped my neck tighter, choking me, as he leaned into my face. His hands were completely cutting off my air. "I can't wait to take you back to the Queen so she can carve out your heart."

Evander felt my magic surge in response and put up an air shield between us, preparing to block my water or ice. But he knew nothing of the fire.

An inferno erupted from me, lashing through his shield as if it had never been there at all.

Evander screamed and staggered back, "You crazy, fucking *bitch*."

I took in deep gulps of air now that I was free of his grip. When he turned back to me, half of his face was charred black along with both of his arms up to the elbows. The skin was gone in pieces, showing the angry red tissue beneath.

Good.

"That's what you planned all along?" I snarled, my hands still aflame, ready for any counterstrike. "To lure me back to Adrienne? You're a *traitor* and your parents would be ashamed."

"My parents were *weak*. They would never do what needed to be done for the continent, to rule like conquerors." His hazel eyes held a darkness I had never seen before. Had he hidden it, manipulating us so effectively we hadn't seen—including his own parents?

"Your parents deserved better than you for a son. They'd be horrified at you now."

"Good thing I killed them then."

The shock of his words made me pause a tenth of a second too long, and Evander blasted me with air. I slammed into a tree, several ribs cracking. Remembering myself, I threw up a shield of fire just in time to evade another of his blasts.

My mind reeled. Evander killed Orelia and Cedric—not Adrienne.

From behind my shield, I saw him go to grab Gemma from where she knelt on the ground. As he reached for her, she cringed away, like she was expecting to be struck.

Gemma. She was sobbing now.

Men like Evander didn't just snap. He murdered his own parents for fuck's sake. He'd put his hands on me, but I wasn't the first he'd done that to.

How long had he been hurting her? There had been no hints, no signs before now—except that wasn't true. He'd grabbed my arm that night in the gardens, the last night I saw him. He'd let go when I pulled back, but his grip had been hard.

And the sirens.

Evander always blanched at their mention, refused to go near the edge of the water...because they attacked males that were violent toward females.

"Do not touch her," I snarled, dropping my shield. A whirling whip of fire flew from my hand. It sliced across his arms, and he screamed. Using wind, he lifted himself into the sky, leaving Gemma behind. Then he was gone, winnowed away.

"Gemma, how long was he hurting you?" I knelt by her side, my ribs searing in pain with every word.

"He would never hurt me, he's my brother," she sobbed. She was shaking so hard she couldn't stand, her legs buckling as she tried.

"Gemma, but you flinched—you pulled away from him."

Her eyes held a sort of blankness, as if she couldn't fully process what I was saying.

Lorraine.

Lorraine was the mindcaster. I wondered if she had coerced Gemma to forget, altered her memories to protect their brother. I wouldn't put it past her.

"Gemma please, come back with me. Let me help you." I reached for her again.

"No, no, no, no." She was hyperventilating, growing pale, and looked to be slowly going into shock. All of this was too much for her.

Shai, Celeste, and August ran into the small clearing then.

"What happened?" Shai spoke first. "We smelled smoke."

August came straight for me. "Nicole, are you hurt?" He knelt beside me, looking at my face then lower, and saw my throat. His fingertips touched my neck gently. I flinched at the sting where Evander must have broken the skin.

August's eyes flickered with lightning, a rage in them as I had never seen.

"I'm okay," I whispered, touching my hand to his arm.

The fury in his eyes didn't dull. If anything, it flared brighter.

"He's dead."

I grabbed his wrist tightly, keeping him from standing and going after Evander. "I can fight my own battles, August."

His chest thrummed with a growl. "Evander Shaw lost the right to keep breathing when he touched you."

"I know that, but he is *mine*. When we find him—and I will—I will rip that hand off and shove it down his throat. Just before I burn him alive."

August's eyes sang in appreciation of my dark words, but the anger didn't abate. He lifted his other hand, his fingers gliding up to cup my jaw, those intense silver eyes still locked on mine.

Shai reached for Gemma to carry her back to the cabin. She didn't acknowledge him as he lifted her, hysterical as she was, her body shaking with the strength of the sobs. He whispered to her gently as he tucked her into his chest. She seemed to calm as his magic fell over her.

August nodded to Shai and Celeste as he and I stood. Tucking me into his side, we winnowed back to the cabin. When we landed outside the cabin's wards, Teale, Damian, and Miranda were waiting for us.

"What happened?" Miranda asked. Damian went to Shai as he held Gemma, assessing her as they walked, his hands glowing gold with his gift of healing.

"Evander attacked me."

"What? Why?" Miranda said, stunned. "I thought Desdemon was Hahnaley's closest ally."

"They were, when Orelia and Cedric were alive." I ground out the words. "Evander is aligned with Adrienne now. When I refused to leave with them, he changed completely. He said he would force me away, let Adrienne cut out my heart."

Fury so thick it was nearly tangible poured off August as he walked close to my side, his hand never leaving my back.

"Why would he align with her? She killed Cedric and Orelia—did he not know?" Miranda continued her questions.

"No, she didn't. Evander killed them himself. He said so."

Everyone paused their walking, looking at me in disbelief.

"How—why?" Miranda got out, unable to form more than those two words in her shock. Shai and Damian continued walking on. Gemma now asleep in his arms.

"I don't know exactly, but I can guess. Imagine this: Adrienne promises him power and magic, more than just the air element. Stolen power she can give him from other High Fae—from his parents even," I said as we followed behind them.

"She can also make him King," August murmured, fury still lacing his voice. "Not just over Desdemon, but the entire continent."

Nausea rose in my gut. Evander had accused August of killing his father for power, all while plotting the same. Orelia and Cedric would have never seen it coming. They loved their children—had always been so kind and trusting. They never would have suspected him capable of such a thing.

My head spun as I thought more about the treaty celebrations, in my head going over every interaction with him, every observation, looking for the signs we'd all missed.

I stopped walking. "The necklace."

"What necklace?" August paused with me.

We'd reached the cabin at that point. Jophiel and Simon were on the porch waiting. Simon held the door open for Shai to carry Gemma inside. The rest followed.

"The Solstice," I said. "Evander had been all over me that day, would hardly leave me alone."

"I remember." He nearly growled.

"He'd also given me this gaudy necklace that morning in the gardens, had been adamant that I wear it, and was unusually upset when I didn't. What if Adrienne poisoned it?"

August considered. "That sounds like something she would do. If she couldn't incapacitate you with her magic, she'd find another way."

"What if she did the same to Misha, incapacitated her. Julian too, and that's why they've been silent? Miranda has mentioned the possibility before."

He let out a long breath. "Then she's prepared to break it if that's the case." August opened the door to the cabin, holding it open for me as I entered.

Shai sat on the couch, still holding Gemma tight to his chest. Silent tears streamed down her face in her sleep. Damian stood, having ensured she was physically unharmed, and came to me. He healed my ribs and throat quickly until not even a soreness lingered.

Teale joined them, recoiling as her hand touched Gemma's skin. "She feels *wrong*."

Miranda shuddered as well. "Something dark is within her."

"Adrienne has been in her mind," I said. "Her magic, even the natural born abilities, must be tainted by her use of stolen power."

Nature rejects the false one. Teale being part-nymph and Miranda with her inclination for earth magic would be more in tune with the unnatural than the rest of us.

"So it wasn't Lorraine Shaw that made her forget?" Celeste leaned forward from where she sat.

"Lorraine had to have done some of it, Adrienne couldn't always be there to wipe away Evander's actions." I pressed my lips together, thinking it through. "But Adrienne had to have done more while they were in Hahnaley these past two months otherwise you two wouldn't sense her magic on Gemma."

"So what do we do now?" Jophiel stood, pacing. "If Adrienne had Misha, then Evander would have used that to coerce you into his trap. Do we still go to Hahnaley to search for her and Julian in the palace?"

This new knowledge changed nothing for me. I still believed them to be there, hidden away in the palace. Under some poison or curse from Adrienne.

August's eyes read my thoughts. "Yes. Adrienne will now have it confirmed by Evander that Nic is in the North with me. The best place to go is right under the traitor's nose."

CHAPTER 55
Nic

S hai carried Gemma to one of the second-floor rooms with Teale. Miranda trailed behind with a reed diffuser, its scent a concoction of lavender and sage to help her sleep peacefully. Teale would watch over Gemma as she slept, calming her if necessary, as she continued to work through unraveling her memories.

Returning to fill in the rest of us on what he'd seen in her mind, Shai told us of the memories hidden under layers of intricate delusions. Not only had Evander been abusing her for years, but she also had hidden memories from their interactions with Adrienne.

As he finished, Shai left to check on her once more. Even with Teale there, I suspected he would spend the entire night watching over Gemma. Afterward, everyone slowly separated to head to their rooms, including August and me.

I couldn't stop thinking about the way August had looked in the glade, the rage in his eyes. He said he would kill Evander for what he'd done, and I knew he meant every word.

I had to know why.

"What was that about?" I said as we entered his room. August stood at the small table taking off his weapons, his back to me.

Turning to look at me, August quickly waved his hand to put up silencing wards. Good, we didn't need the rest of the cabin hearing us argue any more than they already had.

"What was what about, Nicole?"

"The glade. I've never seen you like that."

August's jaw clenched, his anger hadn't abated at all since we'd returned. "Because against my better judgment, I let you walk off with him. Then not two minutes later he's got his hands around your throat."

I bristled. "After all this time, you still think I can't defend myself?"

"No, that's not—" August took a deep breath as he ran a hand through his dark hair. "I know you can—you did. But Evander threatened you. *Hurt* you. And he got that opportunity because I let you walk away with him. I could never forgive myself if something had happened to you."

"August, what happened to your mother," I swallowed, my mouth suddenly too dry. "—that wasn't your fault. Neither would it have been if Evander—"

"You don't get it." August shook his head, cutting me off. "I will kill anyone that harms you. That even thinks about harming you. I won't apologize for wanting to protect you."

"Why?" I asked, my heartbeat thundering in my ears.

"You know why," August said softly.

I crossed my arms and narrowed my eyes at him, frustrated by his non-response.

"Don't give me that." He stalked toward me, his silver eyes flaming. "You *know* why, but you are too in your own head to see what is right in front of you—what you are to me."

Panic rose in my chest. I couldn't have this conversation—it would shatter me if it wasn't what my heart wanted to hear. Turning, I opened the door, wanting nothing more than to escape this feeling until I could shove it down again.

"No, wait—" August grabbed my arm, turning me back to him. At the same moment, he pushed the door shut again.

"Let go of me," I pushed against his chest trying to dislodge him. He now had his hands on both my arms, holding me to him.

"I *can't*," August whispered, pain lacing in his words. "Don't you understand why—you have to know by now."

I shook my head, not comprehending what he was saying. My heart screamed the answer, but my thoughts shut it out.

"From the very first moment you crashed into my world in that alley, for better or worse, I can't let you go. You can push me, curse me, fight me all you want. But just don't stop...don't walk away. Not now." August said as his silver eyes burned into mine, their intensity leaving me breathless. It felt like they were reaching for my soul, desiring it, demanding it even with all its darkest parts.

But it couldn't be, he couldn't feel that way about me. I wasn't worthy of being wanted, of being seen in that way.

The beach scared me.

The dousing of your fire would be too great a tragedy to bear.

Trust me.

And if I do?

Untrue.

I'd tried for so long to not let it affect me—but August had somehow worked his way under my skin. I would never be free of him. A part of me wanted to rip it off, to claw him out. The other part of me had to know, had to feel what it would be like to give the fire inside me what it wanted, what I'd been fighting since the day I met him.

Even if the result broke my heart.

If this thing between us was going to crash and burn, I might as well go down in flames.

Slowly I ran my hands up his chest to his neck, then around to tangle in his silky black hair. Finally, I stood on my toes and touched my lips to his. August was motionless as I did this, his hands still on my arms. Yet he didn't move to kiss me back.

Oh gods. I'd misinterpreted his words. He'd alluded that he cared for me—but not like this.

Panic and rejection seized in my chest. I dropped my hands and pulled away, wanting nothing more than to sink under the water of my bath and never come out again, to never have to face him after this.

No more than a second after I did so, August finally moved, his grip tightening to prevent my escape. I couldn't look at him. One of his hands let go of my arm, the other still holding me firm, as his fingers lifted my chin.

Then his mouth crashed down onto mine.

August kissed like he was starving and intended to devour me. Relief flooded through me as my hands came back to his shirt, the material fisted in my grip. I returned his ferocity, my mouth opening for him as his tongue slipped in and caressed mine.

He groaned, his hands reaching down to catch the back of my thighs. As he lifted, I wrapped them around him. With a hand, he knocked away the daggers, sword, bow, and arrows. The weapons clattered to the ground, clearing the space for me on the table.

August's hand moved to the back of my head, gripping my hair to hold me in place as his mouth possessed me once more. With my legs still around him, I pulled him tighter into me. His other hand moved to my waist, slowly slipping under my shirt. The feel of his calloused skin shot straight to my core, his touch searing in the best way.

I knew after only one taste of him it wouldn't be enough, it would *never* be enough.

I broke our kiss to catch my breath as his grip in my hair tightened. He took this chance to run his lips down the column of my neck, his other hand stroking up my back. His touch was pure electricity, everywhere he touched my body responded.

"Nicole," he breathed my name against my skin. August returned his attention to my mouth again, and I moaned as he kissed me. Too soon he was pulling back to look into my eyes.

"What do you want?" August asked, his voice hoarse. His eyes burned into mine, a raging silver storm.

"I want you to fuck me," I whispered breathlessly as I leaned forward, my hands threading through his hair as I recaptured his mouth with mine. He chuckled darkly as he pulled back again.

"Oh, I got that, sweetheart." His face broke into his teasing smile. I went to slap his arm half-heartedly for his arrogance. August easily caught my wrist, planting kisses from its pulse point to my inner elbow.

"What I meant is—what does it mean for us?" He asked as his smile faded, becoming more serious. I froze.

I wasn't the one people wanted. My beauty maybe, but me at my core, my heart? No one had ever taken the time to truly know it outside of my family.

Except him.

I wanted everything from August, and to give all of me in return.

The self-admission terrified me. I didn't know when it happened—when it started. All I knew was that August Warin had completely consumed me.

But I couldn't make the words leave my mouth. The walls I'd constructed to protect my fragile heart wouldn't give, wouldn't let any vulnerability escape so I could tell him what I hadn't realized until now...that through all the heartache and grief he'd supported me, held me, protected me, and—

I'd fallen in love with him for it.

He sensed my hesitation, but August just stared into my eyes, waiting for my answer. Eager, but patient. He wouldn't rush this.

"August, I...I don't know." I whispered.

Untrue.

I immediately regretted what I said, for what he might take it to mean. His eyes flashed with an emotion I didn't catch.

I wondered if he could read my face and sense my lie. If he could see through my eyes into my soul that was calling to his—the way he looked at me felt as if he did.

"For tonight then, I'm yours," August said, though he sounded like he'd meant something different. "We'll face everything else tomorrow." He touched my face gently, and I leaned my head into his hand.

"So sweet," he whispered, teasing me. I turned, biting his palm.

August laughed as he pulled me in close again. "There she is...that dragon fire heart."

Grabbing his shirt I pulled him back to me, kissing down his neck that tasted of rain and crackling embers and *him* as my hands moved to the buttons, quickly undoing them. When I finished I pushed it off his shoulders, and he released me to let it fall to the floor. I swept my palms across his chest, along the firm muscles to feel every line and ridge. With every scar, he was beautiful. More so, even.

August reached back for me, both of his hands sliding up my waist as he took my shirt the rest of the way off and tossed it to who knew where. One hand came up to cup my breast, now bared to him, as he planted a kiss on the top of my shoulder. A moan escaped me as I arched into his touch.

"*Fuck*, that sound," he ground out then lifted me, setting me back onto my feet. Once I was standing, his hands went back to my waist. He unbuttoned my pants and kneeled as he pushed them, along with my undergarments, down my legs. I quickly stepped out of them.

Kneeling, he took a second to just look at me. Before I could feel self-conscious August whispered, "So beautiful, Nicole," as he kissed me once on each thigh.

As he stood, August gripped my hips and lifted me back onto the table, his mouth crashing back into mine. With both hands, he pushed my knees wider, settling himself between them. One hand caressed down my waist—lower. I shivered in anticipation.

His fingers finally touched me, parting me. August let out a low growl in approval at the wetness he found there. He continued to stroke, exploring me, but wasn't quite pressing where I wanted it. I shifted my hips in response.

"So impatient," he murmured, gently biting my bottom lip as his tongue flicked against it. Just like it would if his mouth replaced his hand. August was torturing me and he knew it.

In retaliation, I reached down to cup him through the pants he was still wearing. As I ran my palm against him, gripping his length through the fabric, he thrust against me.

He swore, his restraint faltering, as the hand at my thigh tightened and I smiled against his mouth. My gloating didn't last long. August made his way down my neck with open-mouthed kisses as his thumb pushed down on my clit, in the same motion sliding a finger into me. I gasped, my back arching at the feeling.

August began to back up from me. I tightened my grip on his neck, a sound of protest escaping my throat.

"Don't worry, sweetheart, I'm not going far," he chuckled darkly. I reluctantly released him.

Slowly he pushed me to lie back on the table, pressing kisses down my stomach as he went. August took his time as he moved lower, lifting my hips to bring them closer to the edge of the table.

Then he knelt. My hands slid back into his hair as he lifted one of my thighs over his shoulder and his mouth replaced where his hand had been.

I took in a sharp breath and arched in response as he licked me. He placed one hand on my stomach, keeping me locked in place, and continued in long strokes that set my entire body ablaze. Then he ran his tongue over my clit, stroking, and at the same time slid two fingers back inside of me.

The pressure was too much, and I began to shake as he devoured me. He curled those two fingers up and my climax shattered through me, my head spinning. I was trembling, overwhelmed by my orgasm as I tried to sit up, but he kept me pinned down with that hand.

"I'm not finished, sweetheart."

Another shot of desire shot through me at the rasp in his voice, the possessive gleam in his eyes as he waited, his eyes locked on mine. I nodded my consent for him to continue, and August returned to kissing, licking. His fingers never ceased moving inside me. I screamed when I went over the edge again.

August gave me a few more tender strokes with his mouth, each one making me jolt at the sensitivity before he slowly rose from the floor. He gave me a slow, smug smile as he licked his fingers.

Stars above, I was going to eat him alive.

I clung to him as he kissed me again, at the same lifting and carrying me to the bed.

He set me down on the edge with a gentleness that contradicted the absolute war his mouth had just raged on me. August was still standing as I reached for the button on his pants. His hands grasped mine, making me pause.

"Are you sure, Nicole?" His eyes were intense, pleading. I could tell he wanted this, but he would stop if I asked him to.

"Very," I breathed in response. He leaned forward, his hand coming to my hair, and planted a kiss on my head. Then he gripped my hair tighter, almost to the point of pain. The sensation shot desire straight through my core.

"Then take me out."

Fuck me, when he used that voice.

I obliged and undid the buttons, sliding down his pants as he sprung free. I was in awe at his beauty as my fingers encircled him, giving him a single stroke. Feeling the urge to taste him I leaned forward, taking him into my mouth, my tongue flicking just under the head.

August took in a sharp breath, "Fuck, Nicole. "

I smiled to myself, loving the effect I had and the knowledge that I could unravel him. Loving how my name sounded on his lips. After I pushed him deep into my throat, his hand went to my hair, pulling me away. I frowned up at him.

"As much as I want this, sweetheart, and I do, badly, I'm not going to finish in your mouth tonight," August said as he grasped my waist, and threw me back farther on the bed.

My head hit the soft pillows, and before I could even gasp he was on top of me, his lips finding mine again. The kiss was open and deep, our tongues and teeth clashing. My nails sank into his back as I pulled him closer, grinding into him. I wanted to never let him go for as long as I lived.

My hand reached for him again, wanting him inside me, done with waiting.

Instead August swiftly changed our position. He was underneath me now as he grasped my hips, pulling me up so that I was straddling him, my hands resting on his chest.

"For so long, I've been imagining—dreaming of the way you would move," August whispered with his lips against my throat. My heart soared at the admission. He gripped himself to position it at my entrance. "I'm yours, Nicole."

Then I slowly sank down onto him, moaning at the fullness of it. It took me a second to adjust. I paused, giving myself a moment to get used to the sensation.

"I've got you, sweetheart...I've got you." He whispered, his hands soothing down my back to my hips. "You can take it."

His grip tightened on me, urging me to continue but never pushing. I slowly sank lower, inch by inch, until our hips met. I whimpered as my inner muscles clenched around him.

"August." I didn't recognize my own voice as I spoke—needy and sultry. My hand went to where we were joined. "I can feel you *everywhere*." Soaring through my veins, my heart, my very being.

A shiver ran through him. "Fucking hell, Nicole—what are you trying to do to me?"

Imprint myself on your soul like you've done to mine.

August kissed me again as I planted my hands on his chest and began to move. He groaned, "No dream could ever do you justice."

I had never felt this kind of blinding need before, for his body. For *him*.

I'd pushed August away so many times, and now I couldn't get close enough. It left like my soul wanted to claw out of my body and merge with his, to never be parted.

I'm yours, he said.

Mine, my heart shouted in response. *You're mine—mine—mine.*

August was just as frantic as I was. His hips thrust up to meet mine as our paces and rhythm matched perfectly.

Suddenly he was flipping me off of him, changing our position as he moved on top of me. His mouth found mine again, and he kissed me hard, over and over in his possessive way. His hand came into my hair, gripping at its base near the back of my neck. Not hurting, but just forceful enough to keep me still as he leaned back to hover over me, his face just inches from mine, looking at me with those molten silver eyes.

August had always been beautiful, hating him had never changed that, but as I looked up at him now, seeing the way he looked back at me, watching him become undone in this way—

My back arched as I pressed myself against him, our skin meeting. Gripping my thigh he pushed inside me again, hard, and took my breath away. His eyes never strayed from mine.

I groaned his name, feeling even more full in this position. He growled in satisfaction and kissed me hungrily along my neck. I melted into it—into him.

He thrust into me again and again. One of his hands gripped my hip, keeping me locked into him. The other came up to intertwine with my fingers above my head.

"Say it again," he commanded, and I knew what he wanted.

"*August,*" I said his name as he thrust into me again.

At this, he lost any control he had left. He rocked into me harder, faster, deeper. I wrapped my legs around him and watched his body move above me, pushing me closer to the edge each time he moved. A moan escaped from me as I felt my body traveling toward that peak once more.

"I know, Nicole. I know," August whispered to me gently, his lips pressing to the hollow of my throat.

Then he grasped one of my legs, hooking the knee up higher, somehow going even deeper with the shift. "Show me again how perfect you are when you come for me, Snow."

As August pressed his lips back to mine, my body obeyed. Release crashed over me and I screamed his name. I clenched around him and he followed with his own climax, saying my name like a veneration.

August burrowed his face into my neck, and we remained there, still joined for a few more moments, each panting as we tried to catch our breath. I felt like I could remain here in this exact moment for an eternity and never tire of it. Never tire of being with him. The bond between us burned as we melted together.

Eventually, August pulled out of me and turned us on our side. His arms wrapped around me as he placed soft kisses on my hair, moving down to my temple, cheek, then finally lips. He kissed me gently, tenderly.

My mind raced with what we'd just done, with how I felt. I didn't know how to say everything I wanted to say. To tell him I'd lied, I knew what I wanted—and it wasn't just tonight.

I wanted forever. I thought my heart might shatter if it was ever without his.

"Sleep, Nicole," August whispered to me, sensing that my thoughts were pacing, but unaware of the reason. He cradled me into his chest and tucked me in tight with his arms.

I knew there was no way that was going to happen anytime soon, not with my mind going haywire the way it was. But as August slowly began to caress my back, I calmed, my heartbeat steadying. I breathed in his scent of rain and embers. Sleep found me not long after.

CHAPTER 56
Nic

At dawn, I awoke. Warm, almost too warm—and trapped. But this confinement felt like heaven.

I turned to shift away from the warmth at my back when arms tightened around me. One was under my head coming across my chest, the other hand was on my stomach. They pulled me into a very warm, very hard chest.

I froze as all of the previous night came back into focus.

What have I done?

Last night was the absolute stupidest thing I had ever allowed myself to do. My heart was on a mission to destroy itself.

I've fallen in love with August Warin.

Fuck.

I began to spiral, wondering if he felt the same. I remembered the way he'd acted, the words he'd said, the way he'd kissed me as if it would never be enough—

If he loved you, he would have said it.

I couldn't face this—face him. I needed to get out of here before he woke up. My heart couldn't take being told it was truly just once, that it was just a way for us to cope, to ignore our stress and grief.

So like the coward I was, I waited for him to shift away from me so I could slip quietly out of the bed and out of his arms. Standing, I donned a robe that was hung on the back of the door leading to his bathroom.

I knew it—*I knew it* when I first saw him. Nothing good could come from him. He was too beautiful, I was drawn to him too much. It would only end heartbreak.

I silently snuck into the hall toward Julian's bathroom to bathe and dress. As I passed through the bedroom I'd once used, the one that was still scorched, I paused. I couldn't sleep in August's room now. Not after what we'd done. I was going to have to figure out a new arrangement. Surely someone would let me share their room now that my fire was under more control.

Once dressed, I planned to head out to the woods to train, somewhere I could go alone and chastise myself in peace. I pulled on leather training pants and a long sleeve shirt. As I fastened the knife holster to my thigh, the door swung open with a bang. I grabbed the Galorian silver dagger out of instinct.

I turned in time to see August pin me against the vanity, hands on each side of my waist, my dagger at his throat.

"What the fuck was that?" he said, inches from my face, completely unaffected by the weapon I could have used to kill him.

"What was what August, get off me." I put my other hand on his chest to push him away and realized he was still naked. I would've thought that I would be completely satisfied after the previous night but the sight had me aching again. My body and heart were both traitors. "And put some clothes on, what if someone walked in?"

August ignored me, his eyes boring into mine. "You left."

My heart stuttered in my chest. "You said *for tonight* right? Well the night is over."

I could see his mind working as he mulled over my words. "No."

"No, what?"

"No, it was never just for one night."

My heart swelled, but my mouth couldn't help but continue to self-sabotage. "You can't burst in here and tell me what this is or isn't, August. You don't get to make demands of me like that." I set down the dagger on the counter behind me and tried to push him away again. He still didn't budge.

He gave a long exhale and dropped his head to my shoulder. I felt the brush of his nose running up my neck, the featherlight touch of his lips lingering against my pulse. It took everything in me to keep still, to not respond outside of my heart beating faster.

"You're right." August finally backed up, just a few inches, but his hands didn't leave the vanity on each side of my waist. "Shai just got word from the border, a unit of approximately thirty High Fae from Adrienne's guard crossed over five minutes ago. We think they are the ones the spies reported missing in Sanserria. Shai and Simon are staying to watch Gemma. The rest of us are going. I'd been awoken by the news and was going to tell you until I realized you'd left me." August's silver eyes gleamed with a longing that tore at me as he said it.

You'd left me.

My hand lifted to trace his cheek—his jaw. I would have given anything to see that look leave his eyes. "I'm sorry," I whispered. "I didn't realize..."

I'd envisioned he wouldn't mind at all if I wasn't there when he awoke. I was wrong.

Birds soared in my chest.

"There are apparently many things we need to clarify," August said. "But the matter at the border is urgent, and we need to leave immediately." He said, his eyes asking the question.

Hesitating, I took a breath. "I need to stay in case Gemma wakes up. She can't wake up to all unfamiliar faces, not after she's been so traumatized."

I also wanted to stay because I didn't know how to act around him anymore. I needed the morning to think it through, to clear my head.

"Okay. But this conversation isn't over, Nicole. We're talking when I get back." August moved closer to me again, pinning my hips to the vanity with his. Then he gently took my face in his hands and paused—silently asking permission.

I tilted my face up to his, and August kissed me softly, as if he were still unsure of what my reaction would be. Almost like he was worried I was going to push him away again. The thoughtfulness shattered my resolve, and I kissed him back.

As I felt it would always be with him, the kiss turned searing. His lips and tongue took hold of me again, just like they had last night, and demanded more. And much like last night, I couldn't get enough. I didn't think I would ever be able to.

August Warin had ruined me.

He eventually broke the kiss, but kept his hands on my face and placed his forehead against mine.

"Even if it's only a minute apart, I will miss you, Snow." He whispered his name for me against my lips, the one I'd come to love. Then he turned and walked out, leaving me feeling like I could float away to the stars on happiness alone.

CHAPTER 57

Nic

The five and August left within the quarter hour to handle the guards Adrienne sent across the border. Though outnumbered, I wasn't concerned for them. August wouldn't have gone if he didn't think they could manage it. Not to mention that he could have easily handled the problem alone based on the magic I'd seen him cast in training. I was more surprised thirty was all Adrienne had sent.

Gemma hadn't yet awoken, but Shai was still keeping vigil, the dark circles under his eyes indicating he hadn't slept.

Letting Simon know what I intended to do, I left the cabin, Eve's bow and quiver strung across my back, and went for a walk to clear my mind. I wouldn't go far so I could hear him call for me if Gemma woke, but just far enough that the peace of the woods would help me reel in my scattered thoughts.

You'd left me.

I'm yours.

August said we would talk when we got back, and remembering his words I allowed myself to hope as I'd never done before...that he might be in love with me too.

I heard a rustle in the brush in front of me, just past the cabin's wards, and swiftly drew my bow.

A moment later I saw him, emerging from between two trees. His familiar dark brown skin, black hair, and silver eyes.

"Julian."

I ran to him. "Misha? Is Misha with you?" I looked around after embracing him. *Julian*. He was here. Unharmed and safe.

"She's not with me." His face faltered, eyes gleaming with fear.

Panic rose in my throat, all this time we'd always assumed they were together. "But if she's not with you—"

"We were together but Misha is trapped, stuck. Her magic has been hiding us—protecting us—but she cannot leave where she is, only I could. I finally broke free to find help."

"She's safe?" I whispered.

Julian nodded. "For now, yes."

I let out a breath, grateful and relieved. "We have to go to the cabin. August has been so worried about you. He had to leave, but he'll be back soon. He can help us go to her, and the Seven, and—"

"We don't have time, Nic." Julian cut me off.

"What—what do you mean?"

"Adrienne found us. Misha's power is holding against her, but it's only a matter of time before the queen breaks through her magic's defenses. It's why I left to get help, and thank the gods I found you, but we have to go back. Now. Before it's too late. We cannot wait on my brother and the others to return."

My mind reeled. *Her magic? Was she conscious then? Why hadn't they reached out to us sooner?*

I shook my head. "But Shai is here, all he has to do is call them back and they'll come."

"Nic, *please*. Misha doesn't have much longer. We have to go *now*." Julian clasped my hand in his. I could see the urgency, the desperation in his eyes.

My heart thrashed in my chest. Misha was in trouble. My sister needed me. I couldn't lose her too. "Okay."

Julian let out a sigh of relief. He held my hand tightly and as I let him guide us, we winnowed away.

We arrived in a clearing in the Redwood. As we walked, the forest thinned revealing a little lake to the southeast. It didn't take me long to realize it was where August and I had trained together with my fire.

"The border is just a few more miles south, we'll walk there then we can winnow again once we cross. There is a small hole in the wards we can use." Julian explained.

"Where is Misha exactly?" I needed more information from him. Where she was, how she was trapped, what had happened to them in all this time.

"In Sanserria. After the ball, we were caught within a snare of Adrienne's, but with Misha's magic we were shielded, hidden away. She only recently found us."

None of what he gave me was new information. "And you've been there ever since? How?" I asked as we walked toward the water.

"I've been conscious and hiding, but Misha is stuck in a deep sleep from some enchantment I don't recognize. It was in the combs someone left for her. She thought they were from me and she wore them to the ball. They must have nicked her skin and poisoned her."

I remembered the rose gold combs she'd had her hair pinned back with that night and felt sick to my stomach. The threat to my sister had been right in front of my face.

"There was no way to get a message out so we could come to you?"

"No," Julian shook his head. "Not without getting caught."

I stopped walking. "So you left her there, stuck in a prolonged sleep with no other protection than her magic?" I felt as if we'd made the wrong choice in not waiting, that I had been too eager to go to my sister. All it would have taken was minutes and the others could have been back. "If you'd explained sooner, we could have waited for Miranda she can—"

"Don't act like you care so much, Nic." Julian sneered as he turned on me. "You and my brother weren't so worried about us when you were here fucking all this time."

All the blood drained from my face. "Julian, it—it wasn't like that. We've been searching for you, for any sign. And he and I—"

Julian laughed humorlessly, the sound full of malice. "You are, aren't you? I wasn't sure until I saw your face, but he finally succeeded in bedding you didn't he? My brother is very skilled at stringing pretty words together to lure females into his bed. Though it's usually much too easy, with his face and status as king. You were certainly his greatest challenge, but I assure you it was nothing but a conquest to him. The beautiful but cold princess."

Julian's words struck me—it was exactly what Callum had done. But what I had with August was different...wasn't it?

We reached the edge of the small lake. "I'm going to look around for some food and be back. It will take us more than a day to reach the palace, even if we take turns winnowing." Julian said as he walked off, leaving me in spiraling emotions of guilt and shame.

CHAPTER 58
Nic

S omething was wrong.

The words Julian had said, the way he carried himself, it was all wrong. What had happened to him in the past two months' time? How had he changed so much?

The way he'd spoken to me was completely out of his character. My sister could be blunt, but she would never have fallen in love with a male that could have said such things and meant them. And I knew in my heart that August hadn't lied to me, that he hadn't said those things only to convince me into his bed. I wouldn't let my fear and past take what had formed between us and remember it as something that it wasn't.

There were rocks and boulders all along the shore of the lake, aspen and fir trees towering in the distance. I glanced back the way we came toward the Mountains of Rei, the snow always covering their peaks, even in summer.

As I walked around the shore, waiting for Julian to return, I found a cluster of apple trees. I pulled one of the ruby-red fruit from a branch and walked back toward the water.

Sitting on a boulder at its edge, I wrapped my arms around my knees. I rolled the apple between my palms, considering everything I'd learned from Julian until—I froze.

The lake was unnaturally still, even the plants in its depths did not dance. A chill ran through me.

There were no fish.

No birdsongs. No humming of bees in the wildflowers. No rustle of small animals moving through the brush.

Nature rejects the false one.

Had Adrienne affected Julian in some way—manipulated or poisoned his mind? Did the Redwood sense her magic on him?

Just as I had the thought, Julian returned.

Something was wrong with him, and I couldn't let him take me over the border back into Hahnaley. That was surely where Adrienne and her guard waited for us.

"Here," Julian said, handing me a wrapped cloth of blackberries, walnuts, and wild onions.

"Thanks," I said as genuinely as I could manage, hoping that he thought my hesitation was from the words he'd said earlier and not my suspicions.

I should have known better when he didn't want to alert the others. Julian loved his brother—trusted August with his life. There is no chance that he would have left without wanting his help to extract Misha.

And I was a stupid, idiotic fool that had been blinded by my need to go to my sister.

I would wait for the right moment, walk away, and winnow back to the cabin. Find August and explain. Together we could find Julian again, bringing Shai and Teale, and let them unravel whatever Adrienne had done to his mind.

"Not hungry?" Julian's voice interrupted my thoughts. He noticed I hadn't touched the food he'd given me.

I shook my head, "I'm just worried about Misha." I hoped he would take my words for what they were. He only shrugged and returned to his own eating. I looked too suspicious sitting here so still, but I sure as hell wasn't eating the food he'd given me.

I brought the apple to my mouth.

I took a bite, and the fruit turned to ash on my tongue, longing in my throat. The outside of the apple in my hands was still a gleaming, perfect red, but the core was black and disintegrated. Rotten.

Poisoned.

"Apples always were your favorite, Nic, and I knew you wouldn't eat anything *I* handed you."

I looked at Julian, coughing. He held a small oval mirror in his hands, then spun it thrice. After the last revolution, he was no longer Julian.

Adrienne herself stared back at me now, the red mark of the traitor gleaming on her forehead. "After yesterday, I realized how foolish it was of me to think Evander could be the one to convince you to leave your protection here, though I should have known sooner when you didn't wear that necklace for him at the ball. Such a pathetic little mommy's girl you've always been. Can't take off that cheap keepsake even for a man professing his love." She sneered as her eyes went to the ruby pendant around my neck.

My magic quickly depleted because of whatever poison was in the apple, hollowness filling my chest where it once lived. Not even the rowan berries, wood, or ash had felt like this.

As I choked, still desperately trying to dislodge the piece caught in my throat, I made one last attempt to cast fire at her before my magic ran out, but the air was ripped from my flame, smothering it.

How.

"Ah look at you, it's so fun to finally watch you flounder, Nic." She laughed, clasping her hands together. "I took Orelia and Cedric's magic when their son delivered their hearts, tucking it away for future use." She palmed a gold spiraling-shell pendant around her neck as she spoke. "Evander now has Cedric's power added to his own, but I kept Orelia's for myself. Such powerful control of the air and wind, so much that I can now steal the oxygen from your flames."

My choking was getting worse, beginning to burn. I couldn't understand how she was here, how she'd cast the illusion over me to make me see Julian. I'd always been able to block out the mindcasters, not once had my shields been breached like this.

"Look at that mind, always whirling. You are wondering how I fooled you. Such a smart girl, Nic—too smart. It made you arrogant. But I'll tell you. Every time I take a heart, I imbue the magic into an object." She lifted the small gilded mirror. "A very handy trick this one is, I got it from a lovely selkie, the only transfiguration that could fool someone with shields like yours after your half-breed aunt had you trained against me."

Adrienne's mouth pulled into a snake-like grin. No humor, only malice. "And the only people that little Nic trusts are Alesia and Eve—both dead—Misha. But I would have no reason to get you alone if I appeared as your twin, so her lover, sweet Julian, would have to do. You only recently questioned his intentions, didn't you? I could see your mind over there working through it. Observing me as I was observing you. But I have been watching and waiting for a *long time*, Nicole. Luckily those around you finally started speaking in front of reflections, where they believed their words were safe."

A mirror to create her illusion.

Mirrors and reflections that didn't match.

The shadows, they follow you. The reflections, they watch you.

The warnings from the siren and naiad. That was how Adrienne had found me, how she knew about August and me—godsdamned mirrors she'd enchanted to hunt me. Every reflection was a traitor.

Adrienne went on, "That apple is filled with a special poison of my making. I knew I couldn't incapacitate you with rowan ash after what you did to my guards. I needed something special, something unique, to incapacitate *both* sides of your heritage. I'm rather pleased with how it turned out. And within the minute you will finally be dead, just like your sweet, too trusting father."

Her words sliced through me. Each cough felt like a knife piercing my throat. *She killed Father, too.*

"My Mirror of Sight told me you and your sister's magic would be powerful, but who would have thought, Nic, *fire*?" Adrienne laughed. "But how had your worthless fae grandfather passed you so much power? The male could hardly put a ripple through a pond. He was an utterly pathetic being, begging for his human lover's life over his own before we executed him for his illicit affair. It wasn't conceivable that his half-breed daughters could have been born with so much magic. Though it was clever of your human grandmother to flee to the slums in that distant city, hiding them where we wouldn't bother to search."

My father and grandfather. Two more names to add to the list of those Adrienne had taken from me. My choking grew frantic as my hands clawed at my throat. I stepped back and felt water lapping at my boots as if reaching for me. I reached back, grinding my feet down into the sand and rock. That's when I felt it—

"Once I take your heart, adding power over both fire and water to my collection, I will have everything I need to burn down the defenses around your sister," Adrienne continued. "Then not even August Warin will be strong enough to keep me from taking the continent. Though I am sure he will put up quite the fight, especially in his attempt to avenge his brother and *you*. How heartbroken he will be." Adrienne smiled brightly as she stalked toward me.

The water was now coming to the middle of my shins. To keep her from getting what she so desperately wanted, this was the only way.

Adrienne's smile dropped, realization finally dawning on her face, but it was too late.

I took another step back and cast myself into the lake.

The water carried me out—father, deeper—below the once serene surface, ripples spilling out from the force of my fall.

Magic poured into and back out of me from the water, at once one with it and its master. As I sank, the surface began to freeze, the crystals forming around me. Adrienne might have been able to fight fire with her stolen air element, but she couldn't breach diamond-hard ice with it.

I saw her above the surface screaming in rage, hitting the surface again and again with her fists, blasting the ice with her stolen air. All to no avail, my ice would not falter—would not yield.

My heart and I were far out of her reach, safe.

As the surface further solidified and the ice thickened around me, my eyes drifted shut and I saw no more.

CHAPTER 59
August

After half an hour at the border, we still hadn't found a single one of Adrienne's guards. Shai hadn't been notified by a break in the wards, rather one of Simon's spies reached out directly as he'd seen them cross, then called us here.

"You are sure you saw them cross the border here?" I asked the spy again, growing impatient.

"Yes, there were thirty of them." The elderly human man's eyes were glassy like he'd drunk too much before breakfast.

I nodded to Teale. "Confirm."

The faerie's face went blank as she looked into his mind, to get some clarification on whatever was going on. A second later she recoiled.

"His mind is wiped," she said. "There are only images of the guards crossing but nothing else. No history. Not even a name."

"What?" Celeste asked, dumbfounded. "That can't be. Sir, what is your name?" She said, turning toward the man.

"Thirty guards came over the border this morning, purple uniforms with white detailing." The man said.

What the hell.

"She asked for your name," I repeated, the word nearly a growl in my frustration.

The man looked from Celeste to me. "Good, you're here. You're the only one that can handle the guards. We needed *you* to come."

None of this made any sense. "Teale, try again."

She did and grimaced. "Nothing. Absolutely nothing. Like Gemma but...worse. At least her memories were hidden. This man has nothing at all in his mind except that the guards crossed the border and you needed to come urgently."

My heart stopped beating. This was a message—just for me.

Adrienne had finally made her move.

"Teale, reach out to Shai. Tell him and Simon to get eyes on Nicole right fucking now."

She did, no questions asked. I could see the pieces clicking together in Miranda's eyes. "Oh gods," she whispered.

"Everyone go back. *Now.*" Seconds later we were winnowing to the wards outside the cabin. As soon as my feet hit the ground, I was running.

Jophiel launched into the sky to get eyes from above. Celeste's golden eagle went as well, cutting off in a different direction.

"What's going on?" I heard Damian ask from behind us.

"It's Adrienne." His mate answered. "She wiped that man's mind and planted those images there as a distraction to draw August out. She's going after Nic."

The cabin was quiet—much too quiet. "*Nicole,*" I tore open the door.

"August," I heard Simon's voice from behind me on the porch. I turned around to face him.

"Where is she?" I roared, unable to contain my panic.

"She went on a walk." Simon's hands were shaking, guilt coated his expression. "Shai just searched. He tracked her scent to the wards. She's not here." The male appeared from the forest edge just then, shaking his head in confirmation. Nicole was gone.

Everything in my world stopped moving.

"I'm so sorry, it was only fifteen minutes ago," Simon said.

I turned to Miranda. "Get Ker."

Familiars had many talents that were little known, one of which being they were one of the few creatures that could track a fae's winnow.

A second later the little black cat jumped onto the porch railing as if she'd heard me call for her. Miranda immediately whispered to the creature to track and find Nic. Then the cat took off, jumping through the air into a winnow that wasn't bound by any ward we could cast.

Now would be the worst part. The waiting.

I didn't know how Adrienne had done it, how she'd hidden herself and convinced Nicole to leave the wards. It was only a matter of time before she killed her for her heart—her magic. I could only hope that Nicole would figure out her scheme, and fight her before it was too late.

"Simon, whatever Adrienne did, this isn't your fault." I turned back to him and Shai. I could see it in his face, no matter what I said he would blame himself. He'd come to love Nic as family. As had the rest of the Seven.

As had I.

Ever since she burst into my life from that alleyway she was all I'd been able to think about. Her, with those deep brown eyes that cut through every defense I'd ever put up, every piece of armor, straight to the ragged soul beneath.

I could understand why she was so angry with me when we'd met, when I wouldn't let her leave that room in the alleyway. But I couldn't let her go. Even then—before I realized what she would come to mean to me.

After just one look in those dark eyes, simmering with the fire she had yet to manifest, I was entranced. I hadn't even seen her face yet, and I didn't realize how gone I already was. Looking back, I didn't know how I could have ever thought my infatuation was temporary—how I could go on without being haunted by her for the rest of my life.

Sitting with Nicole that night under the moon, I wondered how it wasn't obvious to her—that the stars and I would give her anything she wished for. I should have told her then what she was to me.

Now, I might never get the chance.

I took a deep breath, leaning my elbows on the rail as my head fell into my hands. I could still feel her touch, her scent all around me like it was embedded into my skin. Amber and freshly-fallen snow.

"Hey..." Miranda stood beside me as I stared out at the forest, waiting for any sign of Ker's return. I hadn't even heard her approach. She gently touched a hand to my shoulder. "We'll find her. Nic is too smart, too powerful to just be taken like this. However Adrienne lured her away, she won't try anything until she's over the border. Nic will figure it out."

"Adrienne Deimos has killed many, many fae that were cunning and power-ful," I said, standing up fully again.

Miranda shook her head. "Not her. Not Nic. Her power is different, stronger. Adrienne can't kill her outright if she wants her heart. And however she thinks she's going to subdue her, it isn't going to work."

I didn't answer, looking back toward the trees. I could only hope that she was right.

Half an hour later, the black cat appeared.

"They're at a lake in the Redwood," Miranda said as the familiar went to her side. "Twenty miles from here, three miles from the border."

"Let's go," I said, not wanting to waste any more time. I knew the place, I'd taken Nicole there myself, and was already armed from this morning. I wouldn't need my magic to tear Adrienne's head from her shoulders.

"There's more, you need to know this." Miranda shook her head. "Adrienne isn't there, but her guards are, approximately thirty of them from what Ker could see. Alexander is overseeing them. And Nicole, she's..." Miranda hesitat-ed. The worst possible thought went through my mind—that we were too late.

"The lake is completely frozen over, and she is under the ice. The guards are trying to resurrect her from it."

It felt like my soul had been ripped in two.

There was little chance she could survive in the ice that long, even being a watercaster. And I knew Nic had done it to herself to keep her heart from Adrienne, to remain free, like the swan in her story.

"Her magic is still holding strong, she might still be alive, August," Miranda said, hopeful. I didn't say it, but I knew magic and enchantments could outlive their casters, the palace in Sanserria being the prime example.

"We're going there. Now." I said. Even if Nicole was dead, I couldn't leave her in that lake.

"We need a plan, August," Jophiel said as she landed.

"If anyone stands in our way, we kill them. All of them. Now. That is the plan. Shai and Simon will remain here to watch over Gemma. The rest of us are going. Celeste, bring Aetos. Miranda, bring Ker."

I could tell Jo didn't agree with me, but I wouldn't waste another second. I needed to know if Nic was dead beneath the ice or somehow still holding on.

Waiting for me.

Jophiel nodded, realizing it was pointless to argue. Then we winnowed to the lake.

We went from late summer woods into nothing but white. Nicole's magic covered every inch of the lake and adjacent forest in snow and ice. I would have thought it beautiful if I hadn't known she was lying trapped at the bottom.

Remaining hidden in the treeline, we watched and assessed the guards as they unsuccessfully blasted the ice with different magic. Air, earth, and watercasters each took their turns. None of which made a crack in the lake's frozen surface.

As focused on extracting Nicole as they were, none of them noticed the sunny sky turning overcast above them.

Miranda held Ker in her arms. She was the only one of us that had seen the familiar's true form. A part of the witch and familiar's bonding process. But as she set her down on the snow, we all finally saw what kind of monster Ker really was.

The little cat shifted into a beast the size of a horse. Like her other form, she was black. However, in this body, protruding spikes angled down her spine. Her long tail ended in a white-striped point that looked to be venomous. Her feet ended in four pronged toes, each fashioned with large talons I had no doubt could disembowel human or faerie with no hesitation. Last, Ker had an unnaturally large, gaping mouth filled with curved needle-sharp teeth. She bared them as she surveyed the soldiers, her tail flicking restlessly, those intelligent green eyes missing nothing.

I wanted to thank Miranda and all the gods that this creature was attached to Nicole. Ker purred in her presence, curled into her lap as she read by the fireplace. I'd once said that the Briars could tame any monster, but knowing that this creature of nightmares adored her gave me untold comfort.

"Spread out among the trees to catch any guards that might try to escape," I said mind-to-mind with Teale, knowing she would spread it to the others. "Subdue first unless your life is threatened, then we will determine their fate. We respect anyone's wish to surrender." The faerie nodded as she released her translucent gossamer wings, the gold veining glowing in against the snow, and drew her bow.

"Miranda," I turned to the witch, mouthing the words in silence. "Ker goes for Nicole. I want her guarded until we handle this."

The familiar let out a low whine as she paced. She'd understood.

Miranda, Damian, and Teale stalked eastward while Jophiel and Celeste went west, getting into position. Aetos remained seated atop one of the large fir trees in full view of the lake, sending Celeste information.

A minute later when the clouds grew dark and heavy, the wind whistled through the trees as I stepped into the clearing alone.

The Reynian guards went still as I emerged

"August." Alexander smiled as stood on the snow-covered ground next to the lake. The guards parted as I stalked toward him. "How nice of you to join us. I was wondering how long it would take you to discover that trick of my sister's."

"Alexander." Thunder rumbled above. "Leave."

"I don't think I will. I have quite the prize here. It would be a shame to walk away from such a heart, but you already know that." He said, his tone thick with insinuation.

I didn't waste my breath answering. I had no intention of playing his games.

"Nothing to say? Look at you with the thunder and the wind—you're so *tense*." The male laughed. "What *is it* about these half-breeds that have so ensnared you all? Dominic Briar couldn't see straight when Diana was in his presence, and now you are just as affected, just as *desperate* for her daughter. When we break through her ice, I just might have to find out for myself what makes the Sancristas so special." Alexander's blue eyes glittered with cruel intent.

I marked each face that smiled with him, they would receive no mercy either. "Last chance," I said, lightning sparking at my fingertips.

Alexander shrugged. "I've got some new tricks I've been dying to try."

"So be it."

Lightning wreathed each of my arms as a gust of wind blasted out from me, knocking all the guards to the ground. Only Alexander remained upright, having erected a shield of earth and rock between us.

Adrienne wasn't the only one stealing magic.

Half of the guards stood and ran for the trees. The other half, either brave or foolish, charged me.

Ker took off from the forest then, bolting for the center of the lake. Most guards ran from her. The ones that didn't, that thought they could stop her, were turned to bloody ribbons.

In the chaos, Alexander sent hundreds of jagged rocks flying for me. Each piece disintegrated as they met my wall of electricity.

Bolts of lightning broke from one hand, in the other my sword danced, striking down guard after guard. They struck with air, earth, and water, but it didn't matter. Their power wasn't strong enough to block mine.

From the corner of my eye, I saw Ker, standing guard over the ice in the center of the lake, eviscerating any guard that made one last try to break through to Nicole while I was distracted.

The last guard that charged me fell, blade through the chest, and then it was just me and him. Alexander used the stolen earth magic to launch boulder after boulder in my direction, each one shattering to dust as lightning and thunder struck.

The coward began retreating, walking backward over the ice. Alexander was foolish. The further he got from shore, the more distance he put between himself and the earth. The less control he had over the stolen magic.

As I stalked toward him, he panicked. "August. We'll leave. We'll let her go—"

A gust of wind brought him to me. I thought of all the horrible things he and his sister had done. A hundred years ago, now, and every moment in between. I thought of what they planned to do still.

Taking his neck in one hand, I reached up, a bolt of lightning coming into my palm from the sky.

Then I shoved it down his throat.

The guards that surrendered were bound in Miranda's spelled circle of salt, Jophiel, Damian, and Celeste standing guard. The surviving Reynian guards would face interrogation with Shai later. Teale and Aetos remained in the sky, making sure no other attack was coming from the south.

Miranda walked to where I stood over Alexander's body. "He stole the power over the earth, rock and soil, but no plants—nothing alive." She reached for a vial around his neck. "This is where he kept it, the magic among others. I can hear it...screaming." Shuddering, she dropped the glass pendant on the ground and crushed it with the heel of her boot. I could have sworn I heard a sigh of relief with the release.

With Alexander dead and the remaining guards bound, I stepped forward, moving toward the frozen surface of the lake. The others stayed back, letting me approach her alone.

Her magic sang to me, beckoning me forward. A pull I could never resist. My own shifted to mimic hers as soft snow fell from the heavy clouds.

Ker laid over her, again in cat form. She purred, twisting through my legs, before running back to her witch. Her little paws left bloody footprints on the ice.

Beneath ice clear as glass—beneath the summer's snow—she laid. Her long hair, dark as night, waved out around her. Eyes of warmest brown were closed. Long eyelashes fanned her pale cheeks, like moonlit snow.

Nicole.

I knelt and placed my hand on the ice over her face, her magic reaching out toward mine, wanting to join. I let down my barriers as our power merged. As it did the ice slowly receded from my touch. I moved to the side, so I was no longer directly above her as her body was slowly uncovered and raised.

"Nicole," I whispered, lifting her from the icy tomb and pulling her into my chest. She was soaked, but her skin was warm thanks to the flame that lived beneath her skin. Placing my ear over her chest, I listened. Her heart was still beating, slowly, though she drew no breath.

"Please wake up, sweetheart." My voice broke on the last word.

My hand swiped over her lips, the red unnatural. I looked at my fingers now covered in the same color.

Poison.

I grasped her jaw and tilted her head back to look into her mouth. Something was wedged in the back of her throat. Using a tiny gust of wind, I dislodged it. Once loose, Nicole stirred in my arms and began choking. I let her twist away from me as she coughed and finally spit out a single piece of apple, the flesh of it black.

Nicole finally drew in deep breaths, her body shaking. My hands grasped her face so I could see her eyes open and breathing and *alive*.

"August?" she whispered, her voice hoarse.

"You're okay. You're alive." I stared at her, scared that saying the words too loudly would make them untrue.

"Adrienne, she's here." She gasped, her hands clenching on my shirt.

"No, sweetheart, she's gone. Your magic protected you, locked you in the ice. She couldn't get to you." I couldn't stop touching her. Her face, her hair.

Nicole was *alive*.

"She was disguised as Julian, August. I never would have gone with anyone else. You know that don't you?" Her dark eyes pleaded.

"Of course, Nicole" I planted a kiss on her forehead. I would worry about how Adrienne had masqueraded as my brother later.

Nicole pulled back, touching her fingertips to my face. "You came."

"I will always come for you." I kissed her again on the cheek. Then the other.

"August, I was so scared," she said, her palm coming to rest on my chest, over the heart she'd claimed.

"Don't be scared, sweetheart. Adrienne is gone, they're all gone." I'd already watched her get dragged under the waves by the sirens, thought her dead for five days after the Solstice, and now pulled her nearly lifeless body from the ice. I would be damned if I let there be a fourth time that threatened her life.

Nic shook her head. "No. I was scared because I thought I wouldn't get to tell you."

"Tell me what?"

"I knew what I wanted—when you asked me last night. I didn't want just one night, I never did. It was all untrue."

I thought she'd set me on fire last night. I thought that moment would never be matched, but that word did it.

Untrue.

"Whatever divine magic compromises our souls, Nicole, know that yours and mine are the same. There is nowhere you could go that I wouldn't find you, no corner of this earth you could be that I wouldn't seek you out. Even if my body was broken, my mind shattered, and I lost all that I am, I would always be wandering, searching for you. Even if I knew nothing else, I will always know *you*."

Nicole's face melted into that heartbreaking smile, the one she'd made me work so hard to see, as she touched a hand to my cheek, cupping my face.

"And I will always love you." She said as her eyes closed again, drifting into an exhausted sleep.

CHAPTER 60
Nic

I awoke curled into August as I laid on my side, my cheek pressed against his chest. His arms wound around me, a hand threaded into my hair at the base of my skull. August's deep breaths of sleep warmed the top of my head.

I craned my neck to the window for an indication of the time, the golden light telling me it was nearing sunset. As I shifted, his arms tightened around me.

"Hi," I whispered.

August pressed himself up onto an elbow, further looking me over as if he couldn't believe that I was here—that I was real. "You're okay," he whispered back, more of a statement than a question, but I nodded anyway. His hand came to my face to brush back my hair. "I had Damian look you over when we returned, making sure you were unharmed besides the poison. Miranda has been analyzing that bit of apple ever since."

"Adrienne said a lot of things to me, August. I need to tell you—tell everyone." I shifted to get up.

August pulled me back with the arm still at my waist. "And you will. But rest a little longer, sweetheart. Then we'll reconvene with the others to discuss what you know."

"I can't rest anymore," I said, frowning. After the poisoning, I'd laid still much too long.

His eyes darkened slightly. "It should offend me you are always trying to leave this bed with me," he said as he leaned over me, trapping me with his body.

Warmth flooded my face. "I'm not—"

August smiled, teasing. "It's okay, sweetheart. I know you'll come back," he purred, his face coming to nuzzle into my neck where he planted kisses along my pulse. As if he needed to feel the life beating there. "Because you love me."

"I did say that, didn't I?" I couldn't help but smile back as my hands rose to clasp his face, as beautiful as his soul.

"And I," he planted a kiss on my cheek. "Love," the other. "You," on the top of my nose as a laugh erupted from my lips. August smothered the sound with his mouth, kissing me before he continued. "I think I might have from the very moment I saw you in that alley—felt that inexplicable thread between us pulling me to you."

I saw the devotion churning in his silver eyes. I whispered back, "I think I wanted you so much it scared me...so I hated you instead."

"It's a good thing I was persistent then."

"No," I shook my head. "You backed off when I asked you to the night of the Solstice. You gave me the space I needed. But you've always seen me, August—all of me—and never shied away from it." I ran my thumb over his cheek. "That's why I love you."

August rolled over me then, settling himself between my thighs, his arms a cage around me—the only one I didn't mind confinement in. Then he kissed me, slowly, deeply, and it felt like avalanches were cascading down around my heart.

After several long moments, I reluctantly pulled away. "As much as I love your methods of distraction, we really do need to debrief the others."

August sighed, rolling onto his back. His cage of arms took me with him. "Let me hold you for ten more minutes, Snow. Then we can go," he said, planting a kiss on my head as he tucked me back into his arms. I sighed contentedly as I rested my head against his chest, feeling his heart beat in time with mine.

At dusk, we sat together in the living room on the couch and various chairs, the Seven, Gemma, August, and me. The youngest Shaw sat between Teale and Shai, drawing comfort from them. She was more withdrawn than I'd ever seen her, haunted by her returned memories, but some color had returned to her cheeks.

I shared one of the larger chairs with August, my back pressed against his side and his arm around my waist. After Adrienne's attack, he showed no inclination to leave me alone for even a second. Not that I minded.

None of the Seven commented on it, making me realize how grossly I'd underestimated how obvious the bond between August and I had become, how much he cared for me. They saw it much before I had.

As we sat, I told the others of how Adrienne had used the selkie's stolen magic to lure me away with Julian's face, the poisoned apple, all the things she'd said, and how I'd come to be under the ice.

When I finished, Miranda spoke first. "I evaluated the poison on the apple from your throat. It should have killed you, should have killed *anyone* within minutes. But you didn't die. How, Nicole?"

I shook my head. "I don't know." Not to mention I could stay for longer until the water than most High Fae because of my water element, but never over an hour. None of it should have been possible.

Miranda leaned forward, her eyes catching on my neck. "Where did you get that necklace? I haven't noticed you wearing it before." She pointed to my mother's ruby necklace I was absentmindedly touching.

"It was a gift from my mother before we were born. Both Misha and I have one. I've never taken it off, but all I've worn here are the training clothes. It must have stayed covered."

"May I? You don't have to take it off, I just want to touch it." Miranda said as she reached for it. I nodded my head in permission. She pinched the pendant between her thumb and index finger, examining it. "This wasn't made by any faerie—it's a witch's knot of protection, Nic. It is spelled with enchantments, specifically guarding against poison. If you were ever to be poisoned while wearing this, you wouldn't be killed, only fall into a deep sleep." Miranda explained. "I've only seen a handful in person, but I've studied their lore in texts."

"Alesia said there was a vision my mother had when she learned of her pregnancy, a prophecy, but she never spoke of it. She and my father only learned of it from a note my mother left after she died. But Alé said that Diana hid most of the prophecy's predictions, writing in the letter that Misha and I would find it when we were ready."

Miranda let the necklace go, sitting back. "Diana must have seen that you and Misha would be in danger—poisoning specifically. I wonder if her gift of Sight allowed her to find a witch with the strength to cast it, there wouldn't be many."

My eyes welled up with tears. August's arm tightened around me, steadying me. My mother had seen me and had saved my life. Had saved August's too, seeing a hundred years ago that he would be the one to come for me.

There will come a time when you will repay the favor. When snow falls in summer.

I wondered if she knew then that the one under the ice was her daughter.

"Poor choice by Adrienne in choosing an area by a lake to poison you then," Damian commented.

"Indeed." I smiled. "The pendant kept me from dying, but I still fell into that sleep state. If I had been landlocked, she might have been successful. But my magic was able to bind with the water and protect me."

"What do you mean?" Miranda sat up straighter again.

"Our power is like a well, typically I can feel the bottom when I'm drained, and I did initially after I bit the apple. But when I felt the water, its pull, and submerged myself, that bottom disappeared. My magic felt endless as long as I was connected to it."

Miranda's eyes widened with realization.

"What are you thinking?" August inclined his head to the witch.

"The Sancristas had extraordinarily deep wells of magic, didn't they? In the war?"

He, Shai, Teale, and Jophiel each nodded, confirming.

Miranda shook her head. "I don't think they truly had a bottom to their magic at all. It's why the rowan wood, berries, and ash worked so poorly against them, even more poorly than against other demi-fae. Then Diana gifted her daughters two witch-made amulets—there are too many coincidences. The Sancristas aren't just part human. They are part witch."

"What?" I whispered. Everything she said was logical, but I couldn't wrap my head around it. Until just two months ago I'd thought all the witches were dead. But Miranda had explained then that the witches drew their magic directly from the elements. A conduit. I'd felt that way in the lake, that the magic was flowing *through* me, not *from* me.

Miranda continued, smiling. "I told you once that many witches went into hiding to protect themselves, some stopped practicing altogether. Your human grandmother may have been such a witch and not even realized it. And as humans and High Fae so rarely mate, so rarely produce children, to have two daughters, twins, that are both fae and witch would be exceedingly rare. But it would explain how powerful they were. How powerful you and Misha both are."

"Adrienne mentioned something," I said. "That my High Fae grandfather wasn't powerful at all, she couldn't understand how his daughters were so gifted. But she also said that my grandmother hid them in the slums to keep Diana and Alesia from being discovered. I think Marisela, my grandmother, did know." But she hadn't shared it with her daughters, opting for the protection of secrecy. Diana must have discovered their heritage and kept the secret as well, from Alé and her mate. I wondered how much she left for us hidden back in the palace, for Misha and me to discover when the time was right.

"Is that how you've enchanted me so, *witch*?" August whispered in my ear, low enough that only I could hear. I flushed as the dragons that had taken up residence in my chest since I'd met him brushed their wings against my heart.

August sat back, inclining his head to his spymaster. "Simon, you had news as well."

Simon and I had spoken privately before this meeting, his guilt over my disappearance a burden on him. I'd assuaged that guilt, there was nothing he could have done to keep me from following who I'd believed to be Julian in order to find Misha. Simon would have only come and Adrienne would have killed him in the process. Still, it was hard for me to understand why it continued to shock me, how much these people—my friends—cared. The hug he'd given me reminded me of my father's, and for a moment, it felt like a piece of my broken heart fell back into place. The Seven had become a second family to me. Not to replace the ones I'd lost, but something entirely new.

Simon's eyes met mine before he addressed everyone else. "This afternoon we got some more credible information from our spies about the situation in Sanserria. The missing guards were not those that came with Alexander today as we would have assumed, at least not all of them."

"If they weren't traveling here, then where are they?" Jophiel asked from where she paced behind the couch.

"They're dead," He said simply, and we all went very still. "According to our spies, they've been going into the woods. Very few that do so return. One of our spies in the Hahnaleyan guard finally accompanied them, saw what happened. There are ruins deep in the woods, an old castle that isn't on any map. It's surrounded by vines and thorns, every surface covered. The guards have been working to break through unsuccessfully."

That wasn't right, Misha and I visited the abandoned castle's ruins often. Yes, it was warded to remain hidden, but for those that knew of its existence, it was easy to access. The plant life was wild, but Misha always kept it groomed to her liking. She hadn't been taken long enough for it to reach such a wild state on its own.

My brow wrinkled as I tried to picture it. "What did the thorns look like?"

"They're large, approximately the length and width of two fingers." Simon demonstrated with his hands. "And poisonous, barbed with a paralytic that is lethal almost instantly. The vines also sprout blooms."

My heart beat faster. Hope threatened to fill my chest, but I pushed it down. Not yet, not until I was sure.

"What type of blooms? What color are they?" I leaned forward, my voice betraying my eagerness.

"Pink roses with a yellow center."

I couldn't stop it, my heart swelled, and a smile broke across my face.

"What is it, Nicole?" August asked, not privy where my thoughts had gone.

I turned to him. "Do you remember the dinner in Hahnaley, the one on the grounds by the gardens?" He nodded. "I crafted a throne of ice, but do you remember what Misha did to hers?"

Light sparked in his eyes as he made the connection. "She covered it in thorns...and pink roses with yellow centers."

"*Briar roses.*"

I turned away from him to address the others again. His hand tightened in mine, sharing in my excitement over this revelation.

"My father created them with Misha when we were children. They don't grow naturally, only from their magic. If they are blooming on the ruins, she's *there*. My sister is using the blooms to tell me where she is."

Shai spoke for the first time, Gemma glancing up at him. "How did she get there?"

"The night of the Summer Solstice, Adrienne planned to poison us both. She tried to use Evander to poison me with a necklace, but what she didn't predict was that I wouldn't accept it. The night of the final ball Misha was wearing combs in her hair I'd never seen before. Adrienne admitted to me herself that they were poisoned."

"But then why is Misha in the ruins and not with Adrienne?" Miranda asked.

"Because Misha and Julian couldn't help but sneak off early to Misha's favorite place—the castle ruins. When I was poisoned, my magic found another way, it pulled from the water like Miranda's—like the witches. Misha's magic could have done the same—drawing from the earth to protect herself and Julian. The poison makes her sleep, as I had, but our mother's amulet keeps her alive, the magic continuing to flow through her."

Jophiel stopped her pacing, leaning her hands on the back of the couch. "So then why hasn't Adrienne collected her?"

"With the guards only recently disappearing, it hasn't been long since she'd learned where they are. And as Adrienne couldn't break through my ice, she can't break past Misha's thorns."

"Simon, you said *many* of the guards died via the thorns, not all." Celeste cocked her head. "What happened to the others?"

"From what our spy saw of them," he swallowed and paled just slightly, "The guards were torn apart like nothing he had ever seen. Their limbs and heads often completely pulled from their bodies."

"Could her vines do that?" Celeste's eyes went wide, with both fear and something like admiration.

I nodded. "Everyone thinks I'm the ruthless sister, but they have no idea what Misha is capable of. They only see the beauty of her magic, her face, and how lighthearted and carefree she is. But my sister has been poisoned, threatened, and Julian with her—who she believes is her mate. So no, it would not be a surprise to learn that her plants were ripping them apart to protect them. Rasalas is likely there as well. I'm sure he's doing his fair share."

"I can't wait to meet that cat," Celeste murmured, smirking as she leaned back into the couch.

"And Adrienne isn't worried that you would recognize this and come for Misha?" Jophiel said.

I shrugged. "She must have been confident that she would get to me before I discovered it. She mentioned wanting to steal my fire specifically to breach Misha's defenses." I turned, facing August again. "But now that we know where Misha is, we can go to her. And Julian has to be there with her."

We found them, my eyes conveyed to him as I intertwined my fingers with his.

We did, Snow. August broke our gaze to say to Simon, "When we arrive in Sanserria we can determine how the ruins are being guarded. Find the best opportunity to go in. We leave tomorrow."

Simon and the others nodded. The decision made.

My heart thundered in my chest. We finally knew where Misha and Julian were. We were going to come for them. I didn't care what we faced when we got there, nothing would stop me.

I'm coming, sister.

EPILOGUE
Misha

A m I dead?

No, I didn't believe so. I thought I was at first.

After the poisoned comb nicked my skin and my power lashed out to protect me, I fell into a dream state. I assumed I had come to where all souls go when they die, before the gods to pass through judgment.

Instead, I woke up here, in purgatory, on a bed of roses in the highest tower of the High King's abandoned castle. Or at least that is what my brain conjured up to keep my consciousness entertained while I slept. I did not know where I really was in reality.

How long have I been here?

An hour...a day...a year...

I wasn't sure. Time meant nothing to me here. I walked through the exterior gardens, *again*, in perpetual dusk. Passing the ivy, the cherry and peach trees full of fruit, the rose vines, their blossoms opening under my touch. I reconsidered, maybe I had passed through judgment.

Though beautiful, this entrapment felt like hell.

Who did this to me?

Whoever it was...they'll be sorry.

Nicky got a bad name for being the aloof sister, the ruthless sister, the cold sister. And it was true, her wrath was nearly unmatched...except by mine. Whoever did this to me was going to wish they'd never been born. The torment I'd experienced in this prison I would recreate tenfold. I would tear them apart slowly, limb by limb, thorn by thorn, until there was hardly anything left for the crows to pick.

My perpetual state of wandering in this hell was only ever briefly interrupted by the nightmares. My family dying around me, my sister and aunts attacked, their blood staining the dark soil around them. I couldn't get to them, could never reach them in time to save them. Watching them die repetitively was slowly tearing me apart. My heart ripped open a bit more with each vision.

I would believe that they were dead except that I could still feel them.

Well, not all of them, but I could feel my twin through our bond. If she was safe, surely the others were too.

My sister and my souls were bonded, the twin pull never absent. As long as she and I both lived, we could sense the other, knowing in our hearts that the other was alive. Though that didn't particularly mean she was safe.

Sometimes I even thought I saw Nic here in the gardens with me. Sometimes it was other places. The darkest part of the forest. A cabin hidden in the woods. An ice-covered lake—

Sometimes I heard her calling my name. I couldn't tell if it was real—if anything was real anymore.

Then my sweet Julian. My love. My mate. So close, but so far from me. Trapped as I was. Not by the poison as I was, but something worse—

I am so sorry, love.

It was all my fault. How could it ever be undone?

My repetitive dark thoughts spurred my anxiety, making it harder and harder to breathe. I took a moment, practicing my deep breathing. I repeated my sister's words, the phrase from a story she'd used to calm me so long ago.

The darker the shadows, the brighter the sun.

I will rise again.

Once my heart rate settled, I slowly made my way back up to the tower, back to my bed of roses and thorns, where even in this dream state I found myself staying more and more, seeking the oblivion of sleep.

The darkness called to me. My despair threatened to consume me the longer I was trapped here, separated from everyone I loved. I needed to stay strong—I couldn't let it take hold of me again.

I walked and walked and walked up the stairs. Around and around and around. Always the same, never changing.

Except today.

A deafening roar cut through the silence. The beast—he could sense her approaching.

I smiled for the first time in an eternity.

She's coming.

ACKNOWLEDGMENTS

At the start of the pandemic, I slowly returned to reading for enjoyment after years of only academia. And as much as I loved these books, I noticed a theme of siblings betraying each other (I'm looking at you, Taryn). Because of this, I wanted to write a different story, a story of sisters that would do anything for each other. This is where Summer's Snow began.

It at its inception is a story of sisters, using the stories of the princesses we'd grown up with. I wanted to take them and make them strong—more than just women awoken by true love's kiss. So this book is for my sister, the Usagi Tsukino to my Rei Hino. We're not true twins, but we are the same age for nine days. I would brave the Redwood and all manner of monsters for you.

I am so thankful for my parents who have always supported me, especially in my love for reading and absolutely unnecessary English minor. My mother that bought me every book and took me to every Harry Potter movie, even if she slept the entire time.

I'm thankful for my friends, Miranda and Darrin, the first two people I ever told about this book after I'd drunk too many glasses of wine at their house. They may have also not so subtly inspired a certain couple in this book.

To Rachel, Alyce, Kenzie, and Abby—my beta readers—thank you all for taking the time to read and give me feedback. Even in that early draft, I cannot believe you all liked it as much as you did. Thank you for loving these characters as much as I do. I apologize again for the heartbreak I caused and promise to give you more Alessia and Eve in the prequel to make up for it.

I have such gratitude and appreciation for my editor, Fiona McLaren. You helped me take this book to new levels so I could better tell these characters' stories. Angela Rizza, my cover artist, who is so ridiculously talented and created the most beautiful cover art I have ever seen. It could not have been more perfect.

Virginia Allyn, you are one of the kindest people I've ever worked with. You created a map beyond my wildest dreams, it is a work of art upon itself. I cannot wait to write more books and beg you to do more illustrations.

Finally to the authors that inspire me. Holly Black who crafts the most wonderful faerie tales and headstrong characters, who knows I exist only because she responded to my tweet once (edit: I met her after this and clammed up too much to tell her about the tweet or how much her writing has inspired me). Silvia Moreno-Garcia who cultivates such a beautifully haunting atmosphere and suspense that I can only dream of doing one day. And Sarah J Maas that made me fall in love with characters again.

Playlist for Summer's Snow

Breakfast – Dove Cameron

Hotel – Montell Fish

Dreaming of You – Selena

you should see me in a crown – Billie Eilish

just friends – keshi

Bow – Reyn Hartley

Take It Slow – Bass Physics, St. Loreto

ANGOSTURA – keshi

ILYSB (stripped) – LANY

Antisocial (with Travis Scott) – Ed Sheeran

Out of Body – Drea Réal

Mean it (stripped) – Lauv, LANY

Hold on – Chord Overstreet

How Do I say Goodbye – Dean Lewis

Heart-Shaped Box – Nirvana

Smells Like Teen Spirit – Malia J

Survivor – 2WEI, Edda Hayes

alright – keshi

All Day – Drea Réal

Better Days – Dermot Kennedy

My Songs Know What You Did In The Dark – Fall Out Boy

Scars – Drea Réal, Prod. By K-Money, St. Loreto

Ocean Eyes – Billie Eilish

Thinking Bout You – rei brown, Joji

Lift Me Up – Rihanna

I Won't Say (I'm In Love) – Susan Egan, Cheryl Freeman, LaChanze, Lillias
White, Vaneese Thomas

beside you – keshi

Forever – rei brown

Get You The Moon (feat. Snøw) – Kina

Could I Be Somebody – rei brown

SOMEBODY – keshi

If You See Her – LANY

Bodies – Drowning Pool

This is Beautiful – Tyrone Wells

Snow On The Beach (feat. Lana Del Rey) – Taylor Swift

evermore (feat. Bon Iver) – Taylor Swift

ABOUT
the
AUTHOR

M y last name is actually not Mannon, but it is a play on my real middle name. I work full-time in healthcare and began writing during the pandemic as a method of escapism. I quickly fell in love with the characters and worlds I created and am excited for others to read about them.

I'm currently drafting the second book to this series, Fall's Thorns, which will focus on Misha Briar and her journey following her rescue. You can follow me at any of the below for updates!

Website: www.carlyhmannon.com

Goodreads: Carly H. Mannon

Instagram: @carlyhmannon

Tiktok: @carlyhmannon

Twitter: @carlyhmannon

Facebook: Carly H. Mannon

Printed in Great Britain
by Amazon

18227302R10264